Sunshine and Showers

Rosie Harris was born in Cardiff and grew up there and in the West Country. After her marriage she lived for some years on Merseyside before moving to Buckinghamshire where she still lives. She has three grown-up children, six grandchildren and two great grandchildren and writes full time.

Sunshine and Showers

ROSIE HARRIS

arrow books

Published by Arrow Books 2009

2 4 6 8 10 9 7 5 3 1

Copyright © Rosie Harris 2005

First published in the United Kingdom in 2005 by
William Heinemann
The Random House Group Limited
20 Vauxhall Bridge Road, London, SW1V 2SA

www.rbooks.co.uk

Addresses for companies within The Random House Group Limited can be found at:
www.randomhouse.co.uk/offices.htm

The Random House Group Limited Reg. No 954009

A CIP catalogue record for this book
is available from the British Library

The Random House Group Limited supports The Forest Stewardship Council (FSC),
the leading international forest certification organisation. All our titles that are printed
on Greenpeace approved FSC certified paper carry the FSC logo.
Our paper procurement policy can be found at www.rbooks.co.uk/environment

Mixed Sources
Product group from well-managed
forests and other controlled sources
www.fsc.org Cert no. TT-COC-2139
© 1996 Forest Stewardship Council
FSC

ISBN 978 0 434 01970 0

Typeset in Palatino by
Palimpsest Book Production Ltd, Polmont, Stirlingshire
Printed and bound in Great Britain by
CPI Mackays, Chatham ME5 8TD

To the Posse –
Pamela and Tony Sak
Sue and Les Cooke
Maureen and John Wilson
Paul and Ann Samways

Acknowledgements

A big thank you to Susan Sandon, Kate Elton, Jo Wheatley, Lucie Bates, Lois Hopkins, Justine Taylor, Lizzy Kingston, Sue Lyne – to name just a few of the wonderful team at Random House – but above all to my brilliant editor Georgina Hawtrey-Woore.

Thanks also to Caroline Sheldon and her staff who work so supportively.

Chapter One

'My mam says you're too pretty for your own good, Sheryl Williams,' Megan Thomas sighed. 'I can't think what she'll have to say when I tell her you're talking of getting married, and to Alun Powell of all people.'

Sheryl sat up and raising both arms lifted her sleek shawl of straight blonde hair from the nape of her neck, and tossed her head provocatively so that it spread out in a dazzling golden spray around her shoulders. Her bright red cotton blouse strained across her pointed breasts, emphasising her slim waist, her shapely arms, and her creamy skin.

It was a Saturday evening in early April and the two girls had not long arrived home from Harveys, the department store in Cardiff city centre where they both worked as counter assistants.

They were exchanging confidences in Sheryl's bedroom, sprawled on the patchwork quilt that Mrs Williams had worked on every evening the previous winter. It was bordered with a wide band of a delicate blue and pink flowered fabric, matching the frilled curtains at the window. It softened the contours of the

1

black iron bedstead and added a pretty feminine touch to the room.

From the reflection in the mirror on the skirted dressing table facing them, it was easy to see that although they were both sixteen Sheryl and Megan were exact opposites.

Their houses, Sheryl Williams's in Thesiger Street and Megan Thomas's in Coburn Street, backed onto each other. The two girls had been inseparable ever since their first day at infants' school, when they had taken an instant liking to one another.

Then, they'd been two wide-eyed frightened tots who'd found strength and comfort from holding hands. Now Sheryl was long-legged, slim, and shapely, with shimmering blonde hair, a perfect oval face, blue eyes, a generous full mouth and a talent for trouble.

Megan was shorter and plumper. Her short brown hair was bobbed and framed her round face. She was sensible, generous to a fault, and her dark thoughtful eyes contributed to the aura of calm, practical assurance about her.

Megan had always had a sobering influence on Sheryl's madcap schemes, and as they were growing up she'd talked her out of trouble more times than she could remember.

'You don't really mean it about marrying Alun Powell, do you?' she frowned.

Sheryl stood up and preened herself in front of the mirror. 'Of course I do. Why don't you believe me?'

'He's not good enough for you, for one thing!' Megan told her firmly.

Sheryl's eyebrows lifted cynically. 'Not good enough! That wouldn't be the little green-eyed monster talking, would it?' she quipped.

'Jealous? Me jealous of him!'

'Well you must admit that he is very good-looking, handsome in fact, quite dashing . . .'

'Take him out of his army uniform and he'd be just an ordinary run-of-the-mill fellow,' Megan told her cuttingly.

'You are jealous! Go on, admit it,' Sheryl persisted, her blue eyes challenging. 'He's better-looking than that bloke you're sweet on, Hadyn.'

'Don't talk daft! I'm not serious about Hadyn Baker. I only go out with him to make up a foursome when you want to go out with Alun. I'm in no hurry to start going steady, because I don't intend to get married and be tied down with a family and domestic chores for years and years. Anyway, looks aren't everything. If I had to choose between Alun Powell and Hadyn Baker then I'd certainly pick Hadyn. He's not only a much nicer sort of person, but he's far more reliable. Alun Powell is a show-off and he's always trying to make an impression, and you know it.'

Sheryl pulled a face. 'You sound like my dad,' she sighed. 'I told him that if he took the trouble to get to know Alun better he'd like him a lot more.'

'I bet that made him laugh!'

'My mam quite likes Alun!' Sheryl pronounced defensively. 'She thinks that he's charming, and a real card.'

'Yes, that about sums him up. Polished and up to every trick in the book!'

'What's that supposed to mean?'

'He piles on the charm and your mam laps it up,' Megan told her. 'Your dad's got more sense than to be taken in! Since he's the one who has to say whether you can get married or not, if he isn't keen on Alun you are wasting your time even thinking about it.'

'You want to listen to yourself sometime, Megan Thomas,' Sheryl jibed. 'You sound like someone's old granny, or a disapproving maiden aunt.'

Megan stood up and made for the door. 'I'm not wasting any more time talking to you about something that can't possibly happen. You don't know when you are well off, Sheryl. You get your own way over most things, you never have to fit in with what others want, not like I have to do in our house. If you had two older sisters and a brother your mam and dad wouldn't spoil you like they do, and I think you are plumb daft to think of getting married and that's that.'

Sheryl shrugged, but there was still a smile on her face as if she was inwardly revelling in something that she wasn't sharing. 'Maybe, we'll see. Are you coming to the dance with me tonight?'

Megan sighed impatiently. 'That's how all this stupidity started, isn't it, Sheryl. I'm beginning to wish we'd never started going to the dances at Maindy Barracks and then you'd never have met Alun Powell and . . .'

'And I'd still be going out on Saturday nights with your Elwyn,' Sheryl finished. She smiled at her reflection and ran her fingers through her hair. 'Your Elwyn's always been crazy about me ever since we were at school. Remember how at one time he used to walk to school with us and insist on taking my hand as we crossed the road?'

'And you used to insist we went to the park so that we could watch him playing footie.'

'I did, didn't I. I had quite a crush on him in those days.' Sheryl sighed. 'Does he still talk about me?'

'I've no idea. You know perfectly well that he's away at the moment doing his police training.'

'Oh yes, I'd forgotten about that. I wonder what he's going to look like in his uniform. PC Plod, who'll walk all over you in his size eleven boots.'

They looked at each other and giggled. 'If I'd married your Elwyn then we'd be sisters,' Sheryl pronounced.

'Well, actually, we would have been sisters-in-law,' Megan corrected her.

'Same difference! I probably would have married him if I'd never met Alun Powell. We used to talk about it sometimes,' she said dreamily.

'Then it's a pity you ever did meet Alun. It's still not too late to change your mind. I think Elwyn still hopes that you'll go out with him again,' Megan added seriously.

Sheryl sighed. 'No, this is the real thing. Going out with your Elwyn was like going out with a brother. Growing up together, and even going to the same school as him, meant that there was no thrill or excitement in it. With our houses backing onto each other like they do I only had to look out of the kitchen window to see him. He was always out in your back garden kicking a ball around, or feeding that black rabbit he kept out there in a wooden hutch.'

'So that makes him like a brother, does it? Well, I suppose when you haven't got any brothers or sisters of your own it probably does,' Megan reasoned. 'The very fact that he did start taking you out on proper dates, though, meant that he saw you as rather more than a sister,' she went on thoughtfully.

'OK, clever clogs. I know you can twist anything round to suit your argument when you want to do so. In fact,' Sheryl's blue eyes gleamed mischievously, 'you are the ideal person to break the news to my mam and dad that I'm thinking of marrying Alun Powell.'

'Oh, no!' Megan made for the door. 'I'm not falling for that kind of flattery. You do your own dirty work.'

6

'Please, Megan,' Sheryl wheedled. 'You'll be able to tell them so much more tactfully than me. If you do it then I'll let you borrow my pink voile dress for the dance at the barracks tonight.'

'No thank you! Anyway, your pink dress is far too long and too tight for me, so I'd look a real frump in it. I'm not even sure at the moment if I want to come to the dance tonight.'

'Megan, you must! I won't be allowed to go if you don't come. You know what my mam's like. She's always going on about us sticking together so that we'll be safe.'

'I know, and that's what we always have done in the past. Now, though, if you are going to marry Alun Powell you won't need me to protect you any longer, will you?'

'Yes, but I told you that Mam and Dad don't know about that yet.' Sheryl smiled archly. 'Not unless you inform them that I'm planning on getting married.'

'Why can't you and Alun tell them?'

Sheryl sighed, puffing her cheeks out in peevish exasperation. 'Alun doesn't know about it yet either, see!'

'What! He doesn't know you are getting married?' Megan's brown eyes widened. 'Does that mean he hasn't actually asked you to marry him?'

'He will!' Sheryl tossed back her hair defiantly. 'It will be tonight at the dance, probably.'

She grinned. 'You will be the very first to know, I promise you.'

Megan shook her head in despair. 'You two deserve each other,' she said caustically.

'What do you mean by that?'

'You both lead people on. You let our Elwyn think you cared for him . . .' She stopped speaking as the bedroom door opened and Sheryl's mother came into the room.

Mrs Williams was in her mid-fifties, an extremely pernickety woman who was always very neatly dressed, a crisp Marcel wave in her short grey hair. In the mornings she wore a wrap-over print overall to protect her smart clothes as she went about her chores. Her house was spotless, furniture and brasses polished until you could see your face in them, and her doorstep and window sills were all scrubbed twice a week with pumice stone.

Before her marriage, which hadn't been until her early thirties, Rachael Williams had worked in David Morgan's, one of the top shops in Cardiff, and she considered it very important to keep up her standards.

No-one ever saw her looking the least bit dishevelled. If someone happened to come to the front door while she was busy at her chores, she always whipped off her apron before she went to speak to them.

She firmly believed that because her husband, Gwynfor Williams, had worked his way up the ladder to become an overseer on the railway, they were a shade above the rest of her neigh-bours. Even the Thomases!

A tall thin man with a thoughtful air about him, Gwynfor lived for his job. When he went to work he always wore a white shirt, a collar and tie and a trilby hat. His shoes were always polished and he looked almost as smart in his working clothes as most other men did in their Sunday best.

Megan's father, Ivan Thomas, was tall and broad-shouldered with massive muscles and a firm, determined face. He worked as a steve-dore at the docks and he set off in the direction of the Pier Head each morning with a muffler round his neck and a snap tin, with his midday meal in it, under his arm. Often when he came home at the end of the day he was covered in grease, or dirt, depending on what cargo he had been unloading.

Megan's mother was plump and with a family of three girls and a son, as well as a husband, to cook and clean for, she tended to take life as it came. Her home was often untidy, but no-one seemed to notice because there was such a warm welcome not only for her own family, but for their friends as well.

Although their houses backed onto each other, the Williamses' house was slightly larger than the Thomases', something which Mrs Williams often pointed out to Sheryl.

'You two girls planning what you are going to wear tonight, are you? I've just bought Sheryl a new pale blue taffeta dress, has she shown it to you yet? I'm wondering if it is a bit too grand, though, for an army hop! What do you think, Megan? Mind you,' she smiled proudly, not waiting for Megan's reply, 'Sheryl is bound to be the belle of the ball whatever she wears, isn't she!'

'Mam! You shouldn't say things like that!'

Mrs Williams looked taken aback. 'Why ever not when we all know it is true? Anyway, I came up to say that I've just made a pot of tea and I wondered if you two girls would like a cup?'

'Thank you, Mrs Williams, but I must be getting home,' Megan told her with a smile.

'So what time are you coming back to collect Sheryl for the dance, then?'

'I . . . I'm not sure. I . . . thought that perhaps we could meet there,' Megan replied uncertainly.

'Go to Maindy Barracks on your own! Oh, surely you're not thinking of doing that! It is so much safer for the two of you to go together.'

'I . . . I thought that perhaps Alun Powell might be coming to collect Sheryl?'

'Alun Powell?' Mrs Williams looked puzzled. 'No, I don't think so, she hasn't mentioned that he's coming to pick her up,' she said, turning to Sheryl for confirmation.

'No, Alun can't get away. He's on duty until half an hour before the dance starts. His friend Hadyn Baker will be on the lookout for us and he'll be expecting us to arrive together,' Sheryl added, looking straight at Megan.

'Oh, that's all right then, as long as you've arranged things properly,' Mrs Williams smiled. 'Do you want your dad to walk as far as the barrack gates with you?'

'No, Mam! That would make us look silly,' Sheryl told her tetchily. 'Megan can call for me at about eight o'clock and then we'll make our own way there.'

'Very well, if that's what you both want to do, but it will be dark by then, remember.'

'We know! And don't go asking my dad to come and meet us, either.'

'Very well, if you say so, my lovely, but I would feel much happier if you'd let him do that.'

'Alun and Hadyn will walk us home when the dance finishes, so you have nothing to worry about,' Sheryl insisted.

'Well, just remember we shall expect you to be back here before midnight.'

'And I suppose you will both be sitting up waiting for me,' Sheryl muttered crossly. 'Can't you understand, Mam, I'm not a schoolkid any longer. I've got a job, I've been working for over a year now, so I'm old enough to live my own life!'

'You're only sixteen,' her mother told her firmly. 'You've a long way to go, and a lot to learn, before you are grown-up.'

'Stop fussing Mam!' Sheryl said irritably.

Rachael Williams shook her head. 'The world's a hard place, as you'll find out soon enough, cariad. Don't be in too much of a rush to grow up. You want to enjoy yourself while you can. Isn't that right, now, Megan?'

Megan smiled uncomfortably. She knew that Mrs Williams meant well, but she also knew that her overprotective attitude only made Sheryl all the more rebellious and even more determined to live life her way.

She dreaded to think about what would happen when Sheryl told her parents that she intended to marry Alun Powell. Mrs Williams would probably throw a fit, because Sheryl was far too young and irresponsible to tie herself down.

Mr Williams would certainly have plenty to say. He was sure to act the heavy father and forbid Sheryl to have anything more to do with Alun.

And they'll probably both blame me for being the one who has led Sheryl astray, because I've been going with her to the dances at the barracks, Megan thought uncomfortably.

Still, she consoled herself, for the time being it was all just hot air on Sheryl's part. After all, she'd admitted that Alun Powell hadn't asked her to marry him yet, so she was simply guessing that he was about to do so.

Chapter Two

It was almost eight o'clock on Saturday evening when Sheryl and Megan set off for Maindy Barracks.

It was a nippy evening for late April and there was a fine mist clouding the air. Both girls were wearing their warm winter coats and they had tied scarves over their heads to protect their hair from the chill dampness.

They found that the hall where the dance was being held was packed. Girls from every district in Cardiff, from Butetown and Grangetown right out to Ely and Fairfield, eagerly looked forward to the dances held there each month.

It had all started about eighteen months earlier. The first dance at the barracks had been a special occasion soon after Armistice Day, to mark the end of the terrible war and to celebrate freedom. It had proved to be so overwhelmingly popular that another dance, to celebrate the start of 1919, had taken place.

Since then the dances had been held on the last Saturday night of each month and because there was no charge for admission, and they knew that they'd find plenty of partners, young girls decked out in their prettiest dresses flocked to them.

Music was supplied by the band of the Royal Welsh Regiment and a local jazz group playing all the well-known dance tunes, together with some of the latest hits. Since all those present were under thirty-five they loved the noise, the excitement and showing off their expertise in the very latest dances.

Sheryl and Megan found Hadyn was waiting for them by the entrance. He pecked both of them on the cheek, but his gaze lingered on Megan, pleasure shining in his dark eyes.

'Where's Alun then?' Sheryl asked sharply.

'He'll be here in a couple of minutes. He didn't come off guard duty until eight o'clock so he's gone to wash and change.'

Sheryl tossed her head in annoyance. 'He should have said he was going to be so late, then we would have taken our time instead of rushing like mad.'

'He'll only be a few minutes so do you both want to go along to the cloakroom and titivate yourselves?'

'Well, I suppose it would help to pass the time,' Sheryl said petulantly. 'I hate being kept waiting.'

'It's not his fault if he's been on duty, and he did warn you about it,' Megan reminded her. 'Anyway,' she smiled at Hadyn, 'by the time we've taken our coats off he'll probably be here.'

Sheryl agreed, but Megan could see she was

14

far from pleased. She was wearing her new blue taffeta dress and Megan knew she had been planning to make a grand entrance, and now it looked as though it was going to fall flat. She'd talked of nothing else as they'd walked along Whitchurch Road and into Maindy Road. Sheryl had even planned that she would slip off her heavy brown tweed coat and let Megan take it along with her own to the cloakroom while she pirouetted onto the dance floor in Alun's arms, making all eyes turn.

As they made their way back to the dance hall Sheryl's good mood was restored as soon as she saw Alun had arrived and was standing talking to Hadyn.

'Sorry I wasn't here to greet you when you arrived, my lovely,' he told her, planting a kiss full on her bright pink lips, and running a forefinger down the side of her face.

She flushed prettily and caught at his hand, pressing it harder against her cheek.

He pulled back his hand and placed it possessively on her shoulder and twirled her round. 'Another new frock?'

Sheryl flicked her long hair so that it fanned around her shoulders, smiling at him as she did so. 'Do you like it?'

'Like it! It's gorgeous . . . and so are you!' he exclaimed as he pulled her into his arms and steered her onto the dance floor.

Haydn smiled at Megan, lifting his eyebrows questioningly. 'Shall we?'

Megan nodded. Sheryl and Alun had already cleaved their way through the mass of dancers and were twirling in the centre of the floor as the band played 'Look for the Silver Lining'.

Knowing that Sheryl was in her element, Megan relaxed and began to enjoy herself. Hadyn was not a terribly good dancer, but he was great company. After a few false starts they managed to match their steps and gave themselves up to the rhythm of the music. Three dances later, when the band took a break, Hadyn escorted her to where refreshments were being served in a room that was normally used as the sergeants' mess.

'Shall we try and find Sheryl and Alun?' he asked.

Megan shook her head. 'No leave them, let's enjoy ourselves. Anyway, there's something I want to talk to you about.'

Hadyn nodded. 'Would you try and find a table then and I'll fetch some drinks.'

Megan waited until she'd almost finished her glass of lemonade before she plucked up the courage to ask him what was uppermost in her mind. 'It's about Alun,' she said hesitantly. 'Has he said anything to you about him and Sheryl getting married?'

Hadyn spluttered into his beer. 'What! Alun get married? He's not the marrying type!'

Megan frowned. 'Are you sure? Sheryl seems to think he is about to propose.'

Hadyn shook his head emphatically. 'Not

him. He likes her, but it's all a bit of fun, the same as it is for us. Like me, he's only twenty. Far too young to be thinking of settling down and getting married.'

'Alun is very fond of Sheryl, though?' Megan persisted.

'Of course he is, but like I said, it's all part of having a good time!' His face became solemn. 'You never know, there might be another war and we'd be the first in the field, so we don't want to make too many plans for the future, now do we, cariad.'

Megan shivered. 'Don't say that! We've only just started to get over the last one when hundreds and hundreds of soldiers were killed.'

He nodded grimly. 'Did you know they're calling it the Great War because it really was the greatest war that's ever been fought? And we missed all the action because our company never went out to France,' he added, his voice tinged with regret.

'Is that what you joined up for, so that you could go and kill people?'

'No, not really.' He looked puzzled. 'I never thought of it like that before. I thought of it as defending my country against an enemy.'

'Does Alun Powell think the same way about things as you, then?'

'Alun! Alun joined the army long before me because he didn't want to go down the pit. He liked the idea of a smart uniform, too, see. All his life he'd only ever had hand-me-downs and his big brother's old boots with the toes scuffed out of them. It seems that's what happens when you're the youngest in the family.'

'So that's why his boots always shine like glass!'

'Yes, he spends hours on them. Spit and polish until you can see your face in the damn things. Same with his buttons and cap badge. Proud he is of them. Mind you,' he grinned, 'it's about the only thing that he does like about the army.'

'Such a free spirit that he's not too keen on the idea of getting married! Right?'

Hadyn frowned. 'Well, I suppose it would depend on the girl and the circumstances.'

'You mean if he was crazy about her, madly in love with her?' Megan pressed.

Hadyn shrugged. 'I can't see Alun ever being that much bowled over. Mind you, it might be different if the girl was in the club. I suppose he'd do the right thing and marry her then.'

Hadyn's words buzzed in Megan's head as she noticed the performance Sheryl was putting on for Alun's benefit. She was fluttering her eyelashes at him, twining her arms around his neck while they were dancing and lifting her face so that their lips met. Megan wondered if all this leading him on was going to have the desired effect.

When the second interval came, and once again the band went off for a well-earned breather, Megan looked around for Sheryl and

18

Alun. She felt puzzled when she couldn't see them anywhere and worried about what they might be up to.

'They've probably already gone for a drink and some grub,' Hadyn told her. 'Stop fretting about them. Now, do you want to come to the mess with me or shall I bring you something back?'

Megan hesitated. She wanted to go with him, but at the same time she wondered if she ought to stay where she was in case Sheryl was still in the room and trying to find her.

'I'll wait here, if you don't mind, my feet are killing me.'

'Fair do's! I'll bring some drinks and whatever else there is on offer.'

Half an hour later, when dancing resumed, there was still no sign of Sheryl. As eleven o'clock approached and the dance drew to a close, Megan began to feel really alarmed. Mrs Williams always relied on her to stick with Sheryl and see she came to no harm, so how could she possibly go home without her?

The final strains of the national anthem were fading away when Megan spotted Sheryl. She was standing by the door, already wearing her heavy tweed coat. Her hair was windblown and damp, almost as if she had been out in the rain.

Alun, standing alongside her, didn't look as bandbox neat as usual and a frisson of alarm tingled in Megan's veins. The two of them had been missing for almost an hour, and by the look of them the reason she hadn't been able to see them on the dance floor was because they'd not been there.

As they walked back to Cathays in a foursome, there seemed to be an uneasy silence. Megan couldn't help wondering if it had anything to do with what had gone on between Sheryl and Alun when they'd been missing.

Had he proposed as Sheryl had expected, she wondered. Was their silence because they wanted to keep their news a secret? Or was Sheryl sulking because everything had gone wrong and Alun hadn't asked the all-important question after all?

She longed to know, but there was absolutely no opportunity to ask Sheryl. Before they reached Thesiger Street they met Mr Williams coming along the road to meet them.

'You two lads had better hot-heel it back to barracks or you won't be in before twelve and then you'll be on jankers tomorrow,' he told them sharply.

'Come on.' He grabbed hold of Sheryl's arm and marched her off without even giving her a chance to kiss Alun goodnight.

Hadyn squeezed Megan's hand. 'See you soon,' he murmured as he turned and walked away with Alun.

'You didn't have to come and meet us, Dad,' Sheryl protested. 'You must have known Alun and Hadyn would walk us home.'

'Yes, and if you'd hung around on the street corner saying goodnight to them then they would have been late back and probably ended up on a charge. I can never understand why you have to stay until the very last minute. You know how long it takes you to get home and that those two chaps have to walk back again after they've seen you to the door.'

'Well they don't mind or they wouldn't do it, would they,' Sheryl argued.

Her father ignored her. 'Do you want me to walk you to your front door or are you going to nip through our backyard, Megan?'

'Well, whichever you like. We pass the top of my street, so I can go the rest of the way on my own.'

'No! You're not wandering round the streets on your own at this time of night, my girl. I either see you right to your front door or you come with us and use the back way home. We didn't make that gate in the party wall for nothing, now did we.'

'Megan will use the back way,' Sheryl told him. 'She hasn't got a front-door key on her.'

'Well surely it will be there, hanging on a string inside the letter box, if she wants to go home that way,' her father argued.

By this time they were already walking down Thesiger Street and Megan could see that Mrs Williams was standing on the doorstep waiting for them.

'Are you going to come in for a cup of tea,

Megan, or do you want to go straight home in case your mam is waiting up for you?'

'Of course she's going to stop and have a cuppa before she goes home,' Sheryl said quickly. 'Her mam never waits up for her, does she Megan? She's not an old fusspot like you two are.'

'I expect she's awake and listening out for her to come home, though. She won't be able to sleep until she knows Megan is safely indoors and in bed.'

'Oh, Mam! You flap like an old hen,' Sheryl told her with an exaggerated sigh.

'Well, come along in then, Megan. It's all made and ready to drink. I even poured a cup out ready for you in case you decided to stop.'

The moment Megan had drunk her tea and prepared to leave, Sheryl stood up and followed her out through the back scullery into the yard.

'Well?' Megan asked, once they were away from the house.

'Well what?'

'What happened? Where on earth were you? You were missing for almost an hour! Did Alun ask you to marry him?'

Sheryl put a finger to her lips as they heard her father coming out into the yard. 'We can't talk now,' she whispered. 'I'll tell you all about it tomorrow.'

Alun Powell and Hadyn Baker were both deeply immersed in their own thoughts as they retraced their steps to Maindy Barracks.

22

Hadyn was remembering his conversation with Megan about the likelihood of Alun and Sheryl marrying. It was something that had never entered his head before. Now he was wondering if perhaps it had been a subtle way on Megan's part of finding out what his intentions towards her might be.

He liked Megan, and enjoyed her company, but he certainly wasn't thinking about marrying her. She was little more than a schoolgirl.

Getting married was something you did when you'd finished sowing your wild oats and you were ready to settle down and have a family. As far as he was concerned, that wouldn't be for a good few years yet. His mam would raise the roof if he went home and told her he was thinking of marriage. The very thought of the look there would be on her face brought a smile to his lips and made him chuckle out loud.

'What you so happy about?' Alun asked. 'Did you get your leg over tonight as well?'

'Duw anwyl! What the hell are you on about, mun. I wouldn't dream of pushing my luck that far and spoiling a good friendship.'

'Probably very wise. That Megan can be a bit frosty sometimes. Not like Sheryl. Now she's hot stuff, I can tell you. Begging for it, that one! No holding back there.'

'Merdi! You're not trying to tell me that you had it away with her tonight?'

'I bloody well did! What's more, she wanted it more than me. Red-hot she is, I tell you.'

'I didn't know you were that serious about her, Alun?'

'Serious? Who said anything about being serious? If I get the chance of a bit of crumpet I grab it. You do the same, don't you?'

'No I damn well don't! What happens if you put her in the club?'

Alun shrugged. 'Up to her to make sure that it doesn't happen.' He tapped the side of his nose with a forefinger. 'There's ways and means of avoiding that, you know, boyo!'

'Well let's hope you've used them,' Hadyn warned him. 'I can't see her dad thinking it much of a laughing matter if you put her in the family way.'

'He won't see my heels for dust if I have,' Alun laughed.

'You'd have a job escaping his wrath. You're in the army remember, boyo. You can't run and you can't hide. They've got all your details on record. If you try and skedaddle then you'll be up on a charge for desertion and you'll probably end up in the glasshouse when you're caught.'

'You're a right morbid bugger tonight and no maybe,' Alun growled. 'What's brought all this on? Are you feeling jealous because I got my end away and you didn't?'

'I didn't even try. You want to watch your step as well, she may have let you have your way tonight, but you'll be dancing to her tune before you know what's happening.'

'What's that supposed to mean?'

'Wedding bells, mun. She'll be expecting you to pop the question.'

Alun hooted with laughter. 'She'll have a bloody long wait then, boyo! I've no intention of marrying her or anyone else. Joining the army was the only way I could see of getting away from home and being my own man without starving to death. I'm not saying I've done the right thing, but it's a damn sight better than going down the pits like my old man and my brothers. Filthy old job that is, and no maybe. Coal smells rank, you know. It smells of poisonous gas, of men's sweat and fear, of death.'

'So you keep telling me.'

'When you step into that cage at the pit head your heart sinks into your guts at the same rate of knots as the cage drops down into the bowels of the earth. Not many of the buggers are warbling then, I can tell you!'

'Perhaps the reason why there's so many pit choirs is because they can't help singing when they come back up to the surface,' Hadyn commented.

'You mean they're so astonished to find that they are back out in daylight and fresh air again, and that there's not been an explosion, that they need to sing?'

'Something like that.'

'Yes, mining's a living death, boyo, let me tell you. If you've never been down into the bowels of the earth, crawling along a narrow seam with only the light clipped onto the front of your safety helmet to see by, then you know nothing about fear.'

'Which is why you signed up,' Hadyn commented neutrally.

'That's exactly why, boyo! Mind you, I can't stand the discipline and all the drilling we have to do. Or those bastard officers who make us grovel and rub our noses in it if we put a foot wrong. I like the comradeship of the men though, and the good food, decent clobber and having money in my pocket.'

'Oh, come on, our pay is pretty meagre!'

'True, but I can spin it out to meet most of my needs. It's a fortune, see, when you've had bugger all. Not having to share my bed with a couple of others, or find my clothes taken by one of my brothers, is another bonus. It's a case of first up is best dressed in big families, see.'

'You told me that was all in the past though, since your family moved out of Abertillery to Ely.'

'When I joined the army I didn't know that was going to happen though, did I? My old man was still working down the pits and so was my eldest brother. Two other brothers were serving in France and they'd said that the army was better than the pits. Mind you,' Alun added bitterly, 'that was before they were killed; now they're probably as deep underground as they ever were.'

'And what about your dad?'

26

'He's got silicosis! Most of the time he's coughing his lungs up. That's why they moved to Ely. No chance of my mam or my three sisters finding work in a pit village. Here they've all got jobs of one kind or another and life's not too bad for them.'

'So all your family have left the pits, have they?'

'Well, one of my brothers is still a miner. He's married and got a couple of kids and is still living in Abertillery. She nags him something silly to get out of the pits, but it's the only life he knows so he sticks at it.'

'Then if you don't want to end up like him you'd better watch your step, mun. If you're not careful, before you know it, you'll find yourself tying the knot and being nagged to death as well.'

Chapter Three

It was Sunday afternoon before Sheryl and Megan were able to catch up on the details of what had happened at the dance the previous evening. They'd seen each other at mid-morning Mass, but there had been too many people around for them to talk privately.

'Come on, let's go for a walk to Roath Park,' Sheryl suggested the moment Megan came to call for her. 'It's the only way we can talk without Mam and Dad listening in to every word we say.'

'Well? Did he propose?' Megan asked bluntly as they walked towards the tram stop in Crwys Road.

'As good as!'

'What does that mean? You were missing from the dance for almost an hour, I was beginning to get quite worried about you.'

'You'd have been more than worried if you'd known what was happening,' Sheryl giggled, tossing her head and freeing her hair from inside the collar of her brown tweed jacket.

'Go on, tell me, I'm listening.'

'I know you are, but I'm not telling you any

more. Let's just say that after what happened Alun Powell will have to marry me.'

'Have to? What do you mean?' Megan stopped dead in the middle of the pavement. 'Oh, Sheryl, don't tell me you . . .'

'Don't looked so shocked,' Sheryl smiled. 'It had to happen sometime, didn't it.'

'You mean you and Alun . . .' Megan hesitated as if she found it impossible to go on. She had only to look at Sheryl's beaming face to know that what she was unable to put into words really had taken place.

'Oh, Sheryl, how could you!' she exclaimed as she started walking towards the tram stop again.

'Easy! It just happened. I'm not telling you all the details, mind.'

'Good, because I don't want to hear them. I think you're . . . you're . . .' She shook her head, completely lost for words.

'Wicked?' Sheryl suggested as a tram came clanging along and stopped.

'No, bloody daft!' Megan said over her shoulder as they climbed on board.

They sat side by side in stony silence until the conductor had collected their fares.

'You didn't really let him, did you, Sheryl?' Megan asked anxiously.

'Of course I did. I bet you would have done the same if Hadyn had wanted to.'

'Not on your life! I want an engagement ring on my finger before I let a chap take any sort of liberties with me. Even then I'd want to have the wedding date all set before going as far as you did!'

'What's a ring, or a piece of paper if it comes to that?' Sheryl said huffily. 'If you love each other that's all that matters.'

'That's what he told you and you were stupid enough to fall for it,' Megan said witheringly. 'He'd say just about anything to get his own way.'

'I wouldn't have given in if I hadn't wanted to,' Sheryl protested.

'I bet he bought you a drink first so that you didn't know whether you were coming or going,' Megan muttered.

'I had two glasses of port if you must know, but then I can take drink, not like you. I remember when you came to our place over Christmas you had one glass of sherry and you went all silly and giggly afterwards.'

'At least I didn't get carried away into doing something as daft as you did last night. What happens if you find yourself preggers?'

Sheryl shrugged her shoulders. 'It means we'll get married sooner rather than later.'

'Oh, he has mentioned marriage then?'

'Well, not in so many words, but we both know that's where all this is leading.'

'You know, but I bet he doesn't. For him, if he's like most men, it's merely a bit of fun. Another scalp to brag about to his mates.'

'You really are horrid these days, Megan. You

make everything sound so sordid and smutty,' Sheryl pouted.

By the time they reached Roath Park they were in the throes of a first-class row. Sheryl resented all the things Megan was implying about Alun. Megan felt furious that Sheryl had been stupid enough to give in to his demands, because she was worried about what the outcome might be.

They walked round the park in moody silence, showing no interest or pleasure in anything, not even in the drifts of yellow and white daffodils or the colourful beds of polyanthus.

When Sheryl announced that she was fed up and was going home Megan made no attempt to stop her. This wasn't the same as their occasional arguments. Sheryl seemed to have completely lost her sense of right and wrong. Megan watched her flounce off in silence, almost glad to see her go. Ten minutes later she decided that there was no enjoyment in walking around looking at the flowers on her own, so she made her way back to the tram stop and went home.

It was almost two hours later, the afternoon light was fading, and the lamplighter had already made his rounds, when Rachael Williams knocked on the back door of the Thomases' house.

'Is my Sheryl here with your Megan?' she asked when Glenda Thomas answered the door.

31

'No, not that I know of.'

'Well, is your Megan here?'

'Yes, she's upstairs in her bedroom.'

'On her own?'

'That's right. She went for a walk with Sheryl this afternoon, but she's been back ages.'

'Sheryl didn't come back with her?'

Glenda Thomas shook her head. 'Hasn't she come home then? Perhaps the two of them have had enough of each other's company after such a late night.'

'No, she hasn't come home,' Mrs Williams said worriedly. 'Will you ask Megan if she knows where she's gone?'

'You'd better come along in. I'll call her down and you can ask her yourself,' Glenda told her.

Megan was equally mystified. 'We went to Roath Park like we often do, but Sheryl decided to come on home,' she told them. 'I stayed on for a bit, but it was so cold that I came home.'

'Did you have a falling-out or something?' Mrs Williams questioned.

'No, not really,' Megan said.

Mrs Williams heard the hesitancy in Megan's voice and probed deeper. 'It's not like the two of you to part company when you are out together, so something must have gone wrong,' she persisted.

'Nothing went wrong. We had a difference of opinion about something, that's all.'

'We've all told you how important it is to stick together,' Mrs Williams stated censoriously. 'If you go off out together then we expect you to come home together.'

'Come on now, Rachael, don't be like that with the girl,' Megan's mother intervened. 'They're not schoolkids any more. They can't live in each other's pockets for the rest of their lives. Megan has told you what happened. Your Sheryl wanted to come home and she didn't so they split. What's wrong with that?'

'Nothing, if I knew where my Sheryl was. She could be anywhere. Cardiff is full of foreign seamen and the like, and you can't help worrying when you have a girl as pretty as she is. She could be picked up by anyone. You hear such dreadful tales.'

'Oh come on, cariad,' Glenda Thomas laughed, 'they went to Roath Park, not down to Tiger Bay.'

'There's criminals about even in Roath Park,' Rachael Williams insisted. 'You ask your Elwyn. I bet he could already tell you tales that would make your hair stand on end, even though he isn't a proper policeman yet. If there weren't any criminals then why would they need great big hulking chaps like him in the police force, tell me that?'

'You'll probably find that your Sheryl has come home while you've been chasing round looking for her.' Glenda Thomas smiled reassuringly.

Sheryl hadn't come home, and an hour later it was Gwynfor Williams who was on the

33

Thomases' doorstep demanding to speak to Megan. He was quite upset and began cross-questioning her like a barrister in his efforts to find out where his daughter might be.

Exhausted by his probing, Megan finally suggested, 'Perhaps you should cut along to the barracks and see if Alun Powell has any idea where she is.'

His eyes narrowed as he stared at her. 'You do know something more than you're telling us, don't you? Did the two of you suggest going for a walk this afternoon to give her the chance to sidle off and meet that soldier chap without our knowing about it?'

'Why should I bother to do that? You know that Sheryl is friendly with Alun Powell.'

'And I also know that she has been forbidden to walk out with him on her own. I don't mind her seeing him when she goes to the dances with you, but I will not have her walking out with him unescorted.'

'She's nearly seventeen, Mr Williams.'

'I don't care if she is seventeen or twenty-seven, as long as she lives under my roof she will comply with my orders,' he retorted firmly.

'It's getting late so perhaps you should go and ask at the barracks,' Ivan Thomas intervened.

Gwynfor Williams turned away abruptly. 'Right, but I'll be back again if I don't find her. I think that you know far more than you are letting on,' he said, looking at Megan accusingly.

Gwynfor Williams's journey to Maindy Barracks proved to be a waste of time. They wouldn't let him inside the gates because he wasn't on official business. The duty sergeant sent someone to enquire about the whereabouts of Alun Powell, but it was fruitless. The report came back that no-one knew where he was because he was off duty and not in his barrack room, and he hadn't told anyone where he was going.

Gwynfor Williams returned home both worried and angry. After conferring with his wife he went back to the Thomases to see Megan. When he told her what had happened at Maindy Barracks she suggested that perhaps he should go back again and this time ask for Hadyn Baker and see if he could tell him anything.

'I think you should be the one to do that,' he scowled. His voice rose angrily. 'Since you were the one who left her on her own, you should be out helping to find her.'

'Hang on a minute.' Ivan Thomas came out into the hallway and stood with arms akimbo, glaring at Gwynfor Williams. 'No bugger talks to my daughter like that, certainly not when she's in her own home and hasn't put a foot wrong.'

'I'm sorry, mun, really I am.' Gwynfor Williams mopped at his forehead with his handkerchief. 'I'm in that much turmoil I hardly know what I'm saying.'

'Well don't shout orders at my Megan as if you were ordering around one of your minions on the railway,' Ivan Thomas growled. 'If you ask her in the right way then our Megan will do all she can to help you find Sheryl, won't you, my lovely?'

'Yes, of course. I'll get my hat and coat and come to the barracks with you, Mr Williams,' Megan said placatingly. 'I'm sure if we can speak to Hadyn then he will be able to tell us where Alun is, and he might even know if Sheryl is with him.'

Megan felt decidedly uncomfortable as she accompanied Sheryl's father to Maindy Barracks. She'd only ever been there to dances, and the thought of asking for Hadyn set off butterflies in her stomach in case he got the wrong idea about her seeking him out like this. She had no idea what the procedure was about visiting soldiers there, or how she should go about finding him.

The sentry on duty was the same one who had turned Gwynfor Williams away earlier, and he was about to do so again when he recognised Megan.

'I've already told your dad that Alun Powell is not around and no-one knows where he is,' he informed her.

'He's not my dad, he's Sheryl's,' Megan said quickly, 'and it's not Alun we're asking for, it's Hadyn Baker. I'm hoping that perhaps Hadyn knows where Alun has gone and also if Sheryl is with him,' she explained.

Hadyn looked uneasy when he came out to the gate to speak to them. 'Alun's mam has been taken ill,' he told them, 'and Alun was given a couple of hours off to go and visit her. I wouldn't have thought he'd take Sheryl along with him though,' he frowned.

'Where do the Powells live?' Gwynfor Williams asked sharply.

'Archer Road in Ely. It's a new housing estate, see. They used to live in Abertillery, but his dad has silicosis and lost his job at the pit so they were moved to the outskirts of Cardiff and . . .'

'We don't need a full history,' Mr Williams snapped. 'Archer Road, Ely, right? Do you know the number?'

Hadyn shook his head. 'Sorry, I don't, not that it matters because they've taken his mother to the Royal Infirmary, see, so it's not very likely that Alun has gone out to Ely.'

'Dammo di! Why didn't you say so in the first place? Come along Megan, we'll go to the hospital and see if they're there.' He grabbed hold of her arm, not giving her a chance to thank Hadyn or say goodbye to him, and hurried her off down the road.

The Powells' house in Ely was not a bit like Sheryl expected it to be. It was part of a new development of corporation houses and still had a raw look about it. In front of each property was a tiny strip of garden bordering the path that led from the pavement to the front door. Some people had planted flowers or shrubs, but the Powells' strip was simply bare earth and weeds.

Sheryl had thrown caution aside and decided to go to the barracks and look for Alun after she'd left Roath Park, because she'd felt so fed up with Megan's attitude that she needed a sympathetic ear.

Although she refused to admit it, she knew that there was some sound sense in what Megan had said about what had happened the night before.

Letting Alan seduce her had been a risky thing to do, but she was head over heels in love with him and there was no doubt in her mind that he was crazy about her too. He'd been so very persuasive and wouldn't take no for an answer. Megan was right, he had bought her a glass of port, two in fact, and she'd been feeling so relaxed that she hadn't taken very much persuading.

He was so good-looking and charming that she was afraid if she did refuse him he might dump her and find some other girl. There were always plenty of them waiting to pounce if they saw a soldier on his own and looking lonely. After all, that was the whole point of the dances – they enabled the soldiers to meet the local girls.

Alun was better-looking and far smarter than most of the other soldiers, and she knew he'd picked her because she stood out from the crowd. To start with he loved her mane of golden hair. Most girls followed the current fashion for short bobbed hair, or even a shingle, but she'd kept hers long.

She didn't go in for tight corsets to try and flatten her curves, either. The first time he'd run his hands over her body he'd whistled appreciatively and told her how gorgeous she was, and said that he didn't like the new flat boyish look.

After that she did everything she knew to tantalise him and please him, until there was no doubt about it, he was as crazy about her as she was about him.

Her dreams of being married and getting away from the restrictions of home life seemed to be coming nearer every time they saw each other. She felt sure that now they had gone all the way in their lovemaking it was only a matter of time before he asked her to marry him.

She'd reached the corner of Crwys Road and could see the barracks up ahead of her when she'd suddenly paused. Flirting and leading him on was pretty daring, but actually going to the barracks and asking to see him was even more outrageous. Supposing they wouldn't let her see him! She was on the point of turning back when to her astonishment and relief she saw him coming down the road towards her.

When he told her that he was on his way home to Ely and asked her to go with him she'd agreed eagerly, confident that he was inviting her to his home so that he could introduce her to his family and that it was all leading up to asking the big question.

When she'd accepted she hadn't realised that he'd been given time off because his mother was ill, and he hadn't mentioned it until they reached Archer Road.

'It doesn't seem right somehow being here when your mam's in hospital,' she said uneasily when he told her that his father had gone to visit her.

He laughed as he slammed the front door shut and slid the bolt firmly into place.

'We could hardly do what we're going to do if she was here,' he grinned, hugging her close and kissing her.

The inside of the house shocked her. Although the property was newly built it looked very neglected, and there was an over-powering smell of stale cabbage.

From the hallway she could see into the living room and there were dirty cups and plates and old newspapers lying discarded on the table and even on the floor. Everything looked dusty and dirty.

It was probably because his mam was ill that the place was in such a state, she told herself, because Alun was always so well groomed, so spit-and-polish clean. She was surprised that he didn't make any excuses about the unkempt appearance of the place, but put it down to the fact that he had other more exciting things on his mind.

'Come on.' He took her by the hand and led her towards the stairs.

She tried to draw back, but he wasn't having any of it. At the top of the stairs he pushed her into one of the bedrooms then pulled her hat off, tossed it onto a chair and began unbuttoning her coat.

'Alun . . .'

He pulled her possessively towards him, covering her mouth with his and preventing her from saying anything more.

Still holding her tightly he wriggled out of his jacket and dropped it on the floor, unbuttoned his trousers and tossed them on the pile, then forced her backwards onto the bed, scrunching her dress up to her waist as he did so.

She tried to struggle, to resist what was happening, but his heated declaration of how much he needed her swamped her mind.

It was mad passion, she told herself. He found her so irresistible that he couldn't help himself.

It wasn't exactly as she'd dreamed, there were no tender words of love, just sheer physical taking followed by an enormous sigh of pleasure and then abrupt abandonment.

'Dammo di, you're a hot little number and no mistake,' he chuckled when she tried to draw him back into her arms, wanting to hear some declaration of his feelings for her. 'Little glutton for it, aren't you! Well, I'm knackered out!'

He reached for his khaki trousers and pulled out a packet of Woodbines. He lit one up and drew deeply on it. 'No repeat performance, I'm afraid. What with last night and now, I would have thought you'd be satisfied,' he guffawed, exhaling a cloud of blue smoke.

She blinked away her tears, not knowing how to explain that it wasn't the physical act she wanted, but sweet words, some sensual stroking, and shared tenderness.

'Come on,' he slapped her bare thigh playfully, 'get your things on. With any luck we can be out of here before my old man gets back from the hospital.'

Chapter Four

Gwynfor Williams couldn't believe what he was hearing when he was told that Sheryl had gone to Alun's home in Ely with him. He ranted non-stop, blaming Rachael for not exercising more control over their daughter, until his wife pointed out it was Megan Thomas who was at fault for not staying with Sheryl when they went out.

'I've told them over and over again that they must stay together and not go wandering off on their own.'

'Then it doesn't look as if they take any notice of what you say, does it?'

Sheryl blamed everyone except herself. She was alternately weepy, and sorry about what had happened. When her parents, ignoring her lamentations, said that she wasn't to see Alun Powell again, she became defensive and rebellious.

When her father insisted that from now on Sheryl stayed home in the evenings and at weekends she cried, she sulked, she stormed and raged. She refused to eat, then, because she felt famished, she crept downstairs in the night and gobbled up anything and everything she could lay her hands on.

43

She refused to go to work, until Megan warned her that unless she sent in a sick note she would lose her job at Harveys.

When she turned up after three days' absence she was so moody and disrespectful to the customers she was told that unless she mended her ways she would be finishing at the end of the week.

The shock of that jolted Sheryl back to reality. She begged Megan to take a message to Alun to warn him about her parents' reaction when they'd found out that she'd been to his home alone. 'Tell him I'm not allowed out and that it might be best if he didn't call round here.'

Megan didn't fancy going to Maindy Barracks again in a hurry, and certainly not on her own. In the end, though, she agreed to do so because at least it would give her a chance to see Hadyn and explain why she might not be at the next dance.

'Alun wasn't there,' she reported back, 'neither of them were. They're both away on some sort of training exercise and might not be back for another four or five weeks.'

'That means they won't be here in time for the next dance,' Sheryl said crossly.

'You probably wouldn't be allowed to go even if they were,' Megan pointed out.

'That's true! Have you told anyone else except me that they're away?' Sheryl asked, her blue eyes thoughtful.

44

'No, why should I?'

'Well, don't! Not a word to anyone, not even your mam! If I pretend to accept my punishment of not going out at night, or at the weekends, then this upset with my parents will blow over. If Alun's going to be away for several weeks then it will all be forgotten about by the time he gets back. I'll be in the clear and we'll be able to go to the next dance at the barracks, and no-one need know anything at all about what has happened.'

Although the weather was warm and sunny, because she wasn't allowed go out with Megan in the evenings Sheryl found that the time dragged. She'd hoped that she might get a letter, or even a postcard, from Alun telling her the exact date when he would be back, but there was no word from him at all.

Each morning when she met up with Megan to walk to work she asked the same question, had she heard from Hadyn, and always received the same answer.

'Deserted us, the pair of them,' Megan laughed. 'Still, that's soldiers for you, I suppose. They get sent off at a moment's notice and there's nothing at all they can do about it.'

'They could still write and let us know where they are,' Sheryl grumbled.

'They're not allowed to do that,' Megan reasoned. 'You know what the army is like about keeping their movements secret.'

45

'In wartime, yes. We've been at peace now for over eighteen months, so surely they don't still need such silly rules.'

'Well, the soldier I spoke to at the barracks did say they'd be back before the June dance, so I suppose we've got to leave it at that.'

Sheryl shrugged. 'It's all right for you, you're not in love with Hadyn Baker like I am with Alun. I miss him so much that I can't sleep. Sometimes in the morning I feel so sick with worry that I can't even eat my breakfast.'

'What's your mam say about that?' Megan frowned.

'She gets very annoyed. When I told her I was pining for Alun she laughed and said it was daft carrying on like that.'

'She's probably right.'

'Maybe she is, but I can't help it, can I. Anyway, it's too hot to eat and the weather is far too nice for us to be going to work.'

'And far too warm to want to go to any dances,' Megan chuckled.

Sheryl was such a model of good behaviour for the whole of May that her plan worked.

Gwynfor and Rachael Williams congratulated themselves on having nipped things in the bud and put matters right by being firm with their daughter.

'If you want to go for a walk with Megan next Sunday then you can,' Rachael Williams told Sheryl. 'We're not trying to make a prisoner of you. We simply wanted you to know for your own good that you have to be careful about what you do and who you see.'

'Does that mean I can go to the dance next month, then?'

'We'll think about it. You behave yourself for the next couple of weeks and I would think it will be all right. You'll have to promise to stay with Megan though, and the pair of you must come home together, not go wandering off on your own.'

'I wasn't on . . .' Sheryl started to argue with her mother and then thought better of it. There was no point in setting her off again on all the dangers of going off on your own with a boy.

The next dance after Alun and Hadyn came back would be the last Saturday in June, and a couple of weeks before that it would be her birthday. Once she was seventeen she'd insist on being treated as a grown-up, and tell her mam and dad they could no longer go on molly-coddling her as if she was still a child.

'Don't forget that Alun and Hadyn will be back in time for the June dance,' she reminded Megan. 'Everything at home is back to normal again now, so there won't be any problem about going to it,' she added smugly.

'You shouldn't make such definite plans,' Megan warned worriedly. 'There is always the possibility that they won't be back, or there might be some other reason why we can't go and then you'll be in such a horrible mood that you'll be unbearable.'

47

Megan's forecast almost came true. Sheryl was far from well in the early part of the last week in June.

'I think I must have eaten something that was off, or on the turn,' she told Megan as they set off for work. 'I was as sick as a dog first thing this morning.'

'You still look a bit pale,' Megan agreed. 'Perhaps it's all the scoffing you do in the middle of the night.'

'No, I stopped doing that ages ago,' Sheryl grinned. 'Anyway, I'm all right now. It went away almost as quickly as it came.'

Sheryl's upset tummy occurred again the following morning, and the next. By Friday Megan was more concerned about it than Sheryl was.

'It's definitely something I've eaten,' Sheryl insisted. 'Mam said I ought to go to the doctor as summer food poisoning can be quite serious. She said she'd come with me.'

'I wouldn't let her do that,' Megan said quickly.

Sheryl's eyes widened. 'Why ever not?'

'Haven't you any idea what it is that's making you sick?' Megan asked cautiously.

'No! If I had I wouldn't want to go to the doctor's to find out, now would I?'

'Well, stop and think. How long is it since you and Alun . . .' She paused, feeling embarrassed and not knowing how to put her suspicions into words.

'What's it got to do with Alun?' Sheryl asked, looking puzzled.

Megan groaned. She knew that as an only child Sheryl had led a very sheltered life, but surely even she knew that morning sickness was one of the first signs of pregnancy.

When she finally explained this to her, Sheryl was outraged.

'Well try working it out for yourself,' Megan snapped. 'You know the date of the dance when it happened the first time, and the date when you went to Alun's house.'

The colour drained from Sheryl's face as she realised the full implication of what Megan was trying to tell her.

'You don't really think I'm pregnant, do you?' she gasped.

'It certainly seems like it.'

By the time they arrived at work they'd gone over the dates and symptoms half a dozen times. Even Sheryl finally accepted that it might be the reason for her feeling sick each morning.

'What on earth am I going to do if I am pregnant? You will help me sort it out, won't you?' she begged Megan on their way home that night.

'The best thing you can do is to tell your mam right away. I'm surprised she hasn't guessed already.'

'I can't do that! She'd be frantic! My dad would half kill me if he heard about what has happened. You know what he's like and the fuss he made when I went missing for a few hours.'

'With good cause by the sound of it,' Megan told her dryly.

'I don't want a lecture from you, Megan Thomas,' Sheryl said huffily. 'Are you going to help me like a true friend or not?' she demanded.

'I really would if I knew what I could do,' Megan assured her.

'You must know a way of getting rid of it,' Sheryl insisted.

Megan's eyes widened in shock. 'You mean have an abortion?'

'Yes, that's right!' Sheryl nodded, her face frightened, but determined.

'Oh, Sheryl, how can you even think of doing something like that? It would be a mortal sin!'

Sheryl's chin went up defiantly. 'No-one else need know.'

'Nonsense. I'd have to tell about what I'd helped you to do when I went to Confession, and you'd have to do the same.'

'I bet you don't confess half your sins, you're not that good a Catholic,' Sheryl said cynically.

'That's not the point. Having an abortion would be a terrible sin. It's a form of murder!'

Sheryl shuddered. 'Then tell me what else I can do?'

Megan's eyes were dark with concern as she saw how distressed Sheryl was. 'Tell your mam what's happened, cariad, that really is the best

50

thing you can do,' she advised gently. 'She'll understand and explain things to your dad.'

'No.' Sheryl shook her head. 'I can't do that, not yet, anyway. I've got to tell Alun first, so that we can plan when we want to be married and tell them together.'

Sheryl's wedding on a grey, muggy day in mid-September 1920 was the direct opposite of the dreams that Rachael Williams had harboured in her mind ever since Sheryl was a tiny tot.

Rachael had envisaged an impressive Nuptial Mass at St Peter's. The sun would be shining and all their relations, friends and neighbours would be there. She had pictured Sheryl, looking unbelievably lovely in a flowing white wedding dress, coming down the aisle on her father's arm.

The lucky groom had always been a misty, ethereal figure. He would be handsome, kind, loving and in a good steady job, so that he could provide for Sheryl in an appropriate manner.

After the ceremony, which would be attended by so many people that the church would be packed to its doors, there would be a wonderful reception. Gwynfor, wearing a morning suit for such a special occasion, would make a stirring speech, expressing his pride and extolling the virtues of their only child.

As it was, Rachael was standing in a dreary register office, while a shabbily dressed clerk gabbled his way through a civil ritual. Gwynfor had refused to attend. In his eyes this was not a proper marriage because Alun Powell was a Methodist and he had declined to change his religion and become a Catholic.

'It is not a marriage in the eyes of God, it's only a civil arrangement to make it legal for them to live together. Can't you see that?' Gwnyfor had said sadly when Rachael tried to persuade him that it was his duty to be there. 'In my opinion you are only condoning this travesty by being present.'

'She is our daughter, after all, Gwynfor. We should both be there to show our love and give her our support.'

'You go if you want to do so. It may help you atone for the guilt you must be feeling about her lax morals,' he said wearily.

Tears blurred Rachael's eyes as she looked at her daughter. How had it come to this? What had gone wrong? Had she failed Sheryl by not pointing out more strongly the pitfalls she was bound to encounter because she was so pretty?

She dabbed away the tears prickling at the corner of her eyes. She'd watched over her so carefully. Perhaps she'd been too good a mother, too protective, she reflected. She had never dreamed that anything like this would happen, not to them, not to her Sheryl.

Gwynfor was quite right when he said that such a wedding was a travesty. She felt some-thing akin to humiliation as she looked at her daughter. The calf-length cream silk dress with its floating side panels, far from concealing Sheryl's swollen breasts and pregnant bulge, seemed to emphasise them in an unseemly manner.

Megan, who was standing beside her, wearing a pale blue dress that was draped to one side, looked trim and elegant when compared to Sheryl.

Rachael bit her lip. It was usually the other way round, Megan seeming plump and dumpy while Sheryl looked so svelte. She still might have done so if she'd chosen the pretty Empire-line white muslin dress I picked out for her when we went shopping, she thought regretfully, but Sheryl had refused to even try it on. 'It looks like a shapeless tent,' she'd said scathingly.

'For the sake of modesty, it's the sort of frock you should be wearing from now until after your baby is born.'

'Mam, this is the Twenties, modesty went out when Queen Victoria died. Alun would have a fit if I turned up in that thing.'

At the time Rachael worried about what other people at the wedding might think when they realised Sheryl's condition. Now she realised her anxiety had been needless, because the only people there were herself, Megan and Hadyn Baker.

As Alun and Sheryl signed the register and he kissed her, Rachael's heart turned over. The deed was done, they were now man and wife, but what did the future hold for them, she wondered.

Alun looked sleek and spruce and well pleased with himself. His cap badge was gleaming, his shoes polished to a mirror shine, his uniform well brushed and pressed.

Hadyn, also in uniform, was similarly smart and well groomed. Alun had the edge on him though, perhaps because he was the better-looking of the two men. If it had been Megan and Hadyn getting married then she'd feel so very different, Rachael mused.

How on earth would Sheryl fare as the wife of a soldier, she wondered. Alun was not master of his destiny, he couldn't live where he wanted to, and as yet he hadn't even been allocated any married quarters.

It meant that for the moment Sheryl would still be living at home with them. She would be there on her own, Rachael thought uneasily, because Gwynfor had put his foot down and refused to have Alun living under his roof.

'As a married man it is up to him to provide a home for his wife,' Gwynfor said stubbornly. 'He's not living here and that's final. Understand?'

For once, all Sheryl's wheedling and cajoling had made no impression. He had remained firm even when she'd started to cry. He had conceded that they could go back to Thesiger Street after today's ceremony for a wedding spread, but whether he would be there or not Rachael had no idea.

There would be no real honeymoon for Sheryl and Alun. They were spending their first night as man and wife at a hotel on Barry Island, a treat Rachael was paying for out of her own meagre savings. Next day Sheryl would return home and Alun would go back to barracks.

Alun had talked about finding some rooms locally, but so far he had not managed to do so. It worried Rachael because she knew it wouldn't be easy to afford anything on a soldier's pay.

Sheryl wouldn't be able to help in any way, because she had already had to give up work. Even though the baby wasn't due for another four months, her supervisor had told her that Harveys didn't feel it was seemly for her to be serving behind a counter in her condition.

Chapter Five

The Williams family were all shocked when Alun went off on manoeuvres two days after he and Sheryl were married. It was bad enough that Sheryl had none of the excitement most young brides enjoyed of moving into her own home with her new husband. This was even worse because they had no idea how long he would be away.

Since she had stopped being sick each morning, Sheryl felt fine, but with no job to go to, she was bored and more than a little resentful about the way things had turned out for her. Only a few months ago she had been looking forward to being seventeen, believing it meant that a whole new world would be opening up. It seemed now as if it had done the reverse and life had closed in on her, making her virtually a prisoner, and she didn't enjoy the situation one little bit.

Now that the excitement of the wedding was over and Alun was absent, she'd begun to feel fat and frowsy. She was also conscious that she was not only losing her shapely figure, but becoming clumsy in her movements. She constantly bumped into things, found sleeping uncomfortable because of her bulk, and was horrified that her feet and legs were swollen to twice the size they'd been before.

That wasn't the worst of it. She found being at home with her mother all day, every day, was an impossible situation.

Sheryl had always dismissed the role of housewife as trivial and inconsequential. Her mother did the shopping and cooked the meals that always appeared on time. She took it for granted that Rachael washed, ironed and mended their clothes and that the house, including her room, was cleaned and polished regularly.

Sheryl had never taken part in the work involved in any of this, happy to accept the fact that her mother liked to do everything herself.

'That way I know everything is done as it should be and in half the time it would take if you did it,' her mother always told her with a dismissive smile, on the odd occasion her father told Sheryl that she should offer to help.

Occasionally, as a punishment, she would be told to tidy up her room. Her mother usually redid it immediately afterwards, though, because she didn't consider it had been done properly.

The only thing Sheryl was ever asked to do was to nip across to the corner shop if they ran out of tea or sugar. Even this rarely happened, because they always had a well-stocked larder. Rachael Williams prided herself on regularly checking what was in her kitchen cupboards, and making a list of the things that were beginning to run low, long before they needed replacing.

Now, because she was at home all day, Sheryl was surprised to find that her mother seemed to take it for granted that she would do her share of the domestic chores. It was not that she minded helping around the house, but her mother was such a martinet.

The schedule for cleaning, washing and shopping was inflexible. Her mother had a strict timetable which seemed to encompass every hour of each day for the entire week, and she refused to deviate from it in any way.

That was bad enough, but there were also the high standards she insisted on. There seemed to be a right and wrong way of doing every chore from washing up to scrubbing the front step. Washing and ironing were the worst of all, and Sheryl found it both laborious and tiring.

It took almost two hours to heat up the water in the copper boiler that dominated one corner of the back scullery. The steam and the strong smell of soap as the whites were boiled for twenty minutes, then lifted out with wooden tongs and scrubbed on the washboard, or pounded in the dolly tub, were overpowering. Then the washing had to be rinsed twice in the stone sink before being put through the huge wooden mangle.

Not only did everything have to be spotlessly clean, but beautifully ironed and folded in a precise way. Any deviation brought criticism and, to Sheryl's intense annoyance, an insistence that it was done again properly.

'You'll have to do these things when you move into your own place,' her mother pointed out, 'so you may as well learn the right way to do them now.'

She did manage to wriggle out of some of the chores, like scrubbing the front step and window sills, and even doing the shopping, because her mother didn't want the neighbours seeing her changing shape. She was afraid that if they did they would start working out when the baby might be due, and then they'd reach the obvious conclusion that Sheryl's marriage had been rather a hurried one.

'You'd better start preparing a layette,' her mother kept warning her. 'You have nothing at all ready. The baby could arrive any time after the eight month, you know, Sheryl, possibly before Christmas.'

Even the stock of terry-towel napkins, tiny vests and all the other paraphernalia failed to bring either of them any delight. As she sat and sewed Sheryl longed to return to the days when she'd been working, her mother had been the one doing all the mundane household tasks, and she'd been free to go out with Megan.

That was another thing that she found irksome. Now that she had plenty of time there was no-one to go out with. Megan was at work and Alun was away. If she asked her mother to go with her she claimed that she hadn't the time to go gallivanting out all the time, because there was far too much to be done in the house.

'Apart from cleaning there's the shopping and the cooking. Your father expects his meal to be on the table when he walks through the door at six o'clock each evening,' she pointed out exasperatedly.

'Surely it wouldn't matter if it was half an hour late?' Sheryl challenged.

'It would to him! He's a man who likes to stick to routine. Come to that, so do I. I like to be finished, the washing-up done and everything put away so that I can be sitting down doing my knitting, or reading a book, by half past seven. A couple of hours in the evening is all the time I have for my own pleasures. Your dad likes to be in bed before ten o'clock on weekdays because he has to be up so early in the mornings.'

Sheryl knew all this, but she found the constant repetition of their dull routine almost unbearable. Her only means of escape was through the door at the end of their backyard to see Megan.

The Thomases' house was not as big as hers and certainly not as well furnished, but for all that the atmosphere was one she enjoyed. Mrs Thomas went along contentedly with whatever was happening around her. There was no strict schedule. If the meal was ready and one of her family was missing, the rest of them went ahead and ate theirs. They didn't wait or make a fuss about it. The latecomer's meal was covered over with a plate, or a saucepan lid, and kept warm over a pan of hot water, or else popped into the oven at the side of the kitchen range.

Mrs Thomas didn't seem to have any strict routine. Sometimes her place was in chaos; often she was cleaning late at night because she'd been occupied doing something else during the day. Megan seemed to give a hand without being asked, and whatever she did to help was never criticised.

Sheryl found it relaxing simply to be there. Megan's mam talked about the baby as if it was something to look forward to, not something to be ashamed about. She even showed an interest in how big Sheryl was getting, as if it was something to be admired and not hidden from view.

Her own mother preferred to ignore the whole business, the same as her father did, almost as if they were ashamed of her being pregnant even though she was married.

Alun Powell's emotions were confused. Newly married, he knew he should have been blissfully happy. In actual fact his responsibilities as a married man were already weighing heavily on his shoulders. Still only twenty, tall, slim and good-looking, in the normal way he would have been playing the field, still be heart-whole and fancy free, enjoying life to the full and taking his pick of all the girls. This had been the case until a few months ago, but all that had ended abruptly when Sheryl had faced him with the news that she was pregnant.

He knew right away that he was in deep trouble. For a start she was barely seventeen, and for another she was a Catholic, which meant that getting rid of the baby was out of the question.

The moment he'd faced her parents his heart sank. Her dad was as stiff and forbidding as any sergeant major. He didn't only condemn Alun's behaviour, he also made it quite clear that a soldier wasn't the sort of fellow he wanted his pretty young daughter to marry.

Her mother was not much better. She was a real fusspot, and up in arms about the terrible scandal she felt sure would ensue when the news that Sheryl was pregnant leaked out.

He'd done the only thing he could do and told them that he and Sheryl were planning to get married. He agreed without any arguing that the sooner they set the date the better. Whatever happened, because Sheryl was so young, he didn't want them complaining to any of his officers that he'd taken advantage of their daughter, or he could end up on a charge.

He'd thought that having offered to do the right thing would keep Sheryl's parents happy, but then they'd started putting difficulties in his way. They wanted him to change his religion and become a Catholic! It seemed that was the only way he and Sheryl could be married in the church her family attended, and have a choir singing and all the trimmings.

When he'd dug his heels in, and said he wasn't prepared to go along with that, Sheryl's father had turned very unpleasant and adamantly refused to come to the wedding unless it was held in the Catholic church.

When Alun had told him that they were going to be married in a register office, Mr Williams had ranted and raved about that not being a proper marriage. He made it crystal clear that he would have forbidden it, but for the disgrace of Sheryl having a baby out of wedlock.

Alun had said nothing about any of this to his own family. He didn't even tell them that he was getting married. As far as he was concerned it was none of their business.

His dad had never approved of anything he did. There had been a rift between them from the moment he'd told him that he wasn't following in the family tradition of going down the pit. After that his dad had given him the cold shoulder and had wanted nothing to do with him. He'd ended up leaving home when he'd been fifteen. Only his mam knew the real truth about why he'd done that.

He'd landed himself in trouble with the law, so before they caught up with him he'd joined the South Wales Borderers. He'd lied about his age, but he'd managed to get away with it. Losses on the Western Front and at Gallipoli had made the army desperate for recruits.

Although he resented being forced into marriage, he'd consoled himself with the thought that Sheryl was a very pretty girl. He knew she was spoilt and self-centred, but he'd thought that would be in their favour. He'd expected her parents eventually to come round to the situation and put the red carpet out for them.

It hadn't been like that, though. The first time he'd gone to Sheryl's home, after he'd insisted that they were going to be married in a register office, Gwynfor Williams had walked out of the room and Sheryl's mam had treated him as if he was a bad smell around the place. Her dad had even said he wouldn't have them living under his roof, despite the fact they would be man and wife.

The trouble was, Alun reflected, he couldn't afford to rent a place and he knew there were no married quarters available. Not that he'd qualify for them even if there were, since the army wasn't aware that he was married.

To give himself time to think what to do, he volunteered for a three-week special course on Salisbury Plain that was due to start immediately after his wedding day. He told Sheryl that he was being sent on manoeuvres and that he didn't know when he would be back. It was

64

dead easy, because no-one at the barracks would tell her where he was, leastways not unless she went there asking for him and told them that she was his wife.

He hoped she wouldn't do that because he was supposed to ask for permission to get married from his commanding officer. He'd been afraid to do so because if the army found out that Sheryl was pregnant, and barely seventeen, it might land him in trouble.

Consequently Alun hadn't been able to arrange for Sheryl to have an army allowance. He wasn't too sure how she was coping for money, since he knew she'd lost her job once her baby began to show. He assumed that since she was living at home her parents were keeping her, but how long that would last he had no idea. From what he'd seen of her father's attitude to their marriage he was pretty certain that, sooner or later, Gwynfor Williams was going to demand that they paid their own way.

An even bigger problem was the question of what was going to happen after the kid arrived. He didn't even want to think about being a dad, he wasn't ready for that sort of responsibility.

When Sheryl had first told him that she was pregnant she hadn't seemed to be any keener than he was to start a family, he reflected, so he couldn't understand why she hadn't had the guts to get rid of it. He was sure that Megan Thomas would know how to go about it. She had her head screwed on, she was down to earth and had plenty of common sense, and her mam was the same.

Glenda Thomas was a real good sort and she always made him and Sheryl welcome, which was more than could be said for Mrs Williams. In fact, ever since he'd returned from manoeuvres, when he did manage to get any time off he and Sheryl usually spent it at the Thomases' place, he thought wryly.

Chapter Six

Sheryl's baby was born in the early hours of Sunday 9th January 1921 after a long and arduous labour. Her contractions had started on the Saturday afternoon while she'd been at Megan's house. She had insisted on Megan coming back to Thesiger Street and staying with her.

Throughout the long, pain-ridden night she had constantly screamed for Alun, but none of them knew where he was. They hadn't seen him for about five days and they assumed that once again he was away on manoeuvres.

'He should be here sharing the responsibility of what is going on,' Rachael Williams exclaimed angrily. 'The army should make special allowances in circumstances like these.'

'If Sheryl had been living in married quarters like she should be by now, they'd probably let him have time off to be with her, I'm sure of that,' Gwynfor Williams declared.

'If she was living in married quarters then they'd probably whisk her off to a military hospital and we'd not have our home turned into this shambles,' his wife complained, her mouth was tight and disapproving.

Molly Mathews, the midwife they'd called in,

was warm-hearted and reassuring, but in Rachael Williams's opinion, she was anything but efficient. Rachael deplored the way Molly had taken over the house and disrupted her neat orderliness. She resented the way Molly had spread herself around the place, her messy paraphernalia overflowing from Sheryl's bedroom to the landing.

Rachael itched to replace the crumpled bed-linen, clear away the soiled towels and the bowl of water that had been used to clean up both the newborn baby girl and Sheryl. To her mind, restoring a semblance of order in the house was far more important than trying to make the mother and baby comfortable, or encouraging the child to feed. It would do so soon enough once it was hungry.

Sheryl's behaviour when she'd gone into labour had shocked her. She realised her daughter was far too young at seventeen to be going through such an ordeal, but she hadn't expected her to carry on the way she had. Her own mother had always said, 'If it can't be cured then it must be endured', and childbirth was one of those things that had to be endured.

She could remember from the time when Sheryl had been born that there was considerable pain and discomfort, and a certain loss of dignity. Even so, she certainly hadn't given way to screaming, or vented her revulsion about what was taking place, as her daughter had done so forcefully.

She'd been utterly ashamed of Sheryl, even though Molly Mathews had assured her that it was better to rant and rave than it was to bottle it all up inside.

'We don't want her turning her milk sour, now do we, cariad, or this poor little baby will end up suffering from colic!' she'd said placatingly.

Rachael Williams's lips tightened, but she kept her thoughts to herself. She'd never heard such nonsense in the whole of her life.

In the morning, as soon as it was daylight, she'd asked Megan if she'd go to the barracks and see if she could find out any news of Alun, and when he would be back from wherever it was he'd been sent.

'He ought to be told about the baby! Sheryl's been calling out for him all night so it might help to settle her down if he was here,' she added hopefully.

'Mr Williams will go with you,' she told Megan quickly when she saw her hesitating. 'I wouldn't expect you to go there at this time of the morning on your own.'

Gwynfor Williams complied with surprising alacrity. After what seemed to be an endless night listening to the commotion his daughter was making, and the constant nagging of his wife, it was like being offered a break for freedom.

Furthermore, he relished the opportunity of having a few strong words with his son-in-law.

He intended pointing out to Alun that it was high time he made a home for his wife and child. The thought of them having to make their home in his house dismayed him more than he cared to admit.

He strode out so fast that Megan found she had a job to keep up with him. It was a sharp cold morning, and frost sparkled on the rooftops and glinted in the puddles on the road.

'Can you slow down a bit, Mr Williams,' she begged. 'The pavements feel so slippery that I'm afraid I'm going to fall over.'

'Sorry, girl! My mind's on other things, see. Here,' he crooked his elbow, 'take hold of my arm, then you'll feel safer.'

He still walked so fast that she was breathless, but at least it meant that she didn't have to talk to him, she consoled herself.

Mr Williams wasted no time on preliminaries when they reached Maindy Barracks, but demanded to see the duty officer.

'I want to speak to Alun Powell,' he told him. 'It's extremely urgent.'

'I'm afraid that's not possible,' the duty officer informed them, 'he's not here.'

'Could we speak to Hadyn Baker, then,' Megan put in quickly.

Again the duty officer shook his head. 'They're both on leave.' He consulted a duty roster. 'They're not due back until 0600 hours on Friday 14th January.'

Megan felt her heart turn over. Alun on leave

and he'd said nothing at all about it to Sheryl, it was unbelievable!

Gwynfor Williams seemed to be equally taken aback. 'There must be some way we can get in touch with him! His wife's just had a baby.'

'His wife?' The officer's eyes narrowed. 'Are you sure you've got the right man? Alun Powell isn't married.'

'He most certainly is!' Gwynfor's eyes flashed with fury. 'He's married to my daughter. You'd better give me his home address.'

'I'm sorry, sir, that's something I'm not allowed to do. I will see that your message gets passed on to Private Powell, though,' he assured him.

Gwynfor Williams was not so easily appeased. Tight-jawed, struggling to hold his temper, he argued angrily, but the officer was implacable. It was against army rules to do so and army rules could not be infringed under any circumstances, not even in an emergency of this sort.

Nola Powell's first instinct when she heard the loud hammering on the front door was to signal to Alun to keep quiet. Then she peeped out through the side window to see who it was.

She hadn't paid the tallyman for three weeks and the last time she had got behind with her payments he had threatened to send in the bailiffs. If that was who was at the door, then she intended to lie low and not answer. With any luck they'd go away before Cradog came home from work, because he didn't know that she was up to her ears in debt. He'd raise the roof if he found out, especially when he discovered she'd been using the money put aside to pay off the tallyman in order to buy extras because Alun was at home.

What else could she do, she asked herself. They only paid soldiers a pittance, so she could hardly ask him to dib up for his keep when he came home on leave. The trouble was he had such a hearty appetite that she spent far more on groceries than usual, as well as buying beer and ciggies for him.

She sometimes wondered if letting him go and be a soldier had been such a good idea, but he'd been determined not to go down the pit.

Now, as she peeped through the curtains and saw that there were two khaki-clad figures on the doorstep, she wondered if they were friends coming to visit him or whether he was in some sort of trouble.

She wasn't left in any doubt. They had spotted the movement of the curtains, and bellowed through the letter box that they knew Alun was there and that they wanted him outside right away.

'Duw anwyl, what have you been up to this time?' she exclaimed in alarm. 'I'll try and stall them to give you a few minutes to get away out the back,' she told him. 'Go on, skedaddle!'

He shook his head. 'I'm not in any kind of trouble, Mam.'

'You mean I can answer the door and let them in?' she said in surprise.

He shrugged. 'You might as well. They won't bugger off until you do, and if you aren't quick about it they might batter the door down.'

From the way they were still hammering on the door she judged he was right.

'All right, I'm coming,' she bawled back at them. 'Dammo di, can't you wait a flaming minute while I put me shoes on!'

Turning to Alun, she mouthed silently at him to get back into the scullery out of sight. 'Let's see what they want you for first, before I say you're here,' she cautioned.

He hesitated, then shrugged and did as she'd advised.

'Are you Mrs Powell, Alun Powell's mother? We've come to collect him,' the older of the two soldiers told her the moment she opened the door.

'Collect him?' She looked the sergeant up and down critically. 'What do you think he is, a bloody parcel?'

'Is he here? We know he's on leave and this is his home . . .'

'That's right, but you don't expect him to be sitting here by the fireside do you? What's this all about, anyway? Why are you in such a hurry to see him? Has war broken out again?'

73

'No, not as far as we know, Mrs Powell, but we do need to see your son as soon as possible.'

'So you said, boyo! Are you going to tell me what it's all about?'

'It's a personal matter . . . a domestic matter.'

'Go on then, I'm his mother, tell me what's wrong. He doesn't have any secrets from me.'

The sergeant rubbed his hand across his chin thoughtfully. 'It's about his wife, she's just given birth and . . .'

Nola Powell's laugh cut him short. 'You've got that all wrong, sonny,' she told him dismissively. 'My Alun's not married, he hasn't got a wife!'

'I think you'll find that he has, Mrs Powell.'

'You check up on your records and you'll see I'm right,' she repeated stubbornly. 'Now if that's all you came to tell us, then you've had a wasted journey. I'll let him know you've called. He'll laugh his socks off when I tell him why,' she chuckled as she started to close the door.

'I think you should tell him to report back to Maindy Barracks at the earliest opportunity. Today if possible.'

'His leave's not up until Friday!'

'We need to see him before then. Understand?'

'Now what was all that about?' Nola Powell demanded, the minute she'd closed the door behind the two soldiers.

'Like you told them, Mam, they've got their facts wrong,' Alun blustered.

'Not them! Come on, out with it. What's been going on?'

One look at his mother's face and Alun knew it was no good lying. He accepted the cigarette she held out to him, and then as briefly as he could he told her about meeting Sheryl and how they'd married in a register office.

'Without even saying a word to me?'

'You'd been in hospital for an op so it didn't seem right to worry you about it.'

'Fair do's, but why the rush?'

'Sheryl was preggers.'

His mother's eyes narrowed. 'So those boyos who came looking for you were telling the truth.'

He nodded.

'So you had to get married, is that what you're telling me?'

He nodded again and helped himself to another cigarette from her packet of Woodbines that were lying on the table.

'Was it too late for her to get rid of it, then?'

'She's Catholic, so it was against her religion to do anything like that.'

Mrs Powell looked puzzled. 'Then how come she got married in a register office?' she asked.

'I wouldn't change my religion.'

'What religion? I didn't know you had any.'

'I put down Methodist when I signed up. It was either that or C of E, and if I'd said that I

75

would have had to go on church parade every Sunday.'

'So where is this Sheryl now?'

'Still living with her mam. I couldn't apply for married quarters because I didn't ask for permission to get married.'

'Well, it looks as though they know now, found you out haven't they, boyo? What happens next?'

He shook his head. 'I don't know. Dropped me in it, hasn't she. I'll probably be court-martialled or something and slammed in the glasshouse.'

'For getting married? Dammo di, what sort of army is this you're in? Surely it's got sod all to do with them whether you are married or not?'

'It's not as simple as that. She's only seventeen . . .'

'Are you telling me she was only a kid of sixteen when you put her in the club?'

'I thought she was older . . . she looks about twenty!'

'Duw anwyl! You're asking for trouble!'

'I know! I'm supposed to ask permission of the commanding officer before getting married.'

Nola's eyes narrowed. 'If you'd done that, told them the truth and so on, then you'd have got an allowance for your wife and somewhere to live. Right?'

He nodded.

She shook her head in dismay. 'You're a

76

bigger fool than I thought you were. And what about the kid? Who's going to bring that up and pay for its keep?'

Alun shrugged his shoulders. 'I'll have to, I suppose. I don't think her mam and dad will let her go on staying with them. They don't like me being there as it is, in case I make the place untidy. A squalling baby in their home will be the last thing they want.'

'So what will you do?'

'I don't know.' He gave her a speculative look. 'I thought that perhaps we could come and live here for a while. I'll get myself out of the army and get a job. What about it, Mam?'

Chapter Seven

Sheryl was secretly relieved when Alun told her that he was leaving the army for good. It meant there would be no more long absences when she had no idea of his whereabouts while he was away on manoeuvres. At last they would be together as a man and wife should be.

He told her that once he was released and had found a job, then they could start making plans for finding a home of their own. She'd have to be patient for a while longer, but knowing that one day soon they'd have their own place would make the waiting bearable. It meant that she'd have time to plan as well as dream about where they would live.

She was sure that her mam would be so relieved to know she would soon be moving out of Thesiger Street that she'd help her to get together all the basic items she was going to need. Her mam had never thrown anything out in her life. She had more sheets, towels and household goods than she could ever use. Every room in the house was cluttered up because they had twice as much furniture as was needed.

Sheryl couldn't wait to move. She was utterly fed up with her mother's niggling ways and constant carping. She seemed to spend her day arguing with her mother, from the moment baby Caitlin woke around six in the morning, crying lustily for her first feed, until she finally settled her down for the night after her last feed at ten o'clock.

In addition, life had become a monotonous round of caring for Caitlin. It was a never-ending routine of changing, feeding, winding her and then repeating it all over again. When Caitlin was asleep and she had the chance to take a rest herself, which she needed when she'd had a disturbed night, her mother would insist that she tidied her bedroom, washed the ever-full pail of dirty nappies or did some other household task.

In the first couple of weeks after Caitlin's birth her mother had done all these chores for her. She had assumed that her mam would go on taking care of them as long as she was living at home, but her mother quickly quashed that idea.

'It's your responsibility, Sheryl, and it is bad enough having you living here and disrupting my routine without me having to shoulder all the extra work that a young baby makes.'

'I feel so tired all the time, though, Mam.'

'At your age? Nonsense! If you feel tired then think how I must feel.'

'You haven't just had a baby,' Sheryl told her sulkily.

Her mother refused to carry on the discussion.

Her answer to any of Sheryl's moans was, 'You should talk to your husband about that. You chose to get married, we didn't push you into doing so, or expect you to ruin your life or ours like this.'

The only concession Mrs Williams was prepared to make was that Sheryl need not pay anything towards her keep while she was still living with them.

'Since it is only going to be a temporary arrangement, you can save whatever money Alun gives you for when you move into your own place,' her mother told her. 'You'll need it then, I can tell you! You've no idea what it costs to put food on the table every day, not to mention all the other things you'll have to buy,' she warned grimly.

Sheryl let it all go over her head. All she wanted was to be with Alun and for them to be on their own. After that she'd work things out for herself.

She couldn't understand why it was taking so long. Alun had told her the week after Caitlin had been born that he intended leaving the army. Now it was April, Caitlin was three months old and he still hadn't done so. He hadn't been sent away on any more manoeuvres but he seemed to be confined to barracks most of the time, so she hardly ever saw him. When she asked, he told her that it was all to do with him working towards his release.

She was conscious that both her parents were

as anxious as she was about the situation. It was a source of disappointment to her that even though Caitlin was now a happy little bundle, with a shock of light brown hair and the biggest blue eyes imaginable, she didn't seem to find very much favour with her grandparents.

Gwynfor Williams practically ignored Caitlin. Rachael Williams seemed rarely to have any time to nurse or cuddle her. Both of them appeared unmoved by her gummy smile, or her gurgles of delight.

Caitlin received more attention from the Thomases than from her own grandparents. Glenda Thomas cooed over her, and noted every tiny change in her development. Ivan Thomas seemed to be equally smitten by her. He stopped whatever he was doing the moment Sheryl walked through the door, so that he could take a look at Caitlin.

Elwyn, who had now finished his police training and was living back at home, was a little more restrained. Apparently he'd been shocked when Megan had told him that Sheryl was marrying Alun Powell.

'Duw anwyl, you don't really mean it, girl, do you?' he said disbelievingly when she broke the news to him. 'What the hell has made her decide to do that?'

He'd looked even more stunned when Megan had told him the reason, and for a long time he couldn't even bring himself to ask how Sheryl was.

Although he didn't openly admit it, Megan knew that Elwyn had had his own sights set on Sheryl. Before he went away on his police training he'd thought she was far too young for any permanent commitment, so he had said nothing.

The baby filled him with awe. Caitlin was so like Sheryl that his interest in her grew, despite his resolve to remain aloof and detached. When Megan informed him that Sheryl was going to move away, as soon as Alun Powell was out of the army and had found somewhere for them to live, he felt quite bereft.

Alun was discharged from the army on Wednesday 18th May 1921 and left Maindy Barracks for the last time.

He had not told Sheryl the exact date, and went straight to his parents' home. He needed time to think and to plan what he was going to do next.

His mother seemed pleased to have him back, but when, once again, he suggested that he and Sheryl and the baby should move in, Nola Powell was not to be won over.

'Diawlch! Never! I've brought you and your brothers and sisters up so don't you think I've seen enough of squalling babas?'

'Caitlin's your granddaughter, Mam,' Alun pointed out.

'That's as maybe, but I don't know your kid's mam, now do I? If you'd married a girl from

Abertillery or even from around here, someone I knew, then it would be different. I would probably have taken you both in for a while to help you get on your feet, but not this Sheryl, she's a complete stranger!'

'Well, she wouldn't be a stranger for long, not if you'd agree to meet her or if she and Caitlin were living here.'

'Dammo di! Can't you get it into your thick skull that I don't want her here? Right little madam she sounds! From what you say about her and her mam this Sheryl would be as finicky as hell and expect me to start changing my ways. Well, I've no intention of doing that, boyo! Not at my time of life. I've had to make too many changes in my lifetime to accommodate this family, and I made the very last one when I upped sticks and left Abertillery. Born and brought up there, and I loved the place, see! Now I'm stuck here in this godforsaken hole with strangers all around me.'

'So why the hell did you move from there?' Alun asked, bewildered.

'It was for your dad's sake, wasn't it. Pride, see! Years to go before he's too old to work, yet if we'd stayed where we were because of the old silicosis he'd have been on the scrap heap, now wouldn't he.'

'If Sheryl and the baby came here to live then you'd have plenty of company. You'd have a family of your own around you again,' Alun persisted.

'Family! Haven't you listened to a single word I've been saying? She's no family . . .'

'She's my wife!'

'Then go and live with her. Rent a couple of rooms somewhere and make a home for her and your babba. Accept the sodding responsibility you've taken on.'

Alun sighed. He knew he'd lost, but he made one last plea. 'Couldn't we live here with you for a couple of months, until I find a job and get on my feet?'

Nola shook her head. 'You had a job, being a soldier. Why chuck that in? If you'd gone about it the right way they'd have given you somewhere to live.'

'Mam, you know why I left the army. I broke their bloody rules and it was either get out or be punished. I was damn lucky that I was at the end of the time I signed on for, otherwise I might have found myself in the glasshouse for God knows how long.'

Nola shrugged. 'There you are then. Break the rules and you have to take what follows, boyo. I know you inside and out and I know this marriage won't last. I don't intend inviting you to come and live here and then find that you bugger off and leave me to support your wife and kid.'

'So you're turning me out? My own mam turning her back on me,' he said huffily.

'That's right. Try her mam, she might be a softer touch than me!'

84

Alun sighed. 'Impossible. I've already told you I couldn't live with her, she's worse than a bloody sergeant major. Whenever she looks at me her face tightens up as though she's swallowing vinegar. Even Sheryl finds it impossible to live with her.'

Nola Powell shrugged her plump shoulders. 'Your Sheryl would probably find fault over living here with me.'

'But unless you give it a try then we'll never know,' Alun persisted.

Nola Powell was not to be inveigled into changing her mind. As she'd already pointed out to Alun, she'd raised a family and now they were all grown-up and independent. For the first time in her life she was free to run her home and her life in her own way. As long as there was a hot meal on the table when Cradog came home, and a clean shirt ready for him when he needed it, he was happy.

She knew that sometimes her standards slipped. She cleaned the place when she was in the mood to do so. Occasionally that wasn't until there was a grey film of dust everywhere, and the room so untidy that she could no longer find anywhere to sit down.

Often when she'd made Cradog's breakfast and seen him off to work, she went back to bed for an hour or two. Or else she simply pottered around, doing nothing in particular, enjoying the peace and tranquillity.

If she wanted to she could spend most of the

day drinking everlasting cups of tea, smoking one cigarette after another and reading the novelettes and women's magazines she was always buying. She'd become so addicted to them that when she started a story she couldn't put it down. Reading was like a drug, taking her out of her drab, mundane existence into other lives filled with love and excitement, bringing back all the wild and wonderful dreams she'd once had, which had never been fulfilled.

'It wouldn't be fair on your dad. He's not well, he needs his rest, so he doesn't want a squalling baby in the house,' she insisted when Alun kept begging her to think about it.

'I'd like you to meet them, though, Mam. You'd love little Caitlin, I know you would.'

'One babba is pretty much the same as any other, unless you're its mam,' Nola replied.

'You'd like Sheryl, too, if you met her,' he persisted. 'She's not a fusspot like her mam.'

Nola shook her head. 'No, I don't want her here.'

Nola had no intention of giving up the freedom she was enjoying by welcoming into her home a girl she didn't know. Once Sheryl got a foot over the doorstep, that would be it. She'd come on a visit and the next thing they would have all moved in.

Nola reached for her shabby old handbag and delved inside it for her purse. Tucked away in the back of it was a well-folded white five-pound note. 'Here,' she held it out to Alun.

86

'Take this and find yourself somewhere to live. I mean it, son, when I say that I don't want you moving in here.'

Alun knew he was defeated. The days when, as the youngest in the family, he was able to twist his mother round his little finger were over. It would seem, he thought resignedly, that he'd have to find a couple of rooms for him, Sheryl and the baby . . . and then he'd have to try and find himself a job.

Chapter Eight

The back bedroom in a shabby terrace house in Angelina Street off Loudon Square was the least inviting place Sheryl had ever seen in her life. Although it was a bright summer morning the room was sunless, airless and dreary. She couldn't believe that Alun thought it was a suitable home for her and their baby.

The furniture consisted of a battered armchair, a ladder-back wooden chair, a three-quarter-size bed, a rickety table and a cupboard built in across one corner of the room. The tall narrow sash window looked out onto a yard that contained piles of assorted junk and one small brick outhouse. Later she discovered that the outhouse was the lavatory; the only one for the whole house.

'We have our own kitchen,' Alun told her. 'Come and look.'

The kitchen was a curtained-off section on the turn of the landing. There was a rusty gas ring and a grime-encrusted brown stone sink with a piece of piping running from it through a hole in the outside wall, so that it could drain down into a grid in the yard below. Attached to the sink was a greasy slab of wood to serve as both a draining board and worktop. Above it were two open shelves and on the other wall there was a lopsided wooden cupboard.

'It's only a temporary home, something for the moment. We'll move into a better place as soon as we can afford it,' Alun assured her.

Sheryl looked around with distaste. She shuddered at the thought of sleeping in the grubby bed, which was probably alive with fleas and bedbugs. Worse still would be trying to prepare their meals in the alcove that served as a kitchen.

She knew that Alun was waiting for her to say something, to accept the home he had found for them. His sharp dark eyes were watching her closely, noting her reactions.

If she said she couldn't live there, how would Alun take it, she wondered. In the last few months they'd had so many problems because they couldn't be together that it seemed whenever they met up there was discord.

Alun had changed so much since he'd come out of the army in May. He still looked smart. He was still so handsome that he set her heart racing whenever she saw him, but there was a difference in his manner. It was especially noticeable in his attitude towards her.

Sheryl blamed it on the fact that they hadn't bonded properly because they weren't able to live together. She felt that he seemed to lack any sense of emotional commitment towards her and Caitlin.

He'd found a job and a home for them both, but she kept asking herself if he still loved her. She ached to be able to be close, to feel his arms around her, his lips on hers, and their bodies united.

She hoped that Alun felt the same and that it was only because her dad refused to let him move into Thesiger Street, and his mother was equally adamant that they couldn't make their home at Archer Road, that they were living separate lives.

Sometimes it seemed to Sheryl that Alun didn't find the situation as hard as she did. He was still living at his mother's place and couldn't understand why she was so disgruntled at having to stay on with her own family. She often cried herself to sleep wondering if he needed her like she needed him. She knew she couldn't stand the uncertainty for much longer.

'You don't seem to understand, Alun, my mam doesn't really like us being there. She wants us out before Caitlin starts crawling all over the place,' she'd told him.

'She's not much of a grandmother, is she?' he taunted.

'No,' she agreed, 'she's far too house-proud. She doesn't like all the mess and paraphernalia that a young baby causes.'

Much as she resented her mother's attitude, Sheryl could understand it. She was also astounded by how much turmoil a baby created.

'Anyway, Alun, I'm fed up of living with my mam and dad. Surely, setting up home together was the whole point of getting married.'

If she refused to accept this room in Angelina Street, what would happen next? If she lied and said that she thought the place was all right, would he bother to try to find them something better? The words stuck in her throat and for once she was pleased when Caitlin started howling.

'I must feed her, she's hungry,' she said, pushing the baby into his arms.

Rummaging in the bags they'd dumped just inside the door, she found the one with the feeding bottle and the tin of powdered milk and took them out. 'I'll need to boil a kettle so I'll make us a cuppa at the same time,' she mumbled as she headed out onto the landing.

The so-called kitchen was worse than she'd envisaged. Not only was the sink caked with grease and grime, but the shelves were studded with mice droppings and there were dead bluebottles and flies trapped in the spiders' webs that festooned the corners of the tiny alcove.

A box of Swan Vestas lay on the makeshift draining board, but they were so damp that it took three attempts before she managed to light the gas ring and plonk the tin kettle on top of it. The gas ran out before the kettle boiled, but she judged that the water in it was warm enough for Caitlin's bottle.

By this time Caitlin was screaming with hunger. Alun snatched the bottle from her and stuffed the teat into the child's mouth. 'Where's that cup of char then?' he asked irritably as the crying subsided.

'The gas ran out before the kettle had boiled. The water was hot enough for her bottle, but not to make any tea for us.'

'Then why didn't you stick some more money in the bloody meter?' he complained.

'I haven't any!'

'Here!' He thrust the baby into her arms, dug deep into his trouser pockets and brought out a handful of coins. 'What does it take? Tanners or coppers?'

Sheryl shook her head. 'I don't know, I don't even know where the money goes.'

'It takes shillings,' he told her when she followed him to see where the meter was. 'You'd better remember to keep a stock of them handy.' He looked in the empty cupboard and at the bare shelves of the grimy kitchen. 'We'll have to get some grub in, there's nothing here to even make a brew. Tell you what, while you finish seeing to the kid I'll go and get some bread and stuff.'

Sheryl nodded, brushing the back of her hand across her eyes to wipe away the tears. She sat down in the battered armchair to finish giving Caitlin her bottle. This wasn't at all how she had expected their arrival at their first home to be. She'd even dreamed of being carried over the threshold, like they did in her favourite magazine stories. She'd imagined the living room would be big and airy with pale yellow walls and flowery curtains at the window. There would be two bedrooms, a large one for them and a smaller one for Caitlin.

Once Caitlin's hunger was appeased she fell asleep, even though she hadn't quite finished her bottle. Sheryl looked round for somewhere safe to lay her down because she desperately needed to go to the lavatory. The only place was the bed, and the counterpane looked so grubby that she hesitated to put her on it.

As there was nowhere else she spread out the shawl she'd been carrying Caitlin in and let her lie on that. Then she covered her over with her own coat and tucked it in around her, hoping that it would stop her from rolling off the bed if she did wake up while she nipped down to the yard. There were three flights of stairs and on each landing turn there was a curtained-off alcove kitchen. Noises came from rooms on each of the floors, and she began to wonder how many people were living in the building.

When she reached the ground floor she had no idea how to get out into the backyard, so she followed the passageway towards the back of the house. To her dismay it led straight into a room and there, stripped to the waist, was an enormous black man. He was standing in front of a cracked piece of mirror that was balanced on the window ledge and he had a cut-throat razor in one hand. He turned abruptly as she opened the door, the razor held aloft.

It took Sheryl all her will power not to scream in fright.

'Good morning,' he nodded to her amicably and scraped the cut-throat razor down the well-soaped left-hand side of his face.

'I'm so sorry, I didn't mean to barge in . . .' She stopped, hardly knowing how to explain where she was going to this half-naked man.

'Walk straight through that far door and you're there,' he told her, continuing with his shaving quite unperturbed.

'Thank you!' She scuttled past him, her heart thundering, and let herself out of the back door. She was still shaking as she picked her way through the mountain of rubbish to the brick outhouse.

Tentatively she lifted the latch and opened the door, then she retreated backwards as the stench hit her nostrils. The place looked filthy, even worse than their room. The wooden seat was cracked and stained and the pan itself so soiled that she felt bile rising in her throat. The urgency she'd felt before was gone, and she was about to turn and rush back the way she'd come when she remembered the man in the back kitchen. She was filled with confusion. What would he think if she did that? He might think she'd been spying on him or something.

Her face screwed up in disgust, she went inside and closed the door. Since it was the only

lavatory there was she'd have to use it sometime, she told herself as she slid home the bolt.

There was a handful of old newspapers,
threaded onto a piece of string, hanging on the
wall beside the pan, so she tore off some strips
and laid them on the wooden seat. She had
never felt so tense in her life. She kept remembering how many other people lived in the same
building, who must also use this nightmare hole.

Alun was sitting in the armchair eating a
hunk of bread and cheese when she got back
upstairs.

'Where the hell have you been? I thought
you'd run out on me and left me holding the
baby,' he joked.

'I went down there.' Sheryl shuddered, pointing out of the cracked window to the yard
below.

He grinned. 'What's the old khazi like then?'

She sat down, her head in her hands, her hair
falling in a tangled mess around her face. 'It's
awful, you've no idea, Alun!' She looked across
at him, her blue eyes filled with disgust. 'We
can't possibly stay here.'

'We'll have to, there's nowhere else we can
go. I'm practically skint. I've had to pay a week
up front for this place, so it's here or out on the
street.'

She moved to where he was sitting and
perched on the arm of his chair. 'Couldn't we
go to your mam and dad's place in Ely?' she
wheedled.

He shook his head. 'I've told you before, my old girl won't have us. She said it's not the sort of place for a baby, not with me dad having silicosis and hawking and spitting all the time.'

'Silicosis isn't catching, is it?'

He shrugged. 'Mam said no and that's it. I've never managed to get the better of her in an argument yet, so no point pushing it. She might come round later on, when she's seen the baby.'

'Could we go and visit her today then?' Sheryl asked hopefully. 'I'm sure she'll change her mind when she sees little Caitlin.'

'Don't talk so daft! I can't spare the money for tram fares all the way out to Ely. I've only a couple of bob left!'

'What about your wages?'

'Wages?' He raised his eyebrows. 'What the hell are you on about?'

'You told me that you had a job to go to when you came out of the army,' she reminded him.

'It fell through,' he muttered, avoiding her eyes. 'I couldn't start as soon as they wanted so they gave it to some other bugger.'

'That's not fair . . .'

'Nothing is in this life, it's time you realised that,' he told her sourly.

'I hate it here, Alun!' She snuggled up to him. 'It's squalid and filthy. It's no place for a young baby.'

'Come on kiddo, stop your nagging and put a smile on your face, it isn't all that bad,' he protested, giving her a squeeze. 'Eat your grub and drink your tea.'

Sheryl picked up the chipped mug and looked dubiously at the orange tea in it. She sipped cautiously, then pulled a face.

'What's the matter with it?'

She shook her head. 'I don't know. It's terribly sweet and tastes awful. Maybe the milk's off.'

'It can't be! I used conny-onny.'

'You mean sweetened condensed milk from a tin?'

'Yes. I thought it would do to spread on our bread as well as using it in our tea when we've nothing better,' he said, a note of defiance in his voice.

Sheryl shook her head and held out the mug to him. 'Do you want this? I don't.'

He snatched it from her and drank half of it down in one gulp, then he nodded towards the wedge of bread and cheese he'd made for her. 'Are you going to eat it or shall I have that as well?'

Wordlessly she pushed it towards him. If she didn't eat or drink anything then she wouldn't have to use the revolting lavatory down in the yard again, she thought childishly.

'Right, please yourself,' Alun told her as he drained the mug and stood up. Still chewing, he made for the door.

'You're not leaving me here on my own, are you?' she asked in alarm.

'I'm off out to see if there's any work going anywhere.'

'So what am I supposed to do?' Sheryl gaped.

He shrugged. 'Whatever married women usually do when they're at home. You can clean this hole up for a start, and then shop for some more food so that you have a proper meal waiting for me when I get back.'

'How can I do any shopping, Alun, when I've no money?'

He counted out some coins for her. 'Here you are. Make it go as far as you can, though, because I don't know when there will be any more.'

'What time will you be back?'

He frowned. 'I don't know, do I! It depends where I go and what happens.'

'Exactly what sort of work are you looking for then, Alun?'

'How the hell do I know! It's a case of mooching around and taking whatever's on offer. I can't afford to be choosy, can I, not now I've got a family to support.'

Sheryl bit her lip to stop herself from saying anything more, since everything she said seemed to annoy him.

As the door closed behind Alun, she looked round the cramped airless room once again. Everything was rickety, lopsided, shabby and dirty. Even the ceiling was stained and there were spiders' webs in every corner.

Mentally she compared it with the comfortable living room at Thesiger Street and felt a lump rising in her throat.

She wondered if her mother would let her move back home if she admitted that perhaps Rachael had been right when she'd said that getting married in such a rush was a mistake. Even her mother's constant carping about cleanliness and tidiness would be preferable to living in this stinking hovel.

Remembering some of the stupid things she'd said to her mother before she left, she bitterly regretted her outburst. It wasn't always wise to speak your mind. She certainly shouldn't have flared up and told her mam to mind her own business and stop interfering over the way she did things for Caitlin. Her mam had meant well and she had done so much for them; she'd even bought her a pram as well as heaps of other things for Caitlin, knowing that at present she couldn't afford them herself.

The trouble is, Sheryl thought unhappily, in the past I've always managed to get my own way over everything, and I've never considered anyone but myself. Megan had told her this many times, told her how lucky she was to be so spoilt. Now she'd upset the apple cart and no mistake!

She daren't even go home on a visit. If she did, her mam probably wouldn't open the door. Her dad had said that it was time for her to go and that he didn't want her there any longer, and she supposed it was what she deserved, she thought ruefully.

It looked as if the only thing to do was make the best of what she had. Perhaps in a week or two's time, if she found her new way of life was completely unbearable, she'd chance going to Thesiger Street. By then her mam would be missing her and Caitlin, so perhaps if she talked to her nicely she would be able to wheedle her way back into her good books.

With any luck she would be able to persuade her mother into letting her move back in. Or, if she refused to do that, she might let Sheryl have some of the pots and pans and bedding that she'd earmarked to bring away with her when she moved into her own place.

Looking back, she could see now that she'd been absolutely crazy to storm out with nothing but her clothes and Caitlin's things.

Chapter Nine

Alun took a deep breath as he escaped from the confines of the house in Angelina Street and turned towards the Pier Head.

The fresh air had a salty tang, although it was laced with a mixture of more unpleasant smells from the litter-strewn streets around him, ones that he didn't even try to identify.

He jingled the coins in the pockets of his grey flannel trousers and felt a surge of excitement as he anticipated how he would spend the rest of the day, knowing he could come and go as he pleased.

After his years as a soldier he had no intention of ever again finding himself in a situation where he had to jump to attention, salute and say 'Yes sir' every time someone spoke to him. From now on he was as free as a bird. No more guard duty. No drill sergeant bellowing orders.

It had sounded so adventurous to sign on, believing he'd be sent over to France right away and become a hero on the battle front. How was he to know that the 3rd Company of the South Wales Borderers would never go overseas but stay cooped up in Maindy Barracks?

They'd called him a soldier, but tea boy,

drudge, boot-polisher, or general dogsbody, would have described his role far better. He'd been at everyone's beck and call, he'd been given the runaround, the most rotten jobs. He was paid washers, and bullied by corporals and sergeants. He might have missed the action but at least he was still alive, he told himself, and resolved to enjoy every minute of his life that he could.

By the time peace was declared he was almost six feet tall, and he'd gained at least two stone in weight. Hard work and rigorous training had developed his muscles and though he was good-looking, and knew it, he was by no means a soft touch.

He lived for off-duty time, chatting up all the local girls, especially the ones who came to the monthly dances at the barracks. He'd fancied Sheryl Williams the moment they met. He liked the way she looked with her long blonde hair, and the way she moved. She was so young and innocent, and so smitten by him, that she'd made him forget the rules of the game were 'love them and leave them'.

Hadyn Baker was partly to blame for the mess he was in now, he thought ruefully. He'd taken a liking to Sheryl's friend Megan Thomas. When both girls had been at the dance the following month, Hadyn, the daft bugger, had said it was fate, so after that they'd gone out and about as a foursome whenever he and Hadyn were off duty.

Getting Sheryl preggers had been one of his greatest mistakes. Why the silly little bitch couldn't have done what most girls of her age did and got rid of it, he couldn't understand. She'd said it was because she was a Catholic, and that her religious beliefs made it impossible to do so.

It hadn't stopped her from insisting that he should marry her though, not even when he told her he was a Methodist and that he had no intention of changing to anything else.

He didn't like her mam or dad and he knew it was mutual. Gwynfor Williams was a pious old sod and he made it clear from the start that he didn't think a soldier was good enough for his precious daughter. Rachael Williams was a snooty old bitch who looked at him as if he'd crawled out from under a stone. She even made him take off his boots at the door, saying that the hobnails would damage her Wilton and dent her polished parquet.

Maybe he should have kowtowed to Sheryl's family. If he'd changed his religion, his in-laws might have been more willing to give them a helping hand. After all, it didn't matter a damn to him what church he went to, it never had. Once he'd dug his heels in, though, pride wouldn't let him change his mind. He didn't intend to let them think they could dictate what he could and could not do.

He couldn't have lived with Sheryl's family, anyway. Her mother's life was as regimented as his had been in the army. She seemed to be intent on dictating what must be done and making sure that everyone else obeyed her.

He'd thought his own mam would cave in and let them live with her, especially since she was missing all her friends and neighbours now that they'd moved to Ely. She'd been equally adamant, though. His mam would probably come round in time, he mused. For the moment, he supposed that he would have to provide somewhere for Sheryl and the kid to live.

He had to agree that Angelina Street was a let-down and that they wouldn't want to stay there for very long. The place was no better than a pigsty, but it was all he could afford. He was used to sharing with a crowd of blokes, but Sheryl had always had her own room and everything posh and lah-di-dah so it must be sheer hell for her. Still, she'd appreciate it all the more when they managed to move on to something better, he thought wryly.

The next thing he'd have to do was to find some work. He wanted something with a bit of excitement attached to it. He certainly didn't want a shop or office job where he'd have to wear a collar and tie and say 'sir' to the boss and turn up on time each day.

He didn't fancy working as a docker. It was not only heavy manual work, but it was too erratic. You hung around the docks waiting for the next cargo boat to arrive, and then you tried to jostle to the front of all the others waiting there in the hopes you'd be picked out by the gaffer in charge. Factory work was out too, because you had to clock on and couldn't leave until the hooter or whistle sounded at the end of your shift.

It was no good thinking about restaurant work, because he wasn't trained to cook and he certainly didn't fancy being a waiter. Which left only bar work. Well, there were plenty of pubs in Tiger Bay, Grangetown and Riverside, so he intended to mooch around and see if he could find one that needed a barman.

Working behind the bar in a pub was a dream he'd had off and on for years. It was one of the best ways he knew of combining work with pleasure. Drinking all you wanted without having to pay for it, and being able to chat up other blokes' birds, sounded to him like the ideal sort of existence.

With a job like that, the fact that he was now married needn't restrict his enjoyment of life. He'd be out every night, having a laugh, cracking a joke, and able to flirt with all the girls. Sheryl could accept it or lump it. He didn't care a damn if she took umbrage and cleared off, he told himself. If Sheryl did leave him then he'd be free again, and that would suit him fine. As for the kid, he'd never wanted to be lumbered with that sort of responsibility. It wasn't in his nature to settle down and become a family man.

There were public houses on every corner in Tiger Bay and over the next few days Alun dropped into all of them, but none of them wanted a barman. He had no more luck in Grangetown or Riverside, and it began to look as if his search for that kind of work was in vain.

Most nights Alun was the worse for drink when he returned to Angelina Street around midnight. Sheryl was either weepy and hysterical, or so angry that she vented her frustration by nagging him.

By the end of their first week in Angelina Street, Sheryl's tumultuous outburst the moment he walked into the room maddened Alun, who was already bad-tempered after a fruitless search for work. It was the last straw, he saw red and retaliated. As well as raging about the situation he found himself in, all because he had become involved with her, he threatened her with a hiding.

His shouting, Sheryl's screaming, and the baby's raucous crying brought curses and protests from other occupants of the rooming house.

Confusion reigned; Alun opened the door to find a gaggle of men threatening to punch his brains out unless he kept the noise down. By the time he had placated all of them, Sheryl had calmed down and had managed to soothe Caitlin with a bottle.

This was her first week in her new home, her first real experience of being married, and she wasn't handling things very well at all. As soon as their neighbours had gone back to their own rooms, grumbling and threatening vengeance if there was any more noise, Alun took her in his arms and did his best to reassure her that things would be OK as soon as he found a job.

By the time Sheryl had settled Caitlin back down she found that Alun had kicked off his boots, dropped his trousers and jacket in a heap on the floor and was in bed lying with his mouth wide open, his snores filling the small room. She'd been so looking forward to them making up with each other. Instead he was too drunk to console her, let alone make love to her.

It set the pattern for the weeks that followed. Alun slept until midday, then he washed, shaved, dressed and went out. He never offered to help with the baby or do anything else. He never said where he was going, but Sheryl knew that once he went through the door he wouldn't be back home again until after throwing-out time.

When he did return, the smell of cigarette smoke on his clothes, and the beer on his breath, were overpowering. There was only one thing that changed from their first week in Angelina Street, and that was that he no longer turned his back on her in bed.

'Come on, we're married aren't we?' he demanded when she tried to push him away.

'I hate it when you reek of beer and cigarettes,' she told him.

'If I've got to feed and clothe you then I want

something in return,' he told her, ignoring her protests.

After that, the overwhelming love that had filled her mind night and day for the handsome soldier who'd swept her off her feet was gone. There were even times when she found herself wondering if she still liked him. In his grey flannel trousers, and flashy ill-fitting jacket, he was no longer the man who had won her heart. The lean features that she'd once thought so handsome now often seemed to be hard and cruel. The tender look of love was gone from his dark eyes, and in its place was something that sent shivers through her. Cold, brutal lust.

She remembered the first time she had seen him dressed in civvies. For a split second she hadn't known who he was. Then the sleek dark hair, the piercing dark eyes and the lean, handsome face had registered. She'd covered her hesitation with a quick forced smile.

'Alun, I didn't recognise you for a moment, you look so different out of uniform,' she'd babbled nervously.

He hadn't answered and she knew that eager though he'd been to get out of the army, he realised that by discarding his khaki uniform he'd changed his character.

All he needs is a muffler knotted round his neck, and a couple of blue scars on his face, and he'd look like any other miner down from the Valleys for a day out, she'd thought critically.

Her parents had been quick to notice the

change too. They hadn't liked the idea of their only daughter marrying a soldier, but they liked this shabby-looking young man even less.

Sheryl wondered how they would feel if they could see the terrible place where she was living now. Tiger Bay had always been regarded as out of bounds for respectable people like the Williams family. It was a place talked about with scorn laced with a trace of fear. It was home to itinerant seamen of all nationalities, the crime centre of Cardiff, the place where policemen patrolled their beat in pairs.

Yet what was she to do? She had no money and she couldn't work, not with a baby as young as Caitlin to look after. She could hardly walk out of Angelina Street because she had nowhere else to go. Not unless she went back to Thesiger Street, and she was afraid to do that because, as the weeks lengthened into months, and there was no word from either of her parents, she was increasingly unsure of what her welcome would be.

Chapter Ten

Alun Powell's life seemed to be in two distinct parts: the time spent in the top back room in Angelina Street with Sheryl and Caitlin, and the time he spent working.

He called it working; he told Sheryl that was what he was doing, but it wasn't what most people would describe as work.

He set off around mid-morning, depending on what time he'd managed to get to bed the night before, whether or not the baby had cried half the night and kept him awake, and what sort of mood Sheryl was in.

She'd changed so much since they'd moved to Tiger Bay that sometimes he barely recognised her as the glamorous flapper who'd flirted with him at the barrack dances. She'd let herself go and had become quite slovenly. Sometimes she looked more like forty than twenty. Her long blonde hair, which she'd once been so proud of, and which had attracted him to her in the first place, was now often dark and stringy with grease, hanging like a dirty old scarf around her shoulders.

Some days Sheryl didn't even have a wash. Her clothes were caked with dirt and grease as well as stained by the baby's vomit. Caitlin was in much the same state. Some days Sheryl didn't even take the trouble to wipe the poor little mite over with a damp flannel. She often didn't bother to dress her and left her for hours in a stinking nappy. The only thing she seemed to do for the kid was feed it, Alun reflected. She probably only did that because sticking a bottle in her mouth was the easiest way to shut Caitlin up when she started squalling. Night or day, it didn't matter when, the bottle was the answer.

As a result, Caitlin was fat, with bloated cheeks and a distended stomach. Alun sometimes wondered if half her screaming was because she was overfed and lacked any regular routine.

Alun's other life was like a breath of fresh air to him compared with Angelina Street. He hadn't had any luck in finding work as a barman, but that had been all to the good as it turned out. Working behind a pub bar he would have earned only a pittance, but by using his brain and spreading his talents around as he did, he had money to burn.

At some of the pubs and clubs he acted as a doorman, and that gave him the opportunity to surreptitiously hand out little packages to the punters as well as to pick up hot racing tips. He also did many other deals which, while they weren't exactly criminal, were quite close to being so.

It had not taken him long to become accepted

by the Tiger Bay boozing fraternity. Army life had accustomed him to mixing with all types, to watch out for danger signs, and so he was able to avoid tricky confrontations. At the rear of many of the pubs, or in a room up over them, there were snooker halls, boxing booths, card schools and opium dens. Little by little Alun gained access to all of them.

Each time he did so he managed to find someone who needed help of some kind and was willing to pay for his services. Sometimes it was nothing more strenuous than placing a bet and being rewarded with a cut of the winnings. At other times it was far more risky. There were men who wanted help to dispose of something they'd acquired in an underhand way; addicts looking for a fix; criminals looking for an alibi.

It took time to prove that he was dependable and could be trusted, but once he'd managed to do so he could pick and choose his jobs. And they were all profitable, he wouldn't take them on unless he was quite sure about that. He liked to spend lavishly, mostly on smart clothes for himself and drinks and smokes for his many new friends.

Alun knew he should be moving Sheryl and Caitlin out of the sordid little room to somewhere better, but he didn't see the point of doing that because he didn't think Sheryl would appreciate it. She had become a slut, there was no other word for it. His own mother had not been house-proud, but she had always kept herself looking decent. Her house might be a bit of a shambles, but she did clean it occasionally.

Sheryl no longer seemed to care about herself, Caitlin or their surroundings. Often when he left around mid-morning she still wasn't dressed, and she was usually back in bed again by the time he got home. They said less and less to each other, except to bicker whenever things went wrong.

He knew she was drinking because he'd found empty gin bottles under the bed. He blamed himself for being too generous with the money he gave her for housekeeping, but otherwise he would have to do the shopping himself and he hadn't the time or the inclination for that.

Once away from their miserable room his life was fulfilling, exciting even. In next to no time he'd picked up girls who were only too pleased to satisfy his needs. He toyed with the idea of finding himself a separate room but that was not the way to deal with things, he decided.

He still had some conscience. He'd been responsible for putting Sheryl in the club, he'd married her, so he was obligated to try and make a go of things.

He planned his strategy carefully. A few more money scoops and he'd be rolling in it, more cash than he'd ever had in his life. Perhaps if they moved out of Angelina Street, Sheryl might pull herself together and smarten up. It was worth a try, he told himself.

At first Sheryl was excited when he told her that they ought to think about moving. Then the arguments started. She wanted to live somewhere near Roath Park, but that was too close to Maindy Barracks for his liking. He refused to consider Cathays because it would be too near to her parents. She rejected Grangetown, Splott and Adamstown, and he objected to both Canton and Ely.

Their arguments escalated until in the end Alun took matters into his own hands and managed to persuade Zakaraki, the owner of the Diawl Coch club in Loudon Square, to let him have the attic rooms up over his premises.

It had taken a lot of bargaining and negotiating. Zakaraki, a wily Sicilian, would only agree to the arrangement if Alun came and worked for him full-time.

'You stay loyal to me, yes?' he asked, his sloe-black eyes glinting fiercely. 'Work for me alone, no deals with other pubs or clubs, yes?'

'That depends on the sort of work you are asking me to do,' Alun told him.

'You will be my right-hand man. You will look after the casino and protect my girls.'

'You mean I'll be the manager?'

'Manager? Yes, if you wish to be called manager that is what you will be, as long as you carry out my orders.'

Alun made a pretence of considering the offer, even though his mind was already made up. He knew that Zakaraki was a power to be

114

reckoned with in Tiger Bay and that overnight he, himself, would become someone of importance.

It took a while to agree on his duties and what he would be paid, but by the end of their negotiations Alun was more than happy. As far as he was concerned his future was assured, he was on the way up.

'I'll get the use of those attic rooms rent-free as well?' he asked.

Zakaraki nodded. 'One thing though, you must use the side entrance in Loudon Place. Your family must never under any circumstances use the club entrance. Do I make myself abundantly clear?'

Loudon Place was close by, but a better area than Angelina Street. The rooms were twice the size of the one they were living in, and there was a proper kitchen. There was also a bathroom and lavatory for their use only.

Alun installed a second-hand double bedstead into the smaller of the two rooms. For the living room he bought a couple of armchairs from one of his contacts at a bargain price, together with a wooden table and four straight chairs.

It was a big improvement on what they had at the moment, he told himself, and if Sheryl didn't like it she could stay where she was in Angelina Street.

Sheryl did like it. 'It's not too bad,' she admitted grudgingly when he took her to see it. She was disparaging about the shabby furniture, so he simply shrugged and let her think that they were renting it already furnished.

'When can we move in?'

'As soon as you like. Right this minute if you want to!'

The move from Angelina Street in September 1922 seemed to put new life into Sheryl. Almost overnight she began to take an interest in her appearance. She washed her hair for the first time in weeks and asked Alun for some extra money so that she could go out and buy a new dress.

Amused, he played along, knowing he could afford to do so. It was just the start. Within a couple of weeks, though, Alun was having to dig deeper and deeper into his pockets. Sheryl wanted new things for the home, for Caitlin, and more and more for herself.

She wasn't an efficient housekeeper, but she certainly tried and he always applauded her efforts. The only trouble was that she wanted him to spend more time with her. Gradually the earlier romantic rapport between them began to re-emerge. When she took the trouble to doll herself up he found himself fancying her again, and she responded enthusiastically.

Pleased though he was by this turn of events, he began to find her needs encroaching on the time when he was expected to be working.

In return for providing him with accommodation Zakaraki's demands increased, but Alun thought it wiser not to confide in Sheryl about these arrangements or even tell her where he worked.

If he did, and she asked questions about what sort of work he did there, he'd have difficulties explaining. He wasn't sure what Sheryl, with her sheltered Catholic background, would think of such activities.

The Diawl Coch Club might look quite respectable from the outside, but this was merely a facade. Everything from prostitution to drug-dealing went on within its doors. It was for this reason that Zakaraki had insisted they must use a completely separate entrance.

Sheryl's manner and behaviour continued to improve. Within weeks of moving into the rooms in Loudon Place she was looking attractive and nicely dressed. Caitlin, who had now turned eighteen months old, was also clean and wearing pretty dresses. She still invariably had either a bottle or a dummy in her mouth, but since it stopped her from crying, Alun accepted that it was necessary and didn't interfere. Anything rather than have the child squalling, because that was something he couldn't stand.

As Sheryl's appearance improved, so did her self-confidence. She even talked about visiting her mam and dad. She'd had no contact with them since the day she'd stormed out of Thesiger Street more than a year ago. She'd not even sent them a Christmas card. Even so, she wanted to try and sort things out between them.

She was also missing Megan and Mrs Thomas, but she'd ignored them both for so long that she felt unsure about what her reception would be if she simply dropped in on them.

Sheryl also wanted to go out more. She wasn't content with pushing Caitlin in her pram up to the Hayes, or even on into St Mary Street or Queen Street. She began to pester Alun to take her out in the evening.

'We can't do that though, can we,' Alun prevaricated, 'what about Caitlin?'

'We'll find someone to look after her for a couple of hours, of course,' Sheryl smiled.

'We don't know anyone we can trust her with though, do we?' he pointed out.

Sheryl didn't argue, but her lips tightened and she flicked back her hair in a defiant manner. A week later she brought the subject up again. This time, when Alun came up with the same reason about not being able to leave Caitlin, she said she had found someone who was willing to come in and look after her while they went out.

'Penny, who works at the newsagents three doors down, said she'll do it,' Sheryl told him.

'She doesn't know Caitlin or anything about her,' he argued.

'What's there to know? Caitlin will probably be asleep when we leave. If I prepare a bottle for her then all Penny has to do is give it to her if she wakes up.'

'It means I'll have to take a night off work, it's an expensive thing to do,' he argued.

She lifted her shoulders disparagingly. 'You're always boasting about how much money you earn, so what does one night matter?'

'It would be easier to go out somewhere during the day.'

'Penny's working then.'

'We'd take Caitlin with us.'

'Oh, Alun, I want to go dancing and have fun, not a trip to Roath Park to feed the ducks,' she wheedled.

It became a bone of contention between them. Sheryl nagged, sulked, cried, and cajoled. In the end, simply to stop the constant bickering, Alun gave in and agreed that they would have a night out.

Sheryl was keen for them to go to some of the places where he had told her he worked, but this was the last thing he wanted.

He suggested going to the pictures at the Odeon. 'Charlie Chaplin is on in *The Kid*, that should be a laugh.'

Sheryl shook her head. 'I don't like him. I'd sooner go to the Empire and see Rudolph Valentino in *The Sheik*.'

'You're too late, that was on last week. It's Douglas Fairbanks in *Robin Hood* this week.'

Sheryl thought about it and then insisted she

wanted to go dancing. So he bought tickets for a special gala dance that was being held at the City Hall.

'What do we want to go there for, we won't know anyone,' she grumbled.

'That's the whole idea, we can enjoy each other's company and there will be no-one interrupting us. If we go to one of the places where I'm known there will be people constantly coming over to talk to us.'

'I want to meet the people you know,' she protested stubbornly.

'I've already bought the tickets for this dance, so do you want to go or not?'

Sheryl gave in, as he knew she would. She insisted on having a new dress. He agreed, but he resolved that there would be no more nights out after this.

Sheryl enjoyed herself and wanted it to become a regular weekly event, but Alun put his foot down.

As a result, the bickering between them increased. He spent even more time working. Sheryl retaliated by bouts of reckless spending. Not content with the shops in Bute Street or the Hayes she went up into the city, to James Howell's, David Morgan's, the Bon Marché and the exclusive shops in the arcades that linked the main shopping areas.

On each trip she bought clothes she didn't need, countless pairs of shoes and expensive outfits for Caitlin, even though she knew the toddler would outgrow them in next to no time.

At first Alun handed over money for these expeditions without any argument. He reasoned that at least it was keeping Sheryl happy, and it stopped her pestering him about meeting people he knew.

It didn't appease Sheryl for very long. She became bored with shopping. Alun's erratic hours and the fact that he always returned home reeking of beer, spirits and cigarette smoke still gave rise to heated rows.

'I don't understand why your clothes always smell so foul,' she grumbled. 'You stink the place out when you come in.'

'I can't help it. At work I'm mixing with people who smoke and drink.'

'If you're working at a pub then why are you so late home? They chuck out at half past ten.'

'You're forgetting about drinking-up time!'

Her blue eyes were stormy. 'I'm forgetting nothing, not even the fact that you are lying through your teeth,' she retaliated. 'You've got another woman somewhere.'

Alun shook his head and laughed uproariously.

'Then where are you until the early hours of the morning?' Sheryl persisted.

'Working! I swear it!'

'The only places open until those hours are clubs. You're staying out at clubs, you lying sod!'

Alun sighed. He was tired of the constant arguing. What the hell did it matter, he asked himself. 'Yes,' he admitted, 'I'm staying out at a club because that is where I work. Happy now?'

Chapter Eleven

Discovering that Alun was working in a club, not a pub, surprised Sheryl, but she was even more amazed when he admitted that it was the Diawl Coch, the club directly under the flat where they were living.

The more she thought about it, the more incensed she became that he hadn't mentioned this to her before.

'If I'd known you were down there I wouldn't have felt so lonely when I'm here on my own at nights!' she stormed. 'I could even have popped down after Caitlin was asleep and we could have had a drink together.'

'I know, and that's what I was afraid might happen, and why I didn't say anything to you about where I was working.'

'Thank you very much!' she snapped, her eyes flashing angrily. 'And why shouldn't I?' She stared at him accusingly. 'Are you ashamed of being seen with me or something?'

'Don't talk so bloody daft,' he laughed, pulling her into his arms and kissing her. 'I can't have you hanging round my neck when I'm working, now can I, that's why I said nothing.'

Her eyes met his challengingly. 'I could

always sit at the bar and have a drink,' she said provocatively.

He shook his head. 'It wouldn't work, cariad. I don't have time to sit and talk.'

'Not even for five minutes? What sort of work are you doing that you can't take a break and chat to your own wife?'

'You don't understand. I'm responsible for greeting people as they come into the club, so I can't sit around in the bar,' he explained.

'A doorman . . . you!'

'I didn't say I was, but what's wrong with that if I am?'

Sheryl raised her eyebrows. 'Back in uniform again, are you?' she jibed.

'Only if you consider that black trousers, a white shirt, a red silk cummerbund and a black bow tie are a uniform.'

Sheryl looked taken aback. 'When do you dress up like that? I've never seen you wearing that sort of clobber.'

'Well you wouldn't. I change into them after I get there and then I put my own clothes back on before I come home.'

'What a waste of time when you are only coming upstairs. Anyway, why go to all that bother, you still stink of cigarette smoke and beer when you come home.'

Alun shrugged. 'I like to keep my home life and my working life separate.'

'Sounds daft to me! Especially since you are only coming back up here. Nearly as stupid as not telling me that you were working down there and not wanting me to spend any time there with you.'

'Well, that's the way it is, Sheryl, and that's the way it stays.'

'It doesn't have to, not now that I know what you're up to,' she protested.

'Oh yes it does!' he said firmly. 'I've kept it from you all this time because I thought you would react like this.'

She frowned. 'What's that supposed to mean?' she pouted.

'I knew you'd get all worked up and cross . . . and you have!'

'No I haven't,' she argued petulantly. 'I'm simply trying to understand why you've had to be so secretive about it all.'

Alun picked up his jacket and thrust his arms into the sleeves. 'I'm off,' he announced, shrugging it into place as he made for the door.

'Wait, I want to talk to you!' Sheryl yelled, running out onto the landing after him.

'I haven't time to stop and talk. Go and see to Caitlin, she's bawling her lungs out.'

'That's you! Always the same! The moment Caitlin starts crying you're away out of it and I'm the one left to see to her.'

Alun didn't even bother to answer. Sheryl flounced back into the room, seething with anger. As usual, Alun had wrong-footed her, and then walked out before she could win the argument.

She brooded about the situation for days. She was used to getting her own way and the more she thought about it, the more the idea of visiting the club appealed to her. If it worked, she could pop down every evening. Half an hour would be a break and give her a chance to meet people, have a drink and a laugh. She couldn't see any harm in doing that.

Finally she resolved to take matters into her own hands. She put Caitlin to bed and then she changed into one of her new frocks, a blue silk one that had a low-cut neckline. She brushed her hair until it was silky and shining and carefully enhanced her make-up.

She wasn't a member, but if Alun was on the door, as he'd claimed, there would be no problem getting in.

Surely he would be able to take five minutes off, long enough to buy her a drink and introduce her to someone she could talk to. She wouldn't be able to stay very long because of leaving Caitlin on her own. Even so, it would be worth it.

Seeing Alun in his working gear would be a laugh. Why he'd had to be so secretive about his job, and where he worked, was beyond her. Alun must realise that she'd had no real life since they'd married, because she never met anyone of her own age. He could be a funny beggar sometimes, she thought dismissively.

She'd been used to going out with Megan a couple of times a week, and it was something she'd missed a great deal since she'd moved down to Tiger Bay and they'd lost touch with each other.

She hadn't wanted to invite her friend over when they were living in a one-room slum in Angelina Street. Now they had a proper living room there was no reason why she shouldn't do so, of course, and they could spend some time down in the club. Megan would like that and she could always nip back every now and again to make sure Caitlin was all right.

The idea cheered her up considerably. A frisson of excitement set her pulse racing. All she had to do was break the ice by dropping into the club now and again to get Alun used to the idea. The first couple of times would be the hardest.

Like so many convoluted plans it went wrong right from the start. The minute she'd changed into her blue silk frock, Caitlin woke up and all Sheryl's efforts to quieten her and get her back to sleep failed dismally. Caitlin refused to have another bottle, and she rejected her dummy. It was nearly an hour later before she'd sobbed herself to sleep, worn out by her own tantrum.

Sheryl settled her back into her cot, annoyed and frustrated by the delay and wondering if she should bother to go down or leave it for another evening.

'There's got to be a first time so it may as well be now,' she told herself out loud as she checked once more that Caitlin was asleep, she let herself out of the side door and walked around the corner to the club.

There was no sign of Alun as she reached the entrance. Instead, two beefy, barrel-chested chaps barred her way. One of them had a cauli-flower ear and looked like an ex-boxer.

'Name?'

Sheryl tossed her hair back and gave the one who had spoken to her a winning smile. 'Where's Alun?' she demanded.

'Alun?' They looked at each other, frowning as though they'd never heard the name before.

'Alun Powell!'

'Who's asking?' one of them questioned cautiously.

'I am!' She flicked her hair again and smiled provocatively. 'I'm his wife.'

She saw the quick exchange of looks before the ex-boxer said, 'Afraid he's not here tonight.'

'Of course he is! I know he is! If you let me in I'll soon find him,' she insisted.

'Sorry! It's not possible to do that, you're not a member, see.'

'I know that, but my husband works here and I want to see him . . . there's something I need to tell him very urgently.'

Again the two doormen exchanged glances, and Sheryl's temper flared as she saw them shake their heads at each other. For a moment she thought of trying to slip past them, but as if reading her mind they stood firm and square, shoulder to shoulder, making it impossible for her to get by.

Biting her lip, she turned and walked away. If they wouldn't let her pass there was nothing she could do about it. She wondered if Alun had deliberately told them not to let her in. When he'd said he met arrivals, he must have meant at a door inside the club. These two bully-boys were obviously selected for their sheer size to keep people out if they weren't members.

She'd failed tonight, but she'd make sure it didn't happen again. She was now more determined than ever that she was going to enjoy the facilities the club could offer.

Alun was annoyed. He couldn't believe that Sheryl had been so pinheaded as to try and get into the club. Surely she must have realised from what he'd told her that such places had rules, and that you had to be a member before you could be admitted.

Gary and Buster had made a mountain out of the incident and regaled everyone with details of what had taken place. They'd all laughed, but Zakaraki had taken him aside afterwards and warned him about future incidents.

He'd pretended to take the ticking-off well and he had apologised profusely, but deep inside he'd been seething.

The moment he arrived home, before Sheryl

129

could reproach him for how she'd been treated, he was on the offensive. Tight-lipped, he berated her for such stupid behaviour.

'What the hell were you thinking of, girl! If I lose my job we'll be penniless, and not only that, we'll be out on the street. The only reason I managed to get hold of this place for us was because I was working for the man who owns it. Upset him and he'll have us out of here before you can say knife.'

'Don't talk so silly, he wouldn't do a thing like that! I only asked if I could have a word with you, Alun,' she told him defiantly.

'Don't you believe it! Why do you think they employ those two hulking monsters on the door, cariad? It's for privacy, see! That's what it's all about. That's why people join clubs like the Diawl Coch. It's because they know they can be safe there and not be pestered by people they don't want to mix with.'

'So you don't want to mix with me, is that it?' she spat at him, her temper rising to match his.

'Don't talk so daft, girl! I'm not talking about us, I'm talking about the rules of the club. I'm trying to explain why you have to be a member in order to get in there.'

'So why didn't they fetch you then?' Sheryl demanded. 'If you'd come to the door I wouldn't have needed to go inside, would I!' she added triumphantly.

Alun shrugged. 'They probably thought I shouldn't be chatting during working hours.'

'How did they know that I only wanted to chat to you? It might have been an emergency, something wrong with the baby . . .'

'Duw anwyl, girl, don't talk such drivel. If it had been anything like that you'd have said so, not stood there arguing the toss with them. You'd have told them what was wrong and then they'd have taken a message.'

'I'll remember that next time!'

Alun's eyes blazed. 'There won't be a next time, get that straight right now.'

'You mean you're never going to let me come in and have a drink?' Her eyes gleamed with anger.

'Dammo di! Are you completely twp, or haven't you been listening to a word I've been saying?'

'I've heard you and I'm not stupid, but it doesn't mean I'm going to take any notice. You're talking rubbish! I'm your wife, Alun, and if you can go in there then so can I.'

'Diawlch! It's members only, can't you get that into your thick head?'

'Then make me a member,' she demanded.

He shook his head despairingly. 'It's not the sort of club where you go for a drink with friends, or where you take your wife or girl-friend.'

'So there's no women allowed in. It's a men's club, right? No women are allowed inside, none at all. Not even a barmaid.'

Alun turned away. 'I'm not standing here

131

arguing with you, I'm going to bed. I've said that you are not to come down there and that's that!'

'You may think it's the end of the matter, but I don't. I intend to get in and I'll succeed. You wait and see,' she taunted.

Alun's temper exploded. 'I said no and that's what I meant. Do you want us to end up back in some dump like Angelina Street again?'

'What we've got now isn't much better,' Sheryl told him scornfully, with an exaggerated shrug.

'Well, cariad, this is the best you're going to get so make the most of it.'

'That's what I was trying to do, by taking advantage of the entertainment right on my doorstep.'

'And what about little Caitlin? Were you thinking about making her a member as well so that you could bring her down with you?' he said sarcastically.

Sheryl's attitude irked Alun. 'You bumptious bitch,' he ranted, 'you don't give a damn about anything, do you?' His mouth tightened as his hand lashed out and slammed across Sheryl's face.

Taken by surprise she fell sideways, catching herself so hard on the corner of the table that she was completely winded and could only gasp like a fish.

When she tried to get up, a searing pain in her chest brought a groan from her.

Alun made no attempt to help her. 'Stop pretending and making such a fuss,' he told her dismissively.

'Help me, Alun. I'm in pain,' she gasped. 'I think one of my ribs is broken.'

He stared down at her in disbelief.

'Please, Alun!' she begged.

He held out his hand to pull her to her feet, but as she tried to take it the pain in her chest was so great that she couldn't even lift her arm.

He stood there, confused. As they heard Caitlin crying he once more tried to help her up, but she turned away and doubled over in pain.

'I'll go and fetch her,' he mumbled.

He hoped that Sheryl was playing up, trying to teach him a lesson. With any luck, by the time he came back with Caitlin she would be on her feet.

When he found her still on the floor, the colour drained from her face, and obviously in considerable discomfort, he accepted that she meant what she said and she really was hurt.

'I think I'd better get you to hospital,' he muttered contritely.

Sheryl nodded, her lips trembling.

'Here,' he laid Caitlin down on the floor alongside her. 'Keep an eye on her then, while I go and see if I can get some help.'

Filled with panic, he ran out into the street wondering what to do. The club was shut, but there was a nightwatchman, so if he could rouse him he could get in and use the telephone to call an ambulance.

He tried to think what he ought to tell them. He didn't want them knowing anything about him hitting her! He'd simply say that she fell and caught herself against the table, he decided.

Chapter Twelve

'You can't come to the hospital with me, Alun,'
Sheryl protested as the ambulance men lifted
her onto the stretcher. 'Who will look after
Caitlin? She can't be left here on her own!'

'I know that, I'm bringing her with me.'

Sheryl tried to argue, to tell him that it would
be better if he stayed there with Caitlin, but the
pain in her chest was so intense that she was
gasping for breath.

As they loaded the stretcher into the ambulance she closed her eyes, trying to ignore the
searing pain, and concentrated on breathing as
shallowly as she could. She sensed that Alun
was sitting close by, holding Caitlin in the crook
of his arm, but she felt too distressed to care.

At the hospital, after she had been given an
injection to ease her discomfort, she floated in
and out of consciousness as a doctor examined
her. When she finally opened her eyes it was to
the sound of a woman's voice which was so
familiar that she thought she must be dreaming.

It still hurt her to breathe. She was conscious
that her chest was tightly bandaged, and she
was in such pain that she almost lapsed back
into unconsciousness.

'Megan? Megan Thomas? Is it really you?' she gasped as she tried to focus her eyes on the round smiling face of the nurse who was bending over her. 'What are you doing here? Why are you wearing that uniform?'

'Sheryl? I don't believe it. I've asked your mam time and again if she had any news of you, or knew where you were living. She said she thought you must have left Cardiff because she hadn't heard from you since the day you moved out. She thought that perhaps Alun had been sent overseas and that you had gone with him.'

'No, I'm still here,' Sheryl panted, struggling for breath. 'Alun isn't in the army now. I'm sure my mam knows that,' she frowned. 'He should be here somewhere, he came to the hospital with me?'

Megan nodded. 'I thought he looked familiar, but I wasn't too sure if it was him or not without his uniform. So I suppose that must have been little Caitlin with him. She's grown so much I didn't recognise her either!'

'She's almost two. Can I see them now?'

'In a minute, cariad. Tell me, how did you manage to crack your ribs so badly?'

Sheryl hesitated, remembering the row she'd had with Alun about her going to the club. 'I . . . I'm not sure,' she prevaricated. 'It's all so hazy. What did Alun tell you?'

'He told the doctor that you fell and caught yourself against the edge of the table.'

'I can't remember clearly, so if that's what he said then that's what happened.' She smiled weakly. 'That's my story, now what about yours?'

Megan frowned. 'What do you mean?'

'I want to know why you've changed jobs and become a nurse?'

Megan shrugged. 'It wasn't the same at Harveys once you'd left. There were no more laughs, and no-one to travel to work with, or to talk over what had happened during the day. I thought it was time to do something completely different.'

'Why nursing though, cariad?'

'Oh, I don't know.' Megan shrugged self-consciously. 'I thought I'd like to do something useful with my life, see,' she murmured, her dark eyes thoughtful.

'After watching me throw mine away, you mean!'

'Oh, Sheryl! I never meant that! You haven't, have you? You are happy?'

Sheryl smiled non-committally. 'It's a completely different sort of life.'

'You must be happy, though! You have Caitlin and from what I saw of her when they brought you in she is absolutely lovely!'

Sheryl nodded. 'She is. So what about you and Hadyn? Are you still going out with him?'

'No!' Megan shook her head firmly. 'After what happened to you I thought it was better not to see him again. We only went out together because he was Alun's friend and I was yours.'

'I thought you really liked each other?' Sheryl frowned.

'Well, we did, but not in quite the same way you and Alun were involved. We were just good friends. We'd split up some time before I decided to be a nurse.'

'There seem to have been a good many changes in your life as well, Megan!'

'Yes, I suppose you could say that, but probably not as many as there have been in yours. You'll have to tell me all your news when you are feeling a bit better. I've been worried because we've not heard a word from you since you left Thesiger Street. You disappeared so completely.'

'Don't! I feel so guilty about it. How are they both?'

'Healthwise they're much the same, but they keep to themselves more than ever.'

Sheryl looked uneasy. 'Was my mam very worried?'

'Well, she seemed to be upset when I asked her if she'd heard from you. Why didn't you keep in touch with them?'

'It seemed better to make a clean break. Neither of them were all that keen on Alun, now were they! They made it very clear that they wouldn't let us live with them. They didn't even make him welcome when he came to visit me. We used to spend more time at your house than with my mam.'

'Yes, I know that, but they're still concerned about you.'

'Which is why I didn't want them to know where I was living, or how things were with us.'

Megan shook her head, her face puzzled. 'So where are you living? Obviously you're still in Cardiff or you wouldn't have been brought in here.'

Sheryl sighed and bit her lip. 'Tiger Bay,' she blurted. 'We started out living in one squalid bug-infested room in a house in Angelina Street, if you must know,' she said defiantly.

'Oh, Sheryl, that's terrible! Are you still living there?'

'No.' Sheryl took a deep breath and winced as her chest burned with pain.

'Look, you really should try and rest,' Megan told her. 'Tell me all about it later on,' she smiled as she straightened the bedclothes.

Sheryl clutched at her arm. 'Don't leave me. I've missed you so much, Megan. I've been so lonely with no-one to confide in. Alun didn't find proper work for a long time and while we were in that horrible room in Angelina Street I wanted to die. There seemed to be nothing to live for, life was so awful.'

'Everything is all right now, though, isn't it?' Megan probed.

'We moved from there a few months ago. Alun found work at a club and we have rooms up over part of it.'

'So everything is fine now, then?'

Sheryl pulled a face. 'The two rooms aren't

bad, but it's still Tiger Bay and not the sort of life I'm used to. I'm so lonely, Megan. Alun works in the club and that means he isn't home until midnight or after.'

'You've got little Caitlin for company, though,' Megan murmured. 'Now settle down and rest, I'll be back again soon.'

Tears sprang unchecked from Sheryl's half-closed eyes. Seeing Megan again was bringing so many memories flooding back. She thought nostalgically of their schooldays and her comfortable home in Cathays where she'd been the centre of attention.

In those days, she'd taken the fact that she had a well-furnished bedroom for granted. She'd even accepted that her mother would clean it. She'd had no responsibilities at all, and yet her eagerness for independence had ruined everything. She hadn't realised, until it was too late, how much fun and freedom she and Megan had enjoyed as they were growing up.

If only she'd listened to her mother and not insisted on going to the dances at Maindy Barracks. That was when things had started to go wrong. She had fallen for Alun because he looked so handsome in his uniform, because it was a challenge to win the heart of a soldier. Giving in to his demands had been her downfall.

Megan hadn't fallen into that sort of trap. She'd had more sense, Sheryl thought ruefully.

Megan had enjoyed being friends with Hadyn, but she hadn't let him take any liberties.

It was no good having regrets now, because it was too late to turn the clock back. There was Caitlin to be considered, she thought as sleep claimed her.

She had no idea how long she was asleep, but suddenly she was wide awake and anxious about Caitlin. Frantically she pressed the bell by her bedside. A nurse in a dark blue uniform came to see what she wanted, and for one frightening moment she wondered if she'd really seen Megan earlier or whether she'd dreamed it.

'The other nurse said that my husband and baby were still here and that I could see them,' she whispered.

'Right. I'll tell Nurse Thomas to fetch them, unless you want to rest quietly for a little longer?'

'I want to see them, to make sure Caitlin is all right,' Sheryl told her worriedly.

'Alun isn't used to looking after her, see. I want to tell him what he must do,' she explained to Megan, when her friend arrived.

'Don't worry. You'll be able to go home in a couple of hours, but you'll have to come back again for a check-up in about a week's time.'

'And will I see you again?'

Megan frowned. 'I'm not sure, it depends on the time of your appointment.'

'We must keep in touch,' Sheryl insisted.

'Of course,' Megan agreed quickly. 'Would

you like me to tell your mam I've seen you?'

Sheryl hesitated. 'No, I'd rather you didn't.'

'Fair do's, but she's been ever so worried about not hearing from you all these months. It would be a relief for her to know where you're living and that you're all right.'

Sheryl shook her head more firmly. 'No, I don't want her to know that I'm living in Tiger Bay. She'd be so terribly upset.'

Megan nodded understandingly. 'Well, think about it. In the meantime I won't breathe a word to your mam, I understand how you feel. You can tell me if you've changed your mind next time we meet.'

'I'll do that,' Sheryl promised, 'but whatever I decide we can both still get together, can't we? We've an awful lot of catching up to do!'

Alun was as startled as Sheryl had been when he realised the nurse who came to fetch him was Megan Thomas.

He gave a long whistle. 'Duw anwyl! A ghost from the past!'

Megan laughed. 'You're making it seem like a lifetime. It's not all that long ago.'

'Well, it feels like a lifetime! You weren't a nurse the last time I saw you!'

'True, though you were still a soldier.'

'Yes, and now you're the one in uniform and very lovely you look in it,' he said admiringly, his eyes lighting up as he studied her. 'Very trim, very smart, bet you have all the doctors chasing after you.'

Megan coloured. 'Stop talking such nonsense, Alun!'

He grinned. Although her voice was severe he could see that her cheeks had turned pink and that she was finding it difficult not to smile.

'You look a real stunner! I wouldn't mind you giving me a bed bath, I can tell you.'

Megan didn't answer. Instead she directed her attention to Caitlin, who was staring from one to the other of them wide-eyed.

'The last time I saw this little bundle of joy she was so tiny that it was difficult to see who she was going to take after in looks. Now there's no doubt about it! She's gorgeous, a perfect miniature of Sheryl except that her hair is a slightly darker colour. She's absolutely beautiful!'

'She can be a little screamer. She demands a lot of attention, the same as her mother!'

'Most little ones do,' Megan said wryly.

'If you say so. How is Hadyn? Are you still going out with him?'

Megan shook her head. 'No, I haven't seen him for ages. We broke it off when we were no longer part of a foursome.'

Alun pulled a face. 'That sounds pretty twp to me, cariad. I always thought that you seemed so suited to each other.'

Megan shrugged dismissively. 'It wasn't daft, it was a mutual decision. We were good friends, that's all. Look, I have to go, I'm needed. I have duties to attend to. Sheryl will be ready to leave quite soon.'

'We'll be meeting up again, won't we? I've missed seeing you, you know. We had some bloody good times together, the four of us, so we must make sure that we stay in touch.'

Megan gave a tight smile. 'Sheryl will have to come back for a check-up in about a week's time, so I'll probably see you again then.'

'That will depend on whether or not I can spare the time,' Alun said evasively.

'Someone will have to come with her. She shouldn't be travelling on her own in case she has a fall or anything.'

'I'll try and remember that, especially if it means I'll be seeing you again!' he grinned.

'I'm serious, Alun. Sheryl will need a lot of looking after for the next few weeks. She certainly shouldn't be lifting little Caitlin, you do realise that?'

He raised his eyebrows. 'I'm afraid she'll have to, I can't be there all the time. Someone has to earn the money.'

'Surely you have friends or you know some-one who can be there to help her with Caitlin?'

Alun's mouth tightened. 'Don't worry about it, we'll manage.'

'She really will need help, Alun. She's going to be in a great deal of pain for a while.'

'Then perhaps you'd better come and give a hand!' he challenged.

'I'd like to, really I would, but I can't take time off work. I haven't been here long enough,' she added worriedly.

'You don't work all the time, Megan. Come on, you must have some free time,' he wheedled. 'Look, girl, I can probably cope during the day, but Sheryl will be all on her own in the evenings. Surely as her best friend . . .'

'I'm sorry, Alun. I daren't take time off because I'm still only a probationer, see . . .'

'That's all right, Megan. I do understand. As I said, we'll manage. We've done so up to now,' he added with a disparaging shrug.

Megan bit her lip. 'Give me your address and I'll see what I can do. Don't mention it to Sheryl though, in case I can't manage anything, and I wouldn't want her to feel I'd let her down.'

Chapter Thirteen

Megan Thomas was extremely worried. Sheryl should have returned so that someone could check that she was making satisfactory progress and ensure that her ribs were knitting together as they should. It was almost six o'clock and even if she did come now she would possibly be turned away, because the outpatients department was on the point of closing.

Megan felt it was very unlikely that Sheryl had left it so late, or that she had forgotten. She thought it more probable that Alun had refused to bring her and she didn't feel well enough to come on her own.

There had been a prickliness about Alun's manner when he'd brought Sheryl in. His tone had been so impatient when he'd spoken to Sheryl, almost as if they'd been quarrelling and not made up afterwards.

He had been so dismissive, too, when he'd been told that Sheryl was going to need a lot of care and help. He didn't show the sort of concern that most husbands would have naturally expressed, and his explanation about how Sheryl had come to have three broken ribs had been far from convincing.

Megan dug down into the pocket of her starched green uniform dress and brought out the scrap of paper on which she'd scribbled down their address, the Diawl Coch club in Loudon Square. Alun had stressed that she mustn't use the main entrance to the club, but a side door that was round the corner.

Megan felt nervous at the idea of going there on her own. She'd never been to Tiger Bay, even though she'd lived in Cardiff all her life. There were so many lurid tales about the dangers to be encountered in that area that she'd always been warned never to venture down Bute Street, or any of the streets off it, under any circumstance.

Since it was already dark she decided that perhaps it would be better to postpone going there until the next day. She didn't have to start work until two o'clock so she would have plenty of time in the morning. Furthermore, it would be much easier to find the place in daylight.

Her qualms about visiting the Tiger Bay area on her own were confirmed next day. Once the tram went past the Custom House on its way towards the Pier Head she saw how everything became so much shabbier. She knew she had to continue down Bute Street, but not how far, so she'd asked the conductor to let her know when they reached Loudon Place. After that it would be easy, she told herself. All she had to do was walk down Loudon Place to Loudon Square and find the Diawl Coch club.

The square consisted of three-storey houses and shops with a scrubby-looking park in the middle, where a few children were playing. There seemed to be quite a lot of people about, every colour and every nationality. No-one took any notice of her as she made her way right round the square, covertly looking for the Diawl Coch club, but unable to find it.

She retraced her steps to Bute Street, and hesitated, trying to think what was the best thing to do. Perhaps she ought to ask for directions, she told herself.

The thought of accosting a stranger in Tiger Bay scared her. I'll walk right the way around again first, and if I don't find the club then I'll go into one of the shops and ask, she decided.

She increased her pace, trying to look as if she knew where she was going. As she brushed shoulders with people she saw some curious looks directed at her. She knew there were merchant seamen of all races living in Tiger Bay, but she'd not expected to see so many African and Indian women and children. Some of the women were dressed in colourful saris, others in long dark clothes. There were even women who had their heads and part of their faces covered over, so all she could see were dark curious eyes staring back at her.

The children were of all colours, shapes and sizes. There were one or two white children playing in the gutters or swinging from ropes tied to the lampposts, but the majority of them looked coloured. Chinese, Indian, African; many of them half-caste. Some of them were in rags, others in strange, colourful dress. Even though it was a cold wintry morning many of the children were running around barefoot, or with their toes hanging out of their broken-down shoes or boots.

As she passed they openly stared at her. In her navy raincoat over her green uniform dress, and with her dark felt hat, black stockings and black shoes, they probably guessed she was a nurse and were watching to see who she was visiting.

She seemed to have been walking around Loudon Square for ever, yet she didn't see how she could have lost her way when she was in a square.

Megan felt so relieved when she finally spot-ted the Diawl Coch that she had to stop herself running towards it. As she drew nearer she remembered Alun had said that she must not go to the club itself, but use the side door.

The outside of the Diawl Coch facing Loudon Square had looked flashy. The side door in Loudon Place was battered and scarred. It looked as though at some time it had been kicked in and had never been repainted.

Megan took a deep breath and rapped as hard as she could on the door. When no-one answered she banged with her fist, but there was still no answer. Tentatively she slipped her hand inside the letter box to see if there was a door key hanging there. Finding there wasn't, she called out Sheryl's name as loudly as she could through the aperture. Her voice echoed hollowly and there was no other sound at all from inside.

Disappointed, she turned away, wondering what to do next. Alun had been extremely insistent that she wasn't to use the club entrance under any circumstances, but since she'd come all this way Megan decided to ignore that warning.

The club also seemed to be deserted, but her persistent hammering on the door finally brought a middle-aged woman to find out what all the noise was about. As she was wearing a coarse sacking apron over her print pinafore, and was holding a scrubbing brush, Megan decided she must be the cleaner.

'I want to see Mrs Sheryl Powell, who lives in the rooms over this place,' Megan explained. 'She's been ill and she isn't answering her door, so do you know if she is in?'

The woman stared at her without speaking, then she turned and bellowed raucously, 'Alun . . . Alun Powell, there's some woman here asking about your missus.'

It was such a long time before Alun answered that she was about to go away. When he did appear he was in his shirtsleeves, unshaven, and there was a cigarette dangling from the corner of his mouth.

He looked taken aback when he saw Megan.

'What are you doing here?' he asked in surprise.

'I came to find out why Sheryl didn't turn up at the hospital yesterday.'

'Didn't she come, then?' He ran a finger round his collar uneasily.

'You must know she didn't,' Megan retorted sharply. 'I told you that you'd have to come with her because she shouldn't be lifting or carrying Caitlin until her ribs have healed properly.'

'Do you chase around after all your patients like this if they miss an appointment, Megan?' he grinned insolently, stubbing out his cigarette.

'Of course not! Sheryl's different, she's my friend. So how is she, then?'

Alun shrugged. 'How do you think she is? She's got broken ribs, hasn't she.'

'I know that! That's why she should have come back to the hospital yesterday, so that someone can check up to see how well she's doing. Are you going to let me see her?'

Alun shook his head. 'I'm afraid I can't help you because she's not here.'

Megan frowned. 'I don't understand. Where is she then?'

'Sheryl decided that she and little Caitlin would go back to her mam's place for a while.'

Megan stared at him in disbelief. 'But they're not even speaking to each other! The last time I saw Mrs Williams she was worried sick about

151

Sheryl because she hadn't heard from her since the day she left home.'

'Well, they're talking now.'

'Good! I'm more than pleased to hear it, but however did it all happen?'

Alun looked uncomfortable. He pulled out a packet of Gold Star cigarettes from his pocket, shook one halfway out and offered it to her. When Megan shook her head he placed it between his own lips and struck a match to light it. 'I couldn't manage to look after both her and Caitlin. It was too much. Now that Caitlin's found her feet, and can toddle around the place, she's into everything, you know how it is. I have to go to work.'

'I thought you told me that you would be able to manage during the day.'

He looked at her from beneath half-closed eyes as he blew out a cloud of smoke. 'Yes, and I asked you if you would come here in the evenings and give a hand, but you didn't bother to do so, did you?' he retaliated reproachfully.

'It wasn't a question of not bothering, I have to work shifts. I've been going on duty at two o'clock and I don't finish until ten o'clock at night. I've called here today on my way into work.'

'Well, if you're on your way to work then you'll have to wait and go and see her tomorrow, won't you,' Alun said teasingly. 'When you do, then you'll be able to find out for yourself how she is.'

Megan bit her lip, reminding herself that it was Sheryl's welfare that mattered and refusing to let him goad her. 'Did you tell Sheryl's mother that she had to come to the hospital today?' she pressed.

'No, I left it to Sheryl to do that. It was no good me saying anything about it. I know from experience that her mother wouldn't listen to a damn thing I said to her. She was too busy telling me how neglected Sheryl was!' He laughed uncomfortably, 'You know what she's like, the old witch.'

'Well, I'm sure Sheryl is in good hands and that her mother will look after her properly as well as taking good care of Caitlin,' Megan said sharply. 'I'll go and see her tomorrow. Is there anything you want me to tell her or will you be going along to see her yourself sometime today?'

'Me seeing her! Not bloody likely,' he guffawed, 'not while she's at Thesiger Street. They've no time for me now, have they? In fact, it's probably much better for all concerned if I keep my distance,' he added cynically.

Megan refused to be drawn into such a discussion. 'So is there any message you would like me to give Sheryl when I see her?'

Alun shook his head, his eyes appraising her.

'Well, I'll tell her that I've spoken to you,' Megan said as she turned to leave.

'Hold on Megan, surely you have time for a drink before you go?' Alun invited.

'No, I really must be on my way, I'm not sure how long it will take me to get to the hospital from here and I don't want to be late for work. It took me a lot longer to find you than I had expected,' Megan replied.

He moved closer and took her arm. 'You can spare ten minutes, surely,' he said persuasively. 'The two of us have a lot of catching up to do, you know.'

Megan suddenly felt uncomfortable. She didn't like the change in Alun's manner. He was still holding her arm, his fingers tightening as he spoke.

'No!' She pulled her arm away. 'I must go, I told you I have to be at work.'

'So have I, but I can spare a few minutes,' he murmured softly. 'Come on, I'll take you up to my place where we can have a chat in private.'

For a brief moment Megan felt tempted because it would give her a chance to see what sort of home Sheryl had, but instinctively she knew she would be walking into trouble. She didn't trust Alun, not in his present mood.

'Please, Megan.' His hand caught at her arm.

'Another time, perhaps,' she said, moving away. Her heart thumping, she hurried down Loudon Place as fast as her feet would take her. She didn't look back until she reached Bute Street. When she did she saw that Alun was still standing on the corner watching her, and she felt a frisson of fear. She didn't know why, but she felt she had escaped from some very real danger.

She resolved she'd go to Thesiger Road first thing next morning and check if Sheryl really was all right.

Chapter Fourteen

Sheryl found that being back in her own bedroom was sheer heaven. Her memories of the squalid room in Angelina Street had nightmare qualities, something that, try her hardest, she knew she would never completely erase from her mind.

The rooms over the Diawl Coch club were better, but could not compare in any way with the comfort of being back again in her old home.

For the first couple of weeks her mother pampered her as she had during Sheryl's schooldays. The harsh disagreements they'd had before she'd left home were all forgotten as if they'd never happened. Rachael took complete charge of Caitlin, as well as supervising Sheryl's recovery.

'You must rest,' her mother insisted. 'The more rest you have, the speedier those broken ribs will heal. I can't think how you came to break three of them by merely falling against a table, mind.'

'I told you, Mam, I fell awkwardly.'

'It was lucky that you didn't have little Caitlin in your arms, that's all I can say. If you had then she might have been really badly hurt. You'll have to be more careful, Sheryl.'

'I didn't do it on purpose, now did I, Mam,' Sheryl pouted.

'I know that, cariad, but I think you must have been careless and not watching what you were doing. Anyway, what's done is done. What you've got to do now is get better as quickly as you possibly can, so you rest up while you have the chance. I'll take care of Caitlin so don't worry about her. She's such a little beauty and she loves her granny so much!'

Her parents had been shocked by both Sheryl and Caitlin's appearance. Sheryl accounted for their bedraggled look by explaining that with her broken ribs she could hardly dress herself, let alone manage a wriggling little bundle like Caitlin.

'Surely Alun could have done more to help you,' Rachael tutted. 'Caitlin's clothes are dirty and she doesn't look as though she's had a proper wash for days. Look how matted her hair is!'

'She hates anyone trying to comb it. I usually have a struggle and Alun simply hasn't had the time to pander to her.'

'She'll let me do it, won't you my little lovely,' Rachael Williams boasted. 'A couple of days here with Granny and she'll be a different child. Neglected she looks at the moment. I'd hate any of the neighbours to see her like this.'

Over the next few days Sheryl took the easy

way out and stayed in bed, saying that she didn't feel well.

'Do you think I ought to get our own doctor in to take a look at her?' Rachael asked worriedly when Megan called round to find out why Sheryl hadn't been back for a check-up as she'd been told.

'There's no need to do that, Mam! Megan will make another appointment for me at the hospital,' Sheryl insisted.

'Well, whatever you think best. I'll look after Caitlin and your dad will go with you. No point in taking Caitlin along to a place like that! She'll be better off here with me.'

'If you are going to look after Caitlin then I can manage quite well on my own. I'm sure Dad won't want to take a day off work,' Sheryl told her.

'How can you go on your own?' her mother scolded. 'You aren't fit to go on a tram in your condition. You need to have someone with you to make sure that you have a seat and that no-one bumps into you.'

Sheryl sighed. It was lovely turning the clock back and being pampered, but she had forgotten how very domineering her mother could be. Her mam meant well, she knew that, but sometimes so much fussing left her feeling suffocated.

When she'd been growing up she'd felt resentful of her mother's possessiveness. Now that she had a daughter of her own she could

158

understand better why she had been like that, but Sheryl still felt that her mother wanted to dictate her every movement.

An only child, all her parents' attention had been focused on her. Her dad had indulged her, especially as she was growing up. He had often slipped her extra pocket money. He was always willing to come and meet her when he knew she was going to be late home. He'd hardly ever told her off, but then he'd never needed to, her mother had done that on a regular basis.

Even though her mam also spoiled her in a hundred and one ways, she'd been quite a stickler when it came to manners and behaviour. A lot of good all that had done when she'd ended up living down in Tiger Bay, she thought ruefully.

She'd been so completely mollycoddled that she'd had no real idea of how to run a home. That was why she hadn't bothered to even try when she'd moved into the room in Angelina Street. There hadn't seemed to be any point, with no proper facilities to do any cooking or carry out the normal things you did in a home. She shuddered at the memory. She never wanted to have to exist like that again. The rooms over the Diawl Coch were better, at least there was a proper kitchen. She still didn't feel it was a real home though, certainly not a place where she wanted to invite her mother.

She snuggled deeper down in her warm soft bed and stretched luxuriously. It might even have turned out all right if Alun had been more reasonable, and not behaved so selfishly. If only he'd let her go down into the club at night and mingle with people, have a drink, and enjoy a bit of life. Instead, she'd been isolated upstairs with only Caitlin for company. By evening she'd seen and heard enough of Caitlin, and wanted a bit of life for herself.

It wasn't as if Alun was any great company when he came home, or during the day before he went to work. At night he was usually stewed to the eyebrows and only wanted to go to bed. In the morning he often had a hangover and stayed in bed until mid-morning. Then he barely had time to get himself spruced up for work.

Being married hadn't been anything like the wonderful experience Sheryl had dreamed it would be. Alun didn't seem to have much time for romantic talk, or the flirting and kissing that had first attracted her to him. In so many ways he was a completely different person from the dashing soldier she'd fallen head over heels in love with and thought she couldn't live without. Now, there were times when she wondered if she'd been too hasty.

The slap across the face that had sent her reeling so violently that she'd crashed into the edge of the table and broken her ribs had been the first time he'd hit her, but it left her scared in case it wasn't the last.

If he behaved like that after being married for only such a short time, what sort of future did they have?

Since she'd been back at home she appreciated so many things which she had taken for granted before. If only she could turn the clock back, she thought ruefully, remembering the days when she and Megan had been inseparable and she'd had a crush on Megan's brother Elwyn.

'You are going to stay here for Christmas, cariad?' Gwynfor Williams questioned hopefully, a fortnight before Christmas.

'Well . . .' Sheryl hesitated. She'd already been there for over six weeks, and she knew that the longer she stayed the harder she would find it to go back to Loudon Place.

'Of course she will,' her mother said crisply. 'She'll have to stay because I've got so many special treats planned for Caitlin for Christmas.'

'Perhaps I ought to go back to spend it with Alun,' Sheryl said dubiously. 'Unless I can ask him to come here for Christmas Day,' she suggested.

There was an uneasy silence and she saw her parents look at each other questioningly.

'Please! I can't stay otherwise, it wouldn't be fair on Caitlin not to be with her father at such a time,' she pointed out.

'Surely Alun will be working?' Rachael said.

Sheryl looked at them uncertainly. 'I don't really know,' she admitted. 'Do clubs keep open on Christmas Day?'

'I'm sure that sort of club does,' her mother declared censoriously.

'They probably do,' Gwynfor agreed, 'and they'll certainly be open on New Year's Eve, there's no doubt at all about that. It's one of the highlights of the year for places like that. Alun will probably be so busy preparing for it that you'll hardly see anything of him. You may as well stay here until all those sort of festivities are over and done with, that's the best plan.'

'I'm not sure, that makes it almost another month,' Sheryl said hesitantly.

'Young Caitlin is better off here being properly looked after in a house that's nice and warm,' Rachael said firmly. 'There's no hurry to decide when you are going back, wait and see what the weather is like. Sometimes it can be bitterly cold in January, there's snow even!'

'You haven't said whether or not Alun can spend Christmas Day here,' Sheryl reminded them.

Again her parents looked at each other, and she knew without either of them saying that they would rather he didn't come.

'Please Mam, Caitlin must be missing him so much, and they should be together on Christmas Day of all times.'

'Have I ever stopped him coming to see her?' Rachael blustered.

'No, but you haven't exactly made him very welcome, have you,' Sheryl commented.

'Well, he never gives us any warning of when he is coming, and you know how I hate being caught on the hop.'

'If you ask him to join us for Christmas dinner then you'll know precisely what time he will be coming,' Sheryl pointed out.

'Yes, I suppose that's true. It would be better to have him sitting down to dinner with us than dropping in casually the minute I am about to serve up, and have the whole meal spoiled.'

'So I can tell him that he's invited?'

'Very well then, but only as long as your dad agrees to that arrangement,' Rachael said rather diffidently.

'So is it all right with you, Dad?'

Gwynfor puffed out his cheeks as though perplexed and ran a hand through his thinning hair. 'Yes, if your mam is happy about that sort of set-up then of course I've no objection.' He cleared his throat awkwardly. 'I don't want him staying the night though, you do understand that?'

Sheryl nodded. 'Thank you, thank you both. I'll let Alun know.'

'So how are you planning to do that?' her mother asked quickly. 'You're not fit enough yet, you know, to go and see him . . . well, not on your own.'

'I'll write to him,' Sheryl promised.

'Very well. That seems the most sensible thing to do. And make it quite clear that he is invited for dinner and nothing else. Tell him to be here promptly at one o'clock on Christmas Day.'

'That's of course if he can manage to get

away,' her father stated. 'You can tell him we'll quite understand if he is unable to come because he is working.'

As she wrote the letter to Alun, Sheryl knew she should be feeling excited that he was going to be there with them for Christmas dinner. Instead she found herself wondering if perhaps it would be better if he didn't come. She was pretty sure there would be arguments between him and her parents. She was also afraid that opinions might be aired and things discussed that would be better left unsaid.

Perhaps, she thought, having stamped and posted the letter, Alun would feel the same and decide he was too busy or make some other excuse not to be there.

To Sheryl's surprise, Alun wrote back by return of post accepting the invitation.

When he arrived, shortly before one o'clock on Christmas Day, he brought a big doll for Caitlin, silk stockings for her, chocolates for her mother and a box of cigars for her father. He also provided a large bottle of wine for them to have with their meal.

By the time Alun left Thesiger Street, shortly before four in the afternoon, the atmosphere had deteriorated from one of cool friendliness to a state of guarded hostility.

Sheryl was well aware that Alun was growing more and more irritated by the way her mother kept comparing Caitlin with what she had been like when she was a toddler.

164

'She's the spitting image of our Sheryl. She's a little Williams all right!'

Each time her mother made such statements Sheryl tried either to laugh it off, or change the conversation to some other topic, hoping that Alun hadn't noticed.

The moment her mother realised what she was doing she started asking Alun directly if he agreed with her. As a result his mood became more and more hostile. When he eventually stood up, saying that he had to go because the club would be opening that night and he had things to get ready, Sheryl felt quite relieved.

She left Caitlin with her mother while she went to the door to see him off. She was hoping that this would give them the chance to have a few private words together, so that she could talk to him about returning home.

Alun shrugged as if he was reluctant even to discuss the matter. 'Hadn't you better ask your mother how long she wants you and Caitlin to stay?' he said. 'She seems to be the one who decides these things, not me.'

'When do you want us to come back, Alun, that's really what matters?'

'Does it? You seem to be very settled in here and loving every minute of it.'

'Mam has been good to me,' she defended. 'It's been wonderful the way she's looked after Caitlin so that I could get plenty of rest and give my ribs a chance to heal.'

'And have they?' he challenged.

'I think so, more or less. I still feel a twinge whenever I try to pick Caitlin up, but that's probably because she's such a plump little bundle these days.'

'Exactly like you were when you were her age, I suppose,' he said sarcastically.

Sheryl felt hot tears prickling her eyes. 'Don't be like that, Alun,' she pleaded. 'My mam's very proud of her, which is why she goes on like that.'

'Is it? I thought she was trying to make it quite clear that I'm of no importance in Caitlin's life,' he said sneeringly. He shrugged on his overcoat, settled his trilby firmly on his head and walked towards the front door.

Sheryl shook her head, blinking back her tears. 'I only came back here because I couldn't look after Caitlin and you said you hadn't got the time to do so,' she reminded him.

'In that case you'd better stay on until you do feel you are fit enough to look after her on your own, hadn't you?'

Chapter Fifteen

It was 23rd January 1923, a fortnight after Caitlin's second birthday, when Sheryl returned to the rooms at Loudon Place. She was aware that if she didn't leave Thesiger Street soon, Caitlin would be completely ruined.

No matter what she told Caitlin to do, her mother seemed to override her. She would either tell her granddaughter to do something different or encourage her to ignore completely whatever Sheryl had said.

Caitlin was so confused about whom she must obey that she was also becoming fretful. Now and again, especially more recently, Sheryl also noticed that she was playing them off, one against the other.

Sometimes Sheryl wanted to laugh, but she realised that would only be storing up trouble for the future. She tried talking to her mother about it, but she took it the wrong way and the atmosphere became increasingly tense until they were barely civil to each other.

She didn't want to fall out with her mother again, so she decided that the best way to solve the problem was to go back to Loudon Place. Whatever things she might say about Alun, she could never accuse him of trying to alienate her and Caitlin. He was more inclined to indulge the child than tell her to do anything.

Sheryl wasn't sure how she felt about returning there. She'd miss the comforts of Thesiger Street and the appetising meals her mam served up every day. She'd tried to learn more about cooking and all the other tasks connected with running a home while she'd been back there. She felt that perhaps if she made a better job of that sort of thing it would please Alun.

She was very conscious that not once since she'd been at Thesiger Street had he said he missed her, not even when she'd asked him at Christmas. It was very humiliating, and not for the first time she suspected that for both of them much of the magic had gone out of their relationship.

She tried not to think about the row that had resulted in her broken ribs and made it necessary for her to leave their home for a while. She was scared that it might happen again.

If Alun ever hit her again, even once, whether it was when he'd had too much to drink or not, then she would leave him. She was quite determined about that. She didn't intend letting him use her as a punchbag.

The fact that he hadn't seemed to miss her at all preyed on her mind. She was very much afraid that it meant he'd found someone else. Well, she wasn't going to stand for that either. She was his legal wife and she wasn't having him playing the field. He had to remember that he was not only a married man, but that he was also a father. It was his responsibility not only to provide for Caitlin but to help bring her up as well.

Although she told herself this over and over again, Sheryl knew quite well that Alun was a law unto himself. If he wanted to go out on the loose, or drink too much, then he would, and nothing she said or did would make any difference. If she reproached him, or even commented on it, in all probability it would only lead to rows between them.

As she dressed Caitlin in the little red woollen coat trimmed with white fur and the white leggings that her mam and dad had bought her for Christmas, Sheryl wondered how much her parents suspected about the problems she was facing.

She couldn't bring herself to confide in either of them about her anxieties, not even tell them the truth about how she'd come to have three broken ribs. She knew that if she did they would retaliate with 'we told you so!' They had never wanted her to marry Alun, and she knew only too well that they wouldn't have let her do so if she hadn't been pregnant.

Alun Powell had ringed Monday 23rd January 1923 in heavy black pencil. Black Monday! It was certainly that as far as he was concerned. It was the day that Sheryl had said she and

Caitlin were coming home. It meant the end of the relative freedom he'd been enjoying since she'd moved back in with her parents.

She'd asked him to go over to collect her and Caitlin, but he'd made it quite clear that he was far too busy for any of those sorts of capers.

'I'll never be able to manage all the cases and Caitlin on my own,' she'd complained. 'I don't want to ask my mam to come with me, because I think it would be too much of a shock for her if she saw the sort of place we're living in.'

He'd refused to rise to her taunts, but he didn't want her mother coming there either, so he made a quick decision.

'Don't worry,' he told her, 'I'll send a man I know, Ieuan Davies, in his motor car to collect you and all your bits and pieces. You should be able to manage, seeing that it will be door-to-door,' he'd added with a touch of sarcasm.

'Don't be daft! He'll never manage to get Caitlin's big pram inside his motor car,' she argued.

'Then leave the bloody thing where it is. She doesn't need it any more.'

'Of course she does! With her little legs she soon gets tired and she's too heavy for me to carry.'

'Don't worry, I'll buy a pushchair for her. One you can take onto the tram when you go into town.'

'Yes? And when will that be?'

'Today. I'll go and get one now. It will be here waiting for you when you get back.'

That had certainly shut her up, and he knew it would be easy enough for him to pick up a second-hand pushchair. Ieuan Davies owed him a favour and he was quite willing to nip over to Cathays and collect them and bring them back.

That was the least of his problems, Alun reflected. It was his private social life that he was going to have trouble rearranging. He'd become so used to coming and going as he pleased, and seeing whoever he liked when he wasn't working.

During the time Sheryl had been away he'd mixed work and pleasure to such an extent that it was difficult to see where one started and the other ended.

The girls who worked at the club were a special breed. They had few inhibitions, were willing to give pleasure whenever it was expected and without any strings attached. They didn't whinge or whine, didn't expect favours, and you knew in advance what the rate was for their services. They bubbled over with goodwill and they always looked stunning.

The girls all knew that he was married, and that his wife was away. Now they knew she was about to come back home and when she did they would respect his domestic privacy, there was no question of that. He would miss the freedom of seeing them whenever he

171

wanted to. During working hours it was not always possible to take advantage of their services. For one thing, he wasn't too sure that Zakaraki would approve and since he was their boss too, his authority had to be observed.

As far as Alun was concerned, after life in the army working for Zakaraki was a piece of cake, because he issued orders as if he was making a mild suggestion. He expected them to be carried out to the letter, though. Failure to do so brought a strong reprimand. He paid well and turned a blind eye to any little deals his employees might arrange with any of the customers.

The one thing he did insist on, though, was that Sheryl must use the separate entrance in Loudon Place. Alun had assured him that he understood and that he considered it to be a perfect arrangement. It suited him down to the ground. He didn't want Sheryl to know too much about what he did when he was working. That was the reason why he'd flared up when he found she had tried to get into the club.

In some ways it would be better to be living completely independent of the club, but if that happened he would have to pay rent. The arrangement as it stood at the moment meant that he didn't have to shell out a penny piece.

He'd neglected their rooms while she'd been away, even though he'd used them as a trysting place when it suited him. To make sure that everywhere was clean, and that there were no traces of the girls he'd taken up there, he asked Annie, the woman who cleaned the club, to go up and give it a thorough going-over.

She'd pulled a face and grumbled about the extra work, but the moment he'd put his hand in his pocket and given her a ten-shilling note she'd changed her tune.

She'd done a spanking good job and it looked a treat now. He only hoped Sheryl would keep up the standard. After a spell with her mother she might have picked up a few homemaking tips. With any luck she might even know how to cook. He was heartily fed up with a diet of bought meat pies or fish and chips.

Sheryl felt apprehensive as the big black Austin car pulled up outside the side door of the Diawl Coch. She had expected Alun to be there waiting for them, but there was no sign of him.

'Sit tight where you are for a moment and I'll see if I can find him,' Ieuan Davies told her. 'I'll nip round the corner and let him know that you're here.'

He was frowning when he returned. 'Alun's busy at the moment, but he'll be with you in about ten minutes so he has asked me to give you a hand up the stairs with your luggage,' he told her as he unloaded her cases onto the pavement.

Sheryl did her best to hold in check the

annoyance she felt. It was no more than she should have expected, she told herself as she lifted Caitlin up into her arms.

'No, no! I'll carry her up for you,' Ieuan Davies insisted. 'Leave all your bags and everything else where they are on the pavement and I'll come back down for them.'

The rooms all seemed so much smaller than she remembered. A fire was burning in the little grate, but even so the room felt cold and unfriendly. Sheryl felt a shiver go through her. It was scrupulously tidy; in fact, it was so spick and span and soulless that it looked like a barrack room, except for the pushchair Alun had bought for Caitlin and which he'd left in the middle of the room so that it was the first thing she saw as she walked in.

Caitlin was bemused by the strangeness of the place and wandered round the room, her thumb stuck in her mouth. She already missed being the centre of things and began to grizzle and make a fuss in order to attract her mother's attention.

Her crying distracted Sheryl. As she'd unpacked the bags and cases she had piled everything up on the table and chairs ready to put away, but now she paused to find Caitlin something to eat to keep her quiet.

It was at that moment that Alun walked in.

'It hasn't taken you very long to make a pigsty of the place again,' he commented. 'It looks like a second-hand shop in here! I was

174

hoping that perhaps you'd pick up some good habits after being at your mam's.'

'And I'm so pleased to see you, too,' she retorted. 'Perhaps if you'd been here when we arrived I would have had the chance to put things away as I unpacked them. Instead I've had to break off to see to Caitlin every couple of minutes.'

'Need a servant, do you!' he smirked. 'I'm not your mam! You are going to have to learn to do things and look after the kid all at one and the same time, like other women do.'

'Well, now you are here you can give Caitlin a bottle while I tidy up and get things straight,' she told him sullenly.

'She shouldn't be having a bottle! At her age she should be able to drink out of a cup. If she has to have a bottle then she's big enough to hold it herself.'

'She doesn't usually have one now,' Sheryl defended. 'Poor little love, she's feeling lost and unhappy because she finds it all so strange here, so I thought a bottle might comfort her. What she really needs is a nice cuddle.'

'Then you'll have to give her one. I've got things to see to, but I'll be back up for some grub before I start work. There's plenty of stuff in the kitchen so rustle me up something tasty. I'll be about half an hour,' he called over his shoulder.

Sheryl felt too choked to answer. This wasn't the sort of homecoming she had envisaged.

175

She'd hoped Alun would be so overjoyed to have them back home again that he'd give her a big hug and shower them both with kisses.

Why on earth had she been in such a hurry to return to Loudon Place, she asked herself. Perhaps her mother had been right yet again! She wished now that she had taken her advice and stayed at Thesiger Street for a bit longer.

Determined to do her best to make things right between herself and Alun, in spite of the bad start, Sheryl scurried around tidying everything away and preparing a meal. She fed Caitlin and settled her down for a nap. Perhaps if she and Alun could have a quiet hour on their own, things would come right, she thought hopefully.

When the half-hour lengthened into an hour and Alun still didn't appear she began to feel angry. She was on the point of clearing the table when he turned up.

There was no word of apology, or even an excuse, as he pulled out a chair.

'Hope my grub's ready as I only have an hour to spare and I need to get changed,' he told her as he sat down.

She dished up in silence. He tucked in without speaking.

'I see you've learnt to cook while you've been at your mam's,' he said appreciatively as he shoved his empty plate aside.

'It was only bangers and mash!'

'You couldn't even cook those properly a few

months ago,' he said scathingly. He pushed back his chair. 'I'll try and knock off early,' he grinned, 'so be sure you're ready to make up for deserting me for the past three months!'

Chapter Sixteen

Finally her first night back home had some of the magic that she had longed for, Sheryl reflected after they had made love. Alun had gone to sleep almost immediately afterwards, but she had lain awake. Cradled in the warmth of his body, she enjoyed the sound of his rhythmic breathing, convinced that he still loved her.

Their lovemaking had been everything she could have desired. Alun had been warm, tender, loving and exciting. It had wiped out all her uncertainty about what he still felt for her. It was so obvious that he had missed her, and she felt ashamed that she had ever doubted his feelings for her.

She thought back over the furtive encounters when they'd been courting. He had been ardent then, but now there was a deeper, more passionate side to his lovemaking.

Caitlin had slept soundly, so nothing had interrupted their emotional reunion. His kisses had been so hungry and eager that she had responded with equal fervour. Their passion had resulted in such an intense crescendo of pleasure that she had succumbed with delight. She'd felt like an insatiable sponge as their naked flesh mingled and the need that had built up while they'd been apart reached fulfilment.

As dawn broke, Caitlin's plaintive cry disturbed Sheryl's blissful sleep. For a moment she lay there, trying to work out where she was. As her leg brushed against Alun he stirred, and muttered something she couldn't catch. Then he rolled over onto his stomach, buried his face in the pillow, and went back to sleep.

As Caitlin's crying became more insistent Sheryl struggled from the warmth of the bed and went to attend to her. From now on, without her mother, it looked as though there was going to be no-one to share this chore with her, she thought resignedly.

Alun slept until mid-morning and then dragged himself out of bed, cursing because it was so late. Impatiently he pushed Sheryl away when she tried to kiss him.

'Not now, I've got to get to work so go and get my breakfast ready,' he told her.

'What time will you be home?' Sheryl asked as she put an egg on fried bread in front of him.

'Late! Certainly not before eleven so don't wait up for me.'

He took a mouthful of food, then waved his fork at her. 'Don't go trying to come down there asking for me, either. Remember I got a bloody mouthing from Zakaraki the last time you did it. You're banned from the club. Do you understand?'

Sheryl didn't answer. Nothing had really

changed, she thought unhappily. She had been so sure that after being on his own for almost three months, and having to look after himself for all that time, things would be different now she was back.

Instead, it seemed they were back to square one again. She was going to be spending not only most of the day on her own, but the interminably long evenings as well. The wonderful feeling of elation that she'd felt after they'd made love the night before began slowly to ebb away.

When she'd been at her mother's place there had always been someone to talk to. Her mother frequently got on her nerves, but at least she hadn't been lonely. She'd been able to see Megan as well when she wasn't working. They'd gone for walks together, and even managed to go to the pictures once or twice while her mother had looked after Caitlin.

As she cleared away Alun's dirty dishes, Sheryl tried to plan what she was going to do from now on. She wasn't going to stay cooped up in two rooms for the rest of her life. She wasn't even twenty until June. She should be having fun, going out two or three times a week, either to the pictures or dancing. Surely Alun must realise that?

Determined to face him and talk to him about it while it was still all so clear in her mind, she resolved to wait up. He'd said around eleven o'clock, but after what seemed like endless hours, it came to half past eleven and he still wasn't home.

It was almost midnight before she heard him coming up the stairs.

'What the hell are you doing still up? I told you to go to bed and not to wait up for me,' he glowered as he took off his jacket and hung it over the back of a chair, and then loosened his tie.

'I wanted to talk to you.'

'Talk to me!' His voice was slurred and his breath reeked of spirits. 'Can't it wait until morning? I've been working for over twelve hours, I'm whacked.'

'You mean you've been drinking and enjoying yourself,' she snapped.

'I keep explaining to you that drinking is all part of the job!'

'And does laughing and talking to the customers go with the job as well?'

'Of course!' He belched noisily. 'What the hell is all this about, anyway?'

'I want to know how many nights you get off a week, so that I can plan where we'll be going when you do.'

Alun stared at her, bemused. 'What the bloody hell are you talking about?'

'I need to know when you will be taking me out, Alun. I can't stay here in this place night after night on my own. I need some fun, I want to go out dancing and to the pictures.'

He laughed sourly. 'How twp can you be?'

'I'm not being stupid, I'm deadly serious.'

'You expect me to take a night off so that I can take you out? Forget it, cariad! If I start asking for time off, Zak will give me time off permanently; he'll sack me! If I lose the job we lose these rooms and we'll be out on the street. I've told you all this time and again. Is that what you want to happen?'

'Of course not! Mr Zakaraki must give you some time off though, Alun. Please,' she begged. 'Ask him. Tell him we need time to be together.'

'Forget it! The only way you'll get the pleasure of my company is in bed, so stop wasting time and get there right now.'

'Oh no!' Sheryl flicked back her hair defiantly. 'If you don't intend taking me out regularly then I certainly don't intend letting you sleep with me.'

She looked at him mutinously, but inwardly she was trembling, scared stiff he might hit out at her like he had before.

He returned her stubborn stare stonily. Then, picking up his jacket from the back of the chair, he turned on his heel and staggered towards the bedroom. 'Please yourself,' he shrugged.

Sheryl remained by the table, shaking, still afraid that he might retaliate in some way. The next minute she heard a commotion coming from the bedroom. Before she could get in there to find out what was happening the door opened and Caitlin's cot, with her still in it, was pushed through into the living room. Then the door between the two rooms was slammed shut again.

The noise and disturbance woke Caitlin and she began to cry. Sheryl picked her up, hugging her close, whispering to her softly to try and calm her down. She made up a bottle and sat nursing her while she drank it, finding comfort from the warmth of the small body pressed up against her own.

When Caitlin eventually fell asleep Sheryl placed her back in the cot and waited to make sure she was settled before she went through to the bedroom.

Alun was already asleep when she crept in under the bedclothes. He stirred and she waited breathlessly for him to speak. When he didn't she slid down beside him, turned on her side with her back towards him, and settled to sleep.

She had barely closed her eyes before Alun grabbed her roughly. Without a word he rolled her onto her back and forced himself on her so savagely that she cried out in agony. This seemed to impel him to become more brutish, as if determined to punish her for daring to oppose him.

Sobbing, Sheryl tried to free herself from his clutches, but he was stronger than her and restrained her easily.

Using every ounce of her ebbing strength she tried to knee him. Alun retaliated by punching her so savagely that she yelled out, convinced that her newly healed ribs were broken again.

She edged away and curled into a ball, hoping it would prevent him hitting her again. With a sneering laugh he lifted his foot and jabbed it viciously into her back, sending her crashing from the bed onto the floor.

She lay there motionless, afraid to move in case he attacked her again. She heard the bed creak and held her breath. When nothing else happened she decided that the noise was only him turning over in the bed.

Sore and aching, she stayed curled in a ball, and waited until she heard him begin to snore. When she judged that he must be sound asleep again she crept across the floor and went back into the living room.

Cold and shivering, her body wracked with pain, Sheryl dragged the red chenille cloth off the table and wrapped it around her for warmth.

She felt too sick and miserable even to make herself a drink. She crouched in the armchair drawn up in front of the dying fire, and wondered what she ought to do.

She couldn't stay here, yet she didn't want to go back to Thesiger Street. After all the bitter things she'd said when she'd quarrelled with her mother about the way she was dominating Caitlin, she knew she would have to apologise and grovel before her mam would let her stay there again.

That wouldn't be the worst part, of course.

If she went back again she would lose all control of Caitlin. Her mother would take over and bring Caitlin up as if she was her child, and she didn't want that. Yet she couldn't stay here because, knowing how volatile Alun became after he'd been drinking, she was afraid of what he might do. Anyway, she reminded herself, she was virtually a prisoner in these rooms, and she didn't want to go on living like that.

She knew she'd have to go back to the hospital to make sure that there was no further damage to her ribs. That would mean telling them what had happened, and she didn't think it would be wise to do that. Yet if she did go, she might see Megan and be able to ask her advice about what to do for the best.

Megan! The moment her name popped into her head she knew exactly what she must do. The answer was to move in with Megan. She was sure Mrs Thomas wouldn't object, not when she explained the situation.

It would only be a temporary measure to give her a breathing space, until she could make some plans. She'd make sure that she got money from Alun for her keep by threatening to tell Mr Zakaraki about his violent behaviour if he refused. One thing she was sure about was that she couldn't go on living with Alun. That was twice he'd hurt her badly, and who knew what he might do in the future? She didn't trust him any more. Next time it might be Caitlin he lashed out at when her crying got on his nerves.

She dozed fitfully, on the alert, listening for any sound from Alun, and wondering what mood he would be in when he woke up.

He seemed to be calm enough next morning. In stony silence she cooked him some breakfast, then left him on his own to eat it. As soon as he went down to the club around mid-morning, she made up her mind to go to the hospital.

She pulled on her winter coat and dressed Caitlin as warmly as she could.

When she reached the hospital she asked for Megan at the reception desk, and her spirits soared when she was told that she had just come on duty.

When Sheryl explained that she had hurt her ribs again, Megan arranged for her to be examined. This time she was told that they were not broken, but there was considerable bruising in the area, and she was warned to take more care.

'You didn't fall again, now did you?' Megan reproached her. 'This was Alun's doing. Come on, admit it!'

'Yes, and I'm afraid to go back because I know it will happen again,' Sheryl confided.

'So what will you do? I suppose you could always go back to your mother's.'

Sheryl shook her head. 'I only left there the day before yesterday. We were constantly having words about the way she was taking Caitlin over. You know what a martinet my mother can be.'

Megan frowned anxiously. 'So what on earth are you going to do now?'

Sheryl bit her lip. 'I don't really know. I was wondering if I could move in with you for a week or two, until I can sort something out?'

'Stay with me?' Megan looked taken aback. 'I'm still living at home!'

'I know that, cariad. Your mam wouldn't mind though, would she?'

Megan looked bewildered. 'I don't know. She's pretty easy-going but . . .'

'Please, Megan. Can we ask her and see what she says?'

'You mean right now?'

Sheryl nodded. 'I'm afraid to go back to Alun and I've explained why I can't go to my own mam's. You're my only hope, Megan, I'm depending on you to help.'

'What about all your things?' Megan prevaricated. 'You'll have to go back and collect those.'

'If your mam says I can stay at your place for a couple of weeks, then perhaps you and me could go together tomorrow and get them,' Sheryl said hopefully.

Megan shook her head. 'It's not a good idea. I don't want to get that involved . . .'

'Please Megan, for old times' sake. We've always been the best of friends. Don't let me down now!' Sheryl begged.

'Look, I've work to do so I can't stand here talking. I'll give it some thought, though, and you come and see me tomorrow morning before

I go to work. I don't start until two in the afternoon.' She hurried away before Sheryl could argue further.

Sheryl's lips tightened as she watched Megan disappear down the long corridor. She made up her mind about what she was going to do. Taking Caitlin's hand she walked out of the building, made her way to where the trams stopped and boarded one going to Cathays.

Glenda Thomas was surprised to see Sheryl in the middle of the afternoon. She'd only that moment sat down to enjoy a cup of tea and read her new copy of *Woman's Weekly*. Hiding her irritation she asked her in, offered her some tea, poured a mug of milk for Caitlin and found her a biscuit.

'Megan's at work, she's on two-until-ten shift so I'm afraid you've missed her, Sheryl.'

'No, I've just spoken to her. I've been at the hospital.'

'Another check-up on those ribs, was it?' Glenda smiled sympathetically.

'Yes and no. Alun thumped me again last night,' she said resignedly.

'Dammo di! That Alun beats you, my lovely!' Glenda exclaimed in dismay. 'Was that how you came to have broken ribs before?'

Sheryl nodded.

'That's shocking, cariad! You only went back to him the day before yesterday, and he's already given you another hiding?' Glenda was horrified. 'That's terrible. Whatever are you going to do?'

Sheryl shook her head. 'I don't really know. I don't want to go back to my mam's because I think they've already had enough of me,' she murmured.

'Rubbish! Your mam will welcome you with open arms when she hears what has happened.'

'I don't want to burden her with my problems. I want to stand on my own feet.'

'That's commendable, cariad, but how can you when you have a little one to look after?'

'I simply want to be on my own, away from my mam and from Alun, to give me time to think and sort myself out,' Sheryl told her, dabbing away her tears with the back of her hand.

'I can understand that, cariad,' Glenda agreed earnestly. 'So what are you planning to do now then?'

'Well, I was wondering if I could stay here with you for a little while, Mrs Thomas. Megan said she wouldn't mind as long as you didn't object? I'll pay my way, of course.'

Chapter Seventeen

Megan tried to hide her annoyance when she arrived home at half past ten that night and found Sheryl sitting in the living room, drinking tea and exchanging confidences with her mother.

'Sheryl and little Caitlin are staying with us for a couple of weeks,' Glenda Thomas told her daughter.

'Oh yes?'

Sheryl had obviously ignored what Megan had said to her earlier in the day and had taken matters into her own hands, even though Megan had made it clear that she didn't think it was a good idea for Sheryl to move in with them.

'She's been telling me all about having to come to the hospital today, because that Alun had beat her up again,' Glenda went on, her voice full of sympathy.

'Yes, Mam, I saw her there.'

'So you know all about what she's been through! Right bastard, that Alun. Fancy him doing that the minute she gets back home. You can't really credit such a thing, can you?'

Megan shook her head. She understood how

Sheryl had managed to get round her mother by telling her a sob story. She only hoped she hadn't led her mother to think that it was her idea, or that she had put Sheryl up to it.

'We'd better not tell Sheryl's mam that she's staying here, mind,' Glenda warned.

'No, Mrs Williams would want to know why Sheryl had decided to come here instead of going back to her place, wouldn't she!' Megan said wryly.

'Oh, it's not that, cariad. It's because Sheryl doesn't want to tell her mam about Alun attacking her because she knows how much it would worry her. She'd make a fuss, see, and Sheryl needs time to get herself together.'

'Your mam's right, Megan. I waited up because I wanted to make sure you didn't mind me staying here. I also wanted to ask you if you'd come to Loudon Place with me tomorrow to collect my things,' Sheryl said pleadingly. 'I'm too frightened to go on my own, see, in case Alun's there.'

Megan shook her head, her lips tightening. She'd already told Sheryl she didn't want to get involved.

'I'm sorry, Sheryl, it's impossible because I'm working again tomorrow.'

'You don't go on duty until two o'clock, cariad,' her mother pointed out.

'I thought we could do it first thing in the morning, as soon as you get up,' Sheryl told her. 'Your mam says I can leave Caitlin with her.'

'That's right, I'll look after little Caitlin while you two go and collect their belongings. She'll be as right as rain here with me, the little love.'

Megan hesitated, but she couldn't see any way out without upsetting her mother as well as Sheryl. 'Do you think we will be able to carry everything?' she hedged.

'I think so, if we walk back. We'll have to bring Caitlin's pushchair so we can pile the cases onto that. We'll be able to manage between us.'

'Then if I'm to be up in time for us to do all that before I go to work, I'd better get off to bed and not sit here talking,' Megan pronounced.

'I've put Sheryl in our Elwyn's room since he's going to be away for a while longer. Sheryl didn't want to go in the back bedroom, see, in case little Caitlin looked out of the window and spotted her mam-gu out in their backyard and called out to her.'

'What about all our Elwyn's things?'

'Oh, I've moved his stuff into the little back bedroom out of the way.'

'What does Dad think about that?'

'He won't mind, it doesn't make any difference to him. Anyway, it's much better for Sheryl and Caitlin to be in Elwyn's room rather than in with you, then if little Caitlin wakes up in the night and starts crying it won't disturb you, see.'

Megan nodded wearily. 'Right, I understand. You seem to have it all worked out.' She yawned as she made for the stairs. 'I'll see you in the morning.'

In spite of her problems Sheryl slept soundly and woke next morning full of optimism. Caitlin, worn out by the day's events, had only wakened once, but when she'd found that she was in the same bed as her mother she'd settled down again without any fuss.

Sheryl felt sure she had done the right thing in taking advantage of Mrs Thomas's hospitality. It wasn't safe for her and Caitlin to go on living with Alun. This was her chance to be away from him and, at the same time, be independent of her own mother. Megan hadn't looked too pleased, but now that the arrangement was made she'd soon come round.

Mrs Thomas was very fond of Caitlin and would want to be involved with her without trying to take her over, like her own mam had done. She wouldn't be criticising all the time about the way she was bringing her up, or trying to advise on what Caitlin should be eating.

Another thing, Sheryl thought happily, was that Mrs Thomas wasn't as fanatically house-proud as her own mam was. Mrs Thomas would understand and make allowances if Caitlin spilt a few crumbs, or upset her drink. She wouldn't scold her and make a fuss about it, or rush to clear it up, making everyone jumpy and on edge.

All Sheryl had to do now was to go and

collect their clothes, and all Caitlin's other bits and pieces.

It was not nearly as easy as she'd hoped. Megan was later getting up than she had expected her to be, and seemed to be in a very disgruntled mood.

Although she had been to Tiger Bay before, Megan was still uneasy about going there. When they got off the tram she clutched hold of Sheryl's arm, and kept looking back over her shoulder nervously as they walked down Loudon Place.

'How can you live in a place like this, it's like being in a foreign country. I haven't seen a single white face since we stepped off the tram,' she shivered.

'Ignore them. None of them will take any notice of you or speak to you.'

'I wouldn't like to live here,' Megan persisted, 'and I certainly wouldn't want to bring a child up in this sort of area. Think about when she has to go to school!'

Sheryl's lips tightened. 'With any luck me and Caitlin won't be living here then.'

Alun didn't approve of what they were planning to do. He made that abundantly clear when Sheryl told him that they'd come to collect her things because she was going to stay with Megan for a while.

'Your home is here,' he declared belligerently. 'Walk out and I might not agree to have you back again.'

'Perhaps I'll decide I don't want to come back,' she told him, tossing her head defiantly. 'I don't enjoy being used as a punchbag, you know.'

He scowled. 'Don't talk so bloody stupid!' he said scornfully. 'We were arguing and I slapped you one. Right? The fact that you fell badly and hit yourself against the edge of the table wasn't my fault. It was an accident. Go on, admit it!'

'That was the first time, but what about what happened the night before last?' Megan asked.

Alun ran a hand through his hair, 'What about it?' he asked, looking puzzled.

'Well, you hit Sheryl again, didn't you?' Megan reminded him. 'She came back to the hospital yesterday with extensive bruising around her ribs.'

'Extensive bruising?' He guffawed loudly. 'Rubbish! A spot of rough lovemaking, that was how that happened. That's right, isn't it Sheryl?'

'You call what happened lovemaking? I'd say it was rape, brutal rape at that.'

'Bloody nonsense!' he stormed. 'Is that what you've been telling Megan?'

'It's the truth!'

'So I got a bit carried away and now you've run home to Mummy,' he sneered.

'No she hasn't. Sheryl is staying at our house,' Megan said quietly.

'That's rather tough on you, Megan. Like taking your work home with you, isn't it?' he jibed. 'A sick woman and a wailing kid.' Alun grimaced.

'So what are you here for?' he asked when neither of them replied.

'I've already told you,' Sheryl said. 'I've come for our clothes, and Caitlin's things and her pushchair.'

He looked so angry that she wondered if he was going to try and stop her from having them. Then he shrugged and waved a hand. 'Take your things, take whatever you want . . . you needn't bother coming back. I don't want you here. After listening to all the things your mother said when I last came to see you, I'm not even too sure that Caitlin is mine.'

'Not yours!' Sheryl felt outraged. 'What on earth do you mean by that, Alun? Of course she's yours. That's the reason why we got married, isn't it?'

'Why you hoodwinked me into marrying you, you mean. How do I know she's my kid? Go on, tell me!'

'Of course she is your child!'

'How do I know? She's nothing at all like me. She doesn't look like me, now does she? Your mam never stopped telling me that she's a perfect little replica of you. "Like having my little Sheryl all over again",' he said, mimicking her mother's voice.

'That will do!' Megan moved closer to Sheryl and put an arm round her shoulders protectively. 'Of course Caitlin is yours. You were the one who got Sheryl preggers, we both know that. You even tried to persuade her to have an abortion.'

'Oh, I remember all the details,' he told her scornfully, 'but it doesn't prove that I am the father, only that she was trying to pin it on me. How do I know how many other squaddies she went out with as well as me? She was a hot little number in those days. Gone off the boil now, mind . . .'

The impact of Megan's hand across his face cut short the rest of his sentence.

'Come on!' Megan grabbed hold of Sheryl's arm, 'let's pick up your stuff and get out of here.'

Alun stood rubbing his jaw, his eyes never leaving them as they packed a couple of suitcases with clothes and toys.

'You'll want someone to help you with that lot,' he smirked as he saw them struggling to carry the cases down the stairs.

'Oh no we won't,' Sheryl told him. 'We're taking Caitlin's pushchair and we'll pile the suitcases on that.'

'And walk all the way from here to Cathays! Have you any idea how far that is?'

'We'll manage all right,' Megan snapped. 'Come on Sheryl, let's get going.'

They were both footsore by the time they reached Coburn Street. And almost the moment they arrived there, Megan had to leave for work.

'You haven't had your meal yet, cariad,' her mother said worriedly.

'I know, but I'll be late if I stop for that now.

I'll get something to eat in the hospital canteen before I go on duty if I have time.'

Sheryl settled into Coburn Street quite happily. She enjoyed the way she was fussed over. Glenda Thomas told her that she was always willing to look after Caitlin in the evenings, so that meant she could go out with Megan.

Sheryl looked forward to them spending quite a lot of time together, but what she hadn't realised was that Megan had a boyfriend.

Owen Pryce was in his mid-twenties, a pharmacist at the hospital where Megan worked. A thin young man with straight fair hair and horn-rimmed glasses, he always had a very serious expression on his clean-shaven face.

Sheryl resented the way Megan built her life around him. Even if they had made arrangements to go out Megan would think nothing of changing their plans if Owen said he was free, or if he turned up on the doorstep without warning.

Mrs Thomas seemed to think the world of Owen. 'He's a lovely chap, see,' she told Sheryl proudly. 'Good job, too, not like that Hadyn fellow.'

'I always thought you really liked Hadyn Baker!' Sheryl said in surprise.

'He was nice enough,' Mrs Thomas admitted, 'but he wasn't a patch on this one. Owen's got a good job, see. He'll make her a great husband. He takes everything so seriously, he's the sort you can depend on to always do the right thing.'

Sheryl nodded in agreement. He was serious all right, she thought critically. He rarely laughed or cracked a joke. She couldn't imagine him doing anything in the least bit rash.

From then on she took a perverse delight in trying to get a laugh out of Owen, when he came to call for Megan. It wasn't easy, but it amused her, especially the alarmed look on his face whenever she flirted with him.

Owen didn't know when she was being serious and when she wasn't. Consequently she teased him more and more. Each time she saw him she took things a little further, became a little bolder and laughed inwardly when she saw how embarrassed it made him.

Megan soon became annoyed by her antics, and complained about what she was doing. She kept asking her to stop it, telling her that Owen found it disconcerting.

Her remarks irritated Sheryl, and in a fit of spite the next time Owen came to the house she flirted with him even more wildly. Brushing up close against him, she fluttered her eyelashes. Tossing back her long hair, she reached up and pulled his head down until their lips met.

She laughed when he pushed her away. When she realised that Megan had seen what had happened, she turned on the charm and tried to make a joke of it. 'Only teasing you, boyo,' she mocked.

Megan was not amused. 'I saw what you did, Sheryl!'

'You heard what I told Owen, then,' she laughed. 'I was only having a joke.'

'Well, it's not the sort of joke I appreciate, and I'm quite sure that Owen doesn't like it either,' Megan retorted.

'Oh dear, naughty, naughty! I promise not to do it again.' Sheryl pretended to be contrite.

'You won't. I'll make sure of that,' Megan told her sharply.

'What are you going to do, stop Owen coming to the house any more?'

'No, of course not. He's always welcome here. You are the one who will be leaving.'

The colour drained from Sheryl's face. 'Now you're the one who is having a laugh,' she gulped.

'No! I mean every word. I want you to leave as soon as you can get packed, and you won't be welcome here ever again.'

'You can't be serious? Where else can I go?'

Megan shrugged. 'Back to Alun, I suppose. That's if he'll have you.'

'You know it's not safe for me to do that!'

'Then you'll have to go to your mam's place.'

'I can't do that either! You know we've fallen out, and she'd be even more angry if she found out that I've been living here.'

'Then you'll have to find somewhere else. It's up to you where you go.'

'I think it's up to your mam. It's her house and if she says I can stay . . .'

'Don't try to talk my mother round, or try to

convince her that you were simply larking about. She's far too fond of Owen to put you before him.'

'Don't be too sure, Megan. She won't want to lose Caitlin, she absolutely dotes on her,' Sheryl said triumphantly.

'Yes, I know she's very fond of Caitlin and that she'll be bound to miss her, but it won't be for very long.'

Sheryl looked bemused. 'What do you mean?'

Megan slipped her arm through Owen's. 'We're getting married quite soon, so it won't be long before my mam will have a grandchild of her own.'

Chapter Eighteen

As the taxi driver dumped the last of her suitcases on the front doorstep of the Powells'
house in Archer Road, Sheryl scrabbled around
in her handbag to try and find enough money
to pay him.

'Look, hang on a minute,' she said apologet-
ically. 'I don't seem to have quite enough
change.'

Picking Caitlin up in her arms she rapped
on the door, her heart racing as she waited
nervously for someone to answer, uncertain of
what sort of reception she would get when they
did.

The heavily built middle-aged woman who
eventually came to the door stared at her questioningly, frowning as she saw the cases piled
up outside.

'Hello, Mrs Powell,' Sheryl smiled. 'I'm
Alun's wife and this is your granddaughter
Caitlin.'

'Oh yes.'

'I know we haven't met before, Mrs Powell,
so I thought it was time that we did,' Sheryl
said lamely, disconcerted by the look of disin-
terest on the older woman's face. 'I'm sure you

must have wondered about us and longed to see your little granddaughter,' she added hopefully.

'Not really, but now you're here you'd better come in, I suppose,' Nola Powell invited grudgingly.

'Thank you!' Sheryl put Caitlin down on the ground and then followed the child as she toddled after her grandmother into the kitchen.

'Hey, missus,' the cabby shouted impatiently, 'what about my money?'

'Mrs Powell, I wonder if you could let me have a quid?' Sheryl asked cajolingly. 'I'll give it back to you later, it's to pay the driver of the taxicab.'

'A quid! Where do you think I can lay my hands on a bloody quid? How much are you short?'

'Three shillings, but I ought to give him a tip . . .'

Nola sighed heavily, then dug around in an old china teapot that was on one of the shelves. 'Here's four bob, that should do you. Go on, take it and send him on his way. The kettle's boiling so bring your stuff inside, and then we'll have a cuppa and you can tell me what's brought you here.'

While Sheryl dragged the cases into the narrow hallway and closed the front door, Nola made the tea and carried it into the living room.

'Sit yourself down then. I'll fetch a cup of

milk and a biscuit for little Caitlin to keep her quiet for a few minutes while we have a chat about things.'

'Thank you.' Sheryl spooned some sugar into her tea and stirred it noisily.

'Steady on, cariad, you'll make a hole in that cup if you're not careful!' Nola took a crumpled packet of Woodbines from her apron pocket and lit one. 'Now, come on, tell me all about it and why you've turned up on my doorstep with all your belongings. Had a row with Alun, have you?'

'You could say that,' Sheryl said tightly, her colour rising.

'I am saying it and I'm waiting to hear what the pair of you have fallen out about this time!'

Sheryl took a mouthful of tea and then winced because it was too hot. 'It was more than just a mere row. Your Alun beat me up! He put me in hospital with three broken ribs.'

'That was months ago! You went back to your mam's until they mended, didn't you? That's what Alun told me when he came to see me.'

'Yes, and the first night I went back to Loudon Place he . . . he attacked me. I had to go back to the hospital the next morning. I thought they were broken again.'

Nola took a noisy mouthful of tea. 'Well, were they?'

'No,' Sheryl admitted. 'This time they were only badly bruised.'

'Well, there you are then, my lovely, a storm in a teacup! One of the ups and downs of married life, see! Everything has been plain sailing since then, hasn't it?'

Sheryl's lips tightened ominously. 'That was only because I had the sense to move out again.'

'Back to your mam? That's no way to have a happy married life, girl!'

'No, I didn't go to my mam's place. I went to stay at my friend Megan's home.'

'Fair do's. So what's happened now?' Nola asked, taking another slurp of tea.

'Well, it was only a temporary arrangement, see, and . . .'

'You've outstayed your welcome and they've asked you to move on.'

'Something like that. I've been staying there for nearly two months.'

Nola nodded. 'So you thought you'd come here and foist yourself on me rather than go home to Alun. Why didn't you go back to your own mam?'

Sheryl felt the colour rush to her face. She took another drink of her tea, to give herself time to think. She wasn't sure whether she should tell Mrs Powell that she couldn't do that because her mam had shown her the door, and she'd never felt so humiliated in all her life.

'All of them fed up with having you, are they?' Nola commented, breaking the awkward silence. 'I take it your mam has had enough of you being back at home with the little one in tow. Alun told me she was one of those house-proud types whose place was so spick and span that it was the same as being back in the army.'

'It wasn't like that . . .'

Nola waved her to silence. 'Don't bother trying to explain. For the little one's sake I'll let you stay, but you'll have to take us as you find us. Keep the kid quiet when my Cradog is around. He can't take a lot of noise. Do your share of helping around the place, and pay your way. Have you got any money?'

Sheryl shook her head.

'Well, I'm not keeping you. You'd better ask Alun for some money pretty damn quick. I don't want any rent from you, but I do expect you to hand over some housekeeping. Oh, and I want that four bob back that I've just let you have, remember that.'

'I didn't want Alun to know that I was here,' Sheryl said nervously.

Nola shrugged her plump shoulders. 'That's up to you. I don't give a damn where you get the money from, but I'm not planning on going without myself to feed you and young Caitlin.'

Sheryl nodded. 'I understand. I'd better get in touch with Alun, I'll write to him tonight and ask him to send me some money.'

'Let's hope he takes some notice, my lovely, otherwise you'll find yourself on your way back to him, bag and baggage.'

Sheryl sensed she wasn't being given a very warm welcome, but at least they'd both put their cards on the table and she knew where she stood. Getting money from Alun, though, was not going to be easy.

She looked round the untidy living room. Nola didn't seem to worry about her home or her appearance. Overweight and flabby, her greying hair pulled back into an untidy bun, she seemed the type who was quite happy as long as she had a fag in her hand, a cup of tea, her nose in a magazine and no-one bothering her.

'You can have our Alun's old room, he only used it when he came home on leave,' Nola told her. 'It's not all that big, mind, but there's a three-quarter-size bed in there. Caitlin will have to sleep with you. If you put her on the inside and push the bed tight up against the wall there'll be no fear of her falling out.'

Nola started spoiling Caitlin from the moment they arrived at Archer Road. When Sheryl complained about the number of sweets and sugar butties that Nola gave Caitlin, her mother-in-law took offence.

'What's wrong in that? The kid's that skinny that she looks half starved.'

'Too many sweet things aren't good for her, they'll rot her teeth.'

'Load of old baloney!' Nola scoffed. 'Toddling round all day with a dummy stuffed in her gob will do far more harm. Never without that damn thing, she isn't. Dirty old habit I call it.'

'It keeps her quiet when Cradog is at home,' Sheryl protested.

'So does a sweet or a sugar butty. And when she's got one of them she isn't sucking on that old dummy.'

Sheryl admitted defeat and let the matter drop. She knew she couldn't afford to get on the wrong side of Nola. Although she'd written to Alun twice asking for money, he hadn't replied, and so she still wasn't able to give her in-laws anything towards her keep.

Nola Powell was well aware of this and, as Sheryl feared, her patience was short-lived.

'If you can't get any reply from our Alun then I'll write to him or go and see him myself,' she threatened. 'You can't go on sponging off me and his dad for ever, you know!'

'I'm not sponging. I'm doing more than my fair share of the cleaning round this place,' Sheryl flared. 'Your house has never looked so spick and span.'

The moment the words were out Sheryl knew she'd made a grave mistake. Nola's face darkened. 'Is that so,' she scowled. 'And who is it that makes all the bloody mess around here, tell me that? It's that mardy kid of yours. Tearing up bits of paper, scrawling all over the walls with her crayons, dropping crumbs everywhere. I could go on and on, but I'll save my breath because you know that's the truth as well as I do.'

'If you didn't keep buying crayons for her and giving her biscuits, she wouldn't be making a mess all over the place,' Sheryl pointed out defiantly.

Once it started there seemed to be no end to their battle of words. Accusations rained like hailstones, pent-up emotions flowed in torrents. Cradog arrived home from work just in time to stop Nola and Sheryl resorting to physical violence.

'Perhaps it's time you moved back with your husband, my lovely,' he told Sheryl. 'All married couples have their differences, you know, especially at first.'

'I'm not going back to be his punchbag again,' Sheryl retorted bitterly.

'No, no! Things will be different this time, you'll see. He's had plenty of time to cool his heels by now, and so have you. It's time the two of you made up, if only for the little one's sake.'

'I'm not going back unless he asks me to,' Sheryl said stubbornly.

Cradog nodded. 'Fair do's. I'm sure he'll agree to that when I've had a talk with him. Leave it to me, cariad. In the meantime, let's call a truce to all this bickering.'

Cradog was as good as his word. The following Monday, around mid-morning, Alun, looking extremely debonair in a smart dark suit, crisp white shirt, gleaming shoes and slicked-down hair, turned up at Archer Road with two bunches of flowers, one each for his mother and Sheryl.

Having kissed them both, he swung Caitlin up into his arms and made a tremendous fuss of her. 'Daddy's come to take you and your mam home, my little lovely,' he stated, looking over the top of her head at Sheryl.

Sheryl bit her lip. This wasn't exactly the kind of apology she'd intended. Nor was it quite the sort of way she wanted him to ask her to come back. Things were now so bad between her and Nola, though, that she thought it was best to give in gracefully.

Nola brewed a pot of tea and sat talking to Alun, leaving Sheryl to collect up Caitlin's things and her own.

'I don't know how we are going to get back to Loudon Place with this lot,' Sheryl grumbled, as she tried to cram everything into the two battered suitcases she'd brought with her.

'They mightn't let us take the pushchair on the bus,' she reminded Alun.

'Don't worry!' He looked at his watch. 'I've got a car coming to pick us up and it should be here any minute now.'

'There's nice! You were quite sure you only had to click your fingers and I'd come back with you, were you?' Sheryl snapped sarcastically.

'Well, you've not got a lot of choice, have

you,' he grinned. 'My dad said you were driving my mam spare and he threatened that he was going to put you out in the street if I didn't come and collect you pretty damn quick.'

Chapter Nineteen

Alun Powell viewed Sheryl coming back to Loudon Place with mixed feelings. He'd been perfectly happy living on his own, spending most of his waking hours in the Diawl Coch. Any spare time he spent in the company of one or other of the girls who worked there. They knew the score. One night of fun and that was it.

As the weeks passed, he'd asked himself over and over again what the hell he could have been thinking about to get himself tied down. Marriage was for middle age, when you were starting to go bald and you were too old, or too paunchy, to play the field. He only had to give a girl the glad eye and she was his. What more could any chap ask for, he thought complacently.

He'd already made two big mistakes in his life, he reflected. The first had been joining the army and having to bow and scrape to the officers and be bullied by corporals and sergeants. The second had been getting married. Now he was making a third one.

In the case of the first two mistakes he'd made, he had no real option, but in the matter of taking Sheryl and Caitlin back he wasn't so sure. His old man turning up at the Diawl Coch had him shit-scared. He'd always been a thorn in the old man's side.

It had been sheer bad luck that it had been Zakaraki himself that his dad had met when he came into the club. Worse still, Cradog had even gone as far as to tell Zakaraki that he wanted to have a word with his son about Sheryl and Caitlin.

Alun managed to get out of it by saying that it was because they were staying with his family for a short break, and his dad wanted to know when he was coming to collect them. It sounded all right to him, but he wasn't too sure if he had managed to pull the wool over Zak's eyes or not.

Time would tell, but he'd have to be on his guard for a while. He'd have to make sure he treated Sheryl better in the future, he thought cynically, and not have her going round with a black eye – or any more broken ribs.

That had been a bad move. He knew he was a bit too quick with his fists, but that was army life for you. He'd learned in the first couple of months that you hit out first and then asked questions. The man who landed the opening blow usually came out on top. Let the other chap win and you were regarded as the under-dog. Once people knew that, they started to put on you, they took advantage of you and made your life sheer hell.

If Zak hadn't been around he'd have shown

his old man the door, told him to mind his own bloody business and not to come round there again. As it was, he'd had to shake his hand and appear hail-fellow-well-met and pleased to see the old bugger.

The first thing he'd done was ask after Sheryl and Caitlin, and enquire if they were enjoying their holiday at his place. He'd even asked when were they coming back and claimed that he was missing them both.

That had taken the wind out of his old man's sails, Alun thought smugly. He'd wanted to laugh out loud when he'd seen the look on his dad's face. He was almost as startled as if someone had punched him one on the nose.

Then, to get him away from Zak, he'd taken him into the club, and a couple of beers later his dad had been putty in his hands. He'd claimed he knew how it was, being tied down so young, and having a kid to support as well as a wife.

He'd let his dad ramble on, only lending half an ear as his old man went back over his life, his early days as a coal-miner, when he'd been struggling to earn enough to keep a wife and three youngsters in food and clothes.

He felt himself becoming irritated, though, when his dad kept going on about the hardships he'd known and the terrible state his health was in because of working most of his life down the pit.

'Cough me lungs up, now, mun, night and morning! That's all the reward I've got for over thirty years down that old pit. Treated no better than the bloody ponies at the end of it. Those poor buggers are turned out to grass when they're too old to work and that's what happened to me, too, boyo.'

After his second glass of beer, not used to boozing in the middle of the day, Cradog became even more maudlin. He even went as far as to admit that Alun had probably made a wise choice in not going down the pit.

Another drink and his mood began to change. He grumbled about having had to move away from all his lifelong friends. He complained about the house he was living in, and then he started to become really bitter about having a young kid living there with her crying and tantrums when he got home at night.

'A man of my age wants a bit of peace and quiet when he comes in, not all that whining and caterwauling. She's a disobedient little madam, your Caitlin is. Takes no notice of what her mam says, or my Nola. She needs her back-side slapping, but those two are soft with her. Pander to her, see, instead of being firm!'

'Caitlin is still not much more than a baby,' Alun protested mildly.

The older man shook his head. 'Your Sheryl says she only gives in to her to stop her crying because she knows it annoys me, but it's the same all the time. Right little handful that kiddy is and no mistake.'

Alun took him for a bite to eat in the hope that it would help to sober him up, and then told him to make tracks for home because he had to get back to work at the club.

'Don't forget now, Dad, that you have to change from the tram to a bus when you reach the city centre. This tram you're getting on now won't take you all the way out to Ely, remember.'

'I know that! I'm not bloody daft, mun,' his father told him irritably.

'I'll be over tomorrow morning to collect Sheryl and Caitlin,' Alun promised.

'Mind you sodding well are! Don't you forget now, boyo, or I'll damn well bring them back here myself. Fed up with the pair of them I am, and that's the truth.'

He'd explained his old man's visit to Zak by saying that Cradog had come to tell him that little Caitlin was pining for him, because she hadn't seen him for weeks, and so he wanted to know if they could come home.

'It's too late to go and visit them when I finish here at night, see, and I'm that damn tired that sometimes I don't waken until it's almost time to be back at work. I have to see to myself, wash out my shirts, clean the place up and all that sort of thing and it all takes time,' he sighed.

'You should have told me, Alun,' Zak reproached him. 'I would have given you a day off to go and see your little girl. It's not right for a father to be separated from his child. You take as much time off as you need tomorrow and go and collect them first thing, no argument now!'

Alun thanked him profusely. He'd had every intention of taking the day off. If it made Zak feel better to think he was doing Alun a favour, though, that was all to the good.

It was high time he patched things up between himself and Sheryl, there was no doubt about that. The only problem now was to make sure that Sheryl toed the line when she got back. No tantrums, no quarrelling, and no attempts to come down to the Diawl Coch in the evenings.

Sheryl found that the first few days back at Loudon Place were like a second honeymoon. Alun couldn't do enough to help her and Caitlin settle back in.

He gave her housekeeping money so that she could stock up the depleted larder, and he'd even given her something extra to go and buy herself a new dress. He went out and bought a drop-side wooden cot for Caitlin.

He'd imposed some conditions, of course, and he'd reminded her in no uncertain manner that Mr Zakaraki had ordered that she wasn't to come down to the club at any time.

She'd retorted that the first chance she had she intended to tell Mr Zakaraki exactly what she thought about such a stupid rule, but when she'd seen how furious that made Alun she'd quickly said that she was only teasing.

She'd been pleasantly surprised when a couple of days later Mr Zakaraki came up to their rooms to meet her. She'd been so taken aback when he asked her if she'd enjoyed her holiday with Alun's family, that she'd forgotten all about asking him if she could visit the club.

He had been very taken with Caitlin. He had beamed the moment he set eyes on her. After that, the conversation had centred around the little girl. He'd told Sheryl that he thought Caitlin was adorable, and he wanted her to promise that she'd never take her away on holiday again, because Alun had been heartbroken without her.

A few days later Zak called with an enormous doll for Caitlin, and a lovely pram for her to push it around in.

Caitlin had been won over and had flung her little arms around his neck and bestowed a smacking big kiss on his swarthy cheek, which had brought tears to his eyes.

So much goodwill also won Sheryl over. 'You needn't worry about me trying to come down to the club any more,' she told Alun. 'I wouldn't upset Mr Zakaraki for the world, not when he's been so kind to Caitlin.'

After that their own relationship seemed to be on a completely new footing. Alun was trying hard to make things right between them.

They were friends as well as lovers and she couldn't believe how patient he was with Caitlin, even when she was having one of her tantrums.

She wasn't sure when, or why, things started to go wrong again. For over a year they were perfectly happy, and then gradually Alun seemed to change.

He didn't hit her, or even threaten her. It was more what he said than what he did. His attitude became cold and critical. He continually found fault with everything she did. She didn't cook the sort of meals he liked, or keep the place as clean and tidy as he wanted it to be. She didn't iron his shirts properly.

It worried her that Alun began to look different. His eyes often had a strange glazed look, and when she spoke to him he stared at her in such a piercing fashion that he frightened her. He started coming home later and later in the evenings, and seemed to be no longer interested in her or Caitlin.

When she attempted to talk to him about it, find out what was wrong, he pushed her away and told her to leave him alone. She tried everything she knew to rekindle the love and affection he'd shown when they'd first returned home from his mother's place, but in vain. He even turned away from her when they were in bed.

Unable to bear the loneliness of her own company, she started taking Caitlin out for long walks. Sometimes, when Caitlin had insisted on taking the doll's pram, if she became difficult, or was too tired to walk any further, Sheryl would be forced to plonk her on top of the doll and push her home in it.

For a long time Alun was unaware of what she was doing. When he found out it took him all his time to control his temper. He hadn't hit her since she'd come back to Loudon Square, but now, as he wrestled with the demons inside his head, it took him every ounce of will power not to do so.

As she listened to him rant and rave, calling her every name he could lay his tongue to, Sheryl wondered if a beating wouldn't be easier to stand than such vile recriminations.

He accused her of every vice and sin possible, but the thing which upset her the most was his repeated declaration that Caitlin wasn't his child.

It wasn't the first occasion; he'd raised this point in the past, but now there was so much more conviction in his voice. It wasn't simply something he was saying to hurt her, or goad her into retaliation. He said it as if he believed it.

Sheryl knew she was courting danger, but she refused to let this go on.

'You know perfectly well that she's yours,' she retorted every time he levelled the accusation. 'It's downright wicked to say things like that.'

'Is she? Can you prove it? She doesn't look

like me. I've got black hair, she hasn't. Hers is light brown! I've got dark eyes, hers are bright blue! I've got a square face, hers is shaped like an egg.'

The list went on and on until in the end Sheryl felt so dazed that she could stand no more, and clapped her hands over her ears to shut out his voice. Whenever she did this he dragged her hands away, forcing her to listen to his catalogue of differences until she thought she was going mad.

Finally, she screamed at him. 'So if she isn't your child then whose kid is she?'

His mouth twisted sardonically, and a crafty look came into his eyes. 'So you're admitting it at last, are you?' he exclaimed triumphantly.

'I'm not admitting anything, I'm asking you a question.'

He laughed derisively. 'It's a question that you know the answer to, isn't it?'

Although she was scared, Sheryl was determined not to give in to Alun's bullying 'So tell me then, who do you think is Caitlin's real father?' she demanded.

'Think? I don't only think, I know just as you do, you little whore.'

'You'd better tell me then, because you're the only man I've ever slept with.' She tried to keep her voice steady, but inwardly she was shaking and terrified.

'Don't think you can pull the wool over my

eyes,' he said scornfully. 'I know you played the field. You might have been chatting me up when you came to the barrack dances, flirting with me and giving me the old come-on. All the time, though, you had another lover in the background, didn't you?'

Sheryl started to shake her head, but Alun wasn't taking any notice. He was completely carried away, his face distorted, ugly, ferocious.

Fear froze her, she wanted to run, to get away from this ranting, raving lunatic, but she was transfixed as she listened to the words spewing from his twisted lips.

'You think I don't know that you were carrying on with Megan Thomas's brother. Bloody cop! Never to be seen, but he was there in the background, wasn't he. Nip out of your back door, run down the yard and sneak into their place through that back gate. How romantic!' His sneer brought spittle to his lips, hate to his eyes.

Sheryl shrank away from him. 'It wasn't like that at all!' Her voice was a mere croak.

'Oh no?' He laughed derisively.

'I agree that Elwyn Thomas was a friend, but that's all he was. I've known him since I was Caitlin's age. He played ball with us, shared his sweets with me and Megan, made sure we weren't bullied on our way home from school.'

'A likely story. Oh, I don't doubt that he did

all of those things. Or that he put you in the pudding club as well. Megan told me you used to knock around with him.'

Sheryl was trembling with distress. 'I've already told you, we were friends from our schooldays.'

'Friends! You were a lot more than that.'

'We weren't and that's a really wicked accusation to make about him,' she gasped.

'He couldn't marry you though, not in time, not before the kid was born. He was away training as a police cadet, wasn't he, and he knew they'd probably kick him out if they heard he'd got a girl into trouble, and that would have been the end of his precious career,' Alun jeered.

'That's utter rubbish!'

'When he turned you down, you thought of the clever trick of foisting it off on me! I fell for it . . . then. Not any longer, though, so what are you going to do about it?'

Sherly took a deep, steadying breath and faced him defiantly. 'I'll tell you what I'm going to do about it, Alun. You are either drunk, or you've been taking drugs of some sort so I'm going to fetch help.'

Before Alun could answer or move, Sheryl had picked Caitlin up and was racing down the steps and into the street. She had no idea where to go or what to do as she ran round the corner and into Loudon Square.

Chapter Twenty

Loudon Square was busy. It was a warm, muggy day in mid-September. School holidays were over so there were not many children to be seen. Men were bustling about their business, some shopkeepers setting out their goods for display on the pavement. Women were cleaning their windows or front doorsteps, talking to each other as they did so, or going off with a bag on their arm to buy food for the day.

In desperation Sheryl headed for the open park in the centre of the square, knowing that it wasn't safe to stay in the same room as Alun while he was behaving so strangely. She realised he must be ill and she was sure he desperately needed some kind of help or treatment.

She wondered if she should ask Mr Zakaraki what she ought to do, but if she did that, and told him how violent Alun could be, then he might sack him. If that happened they'd have no home.

She saw a small knot of people gathered down the right-hand side of Loudon Square, so holding Caitlin tightly in her arms she headed straight towards them. As she ran she could hear Alun calling to her, cursing and threatening her at the top of his voice. Hampered by Caitlin's weight she felt panic-stricken, afraid he would catch up with her before she could reach safety.

When she heard someone else shouting to her to stop and heavy feet pounding the ground behind her, she felt so engulfed by terror that she stumbled and almost fell down. 'Let me go, let me go,' she screamed when a pair of strong arms grabbed her, pinioning her to a standstill.

'Hold on, you're safe now!' A man's calm voice filled her ears as she and Caitlin were held firmly against a broad chest. She struggled wildly to get free until she saw that the man was wearing a dark blue uniform, and realised he was a policeman.

She looked up at him gratefully, her breath coming in ragged gulps.

'Calm down,' he said, slackening his grip, but still holding her arm. 'Try and tell me your name and who you are running away from. I'll make sure they don't harm you or your little girl.'

Before she could convince herself that it was safe to do as he asked, her rescuer uttered a deep guttural groan. The hand that was grasping her arm tightened in a spasm, and then slackened and dropped away.

As though in a dream she saw him crumple onto the ground by her feet, blood seeping through the blue serge jacket. Unable to believe her eyes, she was aware that Alun was standing over him and that he had a knife in his hand. Instinctively she pushed Caitlin's head tight against her shoulder, praying the child hadn't witnessed what had happened.

'Waiting out here for you, was he?' Alan jeered, scowling at her accusingly.

Sheryl shuddered as she looked at her husband's demented face. His eyes were glittering, his breath coming in harsh gasps, his mouth twisted, his whole face distorted. He looked so malevolent that she felt herself wilting under his venomous glare.

'I don't know what you're talking about,' she choked. 'I've no idea what you mean or even who he is.'

Before he could speak there was a commotion all around them as people came running across to where they were standing, to find out for themselves what was happening.

A woman began screaming as she saw the pool of blood that was now staining the ground alongside the policeman. Caitlin, frightened by all the turmoil, began to sob loudly.

More and more people joined them. A shrill metallic whistle cut through the hubbub as a second policeman came pounding across the square. There was a sudden moment of silence as he dropped to his knees to check for a pulse. His face was grave as he stood up and blew another blast on his whistle to summon more help.

As he did so, he saw Alun still standing there with a knife in his hand. 'Did you do this?' he asked accusingly, indicating the body of his colleague lying unconscious on the ground.

Alun looked at him scornfully. 'I did, and with bloody good reason.'

The second blast on the police whistle had brought additional back-up. A constable and a sergeant, who had been patrolling close by in Bute Street, came hurrying to the scene.

The crowd had now trebled in size. The majority were women, and they stared in horror at what had happened. The Catholics amongst them crossed themselves and murmured a prayer or two. Many of the others turned their heads away, their eyes filled with tears, unable to stand the dreadful sight in front of them.

Some of the Somali women started keening loudly as they stared down at the inert figure on the ground. Others wrapped their robes more tightly around their bodies, or covered their faces in an effort to shut out what they were seeing.

Many of them muttered amongst themselves. Those at the back started pushing and shoving to get closer to the scene. All the time the crowd was growing larger and larger as news spread of what had happened. Men in the cafes in Bute Street, and even from the nearby tenements, came rushing along to witness for themselves what was going on.

Alun suddenly seemed to realise the dangerous predicament he was in and furtively he started to edge away, trying to lose himself in the crowd.

Sergeant Pearce frowned as he heard the swelling roar of voices. He was well aware that the situation could easily get out of hand unless he acted quickly to calm matters down.

'Arrest that man, Constable Jenkins, before he scarpers!' he instructed one of the officers, indicating Alun with his truncheon.

Constable Jenkins stared down at the body of his colleague, shaking his head in disbelief as he slipped handcuffs on Alun and formally charged him.

Sergeant Pearce then began to try to move the crowd back. 'There is nothing else to be seen, so be on your way, please. Come along now,' he chivvied, 'clear the way, the ambulance will be here any minute so make room for it to get through.'

The constable who had arrived on the scene with the sergeant moved towards the crowd to try and enforce the instruction. As he did so he stopped and stared at Sheryl as if he recognised her. Then he frowned uncertainly, because it was difficult to make out her features.

Her hair was hanging in damp strands that practically obscured her face, and her entire body was shaking so uncontrollably that her shoulders were hunched forward. The child with her was also crying and clinging tightly to her.

'Sheryl . . . is it really you?'

She pushed her hair aside and peered up at him. 'Elwyn?' Her voice trembled with emotion and surprise.

'Duw anwyl! Sheryl! What happened? How do you come to be involved in all this?'

'Oh, Elwyn, I'm so glad you're here.' She hugged Caitlin closer. 'You must help me,' she pleaded. 'I'm so scared, I think Alun wants to kill me!'

'Try not to get upset,' he told her, patting her shoulder consolingly. 'Everything is going to be all right. He's under arrest now so he won't be able to hurt you. Here, let me take the little one for a moment. You're squeezing her half to death.'

Gently he freed her gripping fingers, shushing and soothing the child to try and calm her and to stop her from crying.

A look of consternation appeared on Alun's face as he heard the exchange between Elwyn and Sheryl.

'Did she call you Elwyn? Are you Elwyn Thomas?' he challenged, trying to pull away from the policeman holding him. 'If you're Elwyn Thomas then who the hell is this bugger?' He stabbed at the body lying on the ground with the toe of his boot.

The policeman who'd put handcuffs on Alun jerked him back savagely. 'That'll do. Now, I'm warning you to behave and that the less you say the better it will be for you.'

Alun tried to shake him off, but Constable Jenkins was by far the stronger and only tightened his grip and jabbed Alun roughly in the side with his truncheon.

'You attacked that poor policeman who's lying there because you thought he was Elwyn Thomas?' Sheryl caught her breath, staring at Alun in disbelief.

'The fact that he was out here waiting for you, and the way you ran into his bloody arms, what else did you expect me to think?' Alun snarled, his face puce with anger.

'It wasn't like that at all!' Sheryl gasped. 'I ran from the house with Caitlin and out across the square to try and get help because you were acting so strangely that I was afraid of what you were going to do to us.'

'Are you saying that you didn't come out to meet up with Elwyn Thomas?' Alun snarled.

Sheryl shook her head wearily. 'I've told you repeatedly that I haven't spoken to Elwyn since long before we were married. Whatever made you think otherwise?'

'Because he's the father of the bloody kid he's holding in his arms, and don't try to tell me any different!'

'Of course he's not! Caitlin is your child. I've also told you that over and over again!' she sobbed, reaching out for Caitlin and taking her back from Elwyn.

'Words! Bloody words! You don't think for one moment that I believed you, do you? She doesn't even look like me!' Alun countered, his voice rising to a roar.

'That will do!' The constable who had handcuffed Alun jerked him sharply by the arm to one side as an ambulance arrived. He forced him to stand perfectly still as the dead policeman was stretchered into it.

Almost simultaneously a large blue van with darkened windows arrived in the square and pulled up behind the ambulance.

The crowd surged forward, a tide of humanity, avidly observing all that was going on.

Sergeant Pearce directed operations. He gave orders that the body of the policeman was to be taken to the morgue so that it could be examined by a police surgeon. He then instructed that Alun Powell, the man they had arrested, was to be loaded into the Black Maria and taken straight to Cardiff jail.

'Do I gather that you know this woman who was involved, Constable Thomas?' he asked, looking across at where Sheryl was now huddled on the low wall that separated the park area from the roadway. Caitlin was clinging to her skirts and the crowd was pressing closer, staring at her curiously as they surrounded her.

'I've known her all my life,' Elwyn told him.

Sergeant Pearce nodded thoughtfully. 'Her husband seems to think you have something going on with her?'

'There's no truth at all in that,' Elwyn assured him.

231

'How well do you know Powell? He obviously mistook Constable Richards for you. You were the one he intended knifing. Have you any idea why?'

'No, Sergeant. I've only met him once before, but his wife, Sheryl, has been a lifelong friend of my sister's.'

'So you had no idea that this was where she was living?'

Elwyn hesitated. 'My sister did say that since her marriage she was living in Tiger Bay. I believe they have rooms above the club where her husband works.'

Sergeant Pearce thoughtfully tapped his truncheon against the side of his leg, as if considering the facts and finding it difficult to reach a decision.

'We'll have to take her along to the station so that she can make a statement about what led up to this state of affairs,' he pronounced finally.

'Yes, Sergeant, I understand. After that, will it be all right if I take her back to my mum's home?'

Sergeant Pearce frowned uncertainly. 'Is that wise?'

'I can't leave her on her own, not here in Tiger Bay at a time like this . . .'

'If you are off duty when she has finished making her statement, then I suppose it is up to you,' Sergeant Pearce said cautiously. 'Be careful though, Constable Thomas,' he added grimly. 'In my eyes you are still only a raw recruit and this is a murder, and you already seem to be embroiled in what has happened here.'

Chapter Twenty-One

When she returned home from the police station after making her statement, Sheryl spent the rest of the day huddled indoors cuddling Caitlin, alternately sobbing herself and trying to stop Caitlin from crying. Elwyn had offered to take her back to Cathays, but she'd refused, knowing she wouldn't be welcomed by her own mum and dad or by his.

She couldn't believe what had happened. It was like a bad dream, one she couldn't awake from no matter how hard she tried.

She kept worrying about what would happen now. They'd charged Alun with murder and there was no way he could deny it, because there had been far too many witnesses. They'd all been eager to give their version of the way he had stabbed the police-man from behind, allowing him no chance to defend himself.

As Sheryl had walked down Loudon Place on the way home people had stared at her with a mixture of curiosity and suspicion, but no-one had spoken to her.

The news had already reached the club, and one of the doormen was waiting outside the side entrance to tell her that Mr Zakaraki wanted to speak to her.

She'd waved him away, rushed past him and pushed Caitlin ahead of her up the stairs to their own rooms.

Half an hour later, she'd heard someone come up and rap on the door, but she took no notice. She'd given Caitlin a biscuit and cradled her in her arms, shushing her to keep quiet until she heard the footsteps retreating. Then she'd hugged Caitlin even tighter, tears of relief streaming down her face.

Sheryl knew that she'd have to face Zakaraki, and the rest of the world, sooner or later, but for the moment she wanted to be on her own. She'd hoped that for the rest of the day, because he didn't have Alun there working for him, he'd be too busy dealing with matters relating to the club to bother about her.

Nevertheless she was filled with apprehension about what he had wanted to see her about. It might only be to hear first hand her account of what had happened earlier. Or it could be that he had already been told all the details and wanted her out of the building, fearing for the effect on the club if he was known to be harbouring the wife of a murderer.

If it had been anybody other than a policeman, things might not have looked so bad. People in Tiger Bay were used to the odd fight that culminated in stabbing, knocking out, or even a killing. The men involved were usually coloured seamen, rough dock workers, or miners down from the Valleys for a night out who, under the influence of too much booze, made some ribald comment that inflamed one of the locals.

But there would be no leniency from the law when it came to knifing a policeman, especially under the circumstances. Alun couldn't claim it was accidental. He'd made it quite clear to everyone that it was intentional. The fact that he'd mistaken the identity of the constable in question was unlikely to make any difference to his punishment when he was brought to trial, because it was an unprovoked murder of the worst kind.

Sheryl wondered how Alun had known that Loudon Square was part of Elwyn's beat. He had never mentioned to her that he had seen him there. She certainly hadn't known, but then she hadn't spoken to any of the Thomases since she'd moved out of Coburn Street more than a year ago. She wondered if, as part of his duties, Elwyn had been into the club and that was what had started Alun off on his wild accusations.

Her life, she reflected uneasily, seemed to be going from bad to worse. She'd fallen out with her own mam, she'd quarrelled with Megan and the Thomases, and Alun's mam didn't want her living with them. Now, with Alun in jail, if Zakaraki turned her out she really would be homeless.

Another problem was what she was going to

do about money. She reached for her handbag and delved inside for her purse. Tipping out the contents into her hand, she groaned as she saw how little she had.

There wasn't very much food in the larder, either. She needed bread, tea, milk and some more biscuits for Caitlin. She counted her money over again and decided to go out and buy these and a bag of chips. She'd eaten nothing since early morning and now she was starving hungry. Perhaps she would be able to think more clearly once she'd had something to eat.

Loudon Square was still busy as she made her way to one of the small general stores, so she was careful to avoid eye contact with anyone. When she stepped inside the shop it was obvious, from the way the customers all stopped talking, that they had been discussing what had happened earlier in the day.

The crowd parted, the coloured women drawing their long dresses or saris tight to their bodies as if to avoid contact with her. The atmosphere felt so hostile that Sheryl almost turned and went out again. Knowing that if she did it would mean that both she and Caitlin would have to go hungry, she held Caitlin tightly by the hand and walked up to the counter.

No-one spoke. Sheryl asked for the items she required and the Bengali who was serving collected them together on the counter without saying a word.

Sheryl opened her purse, counted out the money and held it out. The man hesitated, then indicated for her to place it on the counter. He dropped it in the till and placed her change on the counter, still without saying a word.

It was only a few pence, but Sheryl scrabbled it up and put it back in her purse, knowing she might need it. In silence she left the shop. As she closed the door behind her she heard the outburst of chatter resume like the jabbering of monkeys at the zoo. Although she tried to tell herself it didn't matter that they'd shunned her, she felt tears stinging her eyes and she brushed them hurriedly away with the back of her hand.

The smell from the fish and chip shop drew her like a magnet. There were already people inside waiting to be served and she hesitated, wondering whether she could face any more curious stares and silences, or if she should go straight on home. Then, summoning up her courage, she took a deep breath and walked in. She knew by sight many of those who were waiting and one or two of them nodded, but they made no attempt to start a conversation. The woman who was about to be served murmured something to the man behind the counter and he looked directly at Sheryl, lifting his eyebrows enquiringly to hear her order. The others moved aside to let her approach the counter.

Her face flaming with embarrassment, Sheryl asked for two pennyworth of chips.

'Stick her in a bit of cod for the kiddy, poor little mite she looks half starved.'

Sheryl spun round, intending to tell the woman who had spoken to mind her own business. When she saw the kindly smile on the wrinkled Somali face, she softened and thanked her instead.

'Not your fault what your hubby did, my lovely, so don't take it to heart,' another woman said, patting Caitlin on the head as they passed her on their way out.

The hot food put new life into Sheryl, but it didn't bring any solution to the problem of her future. She was still thinking about it when she heard footsteps outside and a hammering on the door.

Hushing Caitlin to keep quiet she remained motionless, afraid that it might be Zak again and hoping he would soon go away.

When the banging came a second time, followed by a familiar voice calling out her name, her heart thundered with relief. She unlocked the door, desperately hoping that Elwyn had come with news about Alun.

To her surprise he was in civvies: grey flannel trousers, and a brown tweed jacket. He looked much less threatening and more like the chap she'd thought of as a boyfriend when she'd been growing up, before she'd met Alun.

'Can I come in?'

'Of course. I've kept the door locked because . . .'

'Yes, I know. Very sensible after what happened earlier today. No-one has bothered you, have they?'

She shook her head. 'No, when I went to buy some groceries the people simply didn't speak at all, except one old woman in the fish and chip shop.'

He nodded. 'They're all afraid of being in some sort of trouble because of what happened, that's why they're avoiding being seen talking to you.'

'When it happened they were jabbering away like magpies, all anxious to tell your sergeant about what they had seen,' she said bitterly.

'Only to make sure that we knew how innocent they were, and that they had nothing to do with you or the crime,' he explained. 'Now they don't want you here in their midst, so they're shunning you. They're afraid that if they are seen talking to you, or helping you, they may find themselves implicated in some way. That's why I've come, I want you to pack whatever you need and move out.'

'I can't do that! I've nowhere to go. You know I can't go back to my mother's place, and your mam won't want me after what happened when I was staying there.' She laughed self-consciously. 'I acted a bit daft and . . .'

'Hush! That's what I've come to tell you. Megan says you can move in with her until Alun comes to trial and things quieten down, and you know where you stand.'

Sheryl stared at him wide-eyed. 'Why should she say that? After what I did, I mean. Mind, I never meant to upset her . . . I was only teasing Owen!'

'It's all right, cariad, calm down. Megan's sorry that she sent you packing over it. Now she's had time to think about it she realises that she should have taken it as a joke, and known that you were only teasing. Well, this is her way of putting things right between the two of you.'

'What about your mam though, Elwyn? Does she agree?'

'It has nothing to do with Mam. Our Megan and Owen Pryce are married, see. They have their own place. She says you can move in there with them. Only temporary, like, but it is better than being here on your own, now, isn't it?'

Sheryl held her head between both hands. 'I can't believe this is happening. I've been so worried, Elwyn, that I couldn't think what to do for the best.'

'I know, I understand. Now shall we start getting your stuff together? You probably need to take quite a lot of things for young Caitlin.'

Sheryl nodded. 'There's her pushchair for one thing. I can't manage without that. She still doesn't like walking very far. She always complains that her legs get tired.'

'Right, well you gather all the stuff together, and find your suitcases, and I'll pack them for you. Come on, the sooner we get moving the

241

better. Megan is hoping that you will be there and all settled in before bedtime.'

They worked quickly. Sheryl piled everything up on the table and Elwyn packed it all methodically into the suitcases.

'I think you ought to tell your landlord that you are going to be away for a couple of weeks, don't you?' he said when they'd finished and were ready to leave.

Sheryl nodded. 'Zak has been up to see me, but I haven't answered the door because I don't know what to say to him,' she said nervously.

'Would you like me to go and have a word with him for you, then?' Elwyn volunteered.

'Would you?' She smiled at him gratefully.

He looked puzzled. 'Did you say his name was Zak?'

'We call him that, but his full name is Zakaraki. Alun works for him in the club, you do know that?'

Elwyn nodded. 'Right, leave it with me. Wait here, I shouldn't be more than a few minutes.'

When he returned Elwyn assured her that everything had been settled, and that Zak had agreed he would keep the rooms for her until after they'd heard what was happening to Alun.

'If you're ready then we'll be on our way,' he said, picking up the larger of the cases. 'I'll carry this down first and then I'll come back for the rest of your stuff. You take Caitlin downstairs and wait for me.'

Sheryl nodded, then reached out and placed

a hand on his arm. 'Thank you Elwyn, I don't know why you should be so good to me, especially since it was you that Alun intended to stab.'

He laughed self-consciously. 'It's Megan you have to thank. She's the one who insisted that it wasn't safe for you to stay here, and that you'd better move in with her for a while.'

Chapter Twenty-Two

Megan's new home was in Cyfarthfa Street, off City Road, and was not very far from Roath Park. Although she said nothing to either Elwyn or Megan, Sheryl felt apprehensive about living there because she felt that it was rather too close to Thesiger Street and Coburn Street for her peace of mind.

It meant that she would have to avoid shopping in Crwys Road or City Road, she decided, because she certainly didn't want to bump into either her mother or Mrs Thomas.

'Megan will be glad of your company, it will be like old times for her. She misses the companionship of her colleagues now that she's at home all the time,' Elwyn said as they caught a tram heading for Roath.

'You mean she's given up nursing? I didn't know that.'

'Is it that long since you saw each other?' He looked surprised. 'You won't know then that Megan is expecting a baby in less than a month's time.'

'She's pregnant!' Sheryl smiled to herself, recalling what Megan had said when they had parted just over a year before, when Sheryl had voiced the opinion that Mrs Thomas would miss Caitlin. Of course, Megan and Owen had been planning to get married even then, but so much had happened since that it had slipped her mind.

She didn't even know when the wedding had taken place, and for a moment Sheryl felt hurt that Megan hadn't been in touch with her and asked her to be there. Could she be sure that their rift was healed, she wondered. The very fact that Megan had told Elwyn to bring her to stay had convinced her that all was forgiven, but had it been Megan's idea? Or had Elwyn been the one to suggest it, she pondered.

There was a moment's unease when Megan opened her door to them. Then Megan and Sheryl were in each other's arms, hugging and kissing. When they drew apart they both began laughing and talking at the same time, neither of them pausing to answer the other's questions.

'If you two will let me get by, I'll put the kettle on ready to make us all a cuppa,' Elwyn volunteered.

'Oh, you and your cuppa,' Megan laughed. 'You're a proper old woman when it comes to tea-drinking. Do you know, Sheryl, when they're out on the beat all coppers have special points of call. Certain places where they know they'll be welcome, shopkeepers and the like, who have a cup of tea waiting for them. I bet he's even been calling in on you because . . .'

'While I do that, you could get Sheryl settled into her room,' Elwyn told them, cutting short his sister's banter. 'Poor little Caitlin looks completely worn out, it's been a long day for her.'

'I've had to put Caitlin in with you, Sheryl, and she'll have to sleep in the same bed as you because I haven't a cot big enough for her. I've only got a cradle for the baby,' Megan said.

'That will be fine, in fact it is probably better, because being in such strange surroundings she is bound to find things a bit puzzling for a few days.'

Caitlin had barely said a word, but clung tightly to Sheryl's skirts, sucking her thumb and staring at them all wide-eyed. Sheryl had expected her to recognise Megan, but having seen so many different faces that day she obviously didn't, and wouldn't even accept a biscuit from her.

'Look, why don't I take a biscuit and a cup of milk through to the bedroom with me and let her have them as I undress her. Then as soon as she's finished I can pop her straight into bed,' Sheryl said.

Megan hesitated. 'Owen will be home in about half an hour and . . .'

'Then I'll get her to bed and with any luck she'll be asleep before he gets home. I think she's met enough people today.'

'Yes, that's probably a good idea,' Elwyn

agreed. 'I'll be off, too. Perhaps you'd like an early night as well, Sheryl, since you've also had a long day,' he suggested pointedly.

Catching the message in Elwyn's eyes and guessing what was behind his comment, she agreed. 'You're probably right, Caitlin and me are both whacked. I'll take my cuppa with me, Megan, and we'll catch up on all our news in the morning.'

The look of relief on Megan's face compensated for the fact that it was only nine o'clock. It also made Sheryl wonder once again whose idea it had been for her to come and stay in Cyfarthfa Street. Elwyn had insisted that it was Megan who had suggested it, but having noticed the guarded look on her face when she spoke about Owen, Sheryl wasn't too sure.

Megan need have no worries, Sheryl told herself. She intended being on her best behaviour, she couldn't afford to upset them. Living here was the only alternative she had to staying in Loudon Place, and she simply couldn't face that . . . not at the moment, at any rate.

She hoped that tomorrow she and Megan could resume their friendship, though she doubted if they would be as close as they'd been in their schooldays. Then they'd confided in each other about everything they thought or did.

The new Megan, Mrs Pryce, the recently married woman who was now an expectant mother, was a completely different person from the Megan she'd grown up with and who had shared so much with her.

Over the next few days, Sheryl discovered that Megan had become almost as house-proud as her own mam was. What was even worse, it seemed that Megan's sense of humour had diminished as her size had increased. She fussed about everything she ate and drank, worrying about the effect it might have on the unborn baby.

'Oh for goodness sake, simply carry on the same as you've always done,' Sheryl encouraged her. 'It's not as though you indulge in anything out of the ordinary.'

'That's not the point. Attention to what you eat is very important if you want a healthy child. You should be a lot more careful about the sort of meals you feed Caitlin.'

'As long as I can fill her little belly, and she isn't crying or miserable because she's feeling hungry, that's all I care about,' Sheryl laughed.

'You let her have far too many biscuits,' Megan went on implacably. 'I learnt about these things when I was training to be a nurse. It's all the sweets and cake Caitlin eats that makes her such a little misery.'

'She's not a misery!' Sheryl defended.

'Oh come on, she's always whimpering or whining about something.'

'Only because all of this seems so strange to her. She hasn't settled in yet. She's missing her dad and all her toys and playthings that we weren't able to bring with us.'

'I wouldn't have thought she'd have all that many toys, not the way you've lived, and she should be used to living in different places all the time.'

Their arguments increased. Megan found fault with so many of the things Sheryl did as she tried to help around the house that in the end Sheryl started doing less and less.

By the time Megan's baby, a son, was born three weeks later, Sheryl was doing very little except caring for Caitlin.

'Are you going to get a woman in to look after Megan and the new baby for the next few weeks?' Sheryl asked Owen after the midwife had left.

'Someone to come in and look after her?' he repeated, frowning. 'Why? What will you be doing all day? One of the reasons we agreed that you could come and stay when Elwyn asked was so that you would be here with Megan when the baby arrived,' he told her without preamble.

'Oh, I'm expected to be an unpaid skivvy, am I!' she snapped. 'Elwyn forgot to tell me that bit. I should have known when he said that Megan wanted to put the past behind us that it was too good to be true,' she added defensively.

'You're getting free bed and board for you and young Caitlin, aren't you?' he pointed out.

'I was invited here because I'm an old friend of Megan's. I've known her a lot longer than you have. Megan, Elwyn and me grew up together, in case you didn't know!' she told him heatedly.

'Then in that case you won't mind giving a hand while Megan is confined to bed and needs some help around the place for the next couple of weeks.'

'Don't you mean someone to look after your welfare, Owen, and make sure you're not inconvenienced in any way?' she asked sarcastically.

He scowled. 'I don't want you to put yourself out on my behalf, Sheryl, but I am expecting you to look after Megan and help with the baby for the next couple of weeks.'

'And after that?'

Owen shrugged. 'After that, once my Meg's back on her feet you can do what you like. I hope it means that you'll arrange things so that you can leave.'

'You don't like me, do you Owen?'

'Do you blame me after the trouble you caused when you were living with the Thomases?'

'That was only a joke, I was teasing you! You don't think I'd be interested in someone like you, do you?' she said witheringly.

'No?' He looked at her scornfully. 'I should hope not having seen the type of man you mix with. Take a look at your Alun! Knifes a copper in the back. Sneaks up on him from behind.

Doesn't even give the poor sod a chance to defend himself or run away!'

Sheryl didn't answer. She went into the kitchen and filled the kettle to take her mind off what Owen had said. She couldn't afford to fall out with either Owen or Megan, not at the moment, not until she knew what was happening to Alun.

She wasn't sure if Owen told Megan about their spat, but she was pretty certain he had because in the days that followed Megan became even more picky and fussy.

She knew she wasn't as competent as Megan when it came to doing housework, but she objected to the way Megan continually harped on about how slapdash she was. She tried her best to serve up nice meals, but she wasn't used to cooking the sort of dishes Megan seemed to like.

'I don't know what my Owen makes of your cooking,' Megan told her worriedly, 'he's extremely fussy about his food.'

'I can always go and fetch him some fish and chips, or faggots and peas, if he doesn't like what I've cooked,' Sheryl offered.

'That sort of greasy food is no good at all for him!' Megan snapped. 'Freshly cooked vegetables and top-quality meat is what he expects, because that is what I always serve up.'

When, ten days later, Megan got up for the first time and saw the state her home was in, she burst into tears. It was a Sunday, so Owen was there, and he tried his best to comfort her.

'There's no harm done, my lovely! Nothing has been broken or damaged . . .'

'Everywhere is dirty, though. Filthy dirty! Look at the state of the sink and draining board, and the mess the cooker is in. It . . . it is a wonder we haven't all got food poisoning.'

'We'll soon have it all cleaned up again,' Owen promised.

'Even the cups are dirty!' Megan sobbed. 'My lovely embroidered tablecloth has tea and jam stains all over it and I found it screwed up in a bundle . . .'

'It wasn't screwed up, it was in with a pile of dirty clothes that I intended to wash,' Sheryl contradicted. 'I didn't get time to do it today because your baby was puking all morning and you were shouting your orders, fetch this, fetch that, as though I was a twopenny-bit skivvy,' she added heatedly.

'There's no need to lose your temper, Sheryl. I only asked you to fetch some clean nappies . . .'

'And you kept calling out to me to come and take Caitlin away from the baby.'

'Yes, because she kept on pulling the covers off him,' Megan blazed.

'Oh, so Caitlin was disturbing him, was she! All she wants to do is take a peek at your precious baby, nothing more.'

'I know, and I don't mind her doing that as

long as her hands are clean and her nose isn't running.'

'So now you're finding fault with her as well, are you?' Sheryl bridled.

'Not really, the poor little thing can't help her background, dragged up in the depths of Tiger Bay, now can she. With a mother like you, who had to get married, a dad who was a squaddy and is now a jailbird, you can't expect her to be top drawer, can you. Even her grandparents are ashamed of her and don't want anything to do with her . . .'

'That will do!'

They had been so busy squabbling that neither of them had heard Elwyn come into the room.

'The door was open,' he explained, when they looked startled to see him standing there.

'What are you doing here . . . in uniform? Hoping to get a cuppa, I suppose,' Megan said pointedly.

'No, but I'll have one if it is going. I've come to give Sheryl some news,' he added more seriously.

Sheryl felt a frisson of fear as she looked at his face and heard the gravity in his voice.

'It's bad news?' she asked tentatively.

He nodded. 'I'm afraid so.'

'Go on.' She braced herself, clutching the back of a chair and clamping her lips tightly together, almost as if she was waiting for a blow.

Elwyn hesitated, looking uncomfortable, evidently not knowing how to start.

'Her Alun hasn't been brought to trial already, has he?' Megan said in surprise.

'No,' Elwyn shook his head. 'No, there won't be any trial.'

'You mean they're going to let him go free after what he did?' Megan gasped indignantly.

There was an awkward moment of silence. Then Elwyn reached out and took Sheryl's hands from the back of the chair and held them tightly between his own.

'I'm sorry to have to tell you this, Sheryl,' he said gently, 'but Alun is dead.'

Sheryl looked puzzled. 'He can't be!'

'He was found dead in his cell this morning. He'd committed suicide.'

'How could he do something like that when he was in police custody? They're responsible for his care, aren't they?' she asked in a bewildered voice.

'I know, I know!' As she started sobbing Elwyn took her in his arms, patting her on the back consolingly, almost as if she was a small child.

'We've no idea how it happened, but somehow he managed to cut his wrists. By the time they found him it was too late. The matter will be investigated . . .'

'You mean Alun's dead . . . gone for ever,' she whispered, bemused.

'I'm afraid so, Sheryl.'

She freed herself from Elwyn and pulled Caitlin towards her, then buried her face in the child's soft brown hair, her entire body quivering uncontrollably.

Chapter Twenty-Three

Sheryl spent a troubled night, dozing fitfully, disturbed by frightening nightmares that left her trembling, her body wet with sweat.

She kept thinking that Alun was in the room with her. Sometimes he was laughing or jeering, at other times he was grabbing hold of her, an evil look in his eyes as he either tried to possess her, or else threatened her with his fist. Each time it happened she woke breathless with fear, trying to suppress the screams that rose in her throat until they almost choked her.

Alongside her Caitlin stirred restlessly. She hugged the little body close to her own, finding comfort from its warmth.

The moment the first light appeared between the cracks in the curtains she tucked the bedclothes in tightly around the little girl, and crept from the bed.

Alun is dead, she told herself over and over again, finding it difficult to convince herself that it really was true.

Elwyn had said that Alun had taken his own life. Committed suicide by cutting his wrists! It didn't sound like Alun. Had it been his conscience, she wondered, or had he done it because he couldn't stand being shut up in prison?

Or had it been the realisation that he was bound to be sentenced to death? There was no excuse, or pardon, in the eyes of the law for anyone who killed a policeman.

For a brief moment, Sheryl wondered if someone in the police force had taken their revenge for what had happened to one of their colleagues. She pushed the thought from her mind. What good was there in speculating on such matters? Why would any of them risk their own career in that way when they knew Alun would be sentenced to death anyway?

Alun was dead, that was final, and from now on she would be on her own, except for Caitlin. She had to plan for their future. She couldn't stay here with Megan and Owen because it wasn't working out. None of them were happy with the situation, so there was only one thing she could do and that was leave as soon as she could.

Almost mechanically she began collecting up all their clothes and few belongings, and piling them haphazardly into her suitcases.

As quietly as possible she carried the cases to the front door. When that was done she gently roused Caitlin, pressing a finger on the child's lips to silence any cry she might make.

Whispering words of encouragement, she took off Caitlin's nightclothes and dressed her in warm leggings and the outdoor clothes she'd laid out ready.

Carrying their shoes in her hand, Sheryl guided Caitlin, who was still not fully awake, down to the front door and strapped her into the pushchair.

Having manoeuvred the pushchair out on the pavement she balanced one suitcase across the front of it, then carrying the other one she began to hurry towards City Road. Although it was barely dawn she hoped that she would not have to wait very long for the first tram of the day. She was also hoping that because it was so early, and there wouldn't be many passengers, the conductor would waive the rules and let her take the pushchair on board.

They arrived back in Tiger Bay shortly before seven o'clock. As she walked down Loudon Place she wondered, for the first time, whether her rooms were still available to her.

Zak had promised that she could stay there until after the trial, she reminded herself, and he couldn't possibly know yet about what had happened to Alun. By midday, however, there would no doubt be a banner headline splashed across the early edition of the *South Wales Echo*.

Her rooms were cold, dank and uninviting. Because they had been shut up for so long there was a sour smell about them that made her wrinkle her nose in disgust.

She surveyed her drab surroundings disparagingly. Could she even count on this as her future home, she asked herself, or would Zakaraki turn her out when he heard that Alun had taken his own life?

Caitlin was so worn out that she had fallen asleep the moment she'd placed her down in the armchair, so Sheryl left her there. As a precaution she wedged a straight chair in front of it, so that Caitlin couldn't fall out of it if she stirred or wakened.

Sheryl went into the kitchen to see if there was any tea or Camp Coffee to make herself a drink and found that there were a few spoonfuls of tea in the caddy, enough to brew herself a cup. As she drank it, without milk and sugar because there were neither of those, she tried to gather herself together and plan what her next step should be.

She'd managed to bring the two suitcases up the stairs, but she didn't unpack them. That would be tempting fate. She had to find out first if Zak was going to let her stay there, and she couldn't do that until the club opened.

Mr Zakaraki was surprised to see that she was back, and astounded when she told him about what had happened to Alun.

'Taken his own life! Poor devil, he must have been desperate to do something like that.'

Sheryl nodded, dabbing at her eyes. 'I still can't believe it. I don't know what I am going to do. Are you going to let me stay on here in my home?'

'Of course you can stay on here . . . for the

present,' he assured her. 'After Alun's funeral you must tell me what your plans are for the future. You will have to find a job . . . yes?'

Sheryl looked at him blankly. She didn't know anything about the funeral, or even if there would be one. Since Alun had committed suicide she knew he couldn't be buried in consecrated ground, and she wondered if perhaps the prison authorities kept the body.

Work? She'd never thought about that either, but now it crashed into her brain like a thunderbolt. How else was she going to find the money to feed and clothe herself and Caitlin? Work?

'Yes, I'll have to find a job of some kind,' she sighed. 'I'm not sure what sort of work I can possibly do, though, with a young child to look after.'

'Don't worry!' Zak patted her hand reassuringly. 'Things will work out.'

'I hope so,' Sheryl agreed, 'because I have no-one I can turn to for help.'

'The little one will be starting school soon.'

'She's not five until next January,' Sheryl murmured.

'Perhaps under the circumstances she might be allowed to start school before then,' Zakaraki suggested.

'Do you think so? You mean in September, at the beginning of the new school year?' she added dubiously.

He nodded. 'So when that happens you will

be ready to work for part of the day,' he commented shrewdly.

Sheryl looked startled, not too sure what he was trying to say.

'Without Alun to provide for you and the little one . . .' He let his voice trail off, but he was looking at her speculatively. His deep-set dark eyes seemed to be summing her up in such a calculating manner that Sheryl wondered what was going through his mind.

'Yes,' she agreed cautiously, 'I suppose I will be able to work when she is at school, but as I said before that is only if I am able to find a job.'

'You could always take Alun's place right here in my club.'

'Alun's job?' Her eyebrows went up in surprise. 'I don't even know exactly what he did for you. He always looked very smart, certainly. He said something about being a manager?'

Zakaraki raised his shoulders in a dismissive shrug. 'What does the title matter?' He licked his lips. 'Alun worked for me in all sorts of ways. He looked after my special customers, he did little deliveries for me, he helped with the books. I am sure there are a good many of the tasks he carried out that you could do equally well.'

Sheryl nodded thoughtfully. 'Nothing heavy, mind,' she said. 'And no work in your kitchens or cleaning, or anything like that.'

Zak laughed boisterously. 'No, no, no! You are not cut out for that sort of thing. You wear a pretty frock, silk stockings and smile and you will win over the hearts of all the patrons. They may even think of you as their lucky mascot.'

'Why do you say that?' Sheryl frowned.

'At the gambling tables,' he explained, laughing because she looked so bemused.

'Gambling tables! I didn't know there was any gambling in your club!'

He frowned. 'I can see that Alun did not tell you very much about his work. Perhaps you should come down to the club and see everything for yourself.'

Sheryl gave a short hard laugh. 'I tried to do that once and I was beaten up for my trouble.'

He looked shocked. 'You were beaten up? I do not understand?'

'By Alun!'

Zakaraki sighed. 'He wanted to keep you for himself, that is probably why. My club is filled with men who would find you very desirable. Don't worry,' he added hastily, 'I can assure you that when they know you are under my protection no-one will approach you, so you will be quite safe. Now, what do you say to my suggestion?'

'You mean I could come and work for you if Caitlin goes to school in September?'

He nodded.

'Thank you.' Sheryl smiled gratefully. 'It sounds a perfect arrangement.'

'Then go and enjoy what freedom you have left,' Zak advised. 'A few months from now we will talk again and settle the details.'

'Thank you again.'

He slipped his hand into an inside pocket of his jacket, pulled out a wad of money, and counted out ten white five-pound notes. 'This should keep you in food until then and we will come to a proper arrangement about your wages once you start work, depending on what duties you are prepared to carry out.'

'And I can go on living here?'

'Of course! You will continue to live rent-free, but you must continue to use the side entrance in Loudon Place, exactly as you have always done.'

Sheryl felt in a daze for the rest of the day. She hadn't given very much thought to Caitlin starting school. She was so clinging, so unsure of herself, that Sheryl couldn't bear the thought of her having to do so, especially in the area where they were living. There were so many different nationalities attending the nearby school that she couldn't imagine Caitlin being happy there. She couldn't think of any alternative, though. The law said she had to go to school after Christmas, so would starting a few months early really matter, she asked herself.

If she was working, would she be able to take her to school and collect her at the end of the day, she wondered. There were some rough types in the area and Caitlin had never mixed with other children.

All the criticism she'd had from Megan about the way she was raising Caitlin crowded into her brain, confusing her thoughts. What would Megan, or anyone else who knew them, think when they heard that she had sent Caitlin to school in Tiger Bay? Yet she had no choice. There was nowhere else she could go, and here she had somewhere to live and the opportunity of work.

She wondered exactly what Zak had in mind when he offered her a job. She wished she knew more about the sort of work Alun had done. What on earth had Zak meant when he'd talked of 'deliveries', or when he said she could be a 'mascot' in the gambling rooms?

Surely he didn't expect her to work at night? She'd have to make it quite clear that she couldn't do that. She couldn't possibly leave Caitlin on her own. She wouldn't be able to work at the weekends either, which was probably when he would need her most. Alun had always said that was one of their busiest times.

More than once in the days that followed she toyed with the idea of going back to Thesiger Street. By now her parents were bound to know that Alun was dead. They would even know that he had committed suicide while in custody, because it had been prominently reported in the national newspapers as well as in the *South Wales Echo* and in the *Western Mail*.

She had hoped that her mam or her dad would get in touch with her, and every morning she looked for a letter. They'd never visited Loudon Place, or even contacted her since she'd left Thesiger Street, but it would be easy enough for them to find out her address from the police or the Thomases.

As the days passed and there was no letter, not even one from Megan, she gave up hoping and concentrated on how she was going to manage in the future. Everyone seemed to have deserted her. There had been no word from Nola, either. She knew it was her own fault, and wished she hadn't alienated everyone, but it seemed it was too late now to make amends.

She had expected Elwyn to call to see if she was all right. He must have guessed that she'd come back to Loudon Place. She wished now that she'd left a note for Megan, not simply disappeared, but her mind had been in turmoil after Elwyn had told her the news about Alun.

To prepare Caitlin for the ordeal that lay ahead, she tried to encourage her to help with sorting out her clothes and choosing the ones she wanted to wear when she went to school, but Caitlin wasn't very responsive. She stood beside her, clutching a battered rag doll that Alun had given her, sucking her thumb, but paying no attention to what was going on.

Sheryl talked to her about school all the time, trying to make it sound exciting. She even began walking as far as the infants' school each day, so that Caitlin would know where she might soon be spending her time.

Caitlin showed little interest. She seemed to be missing Alun and frequently asked for him. When Sheryl told her that he'd had to go away, Caitlin wanted to know where he had gone. She kept asking when he was coming home and if he would be back before she had to go to school.

Sheryl avoided a direct answer, because she was sure Caitlin would know from the tone of her voice that she wasn't telling the truth. She hoped that when Caitlin did start school, the different routine would help to fill the void in her life. She would make new friends, perhaps even find someone who would be really close, as she and Megan had been when they'd been growing up.

She realised that Caitlin must feel disorientated. In the past they were continually living with people for a few weeks, or a couple of months, and then either coming back to Loudon Place or moving somewhere else. It was unfortunate, Sheryl thought, that Alun was the only one Caitlin ever asked after, and he was the only one she couldn't answer truthfully about.

September was a wake-up call for both of them. Caitlin was so used to being pandered to and having her own way that she didn't like it when she was made to sit at a desk and behave herself. After being such a solitary child, she found having to mix with almost forty other boys and girls of the same age quite frightening. They sensed this very quickly and began picking on her and teasing her so that Caitlin started sobbing and crying the moment they reached the school gates. She clung to Sheryl, kicking and screaming as her mother tried to leave.

It upset Sheryl a great deal, even though Miss Gibson, her teacher, tried to reassure her.

'Within moments of you leaving, Mrs Powell, Caitlin has dried her tears and is playing happily enough with other children in her class,' the teacher told her.

The first few days, when Sheryl fetched her in the afternoon, however, she found her in tears. Often her clothes were torn or muddied. As they walked home a little knot of her class-mates would follow behind, shouting out rude remarks or throwing things at them.

When Sheryl once again complained to Miss Gibson, she was told not to worry. 'She'll soon settle in. It may take a few weeks, but things will calm down, given time,' Miss Gibson assured her. 'Try not to take too much notice. As an only child she's probably been spoilt. Is her father worried about it?'

'Caitlin's father is dead,' Sheryl said in a clipped voice. She was sure that the teacher must know that, and she wondered if she was merely prying.

'Oh I am sorry to hear that, poor little Caitlin.' She frowned. 'Has he died recently?'

'Yes. Very recently. His name was Alun

Powell, I'm sure you read all about it in the papers.'

Miss Gibson's mouth tightened. 'Yes, of course. I thought the name sounded familiar. Still,' she added consolingly, 'children quickly adjust. Most of the children I teach have to cope with long separations, because their fathers go to sea and are away for months at a time.'

Helping Caitlin to settle into school was not Sheryl's only problem. The moment Caitlin had started school Zak had been quick to remind her that now she was free for part of the day, he expected her to take up his offer of work.

'We'll put it all on a proper basis, negotiate a salary and draw up a list of your duties.' He reached into his inside pocket and brought out some money. Peeling off several notes, he handed them to her. 'Buy yourself some smart clothes for work. A well-fitting black dress that has an eye-catching neckline. You'll need all the trimmings as well, silk stockings, high heels, you know the sort of thing. Understand me?'

'I'm not sure.' Sheryl felt embarrassed by his instructions and also by the large amount of money he'd given her. 'What sort of job are you offering me?'

'Nothing you're not capable of doing,' he assured her, patting her on the shoulder.

'These clothes you've told me to buy . . . I don't understand. I thought you said you wanted me to deliver things for you and help with the books?'

'That's right. You need to look smart, though.' He gave her an appraising glance. 'I'm sure it will be worth it. My clients will appreciate it when you help at the tables.'

'I'm not really interested in being a waitress, I told you that before.'

Zak laughed and squeezed her shoulder encouragingly. 'Forgotten already? I explained it wasn't those sort of tables!'

'You mean gaming tables? I know nothing about gambling . . .'

He laughed again. 'You just do as you're told and we'll get along fine,' he told her. 'The job will be whatever you want it to be, whatever you make it. No-one will force you to do anything you don't want to do.'

Chapter Twenty-Four

By the third week Caitlin seemed to have settled down at school. She was anxious to leave home in the morning, afraid she was going to be late.

'I want time to play with my new friends before the bell goes,' she told her mother impatiently.

Sheryl was relieved by the change in her, until she met the new friends she'd made and then she wasn't so sure. She tried to tell herself that all small children were the same, but she had a great many doubts about whether that applied to Caitlin's friends.

There was only one white child amongst the little group she headed for each morning as soon as she reached the school. He was a sturdy little boy with his hair cut so short that he resembled a shorn lamb. His trousers were patched but otherwise he looked clean and tidy.

The other children Caitlin seemed to favour included a little Chinese girl with her hair in spiky pigtails, and two dark-skinned young girls. One of these had tight wiry curls all over her head, the other one, whose skin was more brown than black, had gleaming straight black hair and blue eyes.

They were not the sort of friends Sheryl would have chosen for her daughter, but there seemed to be nothing she could do about it. She had too many other things to deal with to dwell on it, or give it more than an occasional passing thought.

When Elwyn called to see how she was managing on her own, she put on a brave face and said that everything was fine.

'Megan will be pleased to hear that,' he told her. 'She's been worrying about you.'

Sheryl smiled vaguely but offered no explanation for why she'd left so abruptly, without even leaving Megan a note. Instead she questioned him about his work.

She listened uneasily as he told her that since his beat covered the Loudon Square area, he would make a point of dropping in to see her from time to time.

'I don't think that is a very good idea, Elwyn. Zak mightn't like it, he says it looks bad for business to have a policeman hanging round the place.'

She could tell from his expression that she'd upset him, but much as she wanted to see him it was better that he stayed away, because she knew he would disapprove if she eventually decided to leave Caitlin on her own at night while she went down to work in the club.

As the weeks passed Sheryl's problems

seemed to multiply. She was increasingly worried in case Zak decided she wasn't suitable for the work he wanted her to do. If that happened and he sacked her, he might turf her out of their rooms.

The hours he asked her to work were reasonable enough. She had plenty of time to take Caitlin to school, do the shopping and even tidy up at home before she changed into her smart black dress and put on make-up ready to report for work at the club.

From midday until three o'clock she served drinks to the customers who came into the club's exclusive casino.

'You simply have to look smart, smile, act friendly and watch what is going on,' Zak told her. 'That is all there is to it.'

He agreed without any quibbling that she could leave each day at five minutes to three to collect Caitlin from school. In fact, working for him would have been an ideal arrangement if it hadn't been for his constant requests for her to be there again in the evenings.

At first she had continued to refuse even to consider it. 'I don't want to work in the evenings because I can't leave Caitlin on her own,' she protested.

'I'm not asking you to leave her on her own . . . well, not until after she is in bed and fast asleep. You needn't start work until nine o'clock and you will be finished again by eleven, so what's the problem?'

'Supposing Caitlin wakes up and finds herself all alone? She'd be scared stiff.'

'Nonsense. She's a big girl now! She's at school, no longer a baby who needs you at her side all the time.'

Sheryl faced him angrily, hands on her hips. 'Of course she would need me there if she woke up after a bad nightmare!'

'How often does that happen?' he questioned. 'She might not stir at all, you know.'

'I can't be sure of that. She often wakes up asking for a drink or a biscuit.'

'Well, there you are then.' He beamed happily. 'I have the perfect answer to your problem. All you have to do is leave a candle burning and some biscuits and a glass of milk by the side of the bed, so that she can help herself,' Zak told Sheryl complacently. 'Train her to do it. Try it for a week, or even two or three, and it will become routine.'

'I don't want to do it though, Zak. I would feel I was betraying her trust in me.'

'So you are going to sit at home every night from now until she is eighteen or twenty and gets married?' he said with sour amusement.

'No . . . of course not. But at the moment she is still little more than a baby.'

He looked at her, shaking his head in despair. 'I am only asking you to come down for a short time each evening when we are at our busiest. Why do you think I gave you the money to buy attractive new clothes?'

'So that I could look really smart when I come to work in the club at midday.'

'Yes, and also again in the evenings, that's when I need your help even more! Make it one hour to start with, Sheryl. By ten o'clock that daughter of yours will be so deeply asleep that the chances of her waking will be one in a million.'

Zak, with his warm dark eyes and soft husky voice, could be very persuasive. In the end, Sheryl agreed to give it a trial.

'I'll try it for a couple of nights to see how it goes,' she told him reluctantly.

Zak kissed her enthusiastically on both cheeks, stroking her long hair and laughing triumphantly, knowing that he had won his battle.

For all her initial reluctance, Sheryl found it was exciting to dress up and go down into the club in the evenings. It was so very different from midday and it seemed to give her a purpose in life.

It saddened her to remember that Alun had forbidden her ever to come down there. If he'd been more co-operative they could have found someone to sit with Caitlin in the evenings, and then they could have worked alongside each other. She would have enjoyed that, and it would have meant that they'd have had a lot more money for all the nice things in life that she'd wanted but couldn't afford.

Soon she was going down every evening, but

never for longer than an hour because she still felt uneasy about leaving Caitlin.

The atmosphere was very different from midday because there were so many more people in the casino, women as well as men. Most of them were wearing evening clothes, the women in low-cut gowns, and glittering earrings and necklaces. They looked so glamorous with their stylish hair and their faces made up with powder, lipstick, and rouge. They all appeared so confident and sophisticated as they sat at the gaming tables that Sheryl felt envious of them. She was fascinated by the way they dangled their cigarettes in long elegant holders, languidly sipping the fancy cocktails that the barman mixed so skilfully and which she served to them from a silver salver.

Mostly it was the men who played the tables. The women usually sat there with them, or leant against them looking over their shoulders as they played. Feminine gasps of shock would be heard as the dice stopped rattling, or when a stake was lost. Shrieks of delight ensued after a win, the mound of chips piling up in front of the victorious player.

Zak was always there, spruce in evening dress, wandering round the club, his eyes alert, noting everyone and everything. Sometimes he seemed to be watching Sheryl so closely that she felt uneasy and wondered if she was doing something wrong.

When, a few weeks later, Zak asked her to come into his office, her heart began racing in fear of what he might be going to tell her.

She was trying so hard to organise her life, and she felt she had succeeded. She made sure that Caitlin was well fed, properly looked after and went to school each day. Now, she was filled with a dread that something was going to happen that would change everything.

'Have I done something wrong?' she asked worriedly as she walked into Zak's office.

'Wrong?' Zak looked amused, a broad grin spreading across his swarthy face. 'Not that I know about, Sheryl. Why, do you think you have?'

She shrugged. 'I've noticed that you seem to be watching me a lot lately.'

He smiled enigmatically, then sat tapping his teeth with his gold fountain pen. She grew increasingly uncomfortable.

'So what was it you wanted to see me about?' she asked balefully when the tension became unbearable.

'Well, there are one or two things, Sheryl. To start with, now that you know that once Caitlin is in bed and asleep she doesn't wake up again until morning, how about putting in a little more time working at night?'

Sheryl frowned. She was scared stiff that Caitlin might awake one night and then tell her teacher that she was being left on her own, even though it was only for an hour.

'So far I've been lucky, but I can't take it for granted, now can I?' she countered uneasily.

He didn't answer immediately, but there was a questioning look in his dark eyes that unsettled her further.

'I mean it, Sheryl. You see, I have other plans for you. You don't want to be a cocktail waitress for the rest of your life, do you?'

She shrugged. 'At the moment I'm happy enough with what I'm doing.'

'It's a hand-to-mouth existence for you though, isn't it? I'm sure you'd like to earn more money. You could. A great deal more than you do now,' he murmured persuasively.

Sheryl stiffened, wary about what he might have in mind. 'So how are you suggesting I could do that?' she asked.

'Simply by working longer hours,' Zak told her quietly.

She shrugged. 'Well, I suppose I could work a bit longer each night. Start at half past nine instead of ten. I couldn't come any earlier than that.'

'I see. Half past nine until eleven o'clock,' he murmured reflectively.

'Not every night,' she said quickly. 'I'd find it too tiring being on my feet so much.'

'Well, you needn't worry about that. I wasn't thinking of you being on your feet. I had something quite different in mind!'

Colour flooded Sheryl's cheeks. 'You're not going to get me doing anything like that,' she said huffily.

Zak looked at her. 'Like what?'

'You know what I mean!'

His face darkened. 'Are you implying that this is a knocking shop?' he said angrily. 'Nothing of that sort is conducted on these premises, I can assure you. You've never seen anything that might lead you to think that there is, have you?'

'No!' She shook her head, startled when he put her thoughts into words. 'No, you're quite right, Zak, I haven't. So what else is it that you want me to do? The books?'

He laughed. 'I was thinking about training you to become a croupier.'

'Work on the tables? Placing the bets, you mean?'

'I think that is what a croupier is supposed to do.'

'I'm not sure I could do it,' she gasped. 'I mean, it's a very responsible job, isn't it.'

His smile faded and he nodded gravely. 'And very well paid,' he assured her.

'You'd have to show me what to do.'

'Of course. You'd receive proper training, Sheryl,' he said expansively. 'You'd never be left on your own.'

'Someone would be in the room with me?'

'Yes, either at the table, or watching in the background in case there was ever any trouble. So what do you say? Are you willing to learn the ropes and see if you come up to standard?'

'I'll certainly give it a go,' she said eagerly. 'Is this one of the jobs Alun did when he was working here?'

Zak smiled non-committally. 'I take it that since the idea appeals to you, you are ready to start learning right away. It will soon be Christmas, a very busy period, so I would like you to be trained by then. Achieve proficiency and you will be able to start 1926 as one of my croupiers.'

Learning the ropes, as Zak termed it, took rather more skill than Sheryl had expected. Zak insisted on teaching her himself. His standards were exacting, and there were times when she wondered if she would ever master the techniques involved.

By the time her training was through she knew every move, what to say, how to say it, and even how to deal with awkward customers. He also taught her how to encourage the punters to stay at the table, persuade them to increase their stakes, and how to cajole them into leaving peacefully if they lost all their money.

'I'm going to try you out at midday to start with, Sheryl,' Zak told her. 'That's an easy option. Once you've had some practice then you can work in the evenings.'

It was a few days before Christmas 1925 when Zak told her he was satisfied with her progress and had decided she was ready to work at the tables at night. 'Three evenings a week, how does that sound to you?'

Sheryl felt so overwhelmed that she could hardly think straight. She loved the atmosphere, and the power that swept through her when she was in charge at midday, but she knew that the evening sessions would be much more exciting.

'Fine, but I won't be able to work on Saturday nights,' she told him.

He shrugged, but there was a gleam of anger in his sloe-dark eyes. 'Very well, if that's the way you want it, but what have you against Saturdays?'

'All the other nights Caitlin will be worn out after a busy day at school, so I can be pretty sure that she will sleep through. On Saturdays she stays up late, so she mightn't be asleep when it was time for me to come down.'

He nodded in agreement, but Sheryl could see he wasn't entirely happy about it. 'Isn't it time that you told her you work down here in the evenings?' he commented.

'No, no, I don't want to do that. Caitlin wouldn't understand. If I did tell her she would be frightened at the thought of being left on her own.'

He shrugged. 'That's up to you, of course, Sheryl, but it is time you recognised that Caitlin is quite a big girl now and probably under-stands more than you think she does.'

'She still misses Alun, and now with him gone I don't want to let her down,' Sheryl prevaricated.

Zak moved closer, his hand caressing her long

fair hair. 'Perhaps it is time that you gave some thought to replacing Alun in her life . . . and in yours,' he said softly.

Sheryl pulled back as if stung. 'No, no, I could never do that. It wouldn't be fair on Caitlin . . . not yet, anyway.'

Chapter Twenty-Five

Sheryl loved working at the gaming tables. She knew she looked stunning in her trim little black dress with its décolleté neckline, her face carefully made up to accentuate her eyes and lips and her shining hair.

She was fully aware that every man in the room was eyeing her up, admiring her shapely legs emphasised by her spindly high heels and sheer silk stockings.

Each time she bent over the gaming table, she made sure that her long hair fell forward like a tantalising screen across her face, hiding the cleavage revealed by her low neckline.

Thrilling though this was, it was the power she was able to exercise over other people that Sheryl found really exhilarating. As she pushed a pile of chips across the table and saw their hands reach out so eagerly for them, or raked back a pile to her side of the table and saw the shock and gloom on the loser's face, she felt as if she was influencing their future.

Zak schooled her thoroughly, making sure she knew exactly how long to pause and then glance expectantly at any punter who was losing, silently challenging him to place another bid, before she continued.

She had been so nervous the first night that Zak had insisted she should have a strong drink before she started work.

'I don't drink,' she protested, 'except perhaps a port and lemonade at Christmas.'

'I should hope not,' he laughed. 'The punters won't trust you if they find you smelling of liquor.'

'Then how can I possibly have a drink?' she asked, bemused.

'Try this, it's vodka and tonic,' he invited, holding out a glass that was half full of a colourless liquid. 'No-one will be able to tell if you always drink that, not unless you have too many and fall over, of course.'

She accepted his advice as she had all his other guidance. She found that a drink not only steadied her nerves, but put a sparkle in her eyes and lifted her spirits.

It also freed her of inhibitions and turned her into a flirt. There was no harm in it, she told herself, because it didn't lead to anything. Most of the men knew it was only fun, just as she did. If any of them showed signs of taking her teasing seriously she backed away quickly. After her life with Alun she had no intention of ever getting serious with any man again. Not even with Elwyn, although he was the only man she felt she could trust. She regarded him as a staunch friend, nothing more.

Halfway through most evenings, when she was beginning to flag, she found that another vodka and tonic acted as a pick-me-up. Soon she was never without a glass by her side, sipping it more and more frequently, almost as if it was water, as the evening wore on.

It helped her sleep, as well. She was usually feeling exhilarated when the club closed, even though she was physically exhausted. She kept going over in her mind all the action of the evening, the remarks and quips that had been made, the amounts of money that had changed hands.

A large vodka and tonic before she left the club helped her to wind down. By the time she'd walked round the corner into Loudon Place, and was home, she was ready to fall into bed and drop asleep.

At first, such excesses had no effect on her daily routine. Gradually, however, she found she needed more and more sleep and it became later and later before she got up in the mornings. Often she didn't even bother to get dressed until it was time to do her midday shift at the club.

It meant that Caitlin was up, dressed and had foraged around for something to eat for her breakfast before Sheryl even stirred. More and more frequently Caitlin went off to school on her own, usually without washing her face or combing her hair.

If Sheryl was aware of this she said nothing.

What did it matter, no-one at the school seemed to care very much about what the children looked like. Caitlin had shoes and socks to wear, and many of the others didn't. A dirty blouse or a stained skirt was nothing. At least she wasn't in rags.

Work, and its accompanying supply of generous measures of vodka and tonic, became all Sheryl lived for, so much so that Zak became worried about her. Once or twice he reprimanded her for her unprofessional attitude.

'You can drink all you want to as long as it doesn't interfere with your work,' he warned her.

'I'm not drunk! I know perfectly well what I'm doing,' she told him angrily.

'Do you? Remember you are responsible for hundreds of pounds each night. If any of the punters feels he's been cheated in any way whatsoever, there will be trouble, for all of us.'

'You'd be lost without me here,' she bragged, tossing back her hair defiantly.

'It has taken me a great many years to build up my clientele and I'm certainly not going to risk having all my hard work jeopardised by an employee who is unable to hold her drink,' he stated firmly.

'Are you saying you're thinking of sacking me?' she challenged.

'I most certainly am! If I do fire you, Sheryl, remember you lose your home as well as your job,' he pointed out.

She laughed mockingly. 'You wouldn't be so heartless as to do something like that, not after all the time I've lived here and worked for you.'

'I'm a businessman, Sheryl. If my investments don't make profitable returns then I dispose of them immediately,' Zak told her curtly.

She drained her glass of almost neat vodka and threw the glass to the ground. It crashed in smithereens only a few inches from his feet.

'I won't be bullied or blackmailed,' she told him furiously. 'If that's how you feel about things then I'll go . . . now.'

He placed a hand on her arm warningly. 'That's the drink talking, Sheryl, not you! You've had far too much tonight. Go home, get some sleep and tomorrow will be another day. Simply heed my words, that's all I'm asking you to do.'

'Really! Well, let me tell you what you can do with your job and all the rest of your good advice. I've had enough!' She staggered towards the door, crashing into the side of a table as she did so.

Zak went to help her, afraid she was going to hurt herself, but she pushed him away. 'Keep your pawing hands off me, I won't be mauled by you. We both know that's the real reason why you are sacking me, don't we.'

He grabbed her by the arm. 'I have no idea what is going on inside your head, or what you are trying to accuse me of, Sheryl!'

She had never seen him so irate. Even when

he had been teaching her how to be a croupier, and she had constantly made silly mistakes, Zak had been tolerant and patient. He rarely lost his temper. He could be severe and she knew he stood no nonsense from anyone on his staff, not even from the girls who acted as hostesses. He would sometimes wave his arms in the air, or clamp a hand to his forehead in despair, but she had never seen him lose his temper before and now his complete change of character frightened her.

For a moment she thought he was going to hit her, and remembering the beating she'd suffered from Alun she pulled away, quaking with fear.

She had intended flirting with him, leading him on because she was sure he liked her. She recalled his concern after the news of Alun's suicide. She'd been sure then that he would have taken her in his arms and kissed her if she had let him.

With that in mind, she'd intended to stir up once again the feelings he obviously had for her, to soften him up so that he overlooked her drinking.

He'd warned her countless times over the past six months. Even though she'd tried to control it, she knew she was still drinking too much. More and more she was relying on vodka and tonic to help her through the stress of the evening.

After a few drinks the buzz was there, the

power, the excitement. It made her forget all her problems, even forget she had a child that she was blatantly neglecting.

Caitlin was now as much a street child as any of her schoolfriends. Knowing that her mother wouldn't be meeting her when the school day ended, and that she would be either asleep or drunk when her daughter arrived home, Caitlin didn't bother coming back to Loudon Place, but stayed out with her friends. Sometimes they played in Loudon Square, swinging from ropes tied to the lamppost, joining in the hopscotch or playing with tops or marbles in the gutter. Other times they wandered down to the canal bank, sometimes roaming as far away as James Street, riding with others in the little wooden cart that one of the boys had fixed onto his bicycle.

Those were the quiet times, but on other occasions the mischief was more dangerous. They pinched sweets, apples and buns from the local shops and stalls, and they were chased by shopkeepers and even by the police. They bullied children younger than themselves, or got into fights with other gangs. When that happened Caitlin arrived home with her clothes almost torn off her back. Along with the others, she threw stones and broke windows, tied tin cans to doorknobs and in general made a nuisance of herself.

Miss Gibson despaired of this unruly group. Frequently she sent notes home to their parents

288

warning of the consequences if they continued to behave in this way.

If Sheryl was sober when she received one of these notes she gave Caitlin a talking-to, but if she was drunk she simply screwed it up and threw it away.

She knew that nothing she said would make any difference, because these days Caitlin treated her with contempt. Several times Sheryl had caught her taking money from her purse without asking. When she scolded her for this, Caitlin claimed that it was because she was hungry and there was nothing in the place to eat, so she needed the money for chips.

Usually Sheryl let the matter drop. She knew what Caitlin said was probably true. Working on the tables drained her of every vestige of energy so that she couldn't even think straight.

She wasn't neglecting Caitlin, she told herself, because, as Zak kept saying, Caitlin was no longer a baby. Now at almost seven, she was a hard little nut who was not only streetwise, but, as he pointed out, capable of looking after herself.

Sheryl had never meant to squander all the extra money she earned on booze, but the vodka and tonic perks at the club had become addictive. She really had meant to save the extra money she now earned as a croupier towards a better home for herself and Caitlin.

Instead she had slipped to depths beyond her comprehension. The shopkeepers in Loudon

Square no longer greeted her in a friendly manner. They looked at her as though they despised her. She suspected that some of them even gave their leftovers to Caitlin because they felt sorry for her, she looked so hungry and bedraggled.

The realisation that she had been about to solicit affection from her Sicilian employer sobered Sheryl like a shower of cold water.

She looked at him with loathing. Fat, paunchy, swarthy, with his prominent nose and loose lips, he repulsed her. His outward smoothness, the sharp suit, the manicured fingernails, the big gold watch and the gold chain around his neck, thicker than even his watch strap, stamped him as flashy. Flashy and polished. A smooth operator who cleverly used other people's weaknesses for his own profit.

He'd used Alun. She'd never found out exactly what Alun's job was, but it was probably very similar to her own. He'd succumbed to drink, just as she had. If she didn't pull back now she would find herself sinking even lower and taking drugs like she was sure Alun had done.

Zak was using her. He'd trained her to con money out of the weak-principled men who came into the club. She knew what was in the 'deliveries' she carried out for him. He'd only stopped using her as a go-between to discreetly deliver packages to certain clients when she'd started drinking, and he wasn't sure that she was trustworthy any more.

She saw it now, it was suddenly crystal clear. At the time she'd thought he was interested in her welfare, that he was being kind to try and compensate for Alun's suicide; being nice to her because Alun had worked for him.

The life she'd been living since then had been merely an illusion. She was relieved now that it had come to an end. She'd survive, she'd make sure of that for Caitlin's sake if nothing else.

It wasn't too late, she told herself. If she worked hard she could turn things round and bring Caitlin back into line. She'd care for her properly from now on. She would never leave her on her own at nights again. She certainly wouldn't let her fend for herself any more, or live on other people's scraps and run around with the dregs of Tiger Bay.

Zakaraki's voice brought her back to reality with a jolt.

'I am telling you to go, Sheryl, and to stay well clear of Diawl Coch in future. I no longer require your services. Understand?'

'Really? Not even for doing your precious deliveries?' she asked sarcastically.

Zakaraki's face darkened. 'If you mention anything about those outside this room you will find yourself in serious trouble, I can promise you! Do you understand?'

'Yes, I can believe that, but you'd be in even deeper, wouldn't you?' she smirked.

'I'm warning you, if you try to implicate me in any way, you'll be sorry,' he threatened.

They stared at each other without speaking for a long moment. Zak's face was mottled with rage as he realised the harm she could do. Unless he mollified her in some way she could be dangerous.

'You can stay on in the rooms for the present,' he told her stiffly.

Sheryl nodded but she didn't thank him, even though she felt a surge of relief. There was nowhere else she could take refuge. She turned on her heel and made for the door.

Chapter Twenty-Six

Breaking her drinking habit was harder than Sheryl had ever imagined it could be. She'd heard people in the club saying, when she'd handed them their 'special deliveries' as Zak instructed her, that giving up drugs was almost impossible, because the withdrawal symptoms were so frightening. She'd had no idea, though, that trying to stop drinking was almost as bad.

Although it was early summer and there were days of warm sunshine, she felt cold and was aware of tremors running through her body all the time. She sat hunched in the armchair, or in bed, shaking and shivering and feeling so depressed that she didn't care if she lived or died.

All her good intentions about making a better life for Caitlin seemed to vanish into thin air. She really had meant to do it; even now she wanted to do it, but she had neither the will power nor the stamina to carry through any of her resolutions.

When she woke in the morning her head ached and felt muzzy. She felt so ill, so agitated and quivery, that she automatically reached for anything alcoholic. She knew that what little money she had saved for their future while working as a croupier she was squandering on drink, but she couldn't stop.

Unable to afford vodka, she switched to cheap wine or cider for those few moments of blind oblivion when she neither knew where she was, nor what was going on around her.

When she did come round, she saw the depths she and Caitlin had sunk into so clearly that she was repelled. Caitlin, at six and a half, had become hard-faced, cheeky and uncontrollable. She was a thief, a scrounger and a liar. What was more she was unwashed, had nits in her hair and was dressed in rags.

Unable to face up to her predicament, Sheryl retreated into a shell of apathy and sat for hours aimlessly staring into space.

In her more lucid moments she once again made plans, sensible aims for their future. Then the realisation swept over her that they only had a temporary home, hardly any money left and she had no job.

When she was floating between her drink-sodden state and reality, she often thought about her own childhood. The pampered, protected atmosphere of Thesiger Street seemed like another world.

The comparison made her feel so guilty that she dissolved into tears, and then the only way of getting out of the dark depression that enveloped her was to have a drink.

As her money dwindled she pawned

anything she could lay her hands on. Alun's smart suits and shirts were the first things to go, then her own clothes and finally even Caitlin's toys.

And so it went on. By high summer their rooms were claustrophobic, airless, and so smelly that they were almost unbearable.

Sheryl knew it would be better if she did some cleaning, and resolved to give the place a good scrub after Caitlin went back to school. But when September came she couldn't muster up the energy. She no longer went out to the shops. She sent Caitlin out to scrounge for food and bottles of cheap wine.

Every time she heard footsteps on the stairs she cowered under the bedcovers, afraid it might be Zak coming to tell her to vacate the rooms. Whether it was or not she didn't know, because she never opened the door. She simply stayed motionless until she heard whoever it was go away again.

Sometimes, if the footsteps were heavy, she wondered if it was Elwyn, but although she longed to see him she didn't want him to find her living in such squalor and looking so unkempt.

She'd warned Caitlin she was always to make sure that Zakaraki never followed her up to their flat. If he did she was to run off, play out in the street until he went away and the coast was clear.

Caitlin was sharp, and she knew the score. She also knew better than to say anything to

Zak about how they were managing if she accidentally met him, or confide in anyone else, for that matter.

Sheryl was shocked to the core when one evening she heard Caitlin talking to somebody and realised she'd brought them home with her.

Caitlin came into the room and tried to explain who was waiting outside the door, but Sheryl grabbed hold of her and shook her hard before she had a chance to do so.

'You silly little bitch!' she railed, 'I've told you time and again that you don't bring anyone at all here. Not even those little scruffs you play around with after you come out of school, or any other bugger. Understand?'

Caitlin was sobbing so much that she couldn't answer, and before either of them had calmed down the uninvited visitor had walked into the room.

The sight of her mother-in-law standing there, fat, motherly and with a disapproving look on her face, sobered Sheryl up. She hadn't seen Nola Powell since Alun had come to collect her from Nola's house. She knew she should have got in touch with her, written to her or gone to see her, after Alun had died, but she'd waited for Nola to come to her. When she hadn't done so she'd felt angry and decided not to bother getting in touch either.

Nola looked round at the mess and muddle in the squalid room in disgust, and sniffed disparagingly.

'Duw anwyl, you look bloody awful and so does your place! Are you ill then, Sheryl?'

Guilt spread through Sheryl like a rash. She should have gone to her, told her the news about Alun, explained to her, offered her sympathy. Families should stick together, she reminded herself. Because her own parents had wanted nothing more to do with her didn't mean she had to ignore Alun's family as well.

Nola had taken her in, after all. She'd provided a roof over Sheryl's head when she'd needed one, after her own mam had turned her out.

'Mrs Powell! Nola . . . what are you doing here?'

'Bringing a little present for Caitlin and to find out how you both are. Here, cariad.' She held out a gaudily wrapped parcel to Caitlin, who snatched it from her hand and began tearing off the coloured paper.

'For me?' Caitlin's eyes were glistening excitedly as she pulled out a bright pink woollen jumper. Without waiting for a reply she dragged it over her head, cuddling herself inside its warmth.

'Thanks for that, Nola! She hasn't many warm clothes,' Sheryl muttered. 'Now, do you want a cuppa?' she asked, pulling her soiled wrap around her as she struggled to her feet.

'Not here I don't!' Nola Powell said scornfully. 'I'd probably end up with bad guts if I ate or drank anything in this place. Bet you couldn't find a clean cup if you tried,' she scoffed.

'I can soon wash up a couple,' Sheryl defended.

Nola's lip curled as she looked her up and down. 'When did you last have a wash yourself, or put a comb through your hair then?'

Sheryl raised a hand and ran it over the tangled mess.

'Lovely your hair used to be, girl. Long, gleaming, like sunshine. Now it looks as full of nits as a sheep's back is of ticks. And it is, too, I wouldn't mind betting!'

Sheryl scowled at her in silence.

'Look at your clothes,' Nola went on. 'That old rag you're wearing looks as though it hasn't been off your back for a month. Wallowing in your own mire, you slattern,' she accused angrily. 'Do you ever give that young Caitlin a proper wash? She looks like a little street urchin, but then that's what she is, isn't it?'

Sheryl put her hands over her ears, shutting out the rasping sound of Nola's nagging voice.

Nola went through into the kitchen and put the kettle on. Sheryl heard her moving around in there, the sound of water being poured into the tin bowl, of cups and plates clattering.

'I'll do that,' she said, hauling herself to her feet.

'Stay where you are,' Nola ordered. 'I've nearly done out here. We'll talk about things over our tea.'

298

'So you've condescended to have a cuppa with me, have you?' Sheryl taunted.

'Yes, more fool me!' Nola's voice softened. 'I hope you are going to listen to what I have to say, cariad.'

'Depends what you are going to yatter on about,' Sheryl told her cautiously.

'I feel bad about not coming here sooner to make sure that you and Caitlin were all right,' Nola said as she set the two cups of tea down on the table.

'Why should you?' Sheryl asked resignedly. 'I never bothered to get in touch with you.'

'No, but I can understand that. I was torn in two when I read in the paper about Alun. I don't know which was worse, him stabbing that policeman or taking his own life.'

'One led to the other, didn't it,' Sheryl said morosely.

Nola shook her head. 'I can't understand him going for a policeman like that. Stupid young fool. Attacking a policeman! He might have known they'd throw the book at him for killing one of their own. I can't think why he did it, he must have been out of his mind. What was it Sheryl, drink? Or was he on something of some kind . . . you know what I mean?'

'It was probably drink,' Sheryl said evasively.

'I should have come and looked for you then and made sure you were all right,' Nola repeated.

She took a drink of her tea. 'I couldn't believe

it was little Caitlin when I saw her out in the street. She's changed so much! So filthy dirty that she looks a proper little guttersnipe.' Nola shook her head sadly. 'How could you let her get like this, Sheryl? I know how cut up you must have been about Alun, but how do you think he would feel to see his little girl in such a state?'

'I know, I know,' Sheryl muttered guiltily. She struggled to look Nola in the face. 'I've turned over a new leaf now, though. In a couple of months' time she'll be a different kid. As soon as I can I'm going to get right away from here. Start afresh, a new life. You'll see. I've only hung on in this dump because it was the only way I could keep a roof over our heads . . .'

'You mean because you're working for that Greek fella who owns the club?'

'He's a Sicilian, not a Greek.'

'Same thing. Foreigner, like all the rest that live around here. So are you working for him then?'

'I was. After Alun died he said I could stay on up here and gave me a job in the club.'

'Yes, but are you still working there?' Nola persisted.

Sheryl shook her head.

'Why not? What happened? Did he get fresh with you, want favours?' Nola asked suspiciously.

'No! Nothing at all like that. It was my own fault that he sacked me. I couldn't leave the drink alone and I let it get the better of me, so he didn't trust me to do my job properly.'

'A very pretty picture. So what are you doing now? Have you got another job?'

Sheryl shook her head. 'Not yet. I had to stop myself drinking so that I could start to straighten young Caitlin out. I want to get her back on the straight and narrow first of all, see.'

'You'll never do that as long as you live in Tiger Bay. I hate to have to say it, but she's a hard-faced little madam. You won't change her now in a hurry, not after she's been left to run wild and do exactly what she likes for so long.'

'I will, really I will. I must!' Sheryl insisted shrilly.

Nola shook her head. 'It's over two years since my Alun died. Ever since then you've neglected her.'

'I've had to work, I couldn't be in two places at once,' Sheryl told her sullenly.

'Not while you were doing the sort of job you had. You should have found yourself some other kind of work. Even charring would have been more respectable and you would have been here for Caitlin when she came home from school. Instead you've been working in that awful club where heaven knows what goes on. What sort of example is that for a young child?'

'If all you've come here for is to throw accusations at me, and criticise everything I've done, then bugger off,' Sheryl said wearily.

'No, I came because I wanted to see Caitlin

and make sure she was all right. I want to help, Sheryl.'

'Help! You! There hasn't been a word from you since Alun died.'

'I know and I've said I'm sorry about that, cariad. I really do want to do my bit to help you both.'

'How?'

Nola looked bewildered. 'I don't know, Sheryl. Perhaps for a start you should come back to Ely and live with us?'

Sheryl scowled. 'It didn't work out last time, did it, so why do you think it would work now?'

'Let's try again, cariad,' Nola begged. 'Living in Ely would be a lot better for Caitlin than staying here.'

'No!' Sheryl shook her head disconsolately. 'That would be turning the clock back and that never works, now does it.'

They drank their tea in silence. Sheryl was longing for a real drink, but knew she didn't dare risk it with her mother-in-law there. She wondered how she could persuade her to leave. She wanted to be on her own, her head was aching and she felt weary of the whole discussion and knew it was serving no purpose.

Nola drained her cup. 'I can see we're not getting anywhere.' She shook her head in despair. Then her face brightened. 'I tell you what I can do, Sheryl, I could take Caitlin back home with me. That will give you a chance to pull yourself together. You'll be able to find yourself another job, see. Do that, and then you can move out of here and find somewhere decent for the pair of you to live.'

Sheryl shook her head. 'I don't want to be separated from Caitlin, she needs me now with Alun gone.'

'She'll have me and Cradog. It will be a far more settled background for her,' Nola persisted. 'Come on now, you must see that.'

'I don't know. She still misses Alun. This was his home . . . and hers.'

'My place was his home, too,' Nola pointed out. 'Cradog and me will take good care of her, you'll have nothing to worry about. Come on, my lovely, let's give it a try. It can't do any harm, now can it, cariad?'

'No!' Sheryl seemed adamant. 'I think she'd be unhappy. She'd be living in a strange house, and have to go to a different school. She'd be upset about losing all her friends,' she added lamely.

'Friends! Don't talk such rubbish, girl! They're not the sort of friends you want her to have, surely? She was such a pretty little thing and look at her now. Ashamed to own her I am, and that's a fact.'

'Then you won't want her living with you, will you!' Sheryl snapped.

Nola looked across the room to where Caitlin was lying on the floor colouring in a picture and ignoring them both. 'I'll soon clean her up, a couple of new dresses and you won't know her. Tell you what, cariad, let's ask her what she wants to do.'

Caitlin listened to them both, a sly look on her grubby little face as she weighed matters up.

'Will I be able to come and see my mam if I'm living with you?' she asked Nola.

'Of course you will, cariad! You can come and see her whenever you want to. Or, better still, she can come out to Ely and see you.'

Caitlin looked from her mother to her grand-mother craftily. 'If I live with you will I have a bed of my very own to sleep in?'

'A bed? Better than that, cariad, you'll have a room of your own. All your dolls and toys . . .'

'I don't have any dolls. Mam says only babies play with them,' Caitlin sighed.

'Well, what if I buy you a teddy bear as a present? Would that be all right for a big girl?' Nola asked.

'I'd sooner have a Betty Oxo.'

'You mean one of those big dolls dressed in bright pink velvet?'

Caitlin nodded eagerly. 'The same colour as my new jumper, but with bits of white fur on her clothes . . .'

'I thought you said you were too old for dolls,' Nola interrupted.

Caitlin shrugged. 'Mam said that, not me. It was only because she wanted to sell my dolls for booze money,' she explained.

'I'm sure we can find something to make up for that,' Nola told her quietly.

Caitlin smiled happily, then she looked thoughtful. 'Will I get pocket money, Nana Nola, to spend on sweets and comics if I come to live with you?'

Nola pursed her lips. 'Well, that will depend . . .'

'On what?' Caitlin asked suspiciously.

'On whether you are a good girl and behave yourself, of course!'

Caitlin thought about it for a moment longer, then nodded her head. 'OK, I'll come with you,' she agreed.

Chapter Twenty-Seven

Sheryl felt utterly desolate after Caitlin had left with her grandmother. It seemed as if everyone had deserted her, even her own little girl. She couldn't think of a single person who cared about what happened to her any more.

She knew that it was her own fault, she'd turned everyone against her; not only her own mam and dad, but even Megan . . . and Elwyn. She felt overcome by remorse. How could she have neglected her own child to such an extent? How could any mother behave as she had done?

Seeing the look of surprise on Caitlin's face when Nola had handed her the package wrapped in gaudy paper, and how excited she'd been when she'd opened it and found the pink jumper inside, had cut Sheryl to the quick. She couldn't remember when she'd last given Caitlin a present or bought her anything new. Even her clothes were second-hand.

The jumper hadn't fitted Caitlin very well, it was miles too big, but she'd been so delighted with it that she'd refused to take it off.

'They said in the shop that it was the right size for her age,' Nola had commented, 'but then they didn't know that she was so damn skinny that she's no bigger than a four-year-old.'

That had hurt, too! Sheryl found herself feeling guilty in case the reason why Caitlin was so puny was because of the way she had neglected her. For a long time now she hadn't noticed what Caitlin ate. She left her to fend for herself. Fish and chips was her daughter's staple diet, that and broken biscuits or stale cakes and buns that shopkeepers and stall-holders gave her when they were clearing up at the end of the day.

Sheryl looked round the dirty, shabby room and felt deeply ashamed that her mother-in-law had found her living in such a deplorable state. Nola was not a very conscientious house-wife herself, but her home was like a little palace compared to this place, Sheryl thought contritely.

She was gasping for a drink, but she knew if she gave in and had one then she'd immediately want another, and then a third and so on until the bottle was empty. By that time she'd be in such a deep drunken stupor she would tumble into bed without even bothering to undress.

Determined not to let that happen, she tried to rouse herself to action. She would clean the place up. Even if she only tidied one room and restored some sort of order she'd feel better, she told herself.

Once she'd started she couldn't stop. She found herself moving from one job to the next, appalled at the filth piled up on the floor, and the cobwebs in the corners. She gathered into one huge pile all the old newspapers, magazines and comics. She was shocked when she found discarded dirty knives, fish-and-chip wrappers and stale, half-eaten sandwiches hidden underneath them.

Disgusted by her own slovenliness, she scrubbed and polished until the living room was transformed. She felt a tremendous sense of pride in what she had achieved . . . until she walked into the bedroom. There were soiled clothes thrown into a corner waiting to be washed, and even dirty plates, cups and glasses that she'd pushed underneath the bed.

With a sigh she started to tidy everything away. Tomorrow she'd change the bed linen, polish the furniture and clean the windows, she vowed an hour later. Now, after all her efforts to restore order, she felt dog-tired, so she made herself a cup of Camp Coffee and got ready for bed.

Sheryl was awake early next morning and lay for a moment wondering why everything seemed different. Realising that she was alone in bed, she wondered where Caitlin was. She hadn't heard her getting up and she couldn't hear her in the kitchen.

As she went to look for her, the sight of the newly cleaned living room brought everything rushing back. Heavy-hearted, she remembered that Caitlin wasn't there because she'd gone back to Ely with Nola.

For a moment she felt desolate, and sought out the comfort of the vodka bottle. As she lifted it to her lips the orderliness of the living room reminded her of her resolution. No more drink, no more slovenliness. She was going to pull herself together, get a worthwhile job and provide a proper home for Caitlin.

Determinedly she replaced the vodka bottle in the cupboard. She knew she ought to empty it down the sink, but she couldn't bring herself to be so wasteful. As long as she knew it was there she was more likely to stick by her resolve and not touch it, she told herself. If she tipped it away, and the craving for a drink became unbearable, she would be tempted to go out and buy some more and the cycle would start all over again. If she knew there was some there, she could look at it and use will power not to drink it.

She caught sight of herself in the mirror and shuddered. Her hair was dark with grease and dirt, her face blotchy with stale make-up, and her nightgown grubby and in need of a wash.

First things first, she told herself. A clean home was no good if the woman looking after it was a slut. She'd smarten herself up and then she'd finish the cleaning spree she'd started on last night.

The bedroom was still a shambles, so she

changed her mind and decided to finish cleaning in there before she started on herself.

It was almost midday before the transformation was complete. With her hair washed and gleaming, dressed in a clean blouse and skirt, her face made up and even her shoes shining, Sheryl had to admit that she felt a different person.

The next thing she had to do was find herself some work. She thought longingly of her job as a croupier, and wondered if she could persuade Mr Zakaraki to overlook what had happened and take her back.

There was no harm in approaching him and suggesting it, she told herself. If she didn't ask then she would never know. If she could persuade him to employ her again as a croupier, now that she'd resolved to stop drinking she'd be able to build up a nice little nest egg in next to no time.

Speedily she changed her clothes, this time putting on the black dress that Zak had given her the money to buy. She touched up her make-up, adding more lipstick, brushing her hair again so that it shone like spun silk.

Pleased with the result, she made her way down to the club before her courage failed her.

The doorman gave a soundless whistle as she approached. 'Been taking a bit of a holiday?' he asked, with a broad wink.

'Something like that,' Sheryl smiled non-committally. 'Is Mr Zakaraki in?'

'He most certainly is, he arrived about ten minutes ago.'

'Good! I'll find him, don't you bother,' Sheryl told him quickly, as he went to move inside.

'Well . . .'

'Really, there's no need for you to do so,' Sheryl insisted, giving him a quick smile. 'I know where he will be,' she said as she slipped past him, and through the door that led into the club.

She headed straight for the casino and was rather taken aback to see a tall, curvy redhead preparing the table for the midday punters.

Of course he would have had to replace me, she told herself. How else would he have kept the tables functioning? It didn't mean she wouldn't get her job back! She only had to ask.

Since Zak wasn't in there, she went along to the small private room which he called his office. If he was surprised to see her he hid it well. She wondered if perhaps the doorman had already alerted him that she was in the building.

His face was inscrutable as he looked up at her. He responded to her bright smile and warm greeting with a frigid nod. In silence he studied her, his eyes hooded.

'Can I help you, Sheryl?'

'I hope so, Zak. I'm feeling better now. Fully recovered, as you can see, and ready for work again.'

Zak frowned and pursed his lips, then rubbed a hand over his chin.

'Zak, I'm trying to say that I'd like my job back,' Sheryl explained patiently.

He avoided her gaze. 'I don't know about that . . . you were only part-time and . . .'

'That was all in the past, Zak,' she interrupted. 'Things are completely different now. I can work full-time. Midday sessions as well as evening ones and even Saturday nights if you need me to do so,' she told him eagerly.

Zak raised his eyebrows enquiringly. 'What about leaving Caitlin on her own?'

'That's all sorted out, she's gone to stay with Alun's mother. I have no domestic ties at all, nothing to stop me from working for you full-time.'

'That's if I want you to do so,' he pointed out coldly. 'I sacked you, if you remember.'

Sheryl's smile faded. Zak was putting up much more resistance than she'd expected. She realised that because of her drinking she'd disgraced herself in his eyes, but surely he only had to look at her to see that she'd changed?

'I haven't forgotten all you taught me, Zak, about dealing with the punters, and everything,' she went on persuasively. 'I can go back on the tables right away. I can even start tonight if you want me to do so. Look!' She pulled aside her coat dramatically to show off her black dress. 'I'm already dressed for the part.'

He still didn't respond and Sheryl began to feel uneasy when he didn't even smile, or tell her that she was looking good. Surely he wasn't going to refuse to let her have her job back, or worse, tell her that he didn't want her to work for him again?

'You say you can start immediately,' he murmured reflectively.

She nodded eagerly. She felt almost afraid to speak in case she said something that upset him and made him change his mind. She'd won, she thought exultantly. He'd been testing her, he'd intended giving her back her job all along.

Things were finally going exactly the way she wanted them to. A few months working on the tables and she would have enough saved to go ahead with the rest of her plans. The next step would be to get away from Tiger Bay and find somewhere better to live.

She'd go to see Nola and Caitlin on Sunday and tell them the good news. It would set Caitlin's mind at rest to know they'd be together again very soon. She'd mark down the days on a sheet of paper for her and then Caitlin could cross one out each morning. That way she'd know exactly when she'd be back with her mother.

'So do you want me to start right away then, Zak?' she asked.

He frowned. 'I'll give you a week's trial, Sheryl. Behave yourself and do your work well, and then we'll talk about a long-term arrangement,' he told her in a sharp voice.

'Zak! You know I can do the work, I don't need a trial. Are you teasing me?' she asked, raising her eyebrows questioningly.

313

'No, Sheryl! If you want to be reinstated then those are my terms.'

She pulled a face. 'All right. Whatever you say, you're the boss!' She sighed as she moved towards the door. 'I'll see you out at the tables later on then, when you come to check up on me,' she murmured with a provocative smile.

'Wait a moment, Sheryl. You've already been replaced as a croupier. You'll have to do something else . . . that is, if you are quite certain that you still want to go on working here.'

She bit her lip. This wasn't what she'd had in mind. She thought quickly, and decided that for the moment she'd better go along with whatever Zak offered her. Making her do a week's trial was probably only his way of showing her that he was the boss. If she humoured him over this little whim, it would be easier to talk him into giving her back her old job.

'Of course I do, I love working here. What is it you want me to do, Zak?'

'You will be waitressing.'

Her eyes widened. She couldn't believe what he was saying. 'Waitressing? You mean serving drinks to the customers?'

'That's right. I presume that you do remember how to do that?' he said caustically.

She ignored the sarcasm. 'Of course I do, but it's not the sort of work I really want to do, not with all my experience,' she wheedled.

He shrugged. 'Under the circumstances, that is all I am prepared to offer you,' he told her.

'Either you do that or you can work here as a cleaner.'

'Tell me that this is some sort of joke, Zak, and that it is only for the week's trial,' she challenged, laughing uneasily.

Zak didn't answer.

'You will let me work as a croupier again quite soon?' she persisted.

Zak looked at his watch impatiently. 'That's all I'm offering you, Sheryl. Are you starting work or not?'

Her spirits sank. She wanted to refuse, to turn and walk out, but she realised that she dared not do that. She'd sunk so low in the last few months that her self-respect was at rock bottom. She had no confidence in herself. If she turned down what he was offering, she wasn't at all sure that she'd stand a chance of finding work anywhere else.

Walking into the bar ten minutes later, she felt as if she was choking with resentment. She needed a drink, a really strong vodka and tonic would do the trick, she decided.

Her resolution to stop drinking melted like an ice-cream cornet in the sun. Only this one, she vowed, as she helped herself to a vodka. She needed the boost it would give her to help her cope with the embarrassment that lay ahead. She would have to face up to some stinging wisecracks from many of the regulars, as well as the usual backchat and jibes from the other members of staff.

By the time the evening ended her legs ached and she was so tired she could have fallen asleep on her feet. She had only been kept going by constant sneaky top-ups from the vodka bottle.

She fell into bed feeling angry and defeated. The sort of money she would earn as a waitress was meagre, even with tips. It meant that it would be years, not months, before she could save enough to make a new life for herself and Caitlin.

As long as she had to work in the club's bar, she knew that she would never be able to resist drinking. And why should she try? After all, it was the only consolation she had. What was more, it needn't cost her anything if she went about it the right way.

She laughed to herself. Sneaking nips of vodka was only one way in which she intended to cheat Zakaraki and get even with him for the way he was treating her. She'd make him pay dearly for this.

Chapter Twenty-Eight

Caitlin felt too excited to go to sleep when she went up to bed on Christmas Eve. She'd protested that she wasn't tired, but Nana Nola kept telling her that if she didn't get up to bed and go to sleep she wouldn't get a visit from Father Christmas.

She'd listened to the other children at her new school as they talked about him, even though she was pretty sure that there was no such person. He'd certainly never paid her a visit when she'd been living with her mam. To be on the safe side, though, she decided not to argue with her grandparents, because they seemed to believe in him. Perhaps things were different in Ely and maybe it was the sort of place where he did visit.

She didn't really mind going to bed, because so many wonderful things had happened recently that she wanted to be on her own so that she could think about them all over again.

On the last day at school, before they'd broken up for Christmas, they'd made long paper chains with strips of brightly coloured paper. They'd looked lovely pinned up on the classroom walls. When she'd come home and told Granddad Cradog all about them he'd helped her to make some more, and they'd hung them right across the living-room ceiling.

Afterwards she'd helped him to stick pieces of holly covered in bright red berries behind all the pictures, to make the room look even more Christmassy.

All day Nana Nola had been cooking, baking and planning all sorts of wonderful things for Christmas, so the house was full of lovely cooking smells. She could still get a whiff of them now, even though she was in bed.

Nana Nola had let her help to grease the baking tins and spoon in the filling for the mince pies. She'd also run messages, going with a list to the corner shop for things Nana Nola had run short of or forgotten to buy.

There were all sort of mysterious parcels hidden away at the top of cupboards, so high up that they were out of her reach. She kept wondering what was in them and if perhaps one of them might be something special for her.

She couldn't remember having any presents since her dad had died, not until the day Nana Nola had come to Loudon Place and had brought her the bright pink jumper. She had worn it nearly every day since then, and Nana Nola had bought her a grey pleated skirt to wear with it.

Nana Nola had also borrowed money from the tallyman to buy her some new shoes. Black lace-up ones, and some knee-high grey socks to keep her legs warm now the weather was so cold. As soon as they were paid for she'd fitted her out with a raincoat that had a thick lining inside it to keep out the cold.

She kept asking if her mam would be coming to see her at Christmas and her nana said she thought so, but she didn't know for certain.

She'd only seen her mam once since she'd come to stay with Nana Nola. She kept sending postcards promising to visit them, but she never turned up because either she was too busy working or she wasn't feeling well and it was a long way to come.

Caitlin knew all about her mam not feeling very well. She'd been like that a lot of the time when she'd been living at home with her. Sometimes her mam had been feeling so sick, or had such a bad headache, that she'd still been in bed when it was time to leave for school in the morning.

Her mam was usually feeling better by the time she got home in the afternoon, though, and she would be sitting there having one of her special medicine drinks that always seemed to cure her.

Some of the children at school had said that what her mam suffered from was called hang-overs. They said it was because she drank too much booze, but Caitlin didn't think that was the only reason her mam was ill so much. She thought it was because her mam was sad because of what had happened to her dad.

Her mam had never told her anything about it, but the kids at school had. They'd teased her for ages because they claimed that her dad was a murderer. They said he'd stabbed a policeman to death and that was why he'd been taken away to jail and why he'd killed himself.

She didn't believe them, but she couldn't find anyone to tell her the real story about what had happened and why her dad was dead.

When she'd asked her teacher if she knew what had happened, Miss Gibson had gone red in the face and said she should ask her mother to tell her all about it. Every time she tried to do that, her mam had clammed up and said she had one of her headaches.

Caitlin was glad she was now going to a different school. None of her new classmates knew anything about what had happened, so they didn't ask questions or tease her about her dad. They didn't ask about her mother, either. In fact, none of them said very much at all to her.

She wasn't included in any of their gangs, so she played on her own most of the time. Sometimes it was a bit lonely, but it was better than being teased. She didn't get into any trouble, either.

At her old school she'd always been in trouble. Usually it was because the others dared her to do stupid things. She'd had to do them to stop them teasing her or saying horrible things about her mam.

She hoped that if her mam did come to see them on Christmas Day, she wouldn't have to go back to Loudon Place with her. She liked it here. Nana Nola cooked lovely meals. She even made a bowl of porridge for her each morning before she went to school. It was delicious because she sprinkled sugar on it, and then made a hole in the middle and poured in the cream off the top of the milk until it covered it all over.

'You must have a good hot breakfast inside you when the weather is cold and frosty,' Nana Nola declared. 'Porridge is best because it sticks to your ribs and keeps you warm all day.'

Nana Nola also insisted on her taking a lunch box with a jam butty and a chunk of bara brith or a couple of bakestones to eat at midday. Sometimes she'd also put in some raisins wrapped up in a screw of paper, an apple, or even a couple of toffees, to finish off her lunch.

There was another hot meal when she got home at night. They had to wait for that until Granddad Cradog arrived home from work, but she didn't mind. If she was very hungry there was always a Welsh cake or a piece of home-made gingerbread to chew on.

She'd grown a lot since she'd been living with Nana Nola, and she'd got tubbier. Even her new skirt was getting quite tight around the waist.

Caitlin's eyes grew heavy as she thought about all this. Although she tried hard to keep awake, because there were still so many other things she wanted to think about, sleep claimed her.

When she woke next morning she had to pinch herself to make sure she wasn't still dreaming, because the sock that Granddad Cradog had said she must hang up for Father Christmas to fill was now bulging with presents at the bottom of her bed.

She'd heard some of the kids at school talking about Father Christmas, but she wasn't sure it was true. She thought you had to have both a mam and dad and to be living with them for him to come.

She hadn't even dared to think about it happening because it never had before when she'd been living in Loudon Place, even when she had both a mam and dad, so why should he come now, she asked herself.

He had, though! There was the sock, hanging from the brass rail at the bottom of her bedstead.

She scrabbled down the bed, almost afraid to touch it in case it wasn't real. Excitedly she grabbed hold of it and then ran her hands over it, trying to guess what the contents might be.

Full of wonder she took them out one by one, her amazement mounting as she did so.

She spread everything around her as she sat on the bed. There was a pair of red woollen gloves and a matching red woollen hat, a bar of chocolate, a colouring book, some coloured pencils, and another book full of pictures that

322

changed colour when you painted them with water. Tucked right down in the toe was an apple, an orange, a couple of toffees and a shiny new penny.

She made patterns on the bed with them, arranging them first in a circle and then in a square. Tempted by the toffees, she unwrapped one of them and popped it in her mouth. Then she pulled on the red hat and gloves and marvelled at how lovely and warm they were.

With a deep sigh she debated whether to eat the remaining toffee or have a piece of the chocolate. It was a hard decision, but in the end she couldn't resist the chocolate. She took off her new gloves first, in case she made them messy.

After that she couldn't sleep. As quietly as possible she dressed and crept downstairs. To her surprise Nana Nola was already in the kitchen.

'You're up early,' Nola greeted her. 'Happy Christmas, cariad.'

'Happy Christmas, Nana. He did come,' she said shyly as she kissed her grandmother on the cheek.

Nana Nola looked puzzled.

'Father Christmas! The sock that I'd hung on the bottom of my bed last night was full of presents this morning!'

'There's lucky you are, cariad. Anything nice in it then?'

Caitlin listed all the things she'd found in her

stocking, counting them off on her fingers as she did so.

'I've eaten one of the toffees and a piece of the chocolate bar,' she confessed.

'Well, I expect that was what they were there for,' her nana smiled. 'Now, if you sit up at the table I'll get you some breakfast. Seeing it's Christmas Day it's something special, a poached egg on toast, now what do you say to that?'

Caitlin's eyes widened and sparkled. 'That sounds really lovely because it's one of my favourites,' she grinned happily.

The rest of the day was packed with surprises. There seemed to be visitors arriving all the time. Apart from friends and neighbours who popped in to wish the Powells a happy Christmas, there were her grandparents' sons and daughters. She was told they were her aunts and uncles and that all their children were her cousins. She'd never met any of them before, she hadn't even known that her dad had any brothers and sisters, so she found it all rather overwhelming. She felt sad that her own mam wasn't able to be there with them as well.

So many of the visitors brought her a present that by the end of the day she had a *Schoolgirl's Own* annual, a box of beads to thread, two more sets of coloured pencils, a card game called Happy Families, two jigsaws, and a box of dominoes.

They were all wonderful, but the most

marvellous present she received all day was from Nana Nola. It was a lovely red plaid skirt and a bright red jumper that matched it perfectly. Nana Nola had given them to her right after breakfast and told her to go upstairs and put them on.

When she'd come back downstairs Granddad Cradog had told her she looked really lovely, and then he'd given her another present which he said was also from him and Nana Nola.

She'd felt overwhelmed with happiness when she unwrapped a big fat cuddly teddy bear that had soft golden fur, and shiny black button eyes.

'I know you are a bit old to be having a teddy bear,' Nana Nola told her, 'but I don't suppose you've ever had one before and something to cuddle up to in bed at night is comforting, no matter what age you are.'

Christmas dinner was a tremendous feast. They sat down to roast chicken with roast potatoes, roast parsnips and peas for their main course. To follow there was the steaming Christmas pudding that she'd been looking forward to so much. She'd been allowed to stir it when Nana Nola had been making it, and she'd made a wish while she was doing so. Now she was wondering if her wish would come true.

Granddad Cradog insisted on pouring some brandy, that Nana Nola had given him as his Christmas present, over the top of it. Then they'd all watched with bated breath as he'd struck a match and set light to it. A vivid blue flame had swirled around the top of the pudding and then disappeared so quickly that Caitlin wondered if she'd imagined it.

At tea-time there had been a special cake with white icing all over the top and sides, and a little red robin perched on a wooden log sitting on top. It was so pretty that it had seemed a shame to cut into it. There had also been the mince pies which she'd helped to make.

Caitlin ate so much that she felt she was absolutely bursting. She'd never known such a wonderful day. The only disappointment was that her own mam hadn't turned up. There'd been so many people coming and going all day, though, that it was bedtime before she realised that she still hadn't appeared.

She wasn't going to mention anything about her mam not being there, but Nana Nola did. She had plenty to say and seemed quite annoyed about it. Even when Caitlin told her that probably the reason why her mam hadn't come was she wasn't feeling well because she'd woken up with one of her bad headaches, Nana Nola still went on ranting.

'Yes, too much to drink and so she had a hangover in all probability,' Nana Nola said crossly. 'Still, never mind, cariad, you've had a nice Christmas, haven't you?'

'The most wonderful Christmas ever,' Caitlin told her enthusiastically, and hugged her so hard that Nana Nola said she was choking her to death.

'My mam will come and visit us tomorrow,' Caitlin told her grandparents confidently as she kissed them both goodnight.

Clutching her new teddy bear she went off upstairs to bed, hoping that she was right and that the wish she'd made when she'd stirred the Christmas pudding really would come true.

Chapter Twenty-Nine

Sheryl staggered up the stairs to her rooms, holding on tightly to the banister rail because everything was spinning around her like crazy. Her head was pounding, her feet and legs ached and all she wanted to do was fall into bed – after she'd had another stiff drink.

It had been the busiest night she could ever remember. There'd been people still in the club, drinking and playing at the gaming tables, long after the place was officially closed.

You'd think the buggers had no homes to go to, she thought sourly, as she reached for the vodka bottle and raised it to her lips.

As the neat slug hit the back of her throat she coughed and choked. Then she took another long swig and swirled it round her mouth before swallowing it more slowly.

Recapping the bottle, she pushed it away out of reach. She really had meant to give up drinking, but now she was relying on it more than ever.

The new life she'd planned was as far away as it had always been. The money she'd intended to save for a new start amounted to only a few measly quid.

It was all Zak's fault, she told herself. He'd vowed not to let her work as a croupier ever again and he'd stuck to it. No matter how much she hinted, pestered, or pleaded he still remained adamant that he would only employ her as a waitress – or worse, as a cleaner.

She'd tried looking for some other kind of work away from the club, but she wasn't qualified to do anything else. When she'd applied at some of the stores in the city centre, and said that she'd had experience of serving in a shop, she'd been informed they wanted younger girls.

'Younger! I'm only in my twenties!' she'd told them angrily.

Time and again she was told that she wasn't what they were looking for, and she only had to look in the mirror to see why they said that. She not only looked older than she was, but her face was puffy and raddled and her eyes bloodshot because of her excessive drinking.

Since Zak insisted she had to work as a waitress, she'd paid him back by making free with his vodka. She was pretty sure he knew, but he never said anything about it. It was almost as if he enjoyed seeing her become a soak, drowning her sorrows night after night. One day he'd even taunted her about the way she was going downhill.

She was sure that she was underpaid, but she knew it was no good complaining and that she should be grateful that he employed her at all. Nevertheless, she'd asked for more money, saying that she couldn't even afford to send Alun's mother any money for Caitlin's keep, let alone buy Caitlin any presents to make up for being separated. He hadn't given her a rise, but he'd hinted that he could offer her a money-making opportunity if she was interested.

'You mean back on the tables, working as a croupier again?' she'd asked eagerly.

He'd laughed derisively, quashing her last shred of hope.

'Take a look in the mirror and you'll see that you're not suitable for a job like that – not now! There are other services you could offer, though, that some of our customers might be interested in.'

The leer on his dark face as he said this had told her what he had in mind. He didn't need to put it into words.

She'd turned away, filled with a mixture of self-loathing and anger towards him. Had she really sunk so low that he felt she was that desperate?

In the days that followed, Sheryl found herself drinking more heavily than ever, trying to blot out Zak's unpleasant insinuations. Being on her own didn't help. She was missing Caitlin. Apart from there being no-one to run errands, if her daughter was around she'd have to keep a rein on her drinking, she kept telling herself.

She really had meant to go over to Ely on Christmas Day to see Caitlin. She was concerned about her and wanted to make sure she was still happy living with Nola and Cradog. Christmas Eve had been such a heavy night, though, that she hadn't wakened until after four o'clock the following afternoon.

Her head had been aching so much that she thought it was going to split in two. She'd staggered into the kitchen to find the vodka and drained what was left straight from the bottle.

As the spirit burned its way down her throat she'd found that, far from clearing her head, it made her feel even more woozy.

She started to get dressed, but the room was spinning round and the effort had been too much, so she'd gone back to bed.

She'd only meant to have a short rest, until the world stopped turning, but she had fallen asleep again. When she woke up it was Boxing Day and she had to pull herself together to get ready for work.

Zak had warned her that Boxing Day was going to be busy because most of the pubs were closed, so she knew that if she wanted to keep her job she'd better turn up on time.

Well, it was over now and there would be a lull for the rest of the week, until New Year's Eve, and then all hell would break loose. New Year's Day 1928 was on a Sunday, so people really would be living it up on the Saturday night.

She'd definitely go over to Ely to see Caitlin before then. If she wasn't up in time tomorrow morning, then the next day . . . or the next. It

331

was only the start of the week, so there was still plenty of time. She really would make a special effort to see her before the year ended, she vowed.

Now that Christmas was over, the shops would be open again and everything would be going cheap, so she'd get her a really nice present. She should have wrapped up something and sent it to her for Christmas, but she'd meant to go to Ely before then and pick up a present for her on the way.

Still trying to think what to buy for Caitlin, whether it should be something to play with or for her to wear, Sheryl fell asleep.

Next day she felt so tired that when she finally pushed the covers back and looked out of the window, everywhere was so dull and grey that she went back to bed again. After that she dozed fitfully until it was so late that she barely had time to get ready to start her midday shift.

When she put in an appearance she found the place was in a complete shambles. Zak was running round like a headless chicken. She'd never seen him so disconcerted and worked up.

'Ah, here you are, at last,' he rasped impatiently. 'For some reason Annie hasn't turned up so you'd better find a dustpan and brush and make a start on getting this mess cleared up,' he growled, waving his arms around.

'Me?' She raised her eyebrows, disparagingly. 'I'm not a cleaner . . .'

'No, Sheryl, you're a third-rate waitress who drinks my vodka by the bottleful and never pays a penny piece for it,' he snarled.

'What's that got to do with it?' Sheryl blustered, facing him defiantly, her hands on her hips as though ready for a fight.

Zak came closer, his eyes narrowing as he took a deep breath and glared at her. 'It means if you want me to take no action about all the vodka you've been stealing from me, you'd better put your back into helping to get this place cleaned up before the first customers come in through that door.'

'And if I don't?'

Her voice wavered as she saw the fury on his face. With a noisy sigh she began to clear the tables, prior to turning the chairs upside down on top of them so that she could clean the floor.

'If you want the place ready in time then you'd better give me a hand,' she told him. 'And the barman and anyone else who's here,' she added with a scowl.

She'd always vowed that no matter what happened she would never do the cleaning in the Diawl Coch, but Zak had won.

It was a depressing thought and it put her in a bad humour for the rest of the day. She wondered who had told Zak about the nips of vodka she helped herself to when she was at work.

She kept away from the vodka bottle in the

bar for the rest of the day, in case Zak was still watching her. By the time evening came she was gasping for a drink. Several times she was sorely tempted because she knew she'd emptied her own bottle, so there would be none for her when she got back up to her rooms.

Without her regular stimulus Sheryl felt more tired than ever. To make matters worse, they were not very busy in the club, so the time passed very slowly.

Having to make do with a cup of tea when she'd finished work left Sheryl feeling even more depressed. She slept fitfully, her mind full of self-recrimination for all the things she'd said as well as all those she hadn't done.

She'd definitely go and see Caitlin the next day, she told herself. She'd set off the minute her midday shift was over. She had to change from the tram to a bus when she reached the city centre, so she would pick up a present for Caitlin before continuing her journey out to Ely.

There would be time to have a cuppa and a good long chat with Nola, and find out how things were going, before she had to come back for work. She supposed she ought to take a present of some sort for Nola and Cradog, seeing that it was Christmas-time. It would be a nice way of saying thank you to them for the way they were looking after Caitlin, since she hadn't contributed a penny piece towards her keep.

It was raining so hard on Tuesday, though,

that Sheryl decided she'd better put off her visit for another day. She didn't have an umbrella, or a mackintosh, so she'd be soaked to the skin even before she reached the tram if she ventured out.

As she was on the point of leaving the bar on Wednesday morning, Zak sent a message to say he wanted to see her in his office.

'I'm in a hurry,' she told him. 'I'm going to Ely to see my little girl, I haven't seen her all over Christmas.'

'That's a pity because I had a proposition to put to you, but if you haven't time to discuss it, then . . .' He shrugged expressively.

Sheryl hesitated, her hopes soaring, sure that he was about to tell her that at last she could have her old job back and be a croupier again.

He stood watching her without saying anything as she dithered, unsure about what to do.

Getting back on the tables was so important to her. The extra money would make all the difference to the sort of future she could provide for Caitlin. Another day wouldn't really matter, she told herself. She could go and see Caitlin tomorrow.

Smiling brightly, she gave in. 'So what is it that you have to tell me?' she asked eagerly.

Zak came round to her side of the desk and took one of her hands in his. 'You could be very attractive, you know, Sheryl,' he told her, touching her hair, stroking her cheek. 'You're far too

335

pretty to be working as a waitress – or a cleaner,' he added with a mocking laugh.

'So?'

'Do you remember I told you that I had some other kind of work in mind for you, something that would pay well so that you would be able to buy all those little extras for Caitlin?'

She nodded, her spirits rising. This was exactly what she wanted to hear. 'Go on!' she breathed.

He paused and his dark eyes raked her face. 'I don't want you letting me down . . .'

'I won't, I won't let you down, Zak, I promise you,' she interrupted. 'You'll be proud of me, all I want is the chance.'

He nodded gravely. 'Have you ever done anything like this before?'

She gave him a puzzled look, fearful of what he meant. 'You were the one who trained me to be a croupier!' she said brightly.

'I'm not talking about you working on the tables again,' he said coldly, dropping her hand and moving away. 'I thought I'd made it quite clear to you, Sheryl, that I would never let you have that sort of responsibility again.'

She felt hurt and deflated. 'So what is this other job that you have in mind, then?' she asked in a small tight voice.

He gave her a steely look. 'Are you quite sure you are interested?'

'Go on, I'm listening.'

He walked back to his own side of the desk

336

and sat down in his leather chair. 'How well do you know Stefano Polti?'

She frowned. 'Do you mean that big fat Maltese man who usually sits at the bar?'

Zak nodded.

'The groper! The man who can't keep his hands to himself. What about him? Has he been complaining because I slapped him one the other night when he was trying to paw me?'

'No, he hasn't complained. In fact, quite the opposite. Stefano Polti has taken a liking to you and he asked specially for you.'

The colour drained from Sheryl's face. 'What do you mean by that exactly?'

'Do I need to explain further?' He raised his heavy dark eyebrows. 'Stefano Polti has taken a particular liking to you, he wants to spend more time with you . . . alone.'

'Never! Not for all the tea in China!' Sheryl exclaimed angrily.

Zak gave a supercilious smile. 'We're not talking about tea, Sheryl. We're talking about money. You'd be good at entertaining him, I'm sure.'

'No, never!' She bit down hard on her lower lip to fight back her tears, horrified to think that Zak had this sort of opinion of her.

Zak stiffened. 'Stefano Polti is one of our best customers, Sheryl, so I won't be very happy about having to disappoint him.'

'I'm not prepared to sleep with anyone, him least of all,' she stated angrily.

'The money would be very good, and it would buy heaps of lovely presents for little Caitlin. You would even be able to afford to buy your own bottles of vodka instead of having to steal mine when you think no-one is looking!' he added as an afterthought.

She felt the hot blood rushing to her cheeks and knew she was blushing furiously. There was a look of despair in her eyes as she stared back at him. There was nothing she could say to defend herself.

He smiled grimly. 'I haven't reached any decision about what to do about that as yet. Of course, if you played your cards right, and showed Stefano Polti the sort of good time he wants, then I'm sure I could forget all about the stolen vodka.'

Chapter Thirty

Nola Powell could see that Caitlin wasn't very happy. She'd not said anything, or complained, but there was such a wistful look on her little face. It worried Nola that she was walking round clutching the teddy bear they'd given her for Christmas, burying her face in its soft fur pelt, and talking to it as if she was telling it some deep secrets.

It didn't take very much effort for her to work out that the reason Caitlin was unhappy was because her mother hadn't been to see her all over Christmas.

It was too bad of Sheryl to be so thoughtless, Nola thought angrily. She hadn't even sent the child a Christmas present. What could the woman be thinking about?

If only Alun was still alive. Nola felt sure he would have shown little Caitlin more love than Sheryl did.

She still found it hard to think about Alun. She couldn't credit all the awful things that had happened to him. It was like a bad dream. She blamed it all on the fact that he hadn't followed in his dad's footsteps and gone to work down the pit when he'd left school, like the rest of the men in the family had done.

He claimed he'd been trying to better himself when he'd insisted on joining the army, but he hadn't even seen that through, she thought sadly. He might have done, of course, and made a proper career out of being a soldier, if he hadn't met up with Sheryl when he was stationed at Maindy Barracks.

Nola sighed. Putting Sheryl in the family way, and her barely seventeen at the time, had put the kibosh on everything for Alun. It had completely blighted his entire future.

He'd done the right thing by her, of course. He'd married her before the baby was born and tried to make a home for her. Life in the army hadn't prepared him for the ways of the world, though. Once he'd left the army and there'd been no-one to guide him, or discipline him in the way he'd grown accustomed to, he didn't seem to be able to handle things on his own.

Moving down to Tiger Bay had been his final downfall; there was no doubt about that. Working in that awful club had set him on a downward path. It wasn't called Diawl Coch – the Red Devil – for nothing! Heaven alone knew what went on there with an owner called Zakaraki. She'd never heard a name like that before in her entire life.

She still didn't know the truth about what had gone wrong between Alun and Sheryl, or what she had said or done to arouse him to such a state of mad jealousy. From what she'd read in the newspapers no-one seemed to know if he had meant to knife the policeman, or whether it had been a terrible accident. The case had never come to court, there had never been a trial, so the real truth was never made public. Alun's suicide had caused her to feel an even deeper sense of shame, because in her eyes it was a coward's way out.

Poor boyo! He must have been in absolute torment to take his own life, though, Nola thought sadly.

Perhaps it had all been Sheryl's fault. If Sheryl didn't care enough about young Caitlin to visit her, or bring her a Christmas present, then what sort of feelings had she had for Alun?

Nola sighed. There was definitely something wrong with Sheryl, she reflected. Even her own mam and dad would have nothing to do with her these days. Now what on earth did that say about the sort of person she was?

Nola whipped off her apron. Her mind was made up. She didn't have to stand for any of this. She wasn't going to put up with seeing the youngster with a face as long as a fiddle for one more minute.

'Caitlin,' she called, 'come along, my lovely, get your hat and coat on as quickly as you can, we're going out.'

'Can I wear my new red hat and gloves?' Caitlin asked excitedly.

'Of course you can, cariad.'

'With my new red jumper and plaid skirt and my nice warm raincoat on top I'll look really smart. Where are we going?'

'You'll see, my lovely, all in good time,' Nola told her as she bustled around, putting on her own warm winter coat, a fur cloche hat that she pulled well down over her ears, and her brown fur gloves.

Nola made a quick tour of the house to make sure that all the windows were shut, that the fire was banked up, and that all the taps were turned off. Then she picked up her black leather handbag, checked that her purse, keys and a clean handkerchief were in it, and moved towards the front door.

'Come on then, are you ready or not, Caitlin?'

Caitlin hesitated. 'Can I bring my teddy with me, please Nana?'

Nola frowned uncertainly. Caitlin was almost seven, far too old for cuddly toys of that sort, but the child was looking at her so pleadingly that she hadn't the heart to refuse.

'All right, as long as you don't get tired of carrying it,' she told her. 'We're going on the bus and then on the tram . . .'

'Are we going into town to the shops, Nana Nola?' Caitlin asked eagerly.

'You'll have to wait and see, won't you,' her grandmother told her.

When they reached the city centre they didn't stop even to look at any of the shop windows, but caught a tram. The moment it started to go down Bute Street, Caitlin recognised where she was.

'We're visiting my mam, aren't we?' she exclaimed, her face wreathed in smiles.

When they got off the tram at the top of Loudon Place, Caitlin skipped along at Nola's side in tremendous spirits. She kept jabbering away to her teddy, telling it all about where they were going.

As they walked up the steps to Sheryl's rooms, Nola wondered if she'd done the right thing in bringing Caitlin back here. Supposing she didn't want to return to Ely afterwards? Or, even worse, supposing Sheryl tried to persuade Caitlin to stay with her?

She squared her shoulders and knocked on the door. When there was no answer she felt a sense of relief. She'd become so attached to the lovable little girl that she knew she'd be heart-broken if she lost her company.

'Dear oh dear, cariad, it looks as though your mam is out. There's silly I've been not letting her know we were coming.'

'She's probably asleep,' Caitlin said. 'She often has a nap in the afternoon because she has to go to work again in the evening.'

'You mean she goes out at night and leaves you on your own?' Nola said in a shocked voice.

Caitlin shrugged. 'She only started doing it lately, and she didn't go out until I was in bed and she knew I was asleep.'

'If your mam didn't go to work until after

you were asleep, how do you know that she went out at all in the evenings?'

Caitlin giggled. 'I used to shut my eyes tight and pretend I was asleep because I knew my mam didn't like being late for work because it made Mr Zak very cross.'

Nola banged hard on the door once more. 'Well, it doesn't look as though she's here now. We'll have to come back another day.'

'We could wait a few minutes longer, she's probably only popped out to one of the shops to buy groceries or something.'

'It's too cold to wait out here on the stairs, cariad, we'd catch a chill. Anyway, there's nowhere to even sit down.'

'We could always go inside, I know where the spare key is hidden.'

Before Nola could stop her, Caitlin had thrust the teddy bear into Nola's hands and dashed off to a turn in the stairs. Kneeling and sliding her hand down behind a loose piece of skirting board, she fished around and then scrambled to her feet waving a key.

'Come on, Nana Nola,' she called gleefully as she slipped it in the keyhole and opened the door.

As Nola followed her into the room a blast of fetid air greeted them. Nola looked around in disgust at the dirt and muddle everywhere. Ashes spilled out of the grate onto the lino in a grey mound, the table was laden with dirty dishes, and the floor was covered in crumbs.

344

'Shall I go and see if Mam's still in bed?' Caitlin asked her.

A moment later Nola heard Sheryl's voice mingling with Caitlin's. When she came into the room, Nola drew her breath in sharply. It was a few months since she'd seen her, and Sheryl now looked as if she'd been ill. She'd lost weight, she looked drawn and haggard, as though she had the troubles of the world on her shoulders.

Nola didn't expect her to look contented and smiling, it was too soon after Alun's death for that, but she didn't expect her to look so ill either. Even her skin looked grey. Something was troubling her, something was radically wrong.

'I was coming to see you one day this week,' Sheryl told them. 'I couldn't make it over Christmas because I was working, and yesterday it was raining so hard I decided to put it off.'

'Well, we're here now, so it will save you having to make the journey, won't it,' Nola told her crisply.

'Have you got time to drink a cuppa then?' Sheryl asked.

'I'm absolutely dying for one. Shall I make it while you go and get some clothes on and comb your hair?' Nola suggested.

'No, I'll see to the tea. I'll have to wash up a couple of cups first, see,' she explained with a tight little laugh.

345

'I thought that might be the case,' Nola commented. She peeled off her winter coat and placed it across the back of one of the chairs. 'Go on, I'll wash them up while you go and get dressed, cariad, and then we'll have a good chat.'

For the first five minutes or so, Caitlin dominated the conversation, telling her mother about all the things that had happened on Christmas Day, and describing all the presents she'd received.

'Your comics are still in the bedroom if you want to go and look at them,' Sheryl told her.

As soon as they were on their own she turned to Nola. 'Quickly, while Caitlin isn't here. She seems to be very happy so can she stay with you for a bit longer?'

Nola raised her eyebrows. There was nothing she wanted more, but she couldn't understand how Sheryl could bear to be separated from the little girl. 'Well, I suppose she can, but . . .'

'Please, Nola. It won't be for long. I'm working all the hours God sends to try to get some money together. With Caitlin not here I can work every evening, see.'

'She told me you went to work in the evenings anyway,' Nola remarked.

'She did? Well, she certainly wasn't supposed to know about that. I always waited until she was in bed and fast asleep, and then it was only for an hour or so.'

'She only pretended to be asleep. She told me she shut her eyes tight because she knew you don't like being late.'

'Now that she's staying with you I put in a full evening every night,' Sheryl told her. 'That way I almost double what I can earn. I think I'm going to be able to do even better. Zak's offered me the chance of a job that pays more money, but I can't do it if I have Caitlin here and have to look after her.'

Nola looked at her quizzically. 'Oh yes, and what sort of job is this then?'

Sheryl hesitated, chewing on her lower lip. 'I haven't been given all the details yet, but he's promised me that I will be earning a lot more money.'

'If that Zakaraki is asking you to do what I think he is, then I suppose you will be earning more money than you could ever hope to make by doing an honest day's work,' Nola said tartly. 'You watch your step, though, cariad. You can get yourself into a whole lot of trouble that way,' she warned.

Sheryl felt concerned about what Nola might be thinking. Perhaps she should tell her that it was peddling drugs, she thought worriedly. In Nola's eyes that would be bad enough, but not anywhere near as terrible as selling her body.

'So Caitlin can stay on at your place for a bit longer then?' she asked, bringing the conversation back to the problem uppermost in her mind.

347

Nola pursed her lips. 'I can see why you don't want her here,' she said acidly. 'It's not at all a suitable place for a child like her. She takes too much notice of what is going on!'

'So she can stay with you for a bit longer?' Sheryl persisted.

'What are you two talking about? What are you saying about me?' Caitlin asked, coming back into the room and looking from her mother to her grandmother enquiringly.

'Perhaps you'd better ask her yourself, Sheryl,' Nola suggested.

'Ask me what?'

'We were wondering if you wanted to stay with Nana Nola for a little bit longer, cariad?' Sheryl said.

'Yes, please,' Caitlin beamed. 'I like it in Ely and I like my new school. Nana Nola cooks lovely meals every day. Why don't you come and live there as well, Mam, then we'd all be together?'

Chapter Thirty-One

Sheryl sobbed her heart out the minute Nola and Caitlin left Loudon Place. She cried because Caitlin had seemed so eager to go with her grandmother and she cried because she felt such a failure as a mother. She was frightened about what was happening to her and fearful about what the future might hold.

She had sensed Caitlin's hesitation when she'd come through the bedroom door, and for a moment she'd been afraid that her daughter wasn't going to hug her or even give her a kiss.

She sensed that Nola was shocked at the state of the place. She wondered what Nola would have thought if she'd seen it before she'd done her best to clean it up.

Nola's warning to be careful, the moment she'd said that Zak had offered her a job that would bring her in more money, had made her uneasy. She was afraid from the shrewd look her mother-in-law had given her that she'd suspected what was afoot, and what sort of work Zak had in mind.

The more Sheryl thought about it, the more reluctant she was to go along with Zakaraki's plans. For one thing, she hated Stefano Polti.

349

She found him extremely repulsive in every way. His looks, his manner, his lustful eyes and his foul drink-laden breath sent shudders through her.

She washed her face and began to get ready to go to the club. As she applied fresh make-up she studied her looks carefully. Megan's words from long long ago, when they had been getting dolled up to go to a dance at Maindy Barracks, came back into her mind.

'My mam says you're too pretty for your own good!' Megan had told her, and her voice had been laced with envy. Now Sheryl was the one who envied Megan, so perhaps Mrs Thomas had been right and she should have heeded the warning behind her compliment.

Before Megan married Owen Pryce, she'd tried to make a worthwhile career for herself by training to become a nurse, someone who was respected and held in high regard. In Sheryl's case, for all her good looks, she was now nothing better than a tart working in a third-rate club. What was more, she was living in the most notorious area in Cardiff, probably in the world, she thought despondently.

She went to the cupboard and delved into a shoebox that she'd tucked away at the very back, and brought out the leather purse she kept secreted there.

Sitting on the edge of the bed, she tipped out the contents and counted it over. She checked it three times, unable to believe that there was so little in there. Only ten pounds in notes and less than two pounds in silver and copper. At this rate Caitlin would have left school and be earning her own living before she'd saved up enough for them to move, she thought dejectedly.

She flopped back on the bed and covered her eyes with her hands, screening out the light, shutting out the world, trying to think what she must do.

She had to get away from Tiger Bay for Caitlin's sake, she'd be seven years old in less than two weeks. She was glad that Nola had taken Caitlin back to Ely with her. It was obvious that living in better surroundings was doing her good, she looked twice the child she had been. She'd grown a couple of inches and she'd filled out nicely. She looked more like a girl of her age should, not a half-starved little waif.

Nola had been good to Caitlin, there was no doubt about that. New clothes, sensible shoes, slides in her hair, she looked a treat.

I should have been the one doing those things for her, Sheryl thought uncomfortably. Instead I let her run wild, neglected her, and didn't even cook her proper meals.

She wished that falling in with Zak's immoral suggestion wasn't the only way she could earn enough money to move out of Tiger Bay and become a proper mother to Caitlin.

She didn't mind a spot of flirting when she was working in the club, in fact she quite enjoyed it. When it came to saucy repartee she could give as good as she got. She'd even let the customers go as far as pinching her bum or stealing the odd kiss, but that was the absolute limit. That really was as far as she was prepared to go.

When she went down to the club her mind was still in turmoil about what she was going to say to Zakaraki. If she turned his idea down flat he might be so angry that he'd sack her on the spot. Her only hope was to keep him guessing, play along, let him think she had agreed to his suggestion. Hopefully, before it was time to fulfil any promise he had made to Stefano Polti, she'd be able to find a way out of it.

Keeping Zak guessing might be possible, but would it be so easy to do that with Polti?

As she carried round the trays of drinks that night, Sheryl kept a wary eye out for the man she loathed. Greatly to her relief he didn't come in.

Zak was there, watching her like a hawk, but he didn't say a word to her about what he had proposed.

The same thing happened the following night. She even began to wonder if Zak had accepted that she wasn't prepared to accede to his suggestion, and had dropped the idea.

When he sent for her on the Friday she was so tense as she walked into his office that her chest felt tight and painful. She could hardly breathe.

'We are bound to be exceptionally busy tomorrow night with it being New Year's Eve,' he warned her, 'so you may be working very late indeed. Are you going to be able to manage that?'

She shrugged. 'Yes, I suppose so.'

'You might not be able to get away until the small hours of the morning. Aren't you concerned about having to leave Caitlin on her own for such a long time?'

'She's still out at Ely with her grandmother.'

'Aah!' He looked so pleased that for a moment Sheryl wondered what he was going to say next. She was taken aback when he smiled and then handed her a twenty-pound note.

'What's this, my wages in advance for the next month to make sure I turn up?' she asked sarcastically.

'No, I know I can trust you to do that. The money is so that you can go and buy yourself a really glamorous new dress for tomorrow evening. New Year's Eve is a special occasion, you know. You ought to mark it in some way. 1928 could be your best year ever.'

The subtle implication in his words was all too clear, but she pretended not to notice. She fingered the note, wondering whether to hand it back, then, smiling to herself, decided to take it. If she shopped carefully, what was left over would make a handsome addition to her savings.

'Go and look for your dress tomorrow and don't worry about coming in for the morning shift,' Zak told her.

'Won't that leave you short-handed?'

'We'll manage. Take your time, have your hair done as well. Perhaps you should try wearing it differently, something a bit more sophisticated. I've told you before that you've got the looks, Sheryl, so make the best of them.'

She didn't bother setting her alarm clock when she went to bed, confident that the thought of going on a spending spree would be enough to ensure she was up early.

Since Zak hadn't stipulated that she had to buy a black dress, like she usually wore, she looked for something more colourful. She intended to spend as little as possible, but since it was sale time at all the big stores she went to David Morgan's and Howell's to see if she could find any bargains there, rather than the open market at the Hayes.

Spoilt for choice, she tried on half a dozen lovely dresses. In the end she decided that the one she liked best was in bright red silk with a low draped neckline. It fitted her perfectly. When she ran her hands over her body in a gesture of sensual pleasure, the dress felt as smooth as a second skin.

Remembering Zak's suggestion about changing her hairstyle, she toyed with the idea of having it cut short with a Marcel wave. Then as she twirled in front of the full-length mirror in the dressing room, and saw the way her long hair spread out seductively around her shoulders as she moved, she decided she preferred it as it was.

The money she would have spent on her hair paid for a pair of bright red shoes with very high heels and some sheer silk stockings.

That night she took her time getting ready for work, paying special attention to her make-up. She'd bought a new lipstick, exactly the same shade of red as her dress, and having outlined her mouth with it she smiled triumphantly at the result.

She felt nervous as she walked into the club. She needed a drink, but she knew if she gave way and had one, she'd want another and yet another, so it was better not to have one at all.

When Zak walked over to greet her his eyes narrowed, and she wondered if he was going to tell her she should be wearing black as usual. Instead, he took both her hands in his and looked at her appraisingly.

'My, my. That was a good investment! In a dress like that you should be one of the clients, not a waitress,' he told her.

Her cheeks grew so hot she was sure they were as red as her dress. There was a challenge in his voice, but she didn't rise to it. The barman calling out to her to know if she was ready to take some drinks round saved her from having to answer Zak. With a cool smile she walked over to the bar.

355

Zak had warned they were going to be busy, but even so Sheryl had never seen the place so crowded. By midnight, when the ships' klaxons and the factory hooters started sounding, the entire club was bulging at the seams.

On the stroke of midnight, champagne corks popped like gunfire and Sheryl found that she couldn't dispense the glasses of foaming wine fast enough.

Zak stopped her as she was passing him, and before she could prevent it happening, kissed her on the mouth. The loaded tray she was carrying toppled precariously, but he steadied it.

'Happy New Year, Sheryl!' he murmured. 'You haven't forgotten that 1928 is to be the start of a new way of life for you, I hope!'

Trembling, she backed away from him and as she did so she noticed that Stefano Polti was standing nearby, watching them closely, a smug smirk on his swarthy fat face. She was shaking so much that she had to put the tray down. She felt engulfed by fear of both men. Picking up one of the glasses of champagne, she downed it and reached for another.

Realising that people were looking at her strangely, and that one or two were joking at her expense, she elbowed her way through the singing, cheering throng towards the door.

She needed air, she couldn't take any more. Suddenly the whole evening, as well as her entire life, was a mockery. All she wanted was to get away.

Wiping away her tears with the back of her hand, she headed out of the club and round the corner.

She heard footsteps behind her and someone calling her name, but she ignored them. She didn't want to talk to anyone, she wanted to be on her own.

She ran along the road towards the side door, but she kept tripping up in her treacherous high heels and she knew she was losing ground.

As she started up the stairs she sensed that she was still being followed. The steps behind her increased their pace, and she felt someone grabbing at her ankle. She tried to pull away, but the hand grasping her was like a vice.

She kicked out with her free foot and heard a grunt of pain as it made contact. The pressure on her leg relaxed and she managed to struggle free.

Sobbing noisily, sweat pouring down her spine, she raced for the top of the stairs and the safety of her rooms. Panting with terror, she found her key and tried to open the door, but her hand was shaking so much she couldn't put the key in the lock.

The footsteps had almost reached the top of the stairs and whoever it was would be on the landing alongside her at any minute. She looked over her shoulder and cold fear shivered through her when she saw it was Stefano Polti.

He came right up to her, his mouth twisted into a sneer. 'Teasing little bitch, aren't you?

Well, I've got you cornered now and you're not going to escape me.'

Her mind swam with ugly visions of what might happen next. 'Leave me alone, I don't want anything to do with you,' she said furiously.

'That's not what Zak promised,' he smirked. 'He said you were hot stuff! He also said that you'd show me a good time, so how about it? Let's get started, shall we?'

'Get away from me, don't you dare touch me!' she screamed, cowering back from him as he stretched out a hand towards her.

'Still playing hard to get?' he mocked thickly. 'That part of the game is over. Come on, let's go inside and find out what else you can do apart from kicking and yelling.'

He seized hold of her and his mouth came down over hers, his hot foul breath stifling her screams and practically choking her. At the same time his hands began roaming over her body, cruelly demanding. His breath quickened as his fat fingers pushed up underneath the silky skirt of her dress and made contact with her bare flesh.

Biting, kicking and fighting, Sheryl struggled to push him away. When her nails dug into his face and raked down his cheek he gave a muttered curse and flung her away from him.

Sheryl gasped with relief, but the next minute she felt herself falling. She screamed out, tried to grab at his clothing, but nothing could save her. She went hurtling backwards down the stairs and then came a nerve-jangling cracking noise as she landed on one arm and felt it crumple beneath her.

The pain was excruciating. She tried to move, but she couldn't. The last thing she remembered before she was enveloped in velvet darkness was Stefano Polti's huge face hovering above her.

Chapter Thirty-Two

It was late afternoon before Sheryl came round from the anaesthetic. For several minutes she lay perfectly still, staring up at the white ceiling above her head, then at the pristine white sheet tucked in around her and the blue-and-white check honeycomb cotton bedspread over the top.

Slowly it dawned on her that she must be in hospital, but she had no idea why she was there or when she had been brought in.

When a man's face moved into her line of vision fear flooded through her, receding as quickly as it had come.

This face wasn't swarthy, with fleshy lips and bullet-hard dark eyes. This was a thin kindly face, with anxious eyes, and a firm mouth and chin. The face was slightly wrinkled so he must be middle-aged, or perhaps even older, she reasoned.

Then she heard his voice and immediately recognised it. 'So you are awake at last, cariad,' he murmured softly.

'Dad!' she gasped. 'Is it really you?'

'Yes, cariad, it's me all right. Now tell me, my lovely, how are you feeling? Are you in any pain? Shall I call a nurse?'

'No!' She stretched out a hand to hold his. 'Why am I here?' she asked in a bewildered voice.

'You're in hospital, you've had an accident, my lovely.' He patted her hand consolingly.

It took her a moment to comprehend what he'd said. 'Accident, what happened?' she asked weakly.

He hesitated. 'We'll talk about it later, Sheryl. You need to rest now.'

'I'm terribly thirsty,' she whispered, moving her head from side to side.

'Lie still, cariad, I'll find someone to come and see to you,' he said quickly.

She heard him talking to a woman, but both of them were speaking so quietly that she couldn't hear what they were saying.

The next thing she knew was that a nurse was at the bedside holding a glass of water. 'Feeling thirsty, are we? Well, let's see if I can prop you up so that you can take a sip.'

Her strong arms raised Sheryl up in the bed a few inches and then she wedged a pillow under her neck. She held the glass to Sheryl's lips and encouraged her to drink. 'Take little sips, now. Drink it very slowly.'

As she tried to obey Sheryl felt the whole room begin to spin. When she tried to steady herself she found that she could only move one of her arms. The other one felt as heavy as lead.

'What's happened to me?' she gasped, as she saw that her right arm was encased in a stiff hard plaster cast that covered it from high above her elbow to the tips of her fingers.

'You had a fall and you've broken your arm and wrist,' the nurse told her briskly. 'Nothing to worry about. The surgeons have attended to it.'

'How long will it take to get better? When will I be able to use my hand and arm again?'

The nurse looked uncertain. 'Well, it will take some time, possibly six weeks or maybe a little longer.'

Sheryl stared at her in disbelief. 'How am I going to be able to work?' she asked in dismay.

'Don't worry about it now,' Gwynfor Williams told her quickly. 'We'll talk it over later and sort something out. What about Caitlin though, Sheryl? Wasn't she with you when it happened? Elwyn couldn't find her.'

'Elwyn?' She looked at him, puzzled. 'I haven't seen Elwyn for ages.'

'He found you, cariad, but he said that there was no sign of Caitlin.'

'She's staying out at Ely for a while with Nola Powell, Alun's mother.'

'Now I want you to take these and then you must rest and try and sleep,' the nurse instructed, bustling over and handing Sheryl two small white pills.

Sheryl nodded. When she'd swallowed the pills she held out her left hand to her father. 'Will you still be here when I wake up again?' she asked.

'Yes, my lovely. I'll be right here.'

'And Mam . . . where's Mam?'

He hesitated, a look of deep dismay on his wrinkled face.

'You need to sleep now, like the nurse told you to. We'll talk about it all when you wake up,' he said softly.

'No! I want to know now, Dad. Is she still so angry with me that she wouldn't come here with you?'

'No, my lovely girl! No, it's nothing like that. Your mam . . .' He shook his head as if searching for the right words. The hand holding hers tightened. 'Your mam . . . your mam is . . . she isn't with us any more, cariad.'

Sheryl stared at him in wide-eyed disbelief. 'You mean she's dead? When? How?' She struggled to sit up. 'Why wasn't I told?' she gasped, collapsing back on the pillow.

'She had a heart attack, almost a year ago, cariad.'

'Why didn't you let me know?' she asked reproachfully, her eyes filling with tears.

'I had no idea where to find you, cariad.'

'You could have asked the Thomases. Megan knew where I was living.'

He shook his head. 'Megan and Mrs Thomas wouldn't speak to us, not after the names your mam called her and the things she said about her. Your mam blamed Megan for so many things, see. For you marrying Alun in the first place.'

Sheryl looked bemused. 'It was nothing to do with Megan.'

'I know, I know!' He released his grip on her hand, fished in his pocket for his handkerchief and dabbed his face.

'It's a long story, my lovely. I'll tell you all about it when you've had a sleep and you're feeling stronger. Now you rest and try not to worry.'

Sheryl slept for more than twelve hours. There had been time for Gwynfor to go home, have a nap, change his clothes, eat some breakfast and come back to the hospital.

He was the first person Sheryl saw when she opened her eyes again. When she tried to sit up she found herself hampered by the cumbersome plaster. As she moved it impatiently an excruciating pain shot through her arm, and she let out an exclamation of distress.

A nurse came hurrying to her bedside, bringing more pills, but Sheryl shook her head.

At the moment her head was clear. She knew where she was, and before her senses were once again dulled by painkillers she wanted someone to tell her about the accident that had resulted in her being there, and, in addition, she needed to know about her mam.

She allowed the nurse to prop her up into a sitting position and gingerly moved her broken arm. For the first time she was able to see the exposed part of her hand, and she drew in her breath sharply when she saw the state it was in. Her fingers were such a dark blue that they looked almost black. They were so swollen that she couldn't move them at all.

It made her even more curious to know exactly what had happened. Since her father either didn't know, or didn't want to tell her, she asked the nurse.

'I understand you fell down a flight of stairs, so you must have put out your hand to break your fall,' the nurse told her.

'Have I hurt it very badly?' Sheryl asked worriedly.

'Well, you have some serious fractures. Both of the large bones in your arm as well as some of the smaller ones in your wrist.'

'So is that why my fingers are such a terrible colour and so swollen? Even the knuckles on my hand seem to be blown up. I hate to think what my arm must look like inside the plaster.'

The nurse nodded sympathetically. 'I'm afraid you will have a lot of pain for the next few days.'

'Will the bones in my arm mend properly?' Sheryl asked anxiously.

'They should do. The surgeon will be able to tell you more about it when he comes to see you tomorrow morning.'

Sheryl listened with growing bewilderment. 'How on earth could I have had a fall that did that much damage?'

'That's something we'd like to know.'

The nurse, Sheryl and her father all looked up in surprise. They had been so intent on Sheryl's injuries that they hadn't heard anyone approaching. Now they stared at the tall broad-shouldered policeman who was standing at the foot of her bed.

'Elwyn! What on earth are you doing here?' Sheryl asked.

'Checking the details of your accident. Can you tell me how it happened?'

'I don't remember very much at all about it,' she frowned.

In the last few minutes it had started to come back to her. Loudon Place, the Diawl Coch club and what Zakaraki had asked her to do. With her father sitting there, though, she didn't want to have to reveal any of that because she knew how much it would upset him. She needed a little time to think what to tell him, because everything was still so confused in her mind.

'There was some sort of rumpus in Loudon Square in the early hours of New Year's Day,' Elwyn told her. 'When I went along there with another officer to investigate, we found you lying in your doorway in Loudon Place.'

'You mean I'd fallen down the stairs.'

Elwyn Thomas frowned. 'Did you fall or were you pushed?'

The colour drained from Sheryl's face. She turned to the nurse. 'Could I have a drink of water, please?' she asked huskily.

366

'Yes, of course.' The nurse held a glass to Sheryl's lips and waited patiently while she took two or three tentative sips.

When she noticed that Sheryl was trembling, she insisted on checking her pulse. Frowning officiously, she told Elwyn sharply, 'I think you should leave now, Constable. Mrs Powell needs to rest.'

'Right, I understand.' He put away his notebook and picked up his helmet. 'I'll come back tomorrow. Will that be all right with you, Sheryl?'

She nodded and gave him a weak smile. All she wanted was to be on her own, so that she could sort out her thoughts and get her story right. It was all there in the back of her mind, but everything was so jumbled.

Now that she was reunited with her father she didn't want to lose him again. Knowing what an upright moral man he was, she dared not risk letting him know the sort of life she'd been living, or why Caitlin was with Nola.

There was also the added embarrassment that it was Elwyn who had been sent to question her. She wondered if it really was sheer chance, the same as it had been when he'd come to tell her about Alun committing suicide, or whether he had wanted to see her.

When her father stood up and said he would leave her to rest and that he'd come back in a couple of hours, Sheryl breathed a sigh of relief.

Left on her own, she closed her eyes to try

and recall everything that had happened on New Year's Eve.

She remembered Zakaraki giving her the money to go out and buy a new dress. She'd bought a gorgeous red silk one, and high-heeled red shoes to go with it. She'd spent ages getting herself all dolled up before she went to work at the club.

She'd suspected even then that Zak had encouraged her to dress up so that she would look attractive for Stefano Polti. Recalling what he expected her to do sent shivers through her. Tears stung her eyes. She had never had any intention of going through with it. Never, never, never! No matter what happened.

She knew it had been a hectic night and that she'd been dog-tired when she'd left the club shortly after midnight. Someone had followed her, and she was almost sure that it had been Stefano Polti.

After that things became less clear. She'd made a dash for her rooms, but whoever it was had overtaken her and grabbed hold of her as she went up the stairs.

The memory of hot fetid breath and wet lips covering hers, almost suffocating her, came flooding back. She could remember struggling, her fingers raking down her assailant's face . . . and then everything went blank.

That must have been when she fell down the stairs into a velvet-black darkness that had blotted everything out.

She'd woken up in hospital to find her father sitting by her bedside.

Would Elwyn be satisfied if she told him that, or would he try to probe deeper? Would he want details about what work she'd been doing in the club that night, and also want an explanation about why Caitlin wasn't living with her?

Tears streamed down her face as she realised what a mess she'd made of her life. She thought back to when she had been living at home, and Elwyn and Megan had lived in Coburn Street, with the back gardens between the two houses joined. In those days they had visited each other all the time, using the gate her dad had made in the dividing wall. Now those childhood days seemed a lifetime away.

If only she could turn the clock back, she thought wistfully, and once again be a young girl who hadn't a care in the world.

What was going to happen next? The nurse had said that in a few days, once the effects of the anaesthetic had worn off, she could leave hospital, but where could she go when they discharged her?

As long as her arm was in plaster she was going to need help to cope with everyday living. She certainly couldn't go back to Loudon Place. The only person she could think of who might take her in was Nola, but she already had enough to do with looking after Caitlin.

It had been such a shock finding her father

at her bedside. He was so much gentler than she remembered, as if he too had suffered.

She was saddened to hear that her mam had died. She hoped her heart attack hadn't been brought on by all the worry she'd caused them both. She hadn't known that her mother was in poor health, but thinking back she recalled the change in her after Caitlin had been born, while she'd been living at home waiting for Alun to find a place for them.

Her mother had seemed to lose patience with her, almost as if she resented her being there. At the time she'd thought it was because of the disruption a baby in the house caused, her mother being so house-proud.

She'd seemed a lot more understanding when she and Caitlin had moved back there later, after she'd broken her ribs, but it hadn't lasted.

Her father must find it very strange living alone and having to look after himself. Her mam had always pandered to him. Their home had been run like clockwork, meals always on time, his shirts perfectly ironed. His comfort took precedence over everything.

Now, he must be so desolate being on his own that she wondered if he'd like her to go back to Thesiger Street when she came out of hospital.

Chapter Thirty-Three

Sheryl found that waking up in her own single iron bed, back in her childhood bedroom, was both comforting and reassuring. So much so that she closed her eyes again and drifted into a wonderful blissful state midway between waking and sleeping.

It was three days since she'd come out of hospital, and her arm was still intensely painful. It was the difficulty she had doing simple things that she found the most irritating, though.

Her dad had been absolutely wonderful, taking care of her every need. To her amazement he was looking after himself extremely well. He had even taught himself to cook and seemed to take pleasure from preparing meals for her. She drew the line, though, at asking him to help her to get washed or dressed.

Finding herself back in Thesiger Street made her wish that she could wipe out the intervening years since she'd left there, and make a fresh start.

Her mam had probably been right, she reflected, marrying Alun had been a mistake. She had been far too young to know what she was doing, or realise the tremendous responsibility that having a child of her own was going to be.

She loved Caitlin dearly, but she knew instinctively that she had been a poor sort of mother. Nola Powell was looking after her far better than she had ever done.

When Nola had brought Caitlin to see her in Loudon Place she'd been amazed at not only how well the child looked, but that she seemed to be happier and more full of life than she'd ever been. She'd developed both physically and mentally, and seemed to be very grown-up for her age.

She'd noticed, too, how eager Caitlin had been to go back to Ely with her grandmother. There had been hardly any hesitation at all when they'd asked her.

As things turned out it had been just as well she had gone back with Nola. Heaven alone knows what would have happened to Caitlin if she'd been in bed asleep when I had my accident, Sheryl mused.

She'd had so much time to think back over the events of that night. Elwyn had called in to interrogate her again before she'd left the hospital, and he'd also come to Thesiger Street to clear up a couple of things that he said she hadn't made clear in her statement.

'I don't know why you are making such an issue about all this,' she told him. 'I didn't report it to the police and it's not as if I'm claiming damages from anyone, or anything like that.'

'It was an accident though, Sheryl, reported

to us by a member of the public, so we have to check the details.'

'Well, you're making a lot of fuss about nothing,' she told him dismissively.

'Are we?' His warm brown eyes had stared at her questioningly, as if trying to probe her mind. 'You see, I'm not sure that you've told me the whole story, Sheryl,' he added quietly.

She'd refused to be drawn or to say anything more, but she couldn't suppress the guilty flush of colour staining her cheeks.

'You will try to remember if there is anything else you can tell us?' he pressed, as he closed his notebook. 'I'll pop back again in a few days.'

'I've told you all there is to know, Elwyn,' she said firmly. She was reluctant for him to leave, though. He was not only a tangible link with her childhood days, but the warmth of his feeling for her came through even when he was on duty and behaving in a strictly professional manner.

She was curious to know more about what had happened to him in the intervening years. She didn't even know if he was married. He was so different to Alun, sensible and dependable. If she had never met Alun, then . . . She mentally pulled herself together – it wouldn't do to start hankering back that far.

She found the idea that Elwyn might have a wife and a family of his own quite disturbing, though. She stared at him as if seeing him for the first time. He was certainly very good-looking, with his thick dark hair and warm brown eyes. He was so tall and broad-shouldered that he looked an imposing figure in his dark blue uniform. She noticed that he now had three white stripes on his arm, which meant that he'd already been promoted to the rank of sergeant.

'I'll still come back again to see you in a few days . . . to see if your memory improves now that you are making such good progress,' Elwyn smiled. 'Of course, if you should remember anything else before then you can always send for me.'

She hoped that before he did come back she'd be able to go out and buy herself a new dress and one or two other things she needed. All her own clothes and belongings were still at Loudon Place. At the moment she was making do with clothes that had belonged to her mother. It made her feel uncomfortable to be wearing them, and they also made her look frumpy.

She'd wanted to ask Elwyn for news of Megan and her baby, but she hadn't managed to pluck up the courage to do so. After listening to her father's account of the row between her mam and Megan, and the things that had been said, and the names her mother had called Megan, it didn't seem very tactful to do so.

It also meant reviving the row that had erupted before she'd walked out on Megan only weeks after she'd had the baby. Sheryl felt ashamed of the way she'd behaved then, as she did about so many things she'd done in the past. No wonder she had no friends left . . . except possibly Elwyn.

She admired Elwyn, she always had, right from the time when they were all at school. He had been several classes higher than her, but she'd always looked for him when they were out in the yard at playtime. Whenever he'd seen her he'd always given her a wave and a smile.

There was even a time, when she'd been about fifteen, that she'd daydreamed about him becoming her regular boyfriend, because he'd taken her and Megan to the pictures a couple of times. Then he'd become a police cadet and seemed to spend all his time studying when he wasn't out with his mates.

It was about the same time that she and Megan had started going to the dances at Maindy Barracks. She'd become infatuated with Alun, so she'd given up on Elwyn.

It was because of Alun's jealousy about Elwyn that he'd ended up in jail, she thought sadly. She'd only been teasing when she'd told Alun that Elwyn had once been her boyfriend. She'd never expected him to become so enraged, or so eaten up with jealousy about it.

When she tried to tell him she'd only had a schoolgirl crush on Elwyn, nothing more, he'd refused to listen. His jealousy must have rankled to the point where he'd started saying that Caitlin was Elwyn's child.

It had become a fixation. She didn't know

how he had found out that Elwyn's beat included Loudon Place, because she certainly didn't know about it.

It had been ironic that although it had been Elwyn that Alun had intended to knife, the victim had been the policeman who was sharing Elwyn's beat and who had come to her assistance when she'd run out into Loudon Square looking for help.

Her father listened in sympathetic silence when she eventually told him all this. He knew some of it from what he'd read in the newspapers, but those reports had mostly been founded on rumour and hearsay. It had helped him, he told her, to hear the true facts and her side of the story.

Talking to him about it all had cleared away the last vestige of restraint between the two of them. Age and the loss of her mother had changed him. He'd mellowed so much that she no longer found it difficult to talk to him, as she had when she was growing up. Hesitantly he told her about how the earlier newspaper reports had upset him and her mother.

'The truth of it isn't nearly so lurid as what was printed in the papers,' he commented. 'Those reports upset your mother. Still, I suppose they had to make a sensational story out of what took place, otherwise no-one would bother to buy a copy of the paper.'

'Even before that happened, Mam wouldn't come to see me when I was in hospital after

Alun beat me up the second time,' Sheryl sighed.

'She couldn't bring herself to do so, my lovely,' he answered, his voice tinged with sadness. 'When Megan came to tell us that you were coming out of hospital and that you were going to stay with her and her husband, she turned on the poor girl like a wildcat.'

'I had no idea that Megan had told you!'

'After that your mam changed her mind and wanted you to come here, but we didn't know where Megan and Owen were living and Mrs Thomas refused to tell us. She was afraid that your mam only wanted to go and have a row with them, and because Megan was due to have the baby at any time she didn't want her upset.'

'No-one told me! Megan never breathed a word about all this to me!'

'Your mam worked herself up into a real state over it. She couldn't put it out of her mind that she'd driven you away and that was why you'd turned to Megan. She talked of nothing else. It went on for weeks until she ended up having a heart attack. She was dead within two days!' He mopped his forehead with his handkerchief, as if reliving it all. 'Terrible it was, cariad. She collapsed and never regained consciousness.'

'If only I'd known,' Sheryl whispered contritely.

'After your mam's funeral Mrs Thomas gave me Megan's address, but it was too late, you'd left there. Megan said you'd fallen out with each other and that you'd gone back home to Tiger Bay. I was so upset that I forgot to ask her what your address was. I couldn't bring myself to go back and ask Megan again or even think how to go about finding you,' he said sadly.

She reached out and touched his arm with her good hand. 'I'm so sorry, it must have been terrible for you. You must have hated me, Dad.'

'Hate you? No, cariad, I didn't hate you! I was distressed, though, that things had turned out as badly as they did. Your poor mam took everything so much to heart, see. She worried all the time about what people might be saying. You know how proud she was, and she always wanted everyone to see us all in the best possible light.'

Sheryl nodded in agreement. 'Even before all that, though, she didn't really want anything to do with me after I married Alun,' she murmured.

'She felt he wasn't good enough for you, cariad. After that last time you left home she could never bring herself to talk about you. She would certainly never have visited Tiger Bay!' he exclaimed. 'From the day you left here with little Caitlin she always told people that you were living in married quarters somewhere, and that you weren't allowed visitors because you were being sent overseas at any minute.'

'Why on earth did she have to say something like that?' Sheryl asked in disbelief.

'Pride, of course, my lovely. She meant well,

believe me, so you mustn't feel bad about it. That little bit of deception was only because she wanted other people to think well of you, too.'

'Neither of you ever met Alun's mother,' Sheryl said thoughtfully. 'She's been so good to me, and it's been wonderful the way she's looked after Caitlin these last few months.'

'Why did you send the child away, you've never explained?'

'I . . .' Sheryl hesitated, not sure what to say. She couldn't bring herself to tell him the whole sordid truth, even though she would have found it a relief to unburden herself completely.

'Caitlin went to stay with Nola because I didn't like leaving her on her own when I was working in the evenings,' she said at last.

'Was it necessary for you to work such hours?' her father questioned.

'I wanted to earn as much money as possible so that I could move out and find somewhere better to live. I didn't want Caitlin growing up in Tiger Bay. The other kids that she went around with were such a rough lot, and she was getting to be like them.' She gave a forced laugh. 'She was becoming a proper little street urchin, I can tell you!'

He seemed to be satisfied with her explanation, to her relief. She was thankful that he would never need to know the real reason why she thought it was better to be on her own. The truth would break his heart, she thought ruefully.

In some ways her accident had been a blessing

in disguise, she mused. At least it had saved her from the fate that Zakaraki had in mind for her.

'As soon as I'm feeling a bit stronger, and this arm of mine stops hurting so much, I'll go and fetch Caitlin,' she promised. 'It's her birthday, remember, in a couple of days' time.'

'My granddaughter,' he smiled. 'It seems strange that she will be seven and yet I have never set eyes on her since she was a tiny little tot.'

'I know!'

'Couldn't we ask Mrs Powell to bring her to visit us and we could have a little party to make up for missing her birthday?' he suggested. His eyes lit up as he considered the idea for a minute or two, waiting for Sheryl's answer.

'No, Dad, it's a nice thought, but it might only confuse Caitlin. I've already written to tell Nola about my accident and said I thought it better if she didn't bring Caitlin to see me. I'll wait until I'm well enough to go over to Ely myself.'

'Surely you can explain to her that things have changed and you'd like to have Caitlin here with us,' he protested.

'Not yet, Dad,' she replied, kissing him on the brow. 'Leave it until we know for certain that this arrangement is going to work. After a few weeks you may decide you would sooner be on your own.'

380

Chapter Thirty-Four

Caitlin wasn't feeling as happy as she usually did. She loved being at Nana Nola's house and being made a fuss of, but she was missing her mam.

When they'd gone to see her a few days after Christmas and her mam had asked her if she wanted to stay in Loudon Place with her, or go back to Ely with Nana Nola, she'd said she'd go with Nana Nola. Now she was wondering if she'd made the right choice.

She was enjoying the new school. At first she didn't have many friends, but ever since Christmas she'd had plenty. Nana Nola had insisted she must have a party for her birthday. 'Seven is very special,' she'd told her, 'so invite three little girls and three little boys from your class to come to your party.'

'I don't know any of them that well,' Caitlin told her.

'Then invite the ones you'd like to have as friends,' Nana suggested.

In the end she'd invited seven children, and Nana Nola said that was exactly the right number because that was how old she was.

They'd had a wonderful time, and now some

of her new friends called for her in the morning so that they could all walk to school together. They always asked her to play out with them after school when it wasn't raining or too cold to do so.

'I don't like you being out in the street in the dark, you might come to some harm,' Nana Nola always told her when she asked if she could go out to play.

Occasionally, though, she gave way. 'Well, all right, for half an hour then,' she would concede, 'and then you must come in. Your tea will be ready by then.'

She always went in at the time she'd been told to, but she knew her tea wouldn't be ready because they always waited for Granddad Cradog to come home from work.

That wasn't what was making her unhappy. She knew it was all part of Nana Nola's way of looking after her. She loved Nana Nola very much, but it wasn't the same as living with her mam.

She wondered if she had upset her mam by saying she wanted to stay in Ely, because she hadn't been in touch. There hadn't been a letter or even a card for her on her birthday.

She'd thought about it a lot since the day they'd gone to visit her. Perhaps she should have tried to explain why she didn't want to stay there when her mam had asked her to choose what she wanted to do.

If she had said that it was because she didn't

like being on her own every night when her mam went to work, then perhaps she would have understood?

There were other reasons as well, but not ones she could do anything about. She didn't like her mam always having headaches and not being well enough to get up in the morning. It made her unhappy, too, when she'd come home from school in the afternoon and everything was exactly as it had been when she'd gone out in the morning. All the dirty dishes still on the table, and the whole place smelling stuffy and horrible.

You couldn't tell grown-ups things like that, though, because they thought you were being rude or cheeky.

Everything was so different at Nana Nola's. There were always nice things to eat, her clothes were always washed and ironed ready for her to put on, and Granddad Cradog even polished her shoes until she could almost see her face in them.

She still loved her mam most, though, and missed her a great deal. She wanted to see her, but she couldn't think how to do it without asking Nana Nola to take her to Tiger Bay again, and that might upset Nana Nola.

If only she could magic herself back to Loudon Place, see her mam, make sure she was all right, then return without anyone else knowing.

Every night after she went to bed Caitlin

pondered over this problem. She might never have found the answer if she hadn't spotted a coin lying in the gutter as she was coming home from school.

When she bent down and picked it up she thought it was a penny, and she couldn't believe her eyes when she discovered that it was a florin. Two whole shillings, twenty-four pennies; more money than she'd ever had in her life before!

The florin was coated in mud, so she took it home and washed it until it was clean and shiny. She hid it under her pillow for safety and to give herself time to think what to do about it.

Someone had lost it so she knew she ought to take it to the police station, or at least tell her teacher, or Nana Nola, that she had found it.

The more she thought about it, the more reluctant she was to do that. Keeping it wasn't really stealing, she told herself. What was more, she'd had a brilliant idea about what she would be able to use it for if no-one knew she had it.

When she went to bed that night she worked her plan out in her mind before she went to sleep.

If she told no-one else about the florin, she would have enough money to go on the bus into the centre of Cardiff and from there catch a tram to Loudon Place. She'd be able to see her mam, buy them both some fish and chips, and still have enough money left over for her fares back home.

The only trouble was it would mean taking a day off school, and she knew she couldn't do that unless she took a note to her teacher to ask permission. Either that, or Nana Nola had to send in a message to say that she wasn't well enough to go to school.

She wouldn't be able to do either of those things. It had to be a secret, no-one must know what she was planning to do.

If she told Nana Nola that she wanted to see her mam it might upset her, she might even think she wasn't happy living with her. She'd tell her to wait until Saturday when she was off school, and then she'd take her.

That wasn't what Caitlin wanted, though. She wanted to surprise her mam and go and see her on her own. She wanted to be able to talk to her mam without anyone interrupting, or even hearing what they were saying to each other.

She hid the florin carefully and waited another day to see if she could solve the problem. Then the solution came to her just before she fell asleep that night.

It was simple, she told herself. All she had to do was go into school the same as usual, answer her name when the register was called so that the teacher and everyone else could see she was there. Then, at the end of morning playtime, when the bell went and the others returned to the classroom, she'd hide some-where and wait for a few minutes. After that she would run off and catch a bus into the centre of Cardiff.

Her scheme worked perfectly. Because it was cold and wintry, it seemed quite natural that she had put her coat on when she went out to play. Some of the other girls had done the same thing.

Caitlin managed to hide without anyone spotting her, and she'd left the school before her friends or teacher noticed that she wasn't back at her desk. She was also lucky that she only had to wait a few minutes when she reached the bus stop.

She felt very nervous when she arrived in the city centre. She remembered quite clearly, however, from the trip she'd made with Nana Nola, where she had to go to catch the tram.

Once she was on the tram, and it had trav-elled past the Custom House, she knew she had to get off two stops further on.

She skipped happily down Loudon Place to the side door of the Diawl Coch and went up the stairs.

She hesitated on the landing, not sure if she should knock on the door and wait for her mam to answer, or find the key and let herself in.

It was still only the middle of the morning, so the chances were that her mam would be in bed.

She smiled to herself. If she went in very

quietly she could make a cup of tea and take it into the bedroom, and that really would give her mam a surprise.

The key was where it was always hidden, so she opened the door as quietly as she could and crept inside.

She found that the living room was as untidy as ever, and when she tiptoed through into the kitchen it looked exactly as it always did. There were dirty dishes in the sink and on the table.

She peeped into the larder and found it was empty, there wasn't even any milk or bread. She looked in the tea caddy and found that was empty too.

Disappointed because she couldn't make a cuppa to surprise her mam, she walked back into the hallway and went along to the bedroom.

As quietly as possible she turned the handle and opened the door. Her mam wasn't there.

She sat down on the edge of the bed to try and think what to do. Perhaps her mam had already gone to work, she reasoned, and wondered if she should go down and ask the club doorman.

There was no-one on the door so she went inside and stood there looking around, wondering if she ought to shout out to let someone know she was there.

Before she could do so a woman with a cigarette dangling from the corner of her mouth came through, carrying a brush and some dusters.

'Hey you, what do you think you are doing barging in here like this? Go on, scram!'

'I'm looking for my mam, she works here. Her name's Sheryl Powell.'

The woman eyed her up and down. 'She used to, but she doesn't any more.'

'Do you mean that she's been sacked?' Caitlin asked worriedly.

'She had an accident and broke her arm so they took her off to hospital and she hasn't been back since,' the woman told her.

Caitlin felt shocked. 'I didn't know. No-one told me. Do you know when it happened?'

'Must be a couple of weeks ago. She fell down the stairs. She was probably drunk. Happy now?'

Caitlin felt bemused. 'Which hospital did she go to?' she asked, fighting to keep back her tears.

'How the hell do I know?' the woman said unfeelingly. She puffed on her cigarette aggressively. 'Bugger off, will you, and let me get on with my work.'

Tears streaming down her face, Caitlin stumbled away out into the roadway.

This was to have been a wonderful surprise for her mam, but it had all gone wrong. The only one who'd had a shock was her.

She wandered round Loudon Square for a few minutes, trying to decide what she ought to do next. Then, squaring her shoulders, she went back to the club. This time the doorman was there.

'Here, what do you think you are doing?' he shouted as she tried to slip past him.

'I'm looking for Mr Zakaraki,' she said defiantly.

'What do you want with him?'

'To ask him if he knows what's happened to my mam, and where she's gone,' she sniffed.

'You Sheryl's kid, then? I thought you were staying with your granny over in Ely.'

'That's right, I am.' She stuck her chin in the air defiantly. 'I've come to see my mam, but some woman's just told me that she has had an accident and that she's in hospital.'

'She's right. I'm not sure which hospital they took her to, though. And if I don't know then you can be pretty sure that Mr Zakaraki won't have any idea either. He's not in the club anyway, so you'd better run along. Go on, back to your granny. I wonder she let you come all this way on your own.'

Afraid that the doorman was going to question her further, Caitlin took to her heels.

Nola Powell opened her front door and peered out into the street. Where on earth could Caitlin be, she wondered. It was almost five o'clock and she should have been home an hour ago.

Nola always insisted that if Caitlin wanted

to play out after school, she must come home first and ask permission.

Nola went back in and checked that the meal would soon be ready. Cradog would be home at any minute and she liked to have his meal on the table when he walked in, especially at this time of the year when he was cold as well as hungry.

She waited another few minutes, then she went to the door again and looked up and down the street for any sign of Caitlin.

'I'll give her a jolly good talking-to when she does come home. Worrying me to death like this,' she muttered. 'I'm getting too old for this sort of caper!'

Still, she had to admit, Caitlin was usually as good as gold. She'd been a bit obstreperous when she'd first come to stay, but a few weeks of regular baths, clean clothes and plenty of good food inside her and she was a changed child.

Her teacher said exactly the same. When she'd first attended the school she'd been cheeky, sulky and very disruptive in class. She'd settled in, though, and now she was one of the brightest pupils there.

Knowing how well behaved she was these days, it seemed all the more strange that she wasn't home from school by now.

By the time Cradog arrived Nola was in a real tizzy. 'Where do you think she can possibly be?' she asked him worriedly.

'How the hell would I know, I've only just this minute walked into the house. Have you asked around the neighbours? Have you checked with the kids she's usually with when you let her go out to play after school?'

Nola shook her head, her plump face looking drawn and tense.

'Then I think that's one of the first things we should do,' Cradog told her.

Nola hesitated, torn between worrying about Caitlin and caring for her husband. 'Your meal's ready, do you want to sit down and have that first?' she asked tentatively.

'Might as well. I've taken my coat off now. Let's have our grub, then I'll go back out and scout around. She might even be home by then. You know how much she likes her food and it's perishing cold out, so she'll be starving.'

They sat down to their meal in silence, ears strained to hear the door opening.

'I can't stand this, I'll go and see what I can find out,' Cradog said, scraping back his chair as he pushed his half-eaten meal to one side.

'You haven't had any pudding yet and it's apple pie, your favourite,' Nola told him.

'I'll have it later. When I get back.'

'Yes, all right,' Nola agreed. She pushed back her own chair. 'I'll come with you.'

'No!' He waved to her to sit down. 'You stay here in case she comes back. She might be upset if she finds us both out.'

'Not half as upset as she's going to be when

she does come home,' Nola said crossly. 'Tan her backside for her, I will. I'll teach her to play tricks like this and scare the wits out of the pair of us.'

Chapter Thirty-Five

'There's only one thing for it,' Cradog said worriedly, 'we'll have to call the police and report that Caitlin is missing.'

Nola stared at her husband in despair. 'No sign of her? None of her little friends were able to tell you anything, then?'

'Not a thing! She went to school as you say she did . . .'

'So were you able to find out who she walked home with?' Nola interrupted.

Cradog ran his hand through his thinning hair and scratched his head. 'That's the strange thing. None of them saw her after school. No-one seems to remember seeing her around during their dinner break, either.'

'Yet they say she was at school first thing today?'

'That's right. She answered her name when the register was called and she was there when they had their break at mid-morning. A couple of her friends even remember playing out in the schoolyard with her.'

'So what could have happened to her after that?'

Cradog shrugged. 'I don't know. After the

bell went for them to go back into their class-rooms she seems to have vanished into thin air.'

Nola shook her head, perplexed. 'I suppose we'll have to tell the police about it then, won't we?'

He nodded. 'I suppose so, I can't think of anything else that we can do.'

'I wonder if she has gone to Tiger Bay to see her mam,' Nola said thoughtfully.

'What, on her own?' Cradog frowned. 'Surely she'd have asked you to take her, if she wanted to see Sheryl all that much?'

'I would have thought so, but you know what kids can be like when they get an idea into their heads,' Nola said worriedly. 'It's months since Sheryl came to see her.'

'She writes to her.'

'Postcards! That's not the same as visiting her, now is it.'

'So you are saying that we should go and see if that's where she is?'

'I don't know.' Nola shook her head. 'I would have thought that Sheryl would have brought her straight back if she'd turned up at Loudon Place.'

'Well, that's true,' Cradog agreed. 'She'd know we'd be worried out of our minds.'

'Maybe she couldn't. You know what funny hours she works at that club.'

They stared at each other in silence, not knowing what to do for the best.

'I'd better be the one to go,' Cradog stated.

'You've only ever been there once before, I don't suppose you remember where it is,' Nola protested.

'Of course I do! Anyway, I've got a tongue in my bloody head, so I can always ask, can't I?' Cradog snapped tetchily. 'Every bugger in Tiger Bay will know the Diawl Coch club in Loudon Square, if the place is at all like you keep saying it is.'

'Yes, but don't forget you mustn't go to the club like you did before, the owner, Mr Zakaraki, doesn't like it. You have to go to a side door in Loudon Place. You go up the stairs, there's a sort of landing, and the door to Sheryl's rooms is right in front of it.'

'Don't worry, I'll find it,' he said confidently.

'It would be easier if I went,' Nola argued. 'I know the place, see. What's more, Sheryl will take it better if I'm the one to tell her that Caitlin's gone missing.'

'You go down to Tiger Bay on your own at this time of night!' Cradog guffawed. 'Fine sort of husband I'd be to let you do that, cariad! No, you stay here, my lovely. Caitlin might return of her own accord and if she does she'll be cold and hungry, and probably a bit frightened as well. She'll need you to give her a cuddle and some hot food.'

Caitlin knew that the biggest hospital in Cardiff was the Royal Infirmary in Newport Road. Her mam had taken her there once after she'd had

395

a nasty fall when she'd been playing in Loudon Square, and gashed her knee open on a broken bottle. If her mam had broken her arm then that was where they'd take her, she reasoned.

She wasn't too sure where Newport Road was, but she thought it wasn't very far from the shops and she knew how to get to the city centre. When she got off the tram she would ask someone to tell her the way to the hospital.

It was the middle of the afternoon by the time she found the Royal Infirmary, and it was a complete waste of time.

When she said she'd come to visit her mam, Sheryl Powell, they said there was no-one of that name there. When she insisted that there must be because she'd fallen down some stairs and broken her arm, they looked it up in their files and then said that she'd been sent home a long time ago.

Caitlin kept telling them that she wasn't at home, because she'd just come from Loudon Place and her mam wasn't there.

At first they wouldn't tell her anything else, and then they looked up their records again and said that the address Sheryl had gone to was Thesiger Street. When she'd asked where that was, they said it was somewhere in Cathays.

Caitlin remembered her mam telling her that she had lived in Cathays when she'd been at school, but she didn't know if Thesiger Street had been her address.

She made her way back to the city and walked round looking at shops. She felt hungry so she went into a café and asked for something to eat. The woman behind the counter looked at her suspiciously.

'Where's your mam, my lovely? Not all on your own are you, cariad?'

Caitlin thought quickly. 'My mam's visiting someone in the Royal Infirmary, so she told me to stay here and get something to eat while I was waiting.' She pulled out some coins from her pocket. 'She gave me the money to pay for it.'

The woman smiled. 'That's all right then! Now, what was it you asked for?'

As she munched her way through an iced bun and drank a glass of milk, Caitlin tried to sort out in her mind what she ought to do next. No-one at the club seemed to know anything about where her mam was, or even care about what had happened. Her mam had been in hospital, but she wasn't there now.

She knew she ought to go back to Ely, because school would be over by now and Nana Nola would be getting worried when she didn't come home. Yet it seemed such a waste of a journey to go back without seeing her mam, especially when she'd had an accident and might want Caitlin to be with her.

Her mind made up, she drained the last of her milk. Still chewing her bun, she hurried to the tram stop. She'd forget about Cathays and go back to Loudon Place and see if her mam was home yet. If she wasn't, she'd write a note and leave it for her and then she'd go back to Ely.

When she let herself into their rooms again Caitlin got the shock of her life. The place was transformed. All the dirty dishes had been washed up and put away and the living room tidied. Yet there was no sign of anyone. Her mam must have come back home, after all. She wondered if she was in the bedroom having a nap, or perhaps getting ready for work.

When she opened the door she realised that there was someone in the bed. The covers were all higgledy-piggledy, so it was easy to see that it was a man.

She wasn't sure what he was doing, but she could see that he had no clothes on. There seemed to be someone lying underneath him, and she could hear a woman's voice moaning and giving little shrieks.

Then she noticed the woman's long blonde hair and was horrified. Someone must have broken in while her mam was asleep and was attacking her! Caitlin darted forward and thumped the man between the shoulder blades as hard as she could with her screwed-up fists.

He let out an oath and jerked his head around to see who it was.

As he did so, she recognised Mr Zakaraki.

'Why are you up here and what are you doing hurting my mam?' Caitlin yelled furiously.

She heard the woman gasp and then laugh hysterically. 'I'm not your bloody mam, you silly twp! Now get out of here. Bugger off!'

The woman's arms went round Zakaraki's neck. Pulling his head down and lifting up one of her legs, she twisted it round his back, pinioning him against her.

Zakaraki's arm restrained her. He half rose, pulling the sheet around his naked torso as he turned to face Caitlin.

'Your mother's not here any more, Caitlin,' he said thickly. 'She's gone away, so run along, there's a good girl.'

Caitlin stood her ground. 'No! This is my home! What do you two think you are doing in our bed?'

As the woman started laughing again, Caitlin felt her temper rising. She looked round for something to throw at her. She wanted to hit them, hurt both of them, make them sorry for what they were doing.

Sergeant Elwyn Thomas was at his desk when a call came in that there had been a disturbance in Loudon Square.

'It's not at the Diawl Coch club but in the rooms above it. Some sort of fight.'

'Any other details?'

The constable looked uncertain. 'Well, the information is that someone's gone berserk. Two people have been attacked . . .'

'You mean a drunken brawl?'

'No, not exactly. Our informant said that the assailant was a young kid . . . a young girl in fact.'

Elwyn didn't wait to hear any more. Having summoned one of the beat bobbies to accompany him, he went straight to the Diawl Coch.

'Mr Zakaraki, the owner, has been hit on the head with a heavy flat iron,' the doorman told him.

'We need to see him. Where is he, in his office?'

'No.' The doorman hesitated. 'He's still in the rooms up over, you'll have to use the side door in Loudon Place. I'll show you the way?'

Elwyn and the constable found Zakaraki in Sheryl's living room. The blonde woman with him was vainly trying to stem the flow of blood from a deep gash on his head.

'Who did this?' Elwyn asked as he took a quick look at the injury. 'You'd better give me the details of how it happened and then get to hospital, that wound looks deep enough to require stitches.'

'I'll tell you what happened,' the woman snapped, quivering with rage. 'Some little bitch walked in here off the street and for no reason at all threw a bloody flat iron at Zak. She could have killed him!'

'And you are?' Elwyn asked briskly.

'What the hell does it matter who I am?' the blonde exclaimed indignantly. 'I didn't do it!'

'We might need you to make a statement,

since you appear to be the only witness. Have you any idea who the girl was or what she was doing here?'

'I can tell you who she was, Sergeant,' Zakaraki intervened. 'Her name is Caitlin Powell. She came here looking for her mother, but Sheryl Powell met with an accident a couple of months ago so she's not living here because she is no longer in my employ. The child didn't seem to know this and she seemed to think I had broken into her mother's rooms.' He shrugged. 'You know the rest. She attacked me, threw a flat iron at me.'

Elwyn's face remained impassive as he listened to what Zakaraki was saying. Inwardly he was churning with anger. Far too much about this incident remained unexplained.

Sheryl was going to be devastated when she heard what had happened, he thought worriedly. She had told him that Caitlin was in Ely, being cared for by Alun's parents, so what on earth had she been doing coming all the way over here, on her own, he wondered. If she had run away, her grandparents would be out of their minds with worry.

Leaving the beat constable to finish taking down details about the fracas, he returned to the station to see if there had been any report filed about a missing child that afternoon.

'There's one just come in, Sergeant,' the duty officer told him. 'A little girl has gone missing. Went to school as normal and then sometime during the day did a bunk. No-one missed her until her grandfather reported that she hadn't come home from school. Not from this area, mind, but we've been alerted . . .'

'Did the report come in from Ely? Was it a young girl by the name of Caitlin Powell?'

The duty officer looked surprised. 'Yes, that's right. Have you found her, Sarge?'

'No, but I know where she was last seen. She was the one who caused trouble at the Diawl Coch about an hour ago,' he said grimly. 'What we need to know now is where she went after that.'

Chapter Thirty-Six

Sergeant Elwyn Thomas was off duty, but he still couldn't put work out of his mind. He'd left a message with the duty officer that he was to be informed the moment there was any fresh news about the little girl who was missing, but even that was not enough. He still felt he had to do something more positive.

The obvious thing was to pay Sheryl a visit and see if she knew that Caitlin was missing. If she had already heard about it, she must be very worried, so he'd have to try and set her mind at rest about the situation.

There was always the off chance, of course, that she didn't know yet that Caitlin was missing. Unless the Powells had already been in touch with her, she might still be under the illusion that Caitlin was safe and sound with her grandparents in Ely.

Sheryl would have to be informed, of course. She might even be able to provide some valuable nugget of information that would be crucial in helping them to find Caitlin.

It was obvious to Elwyn the moment Gwynfor Williams answered the door that he knew nothing about what had happened.

Elwyn tried to tell him and Sheryl in as detached and professional a manner as possible what had happened, but it perturbed him to see how utterly devastated Sheryl was by the information.

Gwynfor Williams took the news badly, too. His face was drawn and his brow furrowed. Sheryl was shaking so much that Elwyn desperately wanted to try and comfort her.

'Don't worry, cariad,' he soothed, 'we'll find Caitlin. Every policeman on the beat throughout the whole of Cardiff has been alerted. They'll scour every nook and cranny until she is found. She'll be back home safe and sound in next to no time, you'll see.'

'I want her brought here, not taken back to Ely, mind,' Sheryl pleaded, her face ravaged by tears. 'I won't rest until she's safely under this roof. I want her right here where I can look after her and keep an eye on her myself, do you understand? I'll never trust anyone else to care for her ever again.'

Elwyn fully understood her concern. Much as he wanted to stay there with her, to take her in his arms and wipe away her tears, he knew it was not his place to do so. His job was to get back to his desk, and filter every scrap of information as it came in. With his inside knowledge of the people and places Caitlin knew, he might spot a clue to her whereabouts that others would overlook.

Explaining his intentions to them both, he

promised that he'd be back as soon as he had any positive news.

'Bring my little Caitlin with you, please Elwyn,' Sheryl implored, brushing away her tears with the back of her sound hand.

'I'll do my best. I'm going to Ely first to let the Powells know exactly what is happening and assure them that everything possible is being done. While I'm there I'll tell them that when we do find her we'll be bringing her back here to you. Right?'

'Thank you, Elwyn. Poor Nola and Cradog, they must be worried out of their minds. I'm sure it's not their fault. Nola probably thought Caitlin was safely in school, and never dreamt that she would run away like this. I really don't understand what Caitlin can have been thinking of . . .'

'I'm sure she'll tell you herself the moment we bring her back,' Elwyn said consolingly.

Nola and Cradog were almost as distressed as Gwynfor and Sheryl had been. Cradog gave them details of what he had done to try and find her. Nola felt she must somehow be responsible for what had happened, and alternately blamed the school and then herself for the predicament they were in. Over and over again she repeated, 'However was it that no-one at the school missed her, that's what I can't understand!'

Elwyn had no explanation. He couldn't comprehend either how Caitlin could have left school sometime during the day without any of the teachers noticing. He assured Nola and Cradog that a full enquiry would be made in due course.

'When we find her,' he told them, 'we'll be taking Caitlin straight back to Thesiger Street, because Sheryl is staying there with her father.'

'You will send someone to let us know that she's safe and sound though, now won't you, boyo,' Cradog begged.

'Of course!'

From Ely, Elwyn went back to the police station in Tiger Bay. There was no fresh information so he organised a concentrated search of all the roads around Loudon Square, because he felt sure that Caitlin was still there somewhere.

Even when the beat bobbies reported that there was no sign of her, Elwyn was sure she was still in the Loudon Square area. He suspected that she was bright enough to be wary of any policeman who might be walking around there, so he changed out of uniform and into his civvies before he went out to look for her.

It was a bitterly cold night; there was frost glistening on the road and flecks of snow in the air. Her grandmother had said Caitlin had on a warm raincoat and a bright red woollen hat and gloves, so she would be easy enough to spot. Even though she was well wrapped up, by now she would be feeling cold and hungry. Elwyn was sure that sooner or later Caitlin would move out of her hiding place in search of a hot drink, or something to eat, so he made a point of keeping the fish and chip shop in view as he roamed round the area.

His hunch paid off.

Unable to believe that Zakaraki had told her the truth when he said that her mam was no longer working at his club, Caitlin hung around the square. She knew her mam wasn't at home, but she kept watch, hoping that perhaps she would turn up when it was time for her to start work.

She knew she'd hurt Mr Zakaraki pretty badly so she didn't want him, or the doorman at the club to see her, so she hid in one of the nearby alleyways. When she saw policemen walking round Loudon Square she hid behind some piles of rubbish stacked down the side of one of the shops until they'd gone away.

Elwyn's pulse quickened as he spotted a small figure in a red woollen hat nipping out from a dark entry and dashing across the road towards the brightly lit fish and chip shop.

He walked into the shop behind her, and stood alongside her at the counter where she was waiting for her order of two pennyworth of chips to be wrapped up.

'That's a big meal for a small girl,' he commented as she paid from a handful of pennies that she'd pulled out of her pocket.

She looked up at him and grinned nervously, but didn't answer.

'Is your name Caitlin . . . Caitlin Powell?' he asked.

She darted a startled look at him and began to back away towards the door.

'I used to know your mam when she was about your age,' he said conversationally. 'She used to like fish and chips.'

Intrigued, Caitlin paused. 'You knew my mam?'

'That's right. She was my sister's best friend. Her house backed onto ours, so her dad made a gate in the wall between our two gardens so that they could visit each other whenever they wanted to.'

Caitlin's blue eyes widened. 'Was that when she lived in Thesiger Street?' she asked.

'That's right! So your mam has told you all about those days, has she?'

She nodded. 'Thesiger Street is in Cathays and that is quite a long way from here, isn't it?'

'Yes it is. I'm surprised to see you've come all this way to buy your fish and chips!'

Caitlin frowned suspiciously. 'Why do you say that?'

'Well, isn't that where your mam is living now?'

Her face cleared. 'That's what they told me when I went to the Royal Infirmary to try and find her, but I didn't know how to get there.'

'I could take you there if you like,' Elwyn offered.

Caitlin studied him for several seconds in silence. 'My mam said I wasn't to talk to strangers, so I don't think she would like me to let you do that,' she said as she made for the door.

'I'm hardly a stranger though, am I?' Elwyn pointed out as he followed her into Loudon Square. 'I told you, I've known your mam since she was a little girl. I still live in the house that has a gate that goes into the backyard of her house.'

Caitlin hesitated. 'I don't know your name.'

'It's Elwyn Thomas. My sister's name is Megan. Has your mam ever talked to you about her?'

Caitlin nodded. 'She was at a dance with my mam when my mam met my dad.'

'That's right! Fancy you knowing that!'

'They went to a dance at Maindy Barracks . . .'

'Yes! Your dad was a soldier.'

'I know,' she said excitedly. 'We've got a picture of him in his uniform. He looked ever so smart, but he's dead now, though.' She sniffed.

'That's sad,' Elwyn said solemnly. 'You and your mam must miss him a great deal. Perhaps that is why your mam's gone back to live with her dad.'

Caitlin shrugged. 'Perhaps. I don't know.' She dashed away the tears that were running down her cheeks. 'She didn't tell me that she was going to do anything like that. I thought she was still living here, and I've been looking for her.'

Elwyn nodded understandingly. 'Well, as I said before, I can take you to Thesiger Street to see her if you want me to, otherwise I'll be on my way.'

Still keeping an eye on her, he began to walk away. Seconds later he heard her running after him.

'I'll go with you. I want to see her and I don't know how to get to Cathays,' she panted as she caught up with him.

'If you want me to take you there, you'll have to give me some of your chips,' he joked.

She nodded in agreement. 'We'll share them,' she told him, unwrapping the paper and holding them towards him so that he could have first pick.

Chapter Thirty-Seven

Sheryl stared in disbelief when she answered the door and found Elwyn and Caitlin standing on the doorstep. Laughing and crying at the same time she clutched at Caitlin with her good arm and hugged her close, burying her face in the child's hair as she asked her over and over again where she'd been.

There were tears in Sheryl's eyes when she looked up at Elwyn. 'I knew I could depend on you to find her, thank you so much,' she whispered gratefully.

He nodded. 'She's safe and sound now, so take good care of her, she's pretty special . . . like her mam,' he said softly as his gaze locked with Sheryl's.

He looked away as Gwynfor Williams came into the hallway. 'Dammo di!' Gwynfor exclaimed jubilantly. 'You've found her! Hello, my little lovely.' He ruffled Caitlin's hair. 'I don't suppose you remember me, you were only a babba the last time I saw you.'

Caitlin stared at him wide-eyed. 'Are you my mam's dad then?'

'That's right! I'm Grampy Williams and you

411

and your mam are going to be living here with me,' he smiled.

'I knew you'd find her if anyone could,' Gwynfor said, turning back to Elwyn. 'This calls for a celebration, have you got time for a drink? How about a nip of whisky, boyo?'

'I'd love to have a drink with you, Gwynfor, but I must let them know at the station that Caitlin's been found because there are constables scouring all over Cardiff for her. After I've done that I must go out to Ely and reassure Mr and Mrs Powell that Caitlin is safe and sound. They've already been told that she's been found, of course, but it's been a very worrying time for them as well, you know.'

'Then why don't you pop back again when you're through with all that official business?' Gwynfor urged.

'Well?' Elwyn looked questioningly at Sheryl, as if unsure how she felt about this.

'Please do, Elwyn,' she said softly. 'I'm sure you will want to check that this young lady is tucked up safe and sound in bed after all her adventures tonight,' she added, looking down at Caitlin, who was still clinging to her like a limpet.

He nodded. 'I would also like to make sure that her mam is all right as well, after all the terrible worry she has had to go through.'

Taken by surprise, Sheryl felt the colour rush to her cheeks. 'You go along in by the fire with your grampy will you, Caitlin, while I see Elwyn to the door,' she suggested, as she gently disentangled herself from Caitlin's hold on her.

'Elwyn,' she laid a hand on his arm, 'you will be careful how you explain to Nola why I want Caitlin to stay here with me? Tell her I'm grateful for the way she has taken care of her, and I don't blame either her or Cradog in any way for what happened today.'

'No, it's not their fault,' Elwyn agreed gravely. 'Caitlin was looking for you, she needed her mam, see. She needs a lot of love and looking after, cariad. She's been through so much recently . . . the same as you have.'

Sheryl bit her lip. 'You're probably right. I'll try and be a better mother to her in future,' she said humbly.

'I know you will, but it won't be easy . . . not on your own.'

She smiled wanly. 'I promise I'll do my best. You heard my dad say that we are going to live here with him, and I know he'll do everything possible to help me care for Caitlin.'

'You need support from someone younger than your dad . . . someone who will look after both you and Caitlin in the future,' Elwyn told her gruffly.

She shrugged. 'Whatever happens, I'm going to have to take a new look at my life as soon as my arm is better and I can find another job. I'm never going to go back to Tiger Bay and that sort of life again, no matter what happens,' she said determinedly.

'I'm relieved to hear you say that,' he said. He took her by the shoulders, his dark eyes studying her face intently. 'I'll help you . . . that's if you'll let me.'

She looked startled. 'Do you really mean that, Elwyn?'

His heart melted as she gazed up at him, her eyes wide and trusting. 'Sheryl, I want very much to be a part of this new future you're planning,' he said softly.

'I'd like that!' She smiled warmly, her eyes sparkling.

'Not only must you never go back to Tiger Bay again, but you most certainly mustn't have anything more to do with Zakaraki.'

She nodded in agreement. 'I suppose in some ways I've had a lucky escape, haven't I?'

'You certainly have. Stefano Polti is a nasty piece of work. He's got a criminal record going back years.'

'I can believe it.' She shuddered at the thought of what might have happened to her.

'We can't tie him in to being involved in your accident, unfortunately, so I don't think there is much point in you pursuing it or even accusing him, because it will only be your word against his.'

'I have no wish to do so, I couldn't bear having to relive it all,' Sheryl told him earnestly. 'I want to put it all behind me.'

'So you are going to move in here permanently with your father, are you?'

'Yes, that's what he wants me to do, he's very lonely here all on his own.'

Elwyn nodded. 'I tried to let you know about your mother. I came to your rooms several times . . .'

'And I didn't answer the door,' she said sadly.

'You heard me?'

'I was afraid to open the door. I thought it might be Zak come to turn me out . . . or Polti.'

'Oh, Sheryl, I'm so sorry. If only you'd confided in me before things reached the state they did.'

She shrugged despairingly. 'What could you have done? Anyway,' she gave a wry smile, 'it's all in the past now, isn't it. I'm determined to start afresh – or turn the clock back – whichever you prefer.'

Elwyn smiled. 'Exactly how far back?'

'What do you mean?'

'Are you turning it back to the days when you lived here?'

She nodded. 'Something like that.'

'You mean to the days when you were heartwhole and fancy-free, as they say,' he persisted.

Sheryl frowned. 'Was I ever that?'

'Before you met Alun Powell, I mean.'

Her face creased into a smile. 'So you think I was fancy-free in those days?'

Elwyn looked puzzled. 'There wasn't anyone in your life before Alun, was there?'

'Oh yes!'

He frowned. 'I never knew! Are you going to tell me who it was?'

'You mean you really don't know?' she teased.

'I've no idea. You were with Megan every chance you had. The pair of you lived in each other's pockets while you were at school and then after you'd started work, you used to go out dancing or for walks together whenever you had any free time.'

She didn't answer, but the look on her face made him draw in his breath sharply.

'You mean me? You had feelings for me?' he said in surprise.

'Perhaps I'd better not turn the clock back quite that far then,' she said dryly.

'Don't say that, I'd like it very much if you did,' he told her eagerly drawing her into his arms. 'Yes, Sheryl, I'd like it very much indeed. After we'd left school I'd always hoped you would go out with me; on a proper date, I mean.'

'You never said anything. I was crazy about you when we were at school and growing up. Then you became a police cadet and all you seemed to be interested in was training for that and going out with your mates.'

'Except when I occasionally took both you and Megan to the pictures,' he reminded her. 'I didn't think it was any good asking you to come to football matches with me.'

'I would have gone absolutely anywhere with you if only you'd asked me,' she said dreamily.

He scowled. 'Rubbish! You preferred going to dances at the army barracks with Megan and then you took up with Alun Powell.'

'He was there, you weren't,' she explained. 'He was dashing, flashy and fun. I was impressionable . . . and according to Megan I was also a terrible flirt!'

'In that case, perhaps turning the clock back isn't the perfect answer,' he chuckled. 'Perhaps you should start afresh from now. I'll try my best to get it right this time, Sheryl,' he assured her earnestly.

'It sounds wonderful, but there isn't only me to consider, is there?'

'What do you mean?' he challenged.

'There's my dad and there's Caitlin to think about.'

Elwyn frowned. 'So what's the problem?'

'I can hardly walk away from them.'

'Of course not. I never for one moment thought that you could, or would even want to do so. It doesn't stop us getting to know each other better. Look, Sheryl, there's never been anyone else I've had feelings for,' he told her.

'Why didn't you ever come to see me, then? You never looked me up, not even when your beat was in Tiger Bay and you found out that I was living there.'

'At first I believed that you and Alun were

happily married, so I thought it was better not to. My feelings for you were far too strong. Now, though, I know different. You are free . . .'

'I'm a widow with a young child,' she interrupted.

'After tonight Caitlin will accept us being together, I'm sure of that,' he said quietly.

'And my dad?'

'I've always got on well with him, even when I was a lad.'

Sheryl bit her lip. 'How will your family feel about us being close? I've fallen out with all of them. I treated Megan so badly that I'm sure she'll never forgive me or even speak to me again.'

'She will, and so will my mam. Are you worried about what Nola and Cradog are going to say as well?' he smiled.

'They'll probably be quite understanding and I'm sure they'll always make you welcome, because in their eyes you'll be a hero for finding Caitlin.'

'So it all looks plain sailing then, doesn't it?' he said solemnly, stroking her hair. 'Fresh start it is, then! Are we both agreed?'

'I like the sound of it, but I can't believe it. It's all my dearest wishes coming true. I feel as though I've been living under a dark cloud for the last seven years, and now suddenly the sun is shining once again.'

'Then can we seal that with a kiss, and when I come back in an hour or so for that drink we'll make it a real celebration. While I'm gone you can warn your father that he'd better get used to seeing an awful lot of me in the future, because from now on I'll be coming courting.'